S0-AQM-697

Kisses from Hanna

From Holland to America:
A True Story of Devoted Friendship

The following resources to validate historical events and dates:

Europe Travel Book (AAA). Buffalo, NY. Quebecor Printing Buffalo, Inc. 1995 Edition.

Miller, Francis T. *History of World War II*, Iowa City, Iowa: Riverside Book and Bible House, 1945.

The World Book Encyclopedia, World Book, Inc. 1990.

All letters used with written permission

Reproducing any part of this book is strictly prohibited. Permission for any other use must be granted by the authors:

Carol Cross
1204 Brentwood
Carterville, IL 62918

Jean Ellen Reynolds
905 South Division
Carterville, IL 62918

© Copyright 1996
All Rights Reserved
Printed in the United States of America

Dedicated to
Ruth Sullivan
Herrin, Illinois

Acknowledgments

To Ruth Sullivan for having the foresight to keep these letters over the years beginning in the 1930's; for her willingness to share Hanna's letters; and for her contributions regarding personal information including photos, names, and addresses of Hanna's family.

To the Muijser family in The Netherlands for permission to use Hanna's letters, for sharing photos, and for trusting us to tell her story.

To our husbands, Bud Cross and Ernie Reynolds, for their patience and encouragement to complete a seemingly impossible and unending task. Bud, with his technical expertise, rescued the computer transcriptions many times, and Ernie gave us moral support.

To our editor, Molly Norwood, for guiding us with her experience, excitement, and prodding that made the book possible.

To friends and families who expressed their faith in the story's success and urged us to hasten our work.

To Carolien Gubbels, an exchange student from Grashoek, Netherlands who helped us search for family members and addresses in 1995. She spent her time and resources helping us.

To Jackie Mueller and Inga Hadfield for generous help in translating the French and German passages.

To Jane Robertson, Carterville Public Librarian, for Internet research and resources.

Foreword

My mother Hanna de Bruijn grew up as a single child in a working class family. She was born in Emmerich, Germany, just across the German border, at the outbreak of the First World War. That was because her father, employed by the Dutch Railways, was stationed for a while in that city to join the mixed German/Dutch working groups customary at borderline railway stations. Much later it appeared conspicuous to have "born in Emmerich" in your passport.

My grandparents deliberately chose to have only one child because they themselves did not have any possibility at all for education beyond primary school and they wanted to escape from poverty and large families and give their only child as high an education as possible. Also, they were influenced by optimistic views of that time that education was the key to a better society and to personal happiness and that, of course, a war would be unthinkable if everyone had been adequately schooled. May be naïve from what we now know would happen later, but not unreasonable at that time. It must have been difficult to live up to these expectations.

By going to the Dutch Indies (now Indonesia) my parents not only wanted to escape from the continuing economic malaise in The Netherlands and have a job and marry, but also they deliberately wanted to escape from a new imminent war in Europe.

The contrast between living in Rotterdam with their parents and living in the colonial Dutch Indies employed as an academic at a cane sugar refinery must have been overwhelming. It is reflected in stories I heard as a child. Once my mother had been going out alone for a long walk between the rice fields, she liked long walks and loved nature, had three servants like everybody else, and no obligations. When she approached an older native woman, my mother saw to her astonishment the native woman kneel at the side of the trail until she had passed. She told me that she felt very ashamed and did not dare to go there again. She liked to play tennis at the compound and also once played against the wife of the director of the refinery. Since my mother was good at tennis, she won.

The next day, however, my father was summoned to the director's office and was told that this was not to happen again; the director's wife should always win. In addition, my father was told not to enter the refinery in shorts, however unbearable the heat was, because the native employees would lose respect for him.

After Rotterdam was bombed in May, 1940, all contacts between The Dutch Indies and The Netherlands were cut off and people in The Dutch Indies did not know the fate of relatives and friends in Rotterdam for a long time. Fortunately, my parents in The Indies and their parents in Rotterdam could both contact Ruth Sullivan in the US, a country not at war at that time.

Later it appeared that they also would not escape war after all. Japan, considered a second class nation manufacturing cheap toys and other inferior products, invaded more or less effortlessly the Dutch Indies after having taken Singapore. This was a great shock at that time since white people had been convinced of their own superiority for a long time. My mother's great deception during imprisonment, however, was not the domination of the Japanese and the obligatory bowing, very difficult for women accustomed to their privileged position and superiority, my mother could accept that and just bowed. No, her great deception was that the women in the camp did not live in solidarity, that a hierarchy developed and that as a result, some women were much more equal than other women.

In her letters just after the war, my mother expressed her sincere doubts, to say the least, that the native people in Indonesia could govern themselves. Yet, in later times she told me that, of course, it was silly to expect the Indonesians to like being governed by people from the other side of the world.

After the war, my parents went back to The Netherlands and decided to start enjoying life. My father who initially never intended to be a teacher, started to teach chemistry, and since he enjoyed it very much and since it provided for plenty of free time and long holidays, it fitted perfectly in their plans. It must, therefore, have been very difficult for them, especially at that time, to see that their young daughter was in very bad health and had endured many illnesses, some almost fatal. The first time it happened she could only be saved because a new antibiotic just happened to arrive at the children's hospital where she was nursed.

Yet, my mother would always worry whether she should have waited some more to recover from the famine during imprisonment before having children as she would worry on many things. On the outside she was very sociable, warm, easy in contacting people, good at organizing things, but on the inside always insecure, wondering whether people would really like her. Could it be connected to the high expectations her parents wanted her to fulfill?

— Hans Muijser

God Manipulated Coincidence
September, 1995
by Carol Cross

Talk about putting the cart before the horse! My co-author, Jean Ellen Reynolds, and I had spent portions of seven years transcribing, typing and editing a suit box full of Dutch pen pal letters lent us by Ruth Sullivan from Herrin, Illinois. Having both recently retired, we were determined to complete the project of preserving this unusual story. We had already returned the collection of letters to Ruth who, in turn, planned to send them to her deceased pen pal's family. We now sought the permission of Hanna de Bruijn's family in Holland to include copies of the original letters in our book. We sent a letter to Aad Muijser, Hanna's husband, in Enschede, The Netherlands in the spring of 1995.

Four months later when our efforts to communicate with Aad had failed, we were unsure what conclusions were to be made. We had known the latest 1978 address was outdated, but we needed Aad's signed release and approval to use the letters. We also hoped he would contribute additional information. Did he not want to allow the letters to be made public? Was he ignoring us? Was he ill? Had he even received the letter we had sent? Ruth at that time was ill and away from home, so we didn't bother her.

We contacted a young exchange student who had spent a year in our town and had returned to her native Holland. Carolien graciously searched marriage and birth records and posted Aad's name in a "Missing Persons' Listing". (These are still being used this long after the war by families trying to locate each other.) One must remember most of their records were destroyed during the bombings in the 1940's. She had no luck either. Several anxious months later, my husband and I decided to take one last desperate long shot.

After attending a wedding in England, we flew over to Amsterdam armed only with a 17-year-old address for Aad in Enschede, on the east side of The Netherlands, and the knowledge that Hanna and Aad's son, Hans Muijser and his wife Liesbeth, were believed to be living in Delft on the west. We also knew Hans had his doctorate in Physics. We decided to assume Hans might be on the faculty at Delft University and drove from Naarden back west to Amsterdam, through Leiden, and The Hague meaning to arrive in Delft early in the afternoon in time to check the faculty listings. However, we were caught in traffic in The Hague and finally arrived at a plaza in Delft at 5:00 p.m. I was discouraged and felt we had lost that day and knew we had only one more day to pursue our goal before flying home. The stores around the plaza were already closed with the exception of one brightly lit "Bibliotheek". It was almost like a beacon in that whole darkened square. Trying to salvage something from this leg of the trip, I said to my husband, "Well, we're too late to check at the University, and we can't even get in to see the Delft pottery factory, so let's go look inside that book store before we turn around and go back to the hotel."

When we entered, a kind lady who thankfully spoke English asked how she could help. It turned out this was a public library. I explained that I was from the States and was searching for one person in the country of 15,000,000 and particularly in this city of 89,000. She caught the spirit of our mission and enthusiastically asked what she could do. When I asked to see a phone book on the off chance that Hans Muijser wasn't as common as John Smith back home would be, she looked up the name for me. There was only one! This helpful lady gave me a copy of his section of the city map, wrote down his phone number, and pointed me toward a department store where I could first purchase a telephone debit card and then place the call. I thanked her and told her I hoped if she ever visited our country, she would find the same generous assistance and cooperation she'd given us.

My next concern was the cost of the debit card I needed. Not having bought (nor even seen) one in the U.S. yet, I feared it might be for a month's worth of calling. However, it turned out to be about $3.00. Next, I learned that the phone gave written directions for its usage in four languages. With trepidation I dialed Hans' number. A lady answered in Dutch and immediately changed to English when she heard me ask, "Is this Liesbeth? Is Hans there?" His wife said I must wait four hours before he would return and asked whether this had to do with "the letters". Other than acknowledging that she might know of our mission, she gave me no clue as to Hans' possible reaction to this book we were writing about his mother. She didn't invite us to come to their home, so there was nothing to do but to return to our hotel two hours away and call later. The agony I went through waiting those last few hours! What if seven years of effort had been fruitless? What if Hans, his father Aad, and his sister Ineke absolutely refused to permit Hanna's letters from being used? We would still have the story, but it would have to be told in third person and would lose most of the poignancy of Hanna's quaint

English and personality that came through so clearly in her correspondence.

Finally at 10:00 p.m. I placed the call. Hans was charming and encouraging about the possible book. He offered to meet us the next evening and show us slides of the family. He gave me his father's phone number so I could call the next morning. We wanted to get Aad's blessing as well. Our correspondence had not reached Aad because he had moved three times since he'd been at that former address, and no one had forwarded the letters. When we talked, Aad expressed his doubts about our having the understanding to write of their war traumas. I assured him we would be sensitive and realistic about their stressful experiences over those years when the world was embroiled in World War II. However, we knew only they, through the letters, could accurately record and convey to others the horrors they'd witnessed and experienced.

The next night Hans set up a slide projector in our airport hotel room, and we exchanged information. He showed us scenes and photographs of the family and friends mentioned in the letters. It was very helpful to put faces with the names we had been using. He had never seen the letters kept by Ruth all those years, and he was amazed at the details I knew about his parents' lives that he didn't know. It turned out he was not associated with the University, but with a research organization. Therefore, our timing in arriving in Delft didn't matter that much. Hans offered to have his sister send copies of the photos we wanted included in the book. I was ecstatic to have found him.

Hans phoned Ruth that night to reassure her that the family felt honored to have Hanna's letters and the story of her remarkable life preserved in a book and that they were pleased she allowed us to use them. We have continued to e-mail messages to each other as the manuscript progressed, and Hans asked to be allowed to write the foreword about his mother.

Flying home the next morning my greatest fear was that we might crash before I had time to tell Jean Ellen that I had found the family. It had taken only two days on my first visit to that country! When our editor heard the story of our discovery, she called it a "God Manipulated Coincidence." That, I think, sums it up very succinctly.

Introduction

The authors felt this story had to be preserved and told to the present and future generations. It not only records a profound era in our history, but it exemplifies the indomitable spirit of common people to persevere and survive under very uncommon events and consequences in their lives. Between tears and laughter we have transcribed the letters and bridged the years with explanations of historical significance and commentaries. Hindsight allows the reader to observe changing attitudes and note insights the correspondents were not privileged to have over the 46 years they wrote.

In 1984, the authors heard Ruth Sullivan, a former teacher of the Herrin High School, share her personal, extraordinary story of an enduring Dutch pen pal correspondence describing intimate glimpses into people's lives and a turbulent time in history that spanned five decades. For three years Jean Ellen Reynolds and Carol Cross encouraged, coaxed, and cajoled Ruth to write this unique story knowing that she was quite capable, as a retired English teacher, to author such a book. Finally, in the summer of 1988, she surprised them by offering her suit box of letters and suggesting they write the book themselves. Preferring truth and reality to narrative, the authors encouraged Ruth and Hanna's family to allow others to read their story through the letters that give an account of the sensitive relationship between two women and their families half a world apart. Only Hanna's letters were kept over the years by Ruth.

The pen pals began writing when they were both teenagers in 1933. Hanna lived in Rotterdam, Holland, a port city on the Rhine River and the second largest city in the country, while Ruth lived in Herrin, Illinois, a small industrial, coal-mining town 90 miles southeast of St. Louis, Missouri. At that time Ruth felt that traveling to Europe was about as remote as traveling to the moon would be today—possible, but highly unlikely. A friend of hers already had a Dutch pen pal, and Ruth asked her to get one for her also. She picked Hanna's name from a list probably because it was one she recognized and thought she might be able to pronounce. The name was Hanna de Bruijn. Ruth didn't know too much about Holland except that it had tulips, dikes, and windmills, but she learned much more about Holland's customs and its history in the months and years to follow.

Some background information might be pertinent to set the stage for these initial letters. The whole world was reeling from the effects of the Great Depression. These girls' families were working, middle class people. Entertainment and social activities were very simple and limited to what people could afford with the constant threat or actual loss of jobs. One-third of the work force was unemployed. This was the time of the penny post card and three-cent stamp. Overseas mail traveled two to three weeks by steamship. In the United States a five-room house could be purchased for $700, and school teachers (only men and single women) might be paid by script, if they had a job at all. Married women were not allowed to hold jobs that were needed by the men as breadwinners in the homes. Food lines and soup kitchens humbled many once proud, prosperous people. The tragic farming methods and drought resulting in the Dust Bowl of the West affected Kansas and Oklahoma farmers, but also Illinois women who discovered the red dust infiltrating their homes on hot, dry days. No air-conditioners were available to relieve the heat had they been able to afford such a luxury.

To participate in another's culture and life was a delicious escape from the fears and realities of this period. The World's Fair, held in Chicago, Illinois, the summer of 1933, was one such opportunity.

Hanna's letters also opened new worlds to Ruth. As expected, the two girls first described themselves, their families, homes, and school life. Later they began to share about their customs, friends, and dreams. Hanna wrote in English, one of four languages the Dutch are encouraged to learn. Her style of language has been copied and retained, not to ridicule, but to recognize the difficulty of finding the correct word or expression, especially the idioms that cannot be translated word for word. We respect Hanna's dilemma. Her quaint expressions and creative spellings add charm while reminding us of her struggles. She often misuses past tense verbs and conjunctions ("when" instead of "if"), but these are just mentioned as a crutch to facilitate the reader's comprehension. The style of the later letters greatly improves, but Hanna's unique English is ever genuine and endearing. Ruth could always understand what Hanna meant, but sometimes the expressions were turned around. One time Hanna asked Ruth, "Do you have a club 'on' your school?" The prepositions "on", "at" and "in" didn't have that much meaning to Hanna. Another time she used the expression "laugh at your nose" instead of our common phrase "laugh in your face." When Hanna sent Ruth a clock, she said it "walked well" instead of "ran well."

Certain languages tend to use feminine and masculine endings or assignments to nouns. Hanna writes of "decorating the tree and making _him_ beautiful" and "the crisis of Holland and _her_ results." Also her word arrangements show the differences between English and Dutch when she says, "You must let work your brains", and on taking Ruth's picture to school "to let it see the boys." Parenthetical words have been added by the authors in order to facilitate better comprehension. They are sometimes nothing more than guesses.

Occasionally both girls tried to communicate in French to equalize the challenges, but fortunately for us, English was the dominant language. British spellings often are used such as "colours" and "honours". Great confusion over the variations in the spelling of the two surnames Bruijn (or Bruyn) and Muijser (or Muyser) was explained to the authors. It seems when they wrote cursively, they used the "y", but typed letters showed "ij" since there is no "y" key on their typewriters. It is simple when one has the facts!

While Ruth's letters were not preserved, we often can surmise what she said by Hanna's responses: "You asked about our schools" or "What a lovely compact you sent!"

Aviation was still in its infancy, and heroes are mentioned. The latest inventions were exciting such as the self-filling pen and ham radios.

One time when Ruth asked Hanna how tall she was and how much she weighed so they could compare sizes, Hanna gave her the statistics in centimeters and grams. The U.S. hadn't even begun to think about the metric system at that time.

Hanna's future husband is first mentioned as a fellow student in chemistry and an aficianado of ham radio broadcasting, but not yet by name.

How grateful we are to Ruth for preserving these treasures of personal glimpses into the lives of these families. We feel we have come to know them so well, and have had the added privilege of getting to know some of the remaining family members personally fifty years later. They have communicated with us on telephone satellite connections and computer E-mail—concepts not even dreamed of at the time these young women began writing.

These recent contacts have proven that international friend-ships are still very basic to peace, and the better we know and understand each other, the less chance we will have of putting others through the turmoil these friends endured.

Chapter One

The following begins the actual letters starting in the early 1930's.

27 February, 1933 — Rotterdam

Dear Ruth,

How glad and surprised was I when I found your letter a few days ago. It is so nice and wonderful to have at once a good friend in a strange company (country). Besides it is so romantic, for we have never seen each other, and there is no great chance that we will see each other in the future. For me it is a pity, that I can't write in my own language to you, for it is so very difficult to express your feelings in a strange language, and I am afraid that you will not understand me (my character, I mean) though you understand my words. Before I begin to make acquaintance with you, I must ask you to make my faults of the English language not so very much.

I will begin just as you: I have blue eyes and blond hair. I am not a beauty for I am not slender. The one thing I am proud of is my hair for it has a natural curl. I have eighteen years.

In our country the children go to the public school when they are six or seven years. On the public school they go for six years and then they go to a higher school where they learn the three modern languages: English, French, and German. The things they learn there I will write in the following letter for I don't know the English words for them. Then after 5 or 6 years they have final examination and, when their parents are rather poor, they don't learn further, but when their parents can pay it, they go to the University. In our country are 6 universities in the towns Amsterdam, Rotterdam, Groginger, Utrecht, Delft, and Wageningen, Kymegen. There they can study for their degree—Doctorate or MS.

I had to do my final examination last year. In our class we were with seventeen—4 girls and 13 boys. But the 4 girls and 6 boys did not pass through the examination for it is very difficult and so we must double (repeat) the last class and do our examination again, which begin 23rd of May.

In the large towns as Amsterdam, Rotterdam, etc. we wear modern dress, but in the villages where the farmers and fishers live, they wear the same coupe (type) of dress as their fathers and grandfathers, mothers and grandmothers. They wear the dress that was worn in the fifteenth century. I will send you a few fotographs of this dress. In that feature you can see that the people of Holland are rather conservative. We like it to beware the things and shades of centuries before although at present there come much people who have modern principles and I see this as a happy thing.

I have no brothers and sisters, but in the place of them I have a heap of friends who are always welcome in our house. Then we make music or play bridge or flirt, or we dance while my mother plays at the piano. My father then sits down and looks very happy when he sees that my mother has a pleasure of that for though my father and mother are married for more than twenty years, they are still fond of each other, and though it begins to occur in our little Holland that a husband and wife separate, my father and mother don't think such a horrible thing.

Though I have a heap of friends, my bosom girl friend is Jo Meyer. We tell each other all our grieves, and we love each other very much.

I don't like learning very much, but I am fond of sport. Our national sport is football (soccer). The little boys of 5 and 6 years already are fond of it, and the thing they want is always to have a football.

Then comes swimming. For our country is more water than land, so we have plenty occasion to swim. Naturally you have heard of our Willy den Ouder, Guch Oversloot, and Lus Brann. The latter not a very sympetic (kind or nice) person. And then comes tennis, basketball, cricket, and hockey. I am fond of tennis. For the holidays I spent my whole afternoon on the tennis court, and I am also fond of swimming. But we don't play at school, but we are members of a club.

Next time I will tell you more of my country, my friends and myself. Will you be so kind to write soon? Will you give my kind regards to your friends especially to Helen Bates?

Your friend, Hanna de Bruijn

P.S. I hope you like it, too, to write each month to each other.

Ruth Sullivan
Herrin, Illinois

Hanna de Bruijn
Rotterdam, Holland

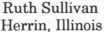

My dear Ruth,

What a lovely girl you are! I am so very enthusiastic about the fotograph you send me. I am sure that when I was (if I were) a boy, I at once had been in love with you in a violent way. So I'm happy to be not a boy (or is it not to be a boy) for otherwise I had to do my utmost to come to you in America, is it not, for I am always told, that love is the strongest feeling people have and nothing can recover you when you have this illness. And then I should have to sing with a German poet:

Da waren zwei Konigs Kinder
Die hatten einander so lief
Sie kounten beisammen nicht Rommen
Das Wasser was viel zu tief.

(There were two kings' children
Who loved each other so much
But they couldn't reside together
The water "between them" was much too deep.)

7

So I was proud on (to have) a friend who was so handsome, and I took the fotograph with me to school to let it see. The boys in our class especially loved it, too, and they were very jealous on me, and they wanted to know your address, too. We had a lot of fun about it. So you must give me the fault (blame me) when you get some day love letters from unknown lovers, but I hope you will not be so angry on me as I deserve them.

Now about English: at the primary school, we go from 6th to 12th years. We learn already arithmetic, reading, and writing in our own language, also Dutch geografy, and history, at the age of ten. We begin learning French at the higher school (12th to 18th years). So I have studied English since 6 years. No wonder that you think we do write rather good, though I am afraid I make a lot of faults, and I do not use the good expressions. But you will warn me, is it not, when I make too much faults, and you will write what serious faults I made in my letters? This is the best method to write better. To understand your letters has no difficulties for me. Do you do your best to write simple words and expressions, or do you write as if I were an American girl, too?

Why don't you try to write a few sentences in French for me? Is it because you are afraid to make faults? Take my example. I write you in a language that is not mine, and you can understand it. And your advantage is that I can't see your faults for French is not my language either. An objection is naturally that you have studied it only six months, but never mind.

So, my chere Ruth, j'espere, que fu escriveras quelgres sentences in francais dans tu lettre prochaime. (I hope you will write some French sentences in your next letter.)

Suppose that it is not so very difficult for you. Then you can say, "Yes, I correspond with a Dutch girl in French, and I can say, "Ja, ik correspondeer met ein Amerikaansch Maisje in het Fransch." I think that to be very proud of or to laugh heartily for it should appear as if we were such haughty clever girls.

I'm glad for you to make such good grades. We also have terms of 3 months, but the last class has two. For 23 Mai we begin already with our final examination. When we have passed through, we are allowed to study on the university. We also study Shakespeare. But the books you read I did not read. We read: The Merchant of Venice, Julius Caesar, and we have just finished Macbeth. I enjoy Shakespeare very much and you? But his work is very difficult and without the help of the teacher, I can't enjoy

8

them very much. The books I read at home when I have time enough are read on the holidays, (you write "vacations", and I could understand it because the Dutch word for holidays is "vacantie" and that resembles on vacations. But is it an American word or is it English, too? It should be funny when (if) the Dutch emigrants had brought it to America). I usually select books of the modern authors, but also of Eng, German, and French authors. Momentary, I am reading The Rosary by T.L. Barclay. Have you read it? I do enjoy it, but I think it too sentimentally (is that good? What a difficulties!)

What a pity that your friend Reathel lives so far from you. My girl friend Jo lives in Schiedam and I in R'dam, but these two towns are but 6 miles from each other, and she comes every day on bicycle to the R'dam Higher School for in Schiedam there is not a good one. We always go to school on bicycle. Holland is the country of the bicycles. Everyone besides babies and old men and women have a bicycle as well in the towns as in the villages. Also the farmers in their national dress have bicycles which is one of the interesting sights for the strangers. Only rich people have a car in Holland for they are very expensive, and the tax to the state is very high. And that young people as Reathel have a car of their own! That does not occur in Holland. But it is very nice to have one, is it not? We only take a car when we go to a ball for then you can't go with a long frock in the tramway.

Naturally, we also have paved roads but not of concrete, but of brick stones. Only a few of the most important roads in the large towns are of concrete. R'dam is one of the largest towns in Holland. In the Middle Ages the town was enclosed by two gates—the East gate (Oostpont) and the West Gate (Delftoche pont). On the other sides were the Kralingsche plas (a lake) and the river, the Haas. Round the town the people has digged canals and on two places there were bridges over them, but at two o'clock at night the bridges were burned up. Before the canals there were the walls with the gates that were closed. No strange people or enemy could enter the town then. In time of war the enemy tried to come over the canals to come through the gates and to enter the town, but the population inside helped the soldiers to beheld their town. Nowadays, the gates are always open, and there are bridges on several points over the old canals, and the town has extended herself outside the gates, too, so that the old gates are now standing in the center of the town. They are fine buildings. Near the

Oostpont is also an old mill. It is very interesting to have a mill in the center of the town on a large square face to face with a large bank on the other side of the square—the old and new things opposite to each other.

My parents have a house on the west side of the town in one of the new built parts about a quarter of an hour by bicycle from the D. pont, and our school is about 5 minutes from the D. pont. From Schiedam where Jo lives, it is 20 minutes to school.

I have sought on a map of the U.S.A. your living town, but I could not find. I only saw the towns Chicago, Peoria, and Springfield. Will you be so kind as to tell me next time where you are living precisely, and how the character of your town is? I should be so glad to know. *(Southern Illinois is situated between the Mississippi and Ohio rivers and the extreme end is quite hilly, covered with trees sheltered in the Shawnee National Forest.)*

I think the Obelisk (a Southern Illinois University yearbook) is a very fine book. At our school we don't have such a thing. Do you have a club on your school? We have. At our school are about 800 pupils. A hundred of them are members of the club which has been founded already in 1917. To become a member of the club one must pay 4 guilders a year. From this money (about 400 guilders) there are given evening parties, excursions, balls, a.s.o. (etc.) Every year in Sept. when the summer holidays are over, the members choose of them as their president, vice president, secretary, vice secretary, treasurer, and second treasurer. Generally the boys of the school are chosen for this job, but this year I am also chosen as the first secretary. So I must write the letters and hire the halls and have a look that the evening parties are pretty. The 8th of March we had such a party. Some of the best actors of the school had to perform a play called "English Without a Master." It was a comedy and the masters and the headmaster and the parents of the pupils who attended the performance had a lot of fun and enjoyed it very much. After the play there was a break and when this was over, there was a school revue written by ourselves and performed by ourselves, too. In that revue the faults and evil habits of masters and pupils were made ridiculous and also was performed what we thought the "ideal school". On the stage were easy chairs and low tables. Each pupil had a cup of tea before him, and the master was doing his best to content them. Fortunately the masters laughed at it, too, and they were not angry. The girls took care for the ballets. Especially our doll dance gave

10

us a great success, and we had to repeat that after the performance. We had a ball, and we enjoyed it very much.

Though I am not very fond of jass bands, I should like to have nice music to dance at. The ball ended at two o'clock. In Holland we dance tango, valse, and fox trot. What do you dance in America, or don't you like dancing?

The farmers in our country don't like the modern dances. At their wedding parties especially they dance the old-fashioned dances. One of them is the horlepipe.

You liked the pictures very much? I'm glad for that, and I have bought for you therefore a few national dresses and a picture of the mill at the Oostpont. This letter has become much too long, but I must tell you such a heap so that we might know each other well. I hope you read it till the end, malgre la quantite (in spite of quantity)!

Your friend, Hanna

P.S. To the honour of the 400th birthday of Prince Willem van Oranje, our greatest prince of the separating war from Spain (1533-1584) the post office in our country gives during 2 months very fine marks (stamps) with the portrait of Willem von Oranje (William I) on it. For this letter you have two of them. Note that they are very fine and that after some years they will be very rare. So if you like marks or if you have friends who like marks, don't forget them!

+ + + + + + +

The Dutch have had many queens in the last century. First, they had Queen Emma who had no sons. Her daughter became Queen Wilhemina and later relinquished her throne to her daughter, Juliana. Just a few years ago Juliana's daughter, Beatrice, ascended the throne. This present generation will probably live long enough to see a king because Beatrice and her husband have three sons.

The girls wore little or no makeup. Even today they wear very little. Ruth's first present to Hanna was a pretty compact. Hanna later told Ruth she didn't use it but took it to school to show her friends. They advised her that Ruth would be a corrupt influence on her life because Americans "paint their faces." If only they could have known how critically important this friendship was to become, the casual usage or non-usage of makeup would have seemed insignificant by comparison.

18 Mai, 1933 — Rotterdam

Dear Ruth,

Received your letter and fotographs and cards and the letter of Reathel which was a very agreeable surprise for me. I'm very glad with the fotos; how beautiful they are! Though I like to write long letters to you and to fancy that I'm speaking to you, this time I can't write so long. You know that we go in for the final examination 23th of Mai and as I failed last year, I must spend as much time as possible on learning. The writing examination is for 9 faculties (the four languages, 4 different arithmetics and biology) and lasts a week. So I hope you will send me a pretty letter in this dull time of learning, for that is a very welcome change for me then.

In as demande, d'ecrire en francais ansn: Je veus commencer a fe faire des compliments de ta manicere d-ecrire francais. J'ai penr, que ji fosse encore plus de fantes que toi et c'est moi qui a edudie plus longtemps ce language. Je trouve le francais le plus difficile car German ressemble le language hollandais et en anglais ilo m'ont pas des conjugims difficiles des verbes. *(Translation: As requested, I write in French thus: I begin by complimenting your style of written French. I have thought this is a little humorous, since I have studied this language longer. I find French the most difficult because German resembles the language of Holland and in English it is not as difficult to conjugate verbs.)*

With kind regards to all your friends, especially to Reathel and with a shake hands for you.

From your friend Hanna

P.S. At this moment my mother comes in my room with your letter of the 5th of May with the pretty pressed flowers and the card and the <u>Egyptian</u> (SIU newspaper). Many thanks. I'm very ashamed that you wrote twice to me though I have not answered you, but you must have pity with me and think that when one must do a final examination in Holland, that it is so difficult that one is in a tangle and one's nerves, too.

+ + + + + + +

Wed. 31 Mai, 1933

Dear Ruth,

Our writing examination is finished now. Though we don't know the grades for it, I believe I have done it rather well. It is possible that you find it nice to know what they did ask us. Therefore, I sent you the examination of French and English. I would like to send you all of it, but you should not be able to read it for, of course, it is in Dutch. I am sorry that I have written above some Dutch words for that is very untidy. Will you be so kind as to send it me back when you have read it, for it is nice later on to have your examination.

Dutch headings: Eindenamen der Hougere Burgerschols in 1933 (Final examination of Higher Schools in 1933)

Muanday 29 Mai nameddag (Monday, May 29 afternoon)
Denadag 23 Mai nameddag (Tuesday, May 23 afternoon)
Engeloch (English)
Fransch (French)

+ + + + + + +

June, 1933

Ma chere Ruth,

Merci bien pour ta jolie lettre de June. Elle etoit si longve et j'aime recevoir des longues lettres, specialime grand elles sont si amnsantes que les tiennes. *(Translation: Thank you for your lovely letter in June. It has been so long since I received such long letters specially grand and more amusing than "thine"—mine.)*

I heard that you made up your mind to visit the World Show in Chicago in your vacation. When you go, you must look at the Dutch stand very well. I should like it so much when you related about it in your next letter. So you amuse yourself at home? I think it very agreeable to be at home again though you miss your school friends. You asked me what I was going to do in my holidays. I am so tired that I think when the oral examination is over and I know if I have passed or failed, I go to bed (for two or three days) to recover and to become the Hanna of before the examination.

But then we step on our bicycles—Jo, I and two friends of us, Adie van Gelder en Rie Kip, and we make a tour through our

13

country. That lasts a fortnight. We don't take very much luggage with us, and we sleep in youth hostels. Do you know what are youth hostels and have you them in America? In Holland the youth often use them. Every day we ride some 60 kms (36 miles) and at dawn (dusk) we reach such an inn. There you meet other holiday makers and together you have dinner. It is all very simple in such a house. All girls together have one sleeping room, and the boys have one too. The next morning you have a breakfast, you do your luggage on your bicycle, you greet the father and the mother, and you thank them for their cares, and you start for a new more or less 60 kms. In Holland are more or less 70 youth hostels so you can choose what ride you will take. It is very funny to be a fortnight with four girl friends and to do what you prefer and to have no parents to look at you. For you it should not be so funny, I think, for you don't see your parents the whole day long and when you have vacation, it should not be agreeable to go away again.

To my regret I can't say to you my measures in inches for I don't know what it is. We have centimeters—breast, 92; hip 87; whole length (height) 170.

Hanna

+ + + + + + +

July 30, 1933

Dear Ruth,

I have passed my examination!!!! I'm so glad. Of course it has helped that you have thought on me when I had it (prayed for me or wished me well.)

The writing examination was very good, but on the oral examination I was so nervous that I made some unexpected faults, but never mind, I have passed and with good degrees.

Now I have two and a half months' vacation, and then I will study gymnastic. The school to do so is in The Hague. That is some 20 miles from Rotterdam, so I will take every morning the train to The Hague and at evening I come back. It is a tiring job, but I like gymnastic, and my parents have no money to let me hire a room in The Hague and to pay board and lodging. When I have studied there some three years, I am able to teach gymnastic on schools.

I'm glad that you think you have made good degrees (grades). We have no "A" or "B", but our degrees are from "0" till "10". When you have a 0, you don't know anything, and when you have a 10, you know all about it. My degrees are usually a 6 or 7. When you have some fours, you fail in your examination. But we have 15 different things to learn so you may have one four and some fives to pass when the rest are 8 or 9.

Our examination is under the suspicion (supervision) of the government so it is very severe and not easy to pass through. At present, when so many people are unemployed, the examinations are more difficult than many years ago for the government is afraid to have many unemployed more.

I have not read the book you did mention in your letter, but I make up my mind to read it for I have a heap of time now that I have vacation.

What a good country is America. Now you say so very simple that you have ridden in an aeroplane! To us that never occurs that school boys and girls ride in an aeroplane for that is so expensive! A ride of a quarter of an hour costs some 30 guilders and then you must know 1 English pound = 12 Dutch guilders. (Approximately in 1934—$9.00)

Love, Your Hanna

+ + + + + + +

August, 1933 — R'dam

My dear Ruth,

When I returned from the youth hostel journey, I found your letter. We enjoyed much on our journey, but we were very tired, too. You asked me if one must pay in the youth hostel. Yes, of course. When you are under the 18 years, you pay 30 cents— 30/100 guilder. And when you are above 18 years, you pay 40 cent; above 23 years, 50 cent a night. You prepare your meals yourselves. Before you go away at morning, you buy a few loaves and when you are hungry, you sit down in the heath or along the roadside or in a meadow and you eat. When you come in at dawn (dusk) to another youth hostel, you pay for sleeping, and you begin to prepare your dinner in the kitchen. Everybody does so. That is very pleasant in such a kitchen.

Saturday I go with Rie Kip to Rockanje (by train). That is a watering place in the southwest of our country (near the Hoek of Holland.) We hired a room with board and lodging. We take our bicycles with us to make trips in the neighborhood, and we go swimming each day. We also take a long chair with us so to sit in the beach. I think it will be pleasant. When Rie and I go to Rockanje, my parents go to Dinant in Belgre (Belgium) to visit the Grottes (caves) of Han. Do you know what they are? I'm sending you with this two pictures about it.

I also send you "tes etoffes" (excuse me, do not know the English word for it) of which I have my frocks. They are not so different of yours, I think. (Etoffes means fabric samples or materials).

Now I made an apron for myself for that I want when I help my mother. I made it of the red "etoffe" with blue "etoffe." Of the black "etoffe" I have an evening dress. My mother makes all our dresses, but in the holidays I am helping her. We also can fruit, but legumes (excuse me again, please, I thought a quarter of an hour, but I could not find the E. word.) too so that in winter time we need not buy them. (Probably peas or beans.)

The children picture cards I am sending you are for Reathel as I promised. Do give her my kind regards.

Your friend, Hanna

+ + + + + + +

After several months of writing, Hanna began studying to be a P.E. teacher and Ruth also was taking college educational courses to be an English teacher, so they had that in common to discuss. In addition, Hanna began talking about a boyfriend, Aad Muijser. (Aad is a common Dutch name and is pronounced "od" with a broad "a" as is Hanna's name.) He began writing to Ruth because he said Ruth was a good friend of Hanna's, and he wanted to get acquainted with her, too.

Aad was a university student, but he was later also in the military. He told Ruth more about the economy and college life.

September, 1933 — R'dam

My dearest Ruth,

You have enjoyed your vacances (vacation), I have heard especially the excursions with your lunch in your pocket. I can

16

appreciate. And then the hay stack party (hay ride). I call it a party for I think it delicious. We don't have such hay stack parties in our country though our farmers have hay stacks, too.

I spent a jolly time in Rockanje with Rie. We swam and we ate and we rode bicycles along the beach and we walked along the beach and we sat down in our swimming dress and we had the sun shining on our body till we were at last as brown as an Indian. Rockanje is not a famous watering place. It is all very simple, but we liked it.

At Scheveningen it is all very luxurious and expensive and modern, and there are many strangers, but in Rockanje we had a dance at night on a farm, and we made the acquaintance of the burgermaster (mayor) of the village. The other farmers there had a music club and one night a week (Wednesday) they played not in a room but in the free air in the center of the village. It was all very lovely.

Very much thanks of the postcards of the World Show. I have enjoyed them. I showed them to all my friends and relatives, and they all were very jealous that I had the occasion to receive such interesting things. I have a friend who wanted to give, I believe, half of his life, when he could go to the Show, but the voyage to it is very expensive so he is not able to go.

You are very enthusiastic about Bulbo (a fleet of airplanes), is it not? Sorry, but I can't deal it (agree) with you. At first the accidents. For our country, too, in Amsterdam one man has found the death. It may be that it is very difficult to fly with so many aeroplanes. I do find it an exercise for the war. Suppose there comes a war when men have done such things. It is an easy matter to fly to America or another country and to let fall poisons.

I believe such things are done for the war and for nothing else, and that aim is horrible. To what all these meetings in Geneve with Bulbo flights and when a Hitler speaks in Germany. Have you heard of the Jews he has took to flight? Many thousands of them came in our country without any penny. But our queen is very lovely, and she has not refused them.

Last week she reigned 35 years over us. We have honoured her in the Stadium in Amsterdam where in 1928 the Olympic plays (games) have been. She sat with her daughter, her husband, and her mother and a great suite in the Royal loge. The stadium was filled. Not one seat was empty. The Dutch youth had an open air play (game) in the Stadium, and when it was done, the queen

17

spoke before the microphone to her people so that everybody could hear her. It was a very fine day.

Do you like these sheets of paper to write on? I got them at the occasion of my 19th birthday on the 19th of Aug. It was just the day that we came back from Rockanje, and my parents surprised me for they had set in my room several bunches of flowers and a beautiful book case. At night we had little party, and I got several things as this post paper. When is your birthday and how many years have you then?

Our "vacancies" are over. I am traveling every day to The Hague to study gymnastic; a friend of mine is traveling each day to Delft (20 miles) with me. He studies there chemistry on the university, and my girl friend Jo is on the bureau. There she is typewriting the whole day. Rie is at home and is helping her mother. Another friend is in Groningen in the northern part of the country. There he lives, for it is too far to travel each day. There he studies for doctor of animals. Do you understand that word? I don't know the good E. word for it?

With many loves and till the next time,
Your friend Hanna

P.S. "Mej" means Mejuffroun—that is the Dutch word for Miss, you know.

+ + + + + + +

October, 1933 — R'dam

My dearest Ruth,

I wished I had received your letter a week before maybe so that I had been in the occasion to wish you good luck with your birthday. Now, of course, I am too late, but never mind; it is meant heartily: many joys in the next year of your life and since it is impossible that you find only joys, I wish you a very few misfortunes. It seems delicious to me to teach children. What is the age of your pupils? Do you like children?

The school where I learn at present also gives practice. Then we must teach an hour children of 6-11 years instead of the gymnastic teacher of some school and in this way we gradually learn teaching. I am very fond of this hour of teaching, but I am sorry that it is only 2 hours a week. The first time I teached, it was a

18

very strange feeling to see all these children (to us the classes consist usually of 30 to 40 pupils) who must do what you ordered them and who looked up to you as if you were a sort of half god, and then to realize that you were a child yourself, too, and looked up to your teachers too; this, I think—so strange, but gradually I will be acquainted with it.

What a lovely thing that you get a salary and that in this time of the crisis. In our country none of the young men and women who have passed their examination of teachers get a place, and everyday teachers who were sometimes more than 20 years teachers are dismissed. The results is that you see in our schools no young teachers, but only men and women "entre deux ages" (between two ages).

Box suppers we don't have to no (know about), but I think we should like it, and I will propose my friends to have such a box supper, an American box supper, too. I do believe it shall be a success.

I hope you soon will fotograph your pupils for I have a desire to know what sort of children they are.

At school I am placed next to a girl who is a socialist. Do you like socialists? I don't like them. At first they will not have a king or a queen, but they will reign themselves. Now it may be a very good principle, but our queen is so lovely and so good and sage and so full of humanity that it is no bad thing at all to be reigned by Her; secondly, they outrage the queen, and when she visits Rotterdam, they begin to riffle and to sing their revolutionary songs; and last it is true that they have fine principles and fine words, but their acts: To mention an example: They say, "We don't like rich men", but the leaders of the party themselves earn large salaries and are some of the richest men in the country.

I have heard of the N.R.A. (National Recovery Administration) and I heard a few days ago that there is chosen a queen of the N.R.A. too, a girl named Ford and no relation of the great auto king, Henry Ford.

What is it to your hobby (custom) in America to choose queens for all sorts of things? What is the duty and the aim of such a queen? Every country seems to have his own hobby which is not to understand by others.

I send you by this a pair of little wooden shoes. The farmers in our country wear these shoes usually; the women of the farmers, too.

I fear that I forget in my last letter to write at my snapshots the names of the girls. Did I send you a girl who was sitting on the grass looking at a map? That was my friend, Rie; the others are of mine. We have hired another house. It is near the station which I like, of course, for now I have not to walk so long before I am in the train to The Hague. The new address is: Stations weg 89 A.

It is to us you could almost say old-fashioned to have cactusses. Do you know what I will say (mean) with this name? I don't know if I use the good word for it. Almost everybody has a box of glass in his room and therein stand the cactusses (cacti). You must have great care for them for they must have a constant temperature and enough food. But when you have great care, you are rewarded in the spring or in the summer with the finest coloured flowers. I will send you a foto of them for I don't press flowers (I cannot for they always become dirty) so I can't send you a real flower. The pressed flowers of you are so beautiful. I have them in a book in my fotobook and when I show my snapshots to a person, always your pressed flowers are admired, too.

Till the next time with great love,

Your friend, Hanna

+ + + + + + +

25 Nov., 1933

Dearest Ruth,

The wooden shoes were in my opinion very fine, especially because they were not new, and they resembled the wooden shoes generally worn although they were much more little. But my mother said the day I would send them to you, "But, Hanna, how dare you to send a pair of old wooden shoes to America? I think Ruth will not be glad to have them, and she will laugh at your nose" (in your face). I thought about it and the result was I did not send them. But I was not content about myself especially because I had promised you them. I did not know what to do until my mother brought me a good idea. You must know that when the time is advanced to December, the time of Nicholaas in Christmas, the shops show all their beautiful things which are bought as presents. My mother walked along these shops and then she saw a shop full of wooden shoes in all shapes and dimenses (sizes). Some of them were used as needle boxes, other as boxes to place flowers in. I will send you such a pair of wooden shoes at Christmas, but I don't tell you now how they are for otherwise it is not a surprise and at us in Holland it is usual to prepare surprises at Christmas. So you will see at Christmas what you get. I regret also I could not place my present for you under the Christmas tree and see your face when you found it, but that is impossible.

Do you have in America a Christmas tree, too? To us everybody has such a tree. A few weeks before Christmas heaps of these pine trees are carried out of the woods and shown in the market place and at several squares by merchants. Everybody if he is not too poor, buys such a tree and carries him in his house. Then the mother and the children make him beautiful with all sorts of cheap glass things and brilliant things. After supper everybody is allowed to see if there are presents for him. I hope you can understand how cozy and serious at the same time such an evening is.

To us December is such a fine month. At first we celebrate St. Nicholaas, a children's feast. I told you already something about it. The children believe each year on 6th December a good old bishop comes from Spain to Holland accompanied by his servant Black Peter. The bishop St. Nicholas rides at night on a white horse over the roofs, and he drops presents in the chimneys for the children. So the children think the horse is hungry. They place in the room under the chimney a wooden shoe with hay. The next morning the hay is gone and a present has come in the place of it. But that is naturally done by father or mother.

Sometimes St. Nicholas and his servant come in the house and bring there the presents. Father or uncle then play for the old bishop. He wears always a red long dress, and he always has a great long white beard. You amuse yourself at such an evening, of course, especially when the children's believing in the St. Nicholaas is so great, and when they don't perceive that it is their father who plays the part of St. Nicholaas.

I have a hard time to read the last time (lately) for it costs so much time to go to school in another city, and it is always late in the evening when I come home. But 22 Dec. we get holidays, and then I will try to read a fine book. Can be I take the same book that you read? Oy He Juif Polonaise by Gil Blas I have read, too.

Ruth, I don't belong to any church. Of course I do believe in the existence of a God, a person, who is good and noble, and who lives in our heart. So I do believe the God is the good and noble part of our soul and the bad part is the devil. Everyone has a part of his soul that is bad and a part that is good, I think.

People who are only good or only bad only occur in bad romans (novels) or in the romans of the 18th century in France as Victor Hugo and others. For that you must read <u>L'Dame</u> <u>Ann</u> <u>Camelis</u>. I hope that you can see out of this that I am not dogmatic. I try to be so good as possible and to struggle with my faults. That is my religion, you know. There are many people who think as I, but there are many, too, who attend a church. The Christian Church (Protestant) is the most common and then the Catholic Church.

The N.R.A. stamp you sent was very fine, my aunt said. But it was a pity that he was torn a little. Will you be so kind as to place such a stamp on your following letter or to send a good one? Then you made my aunt very happy. You must not do it, of course, when the price of the stamp is very high. On the stamp I saw it costs 3 cts, but I don't know how much that is for the wage that you earn is so impossibly high in our country and is only earned by men with very good jobs.

The fotos were very fine, Ruth. What nice children you have in your class. Do you think it a lucky thing that you have a little class?

The magazine I did not receive. To what address did you send them? Perhaps they arrived in the Jan Robellstraat. That would be a pity. I shall go to that street and ask to the people who live there now, if your magazines have arrived there.

Till the next time, my dear Ruth

Your Hanna

+ + + + + + +

9 Dec., 1933

My dear Ruth,

I'm fallen ill last week. I had had a sad feeling a few days and one morning when I sat in the train for The Hague to go to school, I did feel so miserable that I came back with the first train I could catch, and I went to bed. I had a rather high fever. The highest grade was 40 degrees Celcius (104). So my mother sent for the doctor and he said I had to be in my bed for a few weeks. I can't write you what is the name of the illness for I don't know what the English name is for it, but when I am recovered, I shall see in a dictionary. Now the fever is gone, and I am allowed to read in my bed and to write and to knit. Dec. 5 was St. Nicholaas Day. We celebrated it in my room, and all my presents were assembled on my bed. From my mother I got a kalender. My father had given me a fruit basket, and then I got a fish glass with four beautiful fishes in it from a friend of mine. A girl friend gave me a new self-filling pen. We had a fine evening though I was ill.

This morning I got your letter and the packet. I was so glad with the letter for sometimes I have nothing to do, and I can't want from my mother that she is the whole day around me for she has her work in the house. On the packet was written that I was not allowed to unfasten it before 25 Dec. I can hardly wait till then— that is 14 days. What a cozy packet it is. I feel it in my hands, and I admire the beautiful paper around it. What a beautiful custom you have in America to celebrate Christmas and to make it cozy by all sorts of little things! As I am not allowed to unfasten the packet, I can't thank you for it, but that comes later on.

It is beautiful to have radio. Has everyone in your city a radio? We don't have one. My father is very conservative in such things, and he says he will not have that "huempa" music through the radio. He prefers to go to a good concert where he can see the people who play. He can't have that people listen to a fine piece of music through the radio while they drink a cup of tea and talk with each other and that often happens. But when there is given anything in the radio worth hearing, I go to a friend who has a radio and at this way I do hear it.

Some people do amateurism (ham) radio. Do you know what I mean by that? It is so difficult to write you about it for there occur so much difficult words, but I will try. When it is a failure, I will buy some day a great dictionary in which I can see all these words and then I will tell you it good. To us only four associations are allowed to send out music or other things. All people are allowed to receive, but they may not send themselves (broadcast).

But now you can go in for an exam and when you pass, you also are allowed to send out. In our country +/– (about) 50 people have passed that exam especially students in chemisty and physics. Now I have a friend who is a student, too. He studies for this exam and he will go in for it next year and then he can send out too. All these people can talk with each other. You understand? It is a sort of telephone, but for a few people. I am enthusiastic about it. Suppose when it comes so far that the radio can be used as telephone for everyone. Then we, too, can talk with each other! But that will last, of course, heaps of years, and then we only have perhaps sixty or seventy years. But never mind. Out of your letter I read that 25 Dec. is to you the same day as Dec. 5 is to us. What you mention Santa Claus is to us St. Nicholaas and when I say "Sint" in French, it is Saint, and I think when you say "Santa" in French it is also Saint, is it not? I told you already that we also try to make the children better by this man and how he gives them presents. Has your Santa Claus a servant as ours and also a black servant? To us grown up people also celebrate the feast, and do you?

Will you excuse me when my Christmas present comes too late? Now that I am ill, I can't do these things myself and I must ask other people to buy my presents and to send them away. I'm very sorry for that.

I'm glad you also find this season a happy one. But I think it's a serious one, too. The birth of the Christ who was given to the people to wash away their sins I think it a very fine feast and you? That has not to do with any Bible or believing, but everyone must feel that as a thing very beautiful and very fine. The Christ figure is the most beautiful I know, and I wished everyone would follow his example. Then the world was good and as a paradise.

What a happy feeling to get 86 Christmas cards. We don't have that custom in Holland. I think it is not a cheap custom for when you must send all your friends these cards and then all the stamps for it, but that has not to do with the beautiful custom, of course.

Ruth, I wish you have a very merry Christmas and a happy new year. A very happy new year with a heap of happiness and a little accident for no accidents at all, that is impossible and it would not be good for us, too.

So a happy new year for you, your parents, your sisters and brother and your friends (especially Reathel.)

Till the next time,

Your Hanna

Chapter Two

With the beginning of 1934 Ruth and Hanna were feeling quite comfortable with each other. Thoughtful gifts were exchanged and more personal insights were shared such as disappointments, joys, and meaningful relationships—boyfriends.

In 1934 Hitler and a military buildup of the Dutch army were first mentioned. Hanna probably expressed the opinion of the majority of the Dutch people when she said she believed Hitler was too involved with German problems to ever consider invading other countries. She did recognize that one-third of the Germans who vigorously objected to Hitler's policies risked concentration camps, but felt that the remaining Germans were quietly non-supportive. Later she even admired his rebuilding of Germany after the Allies of World War I so "cruelly and needlessly crushed it". (No wonder the United States had such ambivalent feelings about getting involved when those closest to the situation were also misinformed and too trusting.) Hanna later had a complete change of opinion (or perhaps of innocent optimism) after her country and many others became the victims, but hind sight is always better.

Hanna expressed her taste in music and noted that she couldn't understand the sudden impact and response to jazz and the "nigger" players. The term was not meant to be derogatory, but was in common use at that time. Today the terms "Blacks" or "African-Americans" are more appropriate and acceptable.

The Lindbergh kidnapping and killing of the famous aviator's son horrified the world. "Lucky Lindy" had been honored and recognized as the first to fly solo nonstop across the Atlantic in 1927. Five years later when his 20-month-old son was abducted and later found murdered, it was an international tragedy. This man touched both girls' lives. Lindbergh had "barnstormed" throughout Southern Illinois in his earlier days giving rides and demonstrations of flying. (Ruth's first airplane ride was from a field outside her town and cost 50 cents.) His plane had been financed by nearby St. Louis, Mo. businessmen—thus the name "Spirit of St. Louis".

Later the Lindberghs moved to Europe with their second son Jon to try to escape the endless publicity and notoriety. The conviction and execution of the Lindbergh's former carpenter were questioned by Hanna whose country didn't practice capital punishment.

Dearest Ruth,

In your letter of Dec. 25 you touch a subject we did not speak about, but as we consider each other as to belong to our best friends, I must turn over my heart for you.

Yes, I have a "special" boy friend. What did you express this is such a particular way? I did laugh heartily about it. But he is not my "sweetheart" for when we say this word in Holland (also in English) then we say it ironical (I hope you understand what I mean) and I mean it so serious with him, you must know.

His name is Aad Muijser (of course you can't pronounce it, these two a's are very difficult for you, is it not?) When we were on the H.B.S still (this was the school about which I told you last year) he helped me often with my work for I often had difficulties with it especially with chemistry and physics (not with the languages) and with his aid I have struggled through the final examination. But when we worked together in my room, it was that our friendship changed into love. And at one evening Aad said this to me. It was very good that my parents trusted us and never came in my room to see if our behavior was good, for this evening it was not, as it must be.

Since this time it was very difficult to work together, you know, but with the examination in view it was a necessity.

For the holidays we often made a trip together for one day without a chaperone. In Holland we don't have chaperones at all, and, I believe, they don't have in France such old-fashioned things either. This chaperoning belongs to the time of Charles Dickens, I think, and not to ours. We are free in such sorts of things and only our feeling of decency so must say to us what we can do and what we must not do. My father allows that Aad comes to us and that I go often with him to the theatre or to his parents, but though he allows it, he often turns his head and sighs: "Oh, oh, this youth of now-a-days." When he was young, it did not occur that a boy and girl went out together without being engaged.

You must know that in our country we think that the American youth is more free than here. Some people say that the indecency is far too such, and that it often occurs that a young couple go away in a car for a few days to make a trip together, and that nobody says that it is bad. Are you really so modern in

America or not? To us that does not occur, only by very low characters.

Now, Aad is a student of chemistry. He studies at the University of Delft. I am studying in The Hague. We must take the same train in the morning and, therefore, we go together. When Aad goes out of the train in Delft, I have to sit down for five minutes still before I am in The Hague. This train is always full of students. Before Aad is a doctor in chemistry, he has to study 5 years. Do you think it long or not? How long does it last in America before you have a title? When Aad has come through three examinations (every summer one), he is a candidate and then he is allowed to teach chemistry on a H.B.S. but that when he studies still 2 years, he is a doctor, and then you can reach for more, of course.

Do I hear the next letter also more of your friend (meaning a boyfriend), Ruth? I think it is my right now a little.

On Christmas day I opened your packet. I knew there was a compact in it (you wrote it in our letter) but such a beautiful one I had not dreamed about. And with a chain on it! Many thanks of it, Ruth. When (if) you were here, you got a big kiss for it. For you must know that till your packet came, I never possessed a compact at all. To us the powder is not so very often used as to you it seems. I am not the only girl who has no powder stuff. I have some girl friends who walk the whole day with powder and rouge on their faces, but most of us only use it when we go to a party or to the theater. If our skin is too red or not smooth enough, for that aim you need not wear a powder stuff.

But now I have one and such a beautiful one. You understand that I wear it and show it to all my friends, and they laugh and say that this friend has a corruptible influence. When we all have such American friends, we in Holland will look like painted dolls, too. But I know that they don't mean it so, and that they are in their hearts very jealous of such a fine thing. Besides I don't use it the whole day, of course, only when I go out as was my custom before.

I hope the wooden shoe has arrived. My aunt has chosen it so when you don't like it, it is not my fault. She is very glad with the stamps. Do you have still the stamp from the packet I sent you? When (if) you have it, and none of your friends will have it, do you send it then back again? You must know that it is a new stamp of 80 ct, and my aunt, the philatelist, likes to have it, and, of course, you can put him (the stamp) on a letter in Holland, too, but he is rather expensive. But never mind, when (if) you have put it away!

Jo is learning to become a typist. To us it is not so easy to get a job and you must learn and learn and pass several examinations before you have any chance to get a job. All these young people have nothing to do and it is not to be wondered that gradually a revolutionary mind comes in the country especially now we have such an example in our neighborhood viz Hitler in Germany. But, fortunately, there are still people enough who are content with the reign of Queen Wilhelmina, and who admit that she has not the fault of the crisis and her results.

What an event when Lindbergh and his wife came in Holland. Everyone who lived in the neighborhood of Amsterdam, or who had money enough to pay a journey to that city, came to the place where Lindbergh descended. But he was not very fond of all this enthusiasm. He visited the "Palais de la Pain" in The Hague, but that day I was not in The Hague so I did not see him to my regret. What a horrible thing is that with the kidnapping of children! To us it fortunately never occurs. Though I don't think it good that the kidnappers are put to death. To us nobody is put to death for it is our opinion: Nobody has the right to put another to death, and everybody is born free and with the same rights for living. But when they have done anything worse, they are put in prison for their whole life, and I think that is much worse still than put to death. What do you think about this?

Ping pong is to us popular, too. We don't have one, but a friend of mine has one, and it often occurs that on a Sunday afternoon he invites some boy or girl friends, and then we have a pretty match. Even his parents play sometimes with us. Do you play it as tennis? With games and sets or have you another method?

I have let Aad read the part of your letter where you wrote about "your doctor." He said when you write already such long letters to me, how long should they be to him when you love him? Is the doctor your "sweetheart" or not? When he is, I do find it strange that you go to parties and so on with other boys. When (if) I were the doctor, I should not like this, and I am afraid that I should be very jealous when I sat 400 miles from you with the thoughts that you sat in a car with a boy friend. Aad and I always go together to such sorts of things, or I go with Jo or with several friends.

I wonder that the temperature was so low "0" Fahrenheit and that you shake then. To us you can already shake when it is a few degrees beneath zero at the Celcius. If I don't make a mistake, I believe that zero Celcius = 32 degrees Fahrenheit, is it not?

I am recovered again. Last week it froze, and we did skate. In our country with its beautiful lakes and rivers and canals, you can skate everywhere. I do find it a beautiful sport. We have ordinary wooden skates with an iron piece beneath so that the ice and the iron touch each other.

Many people in Holland go in the Christmas holidays to Switzerland. There is snow enough, and you can learn to walk at skis (cross-country skiing). Do you know what I mean by that? In our country often falls snow, but it is so low with no mountains so that you can't ski. Sleigh riding is not so popular to us as skating. Only children do it with little sleighs.

With much love.

Your friend, Hanna

+ + + + + + +

5 March, 1934 — R'dam

Dearest Ruth,

The tough pieces for the report that our school gives before the Easter holidays are over. I hope I made them very well, for I studied hard and long the last weeks. Now a few weeks yet, and it is Easter holidays, and we can repose for a fortnight as much as we desire for you feel at last you become very tired. At first that traveling between R'dam and The Hague and then as much mental work as bodily (or is it corporal) work, and when you are bodily tired, you can hardly let work your brains.

But now an uncle of mine is coming to live in The Hague, and I can go to him when I have some hours free. We have there a military university, you know. Boys who come from the middle schools as H.B.S. can come there to be prepared to go later to the East Indies (Dutch Indies) as an officer. My uncle was teacher there. He had to teach the boys to fence. But the last years no boys were admitted at this school all because the crisis (depression) for the Public Exchequer paid the school and gave in every

29

case a great gratification. Now my uncle is removed to The Hague, and he is there sargeant of cavalry. That is a very amusing job for you must always have care for the horses and make exercises for them and so long as there is no war, it is not a dangerous job. I hope so ardently that there will be no war although I fear for everywhere the countries extend their armies, and in Europe the several countries can't say a good thing of each other. The papers write excitedly things, too, and that is not a good specimen. Even the social democrats (that is the party who has always pled for disarming) have changed their program, and now she is for extending the army. I can't find words for it, but it is bewildering and painful and grievous. And the mere pretext they have for that changing is that we are so in the neighbourhood of Hitler (the Germans are our East neighbours) and that we must be afraid that he will come in our country. But that is a mere pretext for they know too well that Hitler has too much to do in his own country to hold out and everybody in Europe knows that 3/3 of the people in Germany say, "Yes," but that 1/3 does it with conviction and that 2/3 do it with hate in their hearts, but because he knows when he says openly, "No," that he is locked up in a concentration camp. So now I have let stress out of my heart all these objections, and I exhaust myself in excuses to you that I come to you with them, but I think that you understand me too well, and I need such a confidential hour of writing with you for you know I love Aad so much, but over this subject there is no talking with him, for he has yet these old-fashioned ideas about it, and I am sure if there was a war today that he should go to the front the next day. So you can understand when we talk about it that we always get quarrel. He says, "Girls must not meddle with these things for they have not enough reason about it. Besides they are too sensitive and sentimental." Now and then I will defend myself, of course, and we get a quarrel. That is not so very serious because when you have finished, you can kiss it off again, but you prefer someone with whom you can speak without quarreling, is it not?

Yesterday evening I dined at Aad's and after dinner we heard the radio. It was all jazz music. How do you find the hot jazz music? It is very modern to us to love jazz, and when there comes a band in our city, everyone pays expensive seats for it. It seems Beethoven, Bach, and Grieg and so very much others have no place in the Dutch hearts—especially not in the hearts of the youth. But Aad and I belong to those who do not gush with this jazz. I can't find them beautiful. Besides the fine rhythm, I hear nothing but sounds and no music. Last week we went with some eight young people to such a band evening where was only plaid hot jazz. I noticed that the people grew excited and when it was done, they cried, "Bis, bis" and they jumped from their seats as if they were drunken. I mean that this is idiotic and that one can see that this sort of music is very primitive and that it only works on the lower instincts of people and that it is only tensions. I mean the jazz is from the origin of the Africans, is it not? Now to you in America who live with niggers and always you turned your back to them, and now in Europe and can be in America, too, one is drunken of their music and often such a nigger jazz player is the hero of much young girls' dreams to us. They write letters to him, and his portrait is hanging above their beds. What do you think of it, Ruth?

Wednesday our gymnastic club gives a feast. I enjoy from it (look forward to it) days before. I hope it will be good.

What beautiful cuttings (possibly Valentine doilies) you send me. It was a pity that there was no letter in the package for now I did not understand what you meant by it and for what purpose for to us in Holland as we have not such things.

Do you write me soon? With much greetings,

Your Hanna

+ + + + + + +

March, 1934

My dearest Ruth,

I am sorry that you don't love the doctor. I thought you did. I thought I read it between the lines of your letter.

I looked at your face on the piano (it has changed places), and I found that your face was so beautiful and lovely that everybody must love it and as you smiled too charming that you could not send it away. But never mind. Have you enough to your family to love and it is, therefore, that you need not the love of anyone who does not belong in your family?

I think any girl has a heap of love in her heart, and there must be an outlet for it, and it is such a sweet and safe feeling that you have anyone on whom you can stream out all the tenderness of your heart. I am not able to tell you how great my

31

love for Aad is, but he has the greatest part of my heart, you know, although you thrust yourself gradually into the most distant corners of it, too.

At school we get dedictions (assignments); that is, every teacher gives us some work to do. The teacher in pedagogie, for instance, gives us a book about pedagogie to read, and when we have read it, we must make an essay about it. All these assignments must be done before the end of March. So I am very busy this month. When the work is done, I am resolving to make a pouch for you to do (carry) something in when you go out, for instance, your handkerchief and your powder stuff. I will embroider it with silk crosses. Do you that work in America, too? When I make it, what colors do you prefer? The pouch himself is black with black crosses, but the flowers are of another colour.

A few months ago I made a cushion of such work. It lasted (took) very long, but when it was finished, it was very beautiful. But when (if) you like not to have such a thing, you must write it, for then I make, for instance, an envelopment for a book from it or a pocketbook—another thing you like.

Yesterday a job's news reached us. There stood in the papers that a thousand workers of the iron works in Rotterdam should be dismissed at the first (last) of March—1000 unemployed men more! And in Holland it is the duty of the queen to care for these men and their wives and children. They get every week about half of the money from the queen that they got from their employer before they were dismissed. But that costs lots of money and the persons who work and earn money have to pay high taxes +/– 20% of their gain.

Ruth, this time you do not get a long letter for I am so busy, and I have not to tell so much for the last weeks I have worked so hard, and I did nothing else.

You wrote me a long time ago when was your birthday, but I forget it, and I did read all your letters over more, but very volubile and I could not find. Please write the date next time for I should be sorry when I forget the birthday of one of my best friends. Possible that I can make the embroidery work for your birthday.

Aad was very glad to make your acquaintance, too, and shakes hands with you.

Best regards to your friends and a kiss for you.

Hanna

April 15, 1934

My dearest Ruth,

Much thanks for the Easter greeting. I do find it such a kind custom of you. Gradually in our country it becomes fashionable, too, to send each other at Easter time such greetings. The shops buy those cards with English words on them. You can see they have picked up this custom from England and America, and it is not original. Therefore, I do not send such a thing to you.

I hope that you escape the mumps for that is a terrible disease. It occurs in Holland, too.

Yesterday I went to an assembly where a clergyman spoke about Fascism. Do you know what I mean by that? It is the manner of reigning in Italy and Germany. To us a lot of people are partisans of this system so that it is becoming a moral apparition. But the clergyman said that such a system born out of despair cannot help to put away the crisis and the bad times. He said we had to look just now in the Easter days to the little child, born in a stall, later on the man who suffered for the sins of the people—viz the Christ, and when we come so far that we bend ourselves to him and understand his sufferings, the world will be better.

With much love, Hanna

+ + + + + + +

30 April, 1934

My dear Ruth,

This day is the birthday of our princess Juliana. She is twenty-five now. It is 10 o'clock in the morning, and the sunlight shines bright in the room where I am sitting to write to you. Before the window is my fish glass, and the sun shines through it and paints the fishes with all sorts of colours.

In Holland people are always glad when on a national day as it is now, the sun shines. We mention on this day, the sun—"the orange sun", and without an orange sun (orange is the colour of the Royal family), it is not a real feast. When I look out of the window, I see people. Most of them have an orange flower in their buttonhole in honour of the princess, and the little children have an orange scarf or bonnet. It is a pity that the death of our good Queen Emma jumps a shadow over it.

I thank you very much for the clippings out of your papers of her. I let them see to my aunt and do you know what she said? "I think this Ruth must be a very sensible and tender girl. I do think this such an act of sympathy especially when she knows that you are such a partisan of the monarchy." Now, in this way I felt it, too, and I am very grateful to have such a friend. A pity that she lives so far away.

But never mind, you know, I have such a presentiment that we shall see each other on a good day.

The other day I heard about a friend of my father. He went with his wife to America for pleasure. You must know in our country exists an association for traveling. When you are a member of this association, you have many advantages. When you pay a sum of money, you can make a travel with other people you don't know, and a conductor who knows all about traveling goes with this people and takes care for all—for boats, hotels, trains, and so on. Now this man went to America, too, but he went to South American to Buenos Aires. He went with so many people that the travel was not so expensive at all. It is possible that in this way we will see each other, too, is it not, Ruth? Then I jump for pleasure out of my skin, you know.

The symbol +/− means "about" or "almost". I thought this was an international method to use for "about", but it seems that it is not the case. You asked if I have heard of Byrd. My dear girl, I did hear his own voice when he was in the South Pole. You must know the radio association in Holland. The A.V.R.O in Hilversum had taken care for it. We could hear Byrd and the dogs. It was on the short golf (wave). It did not come through very good, and as they spoke English, we could not understand so good for we had difficulties enough to hear the voices. But it was very interesting after all.

What you describe as a carnival is mentioned to us as a fair. On a fair are all these amusements, too. With a carnival we mean a sort of bal-masque, (masked ball) you know.

Years ago, especially in the last century, a carnival went together with a fair, especially in the villages. In the market place there were standing all sorts of amusements as rounds about and barrel organs, and the country folk changed their dress. Girls were dressed in men's dresses, and you saw men who had made of themselves an old wife. It was all very horrible. They all had at evening a mask for their eyes, and they drank till they were dead drunk. Such a fair was also good to fight old bitter strifes, and in the days of the fair, which was in the last week of August, it occurred always that to a fight some men were killed.

Later on the government has forbidden these fairs, and now, you have a remains of it, and that is the bal-masque. You know what a bal-masque is? It is very funny. You go to a ball, but you don't dress in your evening frock, but an old fashioned dress or a fantastic dress. Last year I went to the bal-masque in a short dress made of red silk and with green trousers under the dress down to my shoes. The frock was with yellow threads. It was meant to resemble a tulip. We had such fun these evenings.

Have you ever heard of the great Hingelberg? He conducts an orchestra, and is famous in the whole world. He got in America the Dr. title. Last year he fell ill, but now he is recovered, and yesterday he conducted for the first since after his disease. People cheered him, and he had to say a few words. After the representation the whole stage was full of flowers.

The spring song of Mendelsohn is very fine. I am glad that you can play it. I do often play it. The other pieces that you mentioned, I never played. To this I send you a piece that Aad made. He liked to make music, and some of his songs are very good. You must, for instance, play this piece and write when you think of it. There are words to it, but as you don't know anything of Dutch, you should not understand them.

I hope you write back soon.

With much love from your pal, Hanna

+ + + + + + +

In the next letter Hanna, a Protestant who didn't seem to have a very strong church affiliation, described a visit to Catholic relatives in Belgium. These Lowlands have been under the control of several governments since they often lie in the paths of warring factors. In the 15th century the Hapsburgs of Austria assumed command. When Charles I of Austria became King of Spain, they were allied with the Spanish Empire. Later, it became expedient to divide the northern part, The United Provinces (Holland) from the Spanish Netherlands. Next, the French annexed the southern portion (Belgium) in 1795. Following Belgium's dissatisfaction with France's regime and especially Napoleon's defeat, Belgium and the United Provinces were combined to form the Kingdom of the Netherlands. The first king, William of Orange, faced a Protestant northern territory and a Catholic southern land. In 1830 Belgium became a neutral nation. Both countries have remained monarchies with Dutch (or a dialect Flemish) being spoken in northern Belgium and French in the south. Both countries were overrun during the World Wars, and each is heavily populated so they have much in common.

8 June, 1934 — Rotterdam

My dear Ruth,

Your last letter was one of our intimate talks again. I did enjoy it very much. I did give it to Aad to read, and he enjoyed it, too. Only he did not understand why it took so much time of parting when you had been car riding with your friend, when it is not such an intimate one (close relationship), as you said. But I said to him that he was naughty, and that he had not to say these things because it was already bad to think them. And then he laughed and sighed and said, "You girls, you resemble so much each other in this regard."

I am so glad that you have got such a good job. I am working hard this time. On 28 June our vacances begin till 3 Sept. So in this time I can rest so much as I will. I did make my work very well so I hope that I will pass to the second class. Aad has done an exam a few weeks ago at the University in Delft. It was an exam in chemistry, and he thought he did it very well. About a week he hears if he has passed the examination. The exams in our country especially at the university become more difficult every year. At our school, too, they are very difficult. This year 80% did not come through the final examination.

To my regret Aad and I are not together on a foto. We only have some where we are sitting on a foto with a lot of other boys and girls. You must not forget, we are not engaged, and this is not a custom here to have then fotos of each other. But because you like to have one, I shall do my best to make that you receive one.

Did you hear that Jo is engaged last month? There was a reception where all her friends and her family came, but to my regret, I could not go for I went with my father to Belgium. This country is south of our country.

A sister of my father is living there in a village near the town Anvers. Her husband died for two years (two years ago), but he had so much spared (saved) that she was able to live with her three children in a house of her own with a lawn behind it to be jealous of. So my father and I had a fine day there. The daughter Julia has the same age as I. She is a teacher in feminal handicraft on a girls' school, and she is fond of making beautiful works as embroidered cushions and knitted frocks. The next day we went with the whole family to Mechelen. There my cousin is a friar in the monastery which was built in 1109. It is a very old building, and in the several wars that have been in the several centuries, it has lost some pieces. It the last war there is also a piece that has been ruined. Although my father and I are not katholic, my cousin was so kind to let see us the whole monastery.

In the monastery is also a boys' school. The boys who live there from 6 to 18 have a very strict education. My cousin is the French teacher there, and besides the lessons he has to educate the boys, too. I do find it a very hard life. He is allowed to visit his mother one day in the three years, but he is allowed to receive visits so often as he will. We had dinner in the monastery, and after dinner we went to the train and home.

Aad thanks you for the stamp, and he sends you a flower card. My mother did appreciate your card at Mother's day very much, and she asked me to give you her kind regards.

From me with a big kiss.

Hanna

Early photo of Hanna de Bruijn and Aad Muijser
Rotterdam, Holland

+ + + + + +

20 September, 1934

My dear Ruth,

At first my great joy about your birthday present. It was just what I wanted so much. At my birthday itself there was your letter, and I did read in it how much we approached each other the last year. I have the beautiful box in my writing desk, and you are the first who gets a letter on it. Usually it is a pity to use such beautiful sheets for our letters because we have to say to each other so much and then you need so many sheets.

We enjoyed your letters about the World's Fair at Chicago. The whole family enjoyed it while I read to them. It was a happy thing that there was a Holland stand, too, and that you saw the old Dutch dances.

I had a very fine birthday. From my parents I got a pair of gloves and from Aad a silver bracelet. I had a pouch of the leather of a snake from my aunt and from another aunt a silver pencil. It was all very fine. Besides I got at night a great tart.

You must know to us it is a habit when any one has reached the age of 10, 20, 30, etc. as a "crown" year, he gets at his birthday night a great tart with 20 candles on it. The lights in the room are turned out, and the tart is brought in burning. When the candles have burnt some time, then the tart is cut in pieces and everyone gets a piece. It is a very lovely custom, and everyone appreciates it. My birthday fell on Sunday so that many people visited us, and we had great fun.

In Sept. I went to school again, and I must work hard to come in June, 1935 through the final examination for 80% failed this year. It is hard working. The whole day I am from home except Saturday and Sunday, but I love my studies and that is the principal thing.

Today there was the great sport day in The Hague. All the schools with their pupils from 12-18 years "fight" (compete) that day another on a very great sport ground. The pupils of a school who are the best in athletics must come in the field, and they fight another in springing, throwing spears, 200 m. running, etc. The school who makes the most points has won. Such a match needs a colossal regulator and registration, and every year the school for physical education in The Hague (our school) takes care of it. Everyone of our school from the teachers to the pupils are working that day to set out the fields for running, to conduct the children to their places, to hold the ground free from too many people observing, to make (record) the times they made and the distances they sprang. It was a very fine day. I had the task to conduct the children from one place to another and to take care they held themselves in good condition. When it was done, we had a lunch together, and it was all very funny.

Ruth, I am glad that you have a friend in Chicago who loves to have Dutch stamps. Aad says we shall look for some beautiful stamps—for instance of Dutch Indies, and I will send them next time.

Much love from me and kind regards from Aad and my parents. Thanks for the stamps. Please send the one on this letter back, too?

Hanna

+ + + + + + +

10 Oct., 1934 — Rotterdam

My dear Ruth,

We all "gratulate" you with your birthday, and we want you to have after this year most of very happy years.

The pocket book I promised you has not come ready. I have it so busy, you must know, and it is a very great work on which you must not hurry for then there comes nothing good of it. So when the pocket book is ready, you get it after all.

But now we have a birthday present you shall like much more. Yesterday evening Aad and I went out to buy you a present, and in one of the warehouses we saw a lovely book-marker. I remembered you liked reading books, and so we did buy it. The bookmarker has on it the weapon (shield) of Rotterdam in silver. You must know in our country every city has its own weapon (the origin from the Middle Ages) and Rotterdam has four roaring lions above a half circle. I hope you like the little present. After all it is for you a curiosity, I think. I want for you to have a happy birthday, my dear.

Kind regards of my family and Aad and a birthday kiss of your friend.

Hanna

39

+ + + + + +

A form of censorship already seemed to be in place and tolerated, if not appreciated, which allowed the postal service to open and examine overseas packages to search for items not allowed into the country. This later became very widespread with letters pried into during the German occupation to prevent the Dutch from giving out information that might aid the Allies.

21 Oct. 1934

My dearest Ruth,

I received your candle stick holders, and at first I must thank you for that attention. I was so very happy with them. I do find them so artistic and beautiful, so slender of line and such a fine combination of silver and blue. And then I do like such presents from you because they are so typically American. Everybody here has on its piano or mantlepiece a candle stick holder, but nobody has one of the World's Fair in Chicago!!

We put the one on the piano. We have on the piano a black cloth. On this an urn of deep gray and a few portraits. Now your candle stands on it, too, and does it very well on the black cloth. The other candle we put on the mantle piece, and there it was very beautiful, too. But the same evening my aunt called on us, and she admired your candles so much. She looked at them all the time. Then I got an idea. It cost me a self conviction, but I offered her one of the candles, and she was so glad with it, that I did not regret my offer one moment. I hope you have nothing against it, too.

Besides I thank you for the fotos of you, your sister, and your brother, and I gratulate them on their degrees. The marks (stamps) are very rare here, I understand so I thank you that you sent them. With this letter I send you two marks for your cousin in Chicago. They are of Queen Emma and Queen Wilhelmina, and I expect he does not have them.

I hope you had a happy birthday, and I hope also my present came not too late. I heard the tax become very high, and it is not an exception when they unfasten the parcels and see what it contains. Therefore, it lasts nowadays so long before we get each other's parcels. For instance, your letter in which you wrote that you should send me a surprise about the World's Fair, reached me

40

a week or so ago, and the parcel came yesterday together with your letter of Oct. 6. It seems they unfastened the parcel at the tariff office to see that there was nothing in it what is not allowed to be sent.

The summer here has passed and the beautiful days of autumn too. It is winter time now with cold rains and heavy storms. We searched for our winter clothes again, and we feel very agreeable in it. My mother is knitting a blouse for me of blue wool. I do appreciate such a knitted dress for it is very warm. Do you have knitted blouses? I wear the blouse on a brown skirt, and I think it is a beautiful combination.

The kidnapping history of baby Lindbergh is terrible, and I am glad they have found the mischief maker. I understand that the whole country grieves with the air here, and I wonder how such terrible things can occur in a modern country as America.

At our school we are allowed to give two lessons a week to a class of children to learn teaching. Now there are twenty schools in The Hague, and under the teacher of these schools we give our lessons, and we become (earn) a degree from it. Now I have two schools, and one of these is a school for ragged children.

When they come to school at 9:00 in the morning, they get at first a slice of bread and butter, and then the lessons begin. At 12:00 they don't go home to eat for their parents are so poor that they have not anything, and therefore, the school gives them what they want. The children are very poor and meagre. They are, of course, underfed, and I have such a pity with them. But to teach such a class is very agreeable, you know, for they are very glad when they get a good word or a caressing. Next time I will tell you more about this school when it interests you.

Notice the marks on the envelope. You must give one to your cousin, and one send back. It is of Queen Emma.

Hanna

+ + + + + + +

Again the Christmas customs are described which cause Americans to reflect on the fact that while we may have modified them, most of our traditions are borrowed from Europe.

29 November, 1934

Dearest Ruth,

How do you do, my dear amice? I hope very well. I did receive your last letter, and I enjoyed it very much. It is winter here again and rather cold. We enjoy sitting near the chimney and listening to the radio or reading a book or working on something. The 5th of December it is St. Nicholas, the feast for children, but grown-up people have their joy in it, too, you know. At this evening there are all sorts of raillery. When dinner is over, and we get some time, the feast begins. Every member of the family has made a present for the others, and he gives his present with a little rhyme of raillery. Now you must know I cannot rhyme at all, and so I do sit weeks before to make such a nonsense thing.

Last year on this time I was ill and was in my bed. I'm happy that now this is not the case and that I am so healthy.

Do tell me in your next letter much about your pupils. I am fond, too, of hearing about children and their habititudes. At the school I visited before I went to the school in The Hague was a gymnastic teacher. She was a very lovely woman, and I loved her much. Now and then I call on her. Now she does not only teach gymnastics, but she also teaches them swimming. She asked me to help her with this occupation. Of course, I'm very glad that I am allowed to do it. Every Friday morning I go to the swimming bath, and I try to teach the children swimming. When they can swim, then we teach them difficulties as water springing (diving) and swimming rapidly. It is very amusing, but I am very tired after such a morning.

Now in the middle of February there is a swimming match between the different schools in Rotterdam, and the best of each school are chosen to swim for their school. These girls must be trained. It is all very lovely and the girls themselves are very enthusiastic about it. Next time I will tell you more about it.

Tell your folks hello for me and tell me much about yourself and your folks. Sometimes I have such a strong desire to see your eyes and your face, you know, and then I have nothing but your portraits to look at.

With love, Hanna

+ + + + + + +

Dearest Ruth,

I received your letter in which you wished us to have a happy Christmas.

This morning I went with my aunt in the warehouse to buy you a Christmas present. You know in Holland we do not give each other Christmas presents, but "Sinterklaas" presents. I did think it lovely of you to think of it, but the date is 5 December, you know.

But for you I buy a Christmas present, and I chose a napkin (or serviette) ring to put your napkin in.

My aunt wished to give you a thing, too, she said, for you always had such a care for her stamps, and we saw a lovely spoon, and it is not an ordinary one. You must know, Ruth, it is in relation with the London-Melbourne race. You know about this race: London-Melbourne is as speedy as one could go in an aeroplane. Two Dutch aeroplanes went to the race, too, and one of them, the Uiver (in English "Stork") won the second prize. It is naturally that in Holland we all were very enthusiastic. The newspapers and the radio were full over it , and we did many honor to the brave men.

Now many people buy a spoon, on which the stork is put, and also the name of the race. My aunt hopes that you appreciate it. She at first would buy a lipstick with silver handle for you, but at the last moment, she was not assured you used one, and I did not know either. Do you use such a thing?

At the last evening of the year my mother always makes meat balls filled with roasted apples. That is so the custom of the Dutch mother, you know. We all eat these apple balls with warmed wine and later on we have supper, and we do family games till it is 12 o'clock. How do you spend the last evening of the year, Ruth? Is it an evening for the family, or not? I should like to know it. And then till the next year!

Always loving you, Hanna

A Merry Christmas and a happy new year—

Mrs. N. de Bruijn Rens

Mr. A. de Bruijn

(A married woman added her maiden surname to her husband's.)

Chapter Three

At first the pen pals wrote only about school, family, and social activities. In the late 1930's Hanna and Aad began writing about their concerns with the military buildup of Germany and this rising leader named Hitler. Being just across the border from that country made the Dutch people feel very vulnerable. Every letter Hanna wrote concerned that growing fear. Since Aad was in the Dutch military service, they knew he would have to go to war if Holland were invaded.

However, in America Ruth didn't think anything about it. It seemed so distant that she didn't feel Americans needed to be concerned. Yet a Christmas card from Hanna in 1936 said, "I don't know how you view this season, but we go into the new year with a very anxious heart. For everywhere countries do not trust one another. Weaponed to the teeth, they beware each other, and weaponed peace is a terrible thing. Ruth, when you pray to God, ask Him to take care of Europe, to be merciful that such a terrible war as 1914 doesn't repeat."

14 Januari, 1935 — R'dam

My dear Ruth,

I thank you very heartily for the cedar chest which I received the day before Christmas. I placed it in my bedroom, and I do in it my jeweleries as rings and bracelets. The yellow stripes in it are very beautiful and are in complete harmony with the red colour of the border. My father thinks you spoil his daughter with such a beautiful present for he said that such chests are here in Holland very rare and when you will buy one, you have to pay a large sum of money. But I am fond of such presents which are not to buy in Holland itself and carry the stamp of America.

I am glad you admired our presents, too. Only there is the following drama with the spoon. I told you all about the Uiver (Stork) and his beautiful flight from London to Melbourne and all the souvenirs they made of it. After the flight the same Uiver has to fly again to the Dutch Indies to bring the Christmas post from Holland to the Indies. You must know almost every family has members of it in the Indies. The Dutch Indies being 100 times as large as Holland itself. So it was the (goal) to bring the Christmas post in 4 days to Indies and the answers take back to Holland and arrive in Holland before New Year. But when the Uiver was in the neighborhood of Baghdad, the pilot was surprised by a thunderstorm. The airplane perished with post, passengers, and crew. When we in Holland heard of the disaster, the whole country was in mourning and sorrow. Everywhere the conversation was about the Uiver and pity for the passengers and crew. Many people could not but weep. It was such a dramatic end of the glorious airplane. In such a little country as our Holland we all are so very interested in all what happens. People know each other and when an airplane as the Uiver is built, it at first comes in all the large cities of the country to be shown and admired. So everybody knew the Uiver, had seen it and his crew. We all were so proud of it, and we have jumped and cried when it got the first prize in the handicap race. Now all is sorrow and weeping in Holland especially for the wives and children of the passengers and crew.

I received your letter of 27 Dec. in which you held your promise to tell me all about your Christmas tree. I went with the letter in an easy chair, and I had a free quarter of an hour to read all about it.

There was also a letter for my aunt in it and stamps. She was very glad with both. She is the sister of my mother and already an elderly lady of 50 years. She is unmarried and she cares for herself as a nurse. She often is in our house and every morning she comes to us. Then my mother and she go swimming in a swimming bath 10 minutes from our town. Although she is fifty, in her manners and thoughts, she is very young. She always understands us, sometimes better as our own parents.

Now she is glad to get from America rare stamps, and she thanks you that you will do your best to purchase the stamps of the National Park. It is not her intention to have them fastened together. You are allowed to "fetch" them from old letters. On your last letter there was one of the Nat. Park of 3 cents and to the stamps of your cousin there was one of 2 cents. So that makes eight to make the series complete. But it is very good, too, when you can send her stamps for when she has two of one kind, she gives one to Aad because he is interested, too, in these beautiful stamps. When you look to such a stamp, it is a picture for itself. You must look at each stamp seriously and then you see that they are beautiful, you know. We appreciated the Mother's Day stamp so much and the stamp of Nicholas landing on the shores of Green

Bay in 1634. You must thank your cousin for it and ask him what Dutch stamp he wants to have. Then my aunt or Aad will send them to him.

Aad has a large collection of stamps. He collects since he was eight years old, and sometimes in the school he changed stamps with other boys instead of having (paying) attention to his lessons. Sometimes he buys stamps, but he prefers changing stamps he has 2X (double) for other stamps he does not have.

My aunt does not have a large collection. She is collecting for 2 years, but she is more violent than Aad so it may be that her collection will grow more rapidly than Aad's collection.

I never had an interest for stamps, but sometimes when they show me a very beautiful one, as those you send, I do find them beautiful. But all those stamps with all the presidents, kings, or queens, I do not admire. What do you think about these stamps? Will you have a care that the edges of the stamps you are sending are not damaged for then they are worthless, you know.

I spent the New Year's Eve at Aad's. We had a pretty evening with playing bridge, singing, eating, until it was 12 o'clock. Then everybody jumped at his feet and Aad's father said some words. We all kissed each other and wished a happy new year. So our New Year's Eve does not change so much as yours.

I do not like that you all paint your faces so much. What is your aim? I think if I painted my face, my parents and Aad should be afraid to kiss me and spoil me. We only put a little powder on our noses when we go to a ball or a party and there are many people who do not like this either. But to us only immoral women paint themselves. But our country is often years afterwards with the world's customs. So it is possible that we shall do it after a few years. I am afraid that this letter is too long, but I had to tell so much. Till next time, greetings from my family and Aad.

Your pal Hanna

+ + + + + + +

Sunday, 24 Maart (March), 1935

My dearest Ruth,

I did neglect you in a scandalous way last month, and I pray you to forgive me. Of course, there is a reason for it, for I love you too much to be indifferent as to our corresponding. You must

46

know, the winter is over here, and the spring has come over the country. The temperature is higher, the sun is shining the greatest part of the day, and it seems all very fine. We wear our summer dresses again, and we have the "summer in our heart". But the spring and especially February are dangerous and betraying for at once the weather changes, and it is winter again with rain and snow and windblows. You can understand that such a changing in temperature is dangerous for the health of people. It is in February that one must be full of care for his health and then it is that 3/4 of our people fall ill. It is in this time that babies and old people go to their death. So it was in our country this spring, too, and everybody feels too lame and tired to do anything. So I had a part of this weariness, and I had not the courage to begin an English letter in which I must spend my brains to find the English words. I hope you will forgive me.

Now the spring has come in all his glory and the betraying snow storms are over. In the meadows flourish the daisies, and the children make festoons of them. Out in our low waterful country there flourish the buttercups and the Wlutonntide flower.

I enjoy the friendship between you and your sister Irene and I congratulate her on her degree. It is not so often that sisters are inseparable friends, is it not? It seems wonderful to me to have a sister who is your friend. I can't imagine that because I am the only child of my parents. I sought my friends outside my family circle, but sometimes I felt alone, and I desired such a lovely sister, as you had one.

You asked me to tell you something about the broadcasting conditions in Holland. We have only two broadcasting stations over which 4 broadcasting corporations send their programs. The time is so divided that every corporation has half of a week for broadcasting purposes. These corporations are standed (financed) by the gifts from the listeners. When you have sympathies for one of the corporations, you send the corporation every year a gift , so little or so large as you will.

The four corporations have different principles:
1. Avro -- a liberal corp. to which we give our gift.
2. Vara -- a Labour party corp.
3. N.C.R.V. -- a Christian corp.
4. K.R.O -- a Catholic corp.

I thank you for the Valentine greetings and Aad thanks you, too. It was so amusing, and I am always so glad when I pull such a lovely sheet of paper out of the envelope. You must know I have a place in my cupboard in which I beware (store) all the letters and clippings you send me. Yesterday I had to clear away my cupboard, and I wondered how many letters I have of you. I believe that the clearing away lasted the whole afternoon for I liked to read some of the letters again and to admire some clippings. I made up my mind to beware the letters of the last year and to tear in pieces the older ones for I feared that when I must beware all your letters that my cupboard should be too little after some time.

Now, it is good to me to have a chat with you again, and I hope that your dream of our cycle riding together becomes true in the future. What a pleasure it would be to me to let you see all the fine and splendid places of our country—the Strand and the Sea, the hills and the lakes, and to chatter with you. Only I think that it would be very difficult to me to bring my thoughts in the English words, but possibly we did not need to say so much for good friends also understand each other without words or with few words.

Your friend, Hanna

+ + + + + + +

Evidentially a graphic depiction of the drought conditions of the dust bowls in the Midwest was described, and Hanna was greatly distressed for Ruth's safety. In later years it would be Ruth fearing for Hanna's very life.

Wed., 8 Mai, 1935

My dearest Ruth,

What did I read yesterday in the newspaper? I was so astonished and sad that I must write you immediately. I read there is in Illinois a great famine with 200,000 men, women, and children given to death because there is no help from other countries. Everybody hopes Washington will help the poor afflicted country where is a deficit on all normal lives. I can't really imagine that you should have to carry the disaster, too, but when it is I am very sad and I would if I could help you and your family. But it is possible that the newspaper exaggerates and that this short, but terrible tidings is not quite just. I can feel that to such a disaster all personal desires and interests fall away and that there is but one desire—to come out of this critical state.

So, Ruth, I will not fatigue you by telling about myself, but I will hope you and your country can be saved, and I am sure that you are a girl that is ready to take courage and to behold spirit. I will pray to God to save you and your country, and I hope that when this letter reaches you that you will only have the remembrance to these sad days.

You can be assured that our whole family lives along with you.

A big and strong kiss from your friend, Hanna

+ + + + + + +

May 31, '35 — Rotterdam

Dearest Ruth,

I'm so glad you did not suffer under the circumstances in your country. You can't imagine what stories the newspapers told us and how they exaggerated the condition. But not only the newspapers, the cinemas too filmed the circumstances in Illinois. Thousands and thousands of animals you saw in the meadows where there was no grass growing, and at last they flew the animals to farmers elsewhere to use their food.

Everyday I looked in the newspaper, but there were but few bits of news and when there was anything about Illinois, it was bad news. So you can imagine that we spoke about you and your family. My father, mother, and aunt all knew the positions in Illinois for they had good friends there who had to suffer under a crisis so bad that the positions here in Holland were divine when you compared. So you can understand that when I got your letter Wednesday, I picked up my bicycle, and I went at first to Aad, to tell him and then to my aunt to tell her the lucky news.

I understand all about the plan of Roosevelt, and I am sorry that it was a failure. Now I shall tell you about the positions in our country. The people have generally enough work and money. But there are different groups of unemployed. In the first place, the group of the labourers. Because machines have been imported the last twenty years a great many workers have become superfluous. And in the second place the group of the intellectuals. Young men, who have studied at the university, come very difficult to the work nowadays; so that they earn too little to set up a home of their own.

The unemployed in our country are entertained (supported) by the government. Everybody who is unemployed by the crisis becomes (receives) 20% of his salary he previously earned from the government and when he is economical, he has enough although no luxuries.

I'm glad you amused yourself to the studying of the play with three acts, and I read in the program you played Helen. And then the new job! I believe that I am going to get a rich friend. I'm proud that I hear all these secrets of your job and your sister's marriage and your friend's job. So you see that such a far friend is very easy sometimes for you can spread your heart in hers without danger that she can't hold a secret and tell it in the neighborhood. I fear if I lived some twenty miles from you that you would not have told me for I can never know a secret, and I always tell it to everyone. I don't know how it is possible. I make up my mind to tell nobody, and then in a minute and immediately it is out of my mouth, and I can't take it back.

I do find it lovely of you to send the fotograph of Princess Juliana. She is, as was to read under the foto, a simple girl. The only sorrow is that she is not allowed to marry the man she loves, but it is not impossible that the law changes in this direction.

Aad makes his last exam of this year next Thursday and then he has vacances. My vacances begin 28 June. Then I shall be able to write more interesting letters. For now it is all working and working on and we have not so plenty of time to have excursions or to become adventures. In the vacances I will also have time enough to work your pocket book for I am ashamed of myself so long as it is laying in my work box. To Ruth, good luck with your job and your sister, that I hope her to be very happy with her husband.

Till the next time, Hanna

+ + + + + + +

Wednesday, 3 July, 1935

My dearest Ruth,

At this moment we have vacances. I've progressed to the highest class of the school and the first day of the vacances my aunt and I were traveling to Belgium, that is our neighborland, to the village Spa. Do you know that Spa is the very healthy place and that very many ill people recover there by the sources and the healthy water in Spa.

From here I write you this letter and on the envelope you will see charity stamps. The price of these stamps is for the poor children in the Belgium country and the portrait is of the children of the Royal family, Prince Baudouin, Princess Charlotte, and Prince Albert. My aunt and I amuse ourselves very much here. We do walks and excursions in the neighborhood and we go swimming and sunning.

Kind greetings of my aunt and a big kiss from your friend.
Hanna

N.B. Write your following letters to:
Hanna de Bruijn,
Velsenluststraat 4
Rotterdam
for my parents have changed their house for a new, you know.

+ + + + + + +

Incidents with little meaning or importance to the United States began to occur. In 1922 an ambitious man named Benito Mussolini had become the Premier of Italy toppling the power of the monarchy. He was called Il Duce (the Leader) and organized the Fascists movement which he ruled as a dictator. In September, 1935 his army invaded the Northeastern African country originally called Abyssinia, later known as Ethiopia. This attack was to distract the Italians from their high rate of unemployment and dissatisfaction with the government. The next year he would send 70,000 troops to help a general named Francisco Franco and his rebels during the Spanish Civil War. In 1937 Germany and Italy signed the Rome-Berlin Axis agreement signifying that all of Europe rotated around those two capital cities. These names would become headline news in a few years, but in the mid-1930's they seemed so unfamiliar and insignificant.

Wed., 25 September, 1935

Dearest Ruth,

Many thanks for your cozy letter this week. It is a joy for us—a letter from America. At first I am reading and then when Aad calls on me, he is allowed to read. Mother and Dad, who do not read easily English are told the most interesting things and Aunt Clazien is told the stamp news.

The situation Italia-Abyssinia (Ethiopia) is not very good and the whole world's sympathetic fortunately on Abyssinia's side. Especially England will force Italy to take back his army. But all with all it is a miserable thing and no hope that all will come good again. I fear the war, and I see in your letter that you fear it too. Let us pray for the goodwill of the nations.

I am glad the children in your class love Holland. It is due, of course, to your enthusiasm over Holland. I'm thinking it should be fun when I could send something to the class from Holland for every child a card or anything else. Do write next time and tell how many children are in your class, and if you would like me to send them somewhat.

I'm now studying the last year, and I begin to work hard. Half the population here is without work. It is a bad situation, and a teacher of physical culture is not a necessity. Also I have not so much hope that I will have a job when I am ready with my study. How is it with the physical culture to you? Write me and please send back the stamp on the envelope for my aunt, please.

With lots of love, Hanna

+ + + + + + +

Hanna's special friend, Aad, with other Delft University students, joined the reserve army for a year. Not only did the queen feel it was expedient to prepare a strong defense force, but money for tuition was difficult to obtain. Therefore, the young men took a sabbatical from studies. Aad's chemical major caused him to be assigned to a chemical warfare unit which greatly distressed Hanna. Since Holland is such a small country, Aad was often stationed close enough for Hanna to see him frequently. She asked Ruth to pray for Europe.

52

Aad took the time to answer questions Ruth had posed and to explain the centuries-old reclamation of the Netherlands (Lowlands). As early as 1000 A.D. earthen dikes were built and the winds of the North Sea were used to turn the windmill pumps. Marco Polo is credited with introducing windmills to Europe from Asia. Since the flat Netherlands have few natural barriers, the westerly winds crossing the country are fairly strong and predictable. They provide a dependable source of power to keep the "new" fields dry of seepage water. The "Leak in the Dike" poem by Phoebe Cary illustrates the importance of protecting the dikes once the fields were reclaimed. It is a constant battle to survive "below sea level". Today concrete dikes have replaced the earthen ones and electric power is utilized for the pumps. Nowadays the picturesque windmills have given way to tall poles with propeller-like arms. The reclaimed areas called "polders" are continuing to be developed as fertile soil replaces the salt-laden sea-bottom that has to be leeched out. A new fresh water lake, the IJsselmeer (pronounced a-sel-mer), which was formed by damming the northern end of the former larger Zuider Zee, is shrinking as new areas are drained. Ditches and canals form boundaries for the fields, and few fences are needed to contain livestock except for horses who could jump the narrower waterways. (It was interesting to note that Germany was careful not to destroy the dam during World War II knowing that the land would be much more useful intact.)

Sunday, 15 Nov., 1935
(Letter from Aad)

Dear Ruth,

I just read your letter to Hanna from Nov 1. First I am sorry I didn't sent my birthday congratulations earlier, but perhaps Hanna wrote you I'm under arms now, i.e. I'm bound to serve a year in the Army. The place where we are is Breda, a town about 40 miles from Rotterdam. Perhaps you know that we have conscription in our country.

Every year the government requires a number of men for the army. As I finished the H.B.S. and later on studied chemistry, I'm going to become a reserve gas-officer. After this year's service I'm going to continue my study. Every year (I believe 4) I am bound to come into Her Majesty's service for some weeks for a kind of repetitions. Then gradually I'm going to be reserve-lieutenant and

53

later reserve-captain. Mostly I'm coming home every Saturday and Sunday. And now I spend part of my Sunday morning sending your letter and writing back to you. You will understand that especially the first weeks I hadn't much time to correspond, but now I have the time for it. As soon as I have photos about us I'll send them to you—perhaps with this letter. You write that three things are characteristic for our country—windmills, bulbs, and canals. In great that's true. However, a great part of our windmills has been broken down and replaced by steam engines to get the water out of the lower parts of the country.

In general, you have the following sketch. In early years about in the beginning of our time the second century, i.e. 100 years after Christ has been born, our country looked about like that. The whole Zuider Zee and all these isles didn't exist at all. The whole coast was a long line of dunes from southwest till the extreme east. But gradually these dunes were broken away by the wind and sea. In about 400 A.D. during a great storm the sea carried the dunes into the north west and inundated the country. The soil wouldn't resist the forces of wind and water so gradually the Zuider Zee got its present form. The consequence of it was that except in some very few parts the Zuider Zee never is deeper than about two meters. About 600 A.D. the Zuider Zee reached its present form. People succeeded in bandaging the forces of wind and water by making earthen walls.

There are two reasons why our country lies so low. First that your country falls lower and lower already during centuries. That is also the case of the insistence of the North Sea (Nord-Zee). Second, before people succeeded in bandaging the water also in the country, holes appeared because the water destroyed the soil and dragged it away.

All these holes lay below sea level. In 1600 that ended and there was made the beginning to reclaim these lakes.

In the 19th century the biggest was reclaimed and because the soil of these lakes was below sea level, these inhabitants needed a means to keep the soil dry. That is done by ditches, canals, and windmills. The ancient border of the lake was made into a ring canal from which its drainage is pumped to the rivers (also higher) by engine pumps. I'll try to send you a map in which you can see the form of the ancient lakes. Now we are busy reclaiming the Zuider Zee which is not so easy. When I send the map, I'll enclose some photos which will give you some idea about the work.

The farms are small, John (Aad's uncle) said. That isn't to be wondered at for the density of population is much greater—almost 250 per square kilometer.

Movies in our country mostly last either the whole evening (8:00 - 11:30), or they last from 7:15 till 9:15 and from 9:30 till 11:30. There are also afternoon shows. Further we have movies lasting almost one hour in which they show only journals: UFA.M.Gil, etc. and a small film. They are called cinema in our country. Princess Juliana and Prince Barnard visited the cinema in The Hague sometimes as non-officials. You see on the enclosed print the young couple leaving the cinema under it:

"To the remembrance of the visit of Princess Juliana
and Prince Bernhard to Cinema on 10th September,
1936, the first non-official visit that the young couple
made after the betrothal."

You know that marriage shall take place in January. Our garrison goes to The Hague to be placed alongside the way the Royal Bride and Bridegroom take to and from church.

Till next time, Aad

Queen Wilhelmina   Queen Juliana   Queen Beatrix
(1880) 1898-1948   1948-1980   1980-

Chapter Four

In 1936 Germany hosted the Olympic Games. Hitler used the Games as a political opportunity to try to prove the superiority of the Aryan race. The American Jesse Owens frustrated Der Fuehrer's attempt by being an outstanding Black athlete. Hitler petulantly refused to give him his medals. Again this was setting the stage to designate minorities, the handicapped, mentally unstable, and Jews as scapegoats for the sufferings being borne during the Great Depression.

Mussolini in Italy also made his move to send 70,000 troops to Francisco Franco to support his rebellion against Spain's first democratic republic following King Alphonso XIII's flight in 1931.

Following the Civil War (1936-1939) Franco, now dictator, officially maintained that Spain was neutral early in WWII but actually befriended Germany and Italy. Later in the war it became apparent the Axis Alliance was losing. Then Spain attempted to make friendly gestures to England, USA, and other Allies.

On a happier note the Dionne quintuplets were mentioned. They were the first set of five babies to survive. Born in May, 1934, to Canadian parents, before fertility treatments were available, these little girls fascinated the world. Frequent news updates kept the interested public informed, and even paper dolls were designed to capitalize on such an event.

25 Jan., 1936 — R'dam

Dearest Ruth,

Many thanks about your long and lovely letter which I enjoyed so much. I received your Christmas parcel on the day before Christmas, and I had to pay some centimes for it to the post man. But this was not because you had not done enough stamps on it, for I have always to pay some money when I get a parcel from you. This is for the taxes, you know. I think, you in America have to pay some money too, when you get a little present from here. Let me know next time.

The Christmas vacances were very pretty. We had a Christmas dinner at the home of an aunt and uncle of Aad and this was very funny. Then the Old Year's Eve my father and mother and I went to Aad's home and spent there the evening with some other guests. And this Christmas holidays were to work for me, for I had to do on 5 Jan. an examination on school in some study parts. But in the Christmas time it is very difficult to work for all sorts of funny things happen. So the examination was not a success, although it was not a failure at all.

A girl friend of mine who was at the physical culture school at The Hague too, went with her grandfather and grandmother to America. The old ones had money enough to live their old days where they preferred, and so they sought the best climate. They resolved to live in Los Angeles. They asked their grandchild to go with them, and Mimy Wansinl did go with them. Now she is living in Los Angeles. But it is a long way from you, is it not? For you are living in the middle of America, and she on the west end. Otherwise I should have asked Mimy to call on you. But you see, that it is not impossible that one of us is in the occasion to make a long voyage and so to have the chance, to call on the other. I pray sometimes it will happen very soon, for sometimes I can't bear that I never shall see your face from so near as I will.

I got your last letter, too, with the letter for Aunt Clazien in it. She is very proud of this letter, and she loves you so much as I do. I'm glad you appreciate her little presents and when the postman "stole" the post stamps, he must have been a good collector, for the stamps were rare for America. So he has had a good day, too.

The stamp on this letter is a rare stamp, too, and I hope you are in the occasion to send it back when your cousin will have such a stamp. I will send one for him, too. The stamps are bought for charity. For a stamp of 12 1/2 ct. you must pay 6 ct and the 6 1/2 ct extra are for all sorts of charity for children. You see that a little child is printed on the stamp.

With much regards to your family and Reathel and a big kiss from me.

Your friend, Hanna

+ + + + + + +

Monday, 11 Feb., 1936

Dearest Ruth,

I thank you cordially for your Valentine greeting. What a lovely custom of you to send each year such a beautiful paper with ornaments and greetings.

I did not make the mirror cover myself, but I did buy it in the warehouse. But when I have more time, I should have it made myself. In my room there is a piece of woolwork from which I intended to make a bookcase or pocket book for you, but I do not work much on it, because I have so little time. But one day it will be ready and I will send it to you.

The picture with the five children is lovely. Aunt Clazien could not swing her eyes from it. It is very difficult, we think, to hold five of these children in life (Dionne quintuplets). Are they at the home of their parents, or are they educated by teachers?

It is a fault of your paper to print Princess Juliana of Holland is to wed with Edward VIII, for the law would not permit this. For Princess Juliana is the only daughter and child of Queen Wilhelmina and she has to succeed later on. So it is impossible for her to marry Edward VIII for then two countries should stand under the same royal house. It is more possible that Juliana will marry one of the sons of the royal house of Danemark or Norwige. But, I believe, she likes not to marry a man she does not love and therefore, it is very difficult for her for there are not many princes. And for the prince who married Juliana, it is difficult, too, for Juliana is to become queen and he will be the Second person. It is not for a man to be the Second in a country behind his wife.

Juliana is not a beautiful girl, but she is very lovely, and she has a beautiful character. She is very naturally charming in her manners and conversations, and she can behave as an ordinary girl. She studied at the University of Leiden, and she helps her mother in reigning now.

I am longing to receive your letter in which you will describe the Valentine's box at your school.

The stamps on your Valentine letter were so beautiful. I did give one to Aunt Clazien and one to Aad. Will you do me the pleasure to sent this child stamp back? Note that "voor het kind" means "for the child" and provincials: for hat Kynt.

Many greetings from us all and a kiss from your friend,
Hanna

+ + + + + + +

2 April, 1936

Dearest Ruth
I was so glad with your last letter. I will answer it tonight. You will excuse me when I do not write such interesting letters for

there is not happening anything worth telling here in Rotterdam. I am spending all my time on the coming examination. On 5 Mai is the day when we have the writing part of the examination.

I read in the paper yesterday that Hauptman (Lindbergh kidnapper) will be assassinated tomorrow. It does not seem to me noble to treat him so when the judges cannot prove that he is guilty. To us we have a comdemned cell. Our laws say that the one man has not the right to condemn the other.

The Halloween picture you got was ridiculous! Our whole family has had pleasure over it when I showed it.

I thank you for your piece of paper with the description of our Princess Juliana. It is a nice description, and it is the truth they tell in it.

The spring is in the country again. Everywhere the flowers are growing inches in the very soft weather we had the last days. We are playing basketball and hockey in the open air, and we have a joyous feeling in our bodies.

The only bad thought is the examination on 5 Mai for which we have to work very hard. I hope you will have a thought for me on this day.

These were a few lines to let you hear anything from me. Write me again such a cozy letter as the last. It gives me a few minutes of pleasure. Many greetings from all of us, but especially from me.

Your friend, Hanna

+ + + + + + +

7 Mai, 1936 — R'dam

Dearest Ruth,

At 5 Mai was the writing part of my examination. I was glad when it was done, and I have resolved to take a few days vacances to get new courage to work for the practical part of it. So I have time now to write you and to tell you something of the day of 5 Mai.

The examination was in The Hague, in an old house, the Kuyhts House. Three hundred young people of all parts of the country came there together at 9 o'clock in the morning. There was in the great hall a table for each and there the "asks" were

59

given. We had to make a story about one of the following three subjects:

1. The physical culture of the girl in the last five ages.
2. The influence of the Humanists at the aim of education, especially in relation with the place of physical culture in the education.
3. The principle of the active school in the development of the pedogogy and the influence of this principle on it.

I took the second subject. We had two and a half hours for it. In the afternoon from 2:00-5:00 we had to answer several questions in relation with anatomy and physiology, hockey, and basketball (etc.). You wrote me last time that Naismith had done so much for the basketball sport in your country. I did write it in my examination, of course. Much thanks for this.

I had taken the train from Rotterdam at 6:00 A.M. I was so tired of all these hours of working that I could hardly eat. That night Aad took me with him to the cinema, and we saw a nice film where I forgot my fatigue.

I hope the writing part was sufficient so that I get an invitation to come to the practical part which is in Amsterdam and lasts two days. Tomorrow I begin work again for this part.

Lindbergh has come to Europe, and it seems, that he feels much safer here than in America. He is here incognito, but each time we see fotos of him and his wife in the newspaper. It seems that everybody knows where he is, and this is not the manner to keep his enemies from finding him.

Have you heard of the victory of the armies of Mussolini in Africa? Yesterday Badoglin held his entry into Addis Ababa while the Negus had taken the flight to Palestine. The whole civilized world is angry and ashamed that this deed of Mussolini must happen, but it seems impossible to defy this effort to increase the power of a man who will be never satisfied till he should reign over the whole world.

Holland had also sent an ambulance of the Red Cross organization to Abyssinia. But the ambulance could not help very much although the best doctors of Holland were with it. But they could not come near the victims because the Italians did not respect the Red Cross and fired at them. So the doctors were obliged to come back especially when one of them, Dr. van Scheloen, was fired at by the Abyssians themselves because they thought that he was an Italian. Dr.van Scheloen spoke through the radio, and he described the fate of all those victims of the terrible Italians. By the fire and the gas they were mutilated by the thousands.

We are glad he is back in our good Holland again for his life was not safe during the whole time he was in Abbysinia. The Princess Juliana had her birthday 30 April, and at this occasion she gave all the members of the Red Cross expedition a gold medalion for the work they had done.

You asked if we saw our princess and queen. Yes! Our country is not so large. You can in one day easily travel with the train from the West frontier to the East, and also at one day from the Nord frontier to the Sud. So it is possible when the queen or the princess moves in public that you can see them. And especially the princess is very super and modern. When she went to the University, she had friends among the students and walked and laughed with them in the "herden" shrubs.

I've seen the princess many times. One time I saw her when she was swimming in the sea. I saw her when she was not the royal princess, but when she behaved as an ordinary girl bathes in the water and sun and ate chocolate. It was a fortuity that we saw her then, but it makes what we thought of her much more sympathic than otherwise.

I am glad when you write me soon back.

With greetings from my family and a big kiss from me!

Hanna

+ + + + + + +

19 Juni — R'dam

Dearest Ruth,

All my hard working has not been rewarded. The examination was a failure. We went with fifteen girls to Amsterdam and during two days we were examined. Six of the fifteen passed through, but nine had to do it once more the next year. I had worked so hard, and it was a very big disappointment for me, but for my parents, too, for they had paid for the rather expensive school. Now I would like to have a job for the three holiday months as a lady of company or in a children's house. But it is not so easy to get such a job for there are many others.

61

We have a great feast here in Holland for the University of Utrecht to celebrate her 300th birthday. The stamp you see here expresses the great event. Noctius was the first professor who came to teach at the University. It is a fine stamp for your cousin, but my aunt will be glad too when you send it back when your cousin does not like it.

A good acquaintance of Aunt Clazien, as well as her doctor, should like to correspond with this cousin of yours. He likes to have a chat with him about stamps and when your cousin likes it too, to change stamps. Ask your cousin. The address of the doctor is:

Den Weled Leerg Heer —Dr. v. d. Hove van Genderen
Nienwe Binnenweg — Rotterdam, Holland

The first line of this address is always written when we write to a man with a degree and means "The honorable, much knowing Gentlemen". Do you have in America such a habitude, too?

It is very warm now here, and nobody likes to do anything. Now I have not to do anything, and I am in a holiday, but such a holiday I do not prefer for I must think the whole day about my failed examination.

I was glad about your letters which I got a few weeks ago. Especially the first was so thick and interesting. It was as a chat with you. Now I am ready for some time to work so hard, I can think and do other things, and then I can tell you more interesting things than the past year.

+ + + + + + +

14 Juli, 1936

Dearest Ruth,

My most hearty gratulations with your passed exam. I read your letter and was astonished. How different the instruction in the New World America is from ours. I thank you for this interesting letter. The weeks that followed my failed examination were very sad. I could not come to any work or any pleasure. My parents and friends dared to me that I must do the exam again and that I should pass them. Now I made up my mind to do it again and to go to school again in September. It is a pity when one is 21 years old and without a grade when one has almost the knowledge to have a grade.

For the vacances I have a job. In our country several schools let spare the children some money every week and when the vacances come, they go for that money out of the city for 12 days and in a summer camp to get there fresh air and brown sun-burned faces. Such a camp is settled in the place Breda where 300 girls come in August together. For these girls must have some guide and instruction and several leaders are engaged. I also have a job as a leader. I have then over 20 girls to care for to make walks and marches, to play basketball, hockey, and other plays, and to see if they do not eat too little. This is a very jolly job. Have you in America such camps, too? Tell me next time.

We get your portrait, and we admired it by turns. It is a very beautiful face that looks from the portrait, but there is such a serious feature in it that I am afraid that my dear Ruth has some sorrow the last years. For the portrait, you sent me a few years ago had this feature not at all. That was a laughing, gay and light-hearted Ruth. The light-hearted Ruth was standing all these years on my writing desk, but now I have got a new portrait. It changed, and the serious Ruth is standing on the old place on the writing desk. But I must say to you, I miss the laugh, and I begin to desire that the light-hearted Ruth is on the table again. Mother and Father and some friends also said that there was a great difference in the two portraits. But I said it came because you had such a serious time behind your back with this examination. But I will be glad, too, when you will send on a day a little snapshot with your old laughing face.

Have you heard of the Erasmus rememberance in Europe? These are post stamps with his face on it. I think I will send you one next time. This time it is a stamp of Joetins, the first teacher in Ubrecht's High School. Aad will write you some day over his studies and the University life in Delft.

Till the next time—love.

Hanna

+ + + + + + +

21 August, 1936

Dearest Ruth,

First I must gratulate you on the marriage of Irene although I understand that it is a great loss for you, and that you will miss her in your home. But it is her destiny and happiness to live near her husband. In this letter I am including a little card for her and her husband to gratulate them. Will you be so kind and give it her when you call her on? I read the announcement of her marriage in the card and also in the paper you sent me. I read with pleasure the great article about her. Is she such an important person that the papers tell lots about her marriage?

Then I must thank you for the birthday greeting and the card you sent. Those greetings from far away that span the miles between us are appropriate. I'm glad you appreciated the foto.

We are now home after having a beautiful voyage, and I'm sending you a few fotos more. I put your fotos in my fotobook. I have many now of you, your family, and your friends, and the car of Reathel. It helps me to imagine how you live there.

I had a very fine birthday, and I got many presents. From Aad I had a book and from my parents a chair for my room. I also got many little beautiful things as flowers, writing papers, and handkerchiefs. We had a little party at evening where we talked a little and had some music. It was my 21st birthday, and I begin to feel very old.

Thank you for the stamps. They were very fine. I'm beginning to feel enthusiasm for stamps too now that I see how much other people care for them. Do you feel that way too?

I'm sending you a little bookmark from Spain.

I'm your friend, Hanna

+ + + + + + +

13 Oct., 1936

Dear Ruth,

It is a long time ago that I came to you to have a chat. In this time I got two letters from you. But it is that I were so very busy that I did not come to write. My vacances were very full, and I amused myself with the children in Gels Ryen. Later on I was with Aad in Nordujk, a watering place on the Nord Sea. I will send you next time some fotos about it.

The friend of my Aunt Clazien, Dr. van de Hove van Gendere who was to change stamps with your cousin was last week under a car. He had such a serious brain wound that he died a few hours after the accident. It was a disaster for his family and his friends. But his patients, too, had many sorrows about it for he was a nerves doctor, and for many people he had been a support in life.

Aunt Clazien and I went to the funeral, and it was all very sorrowful. She asked me to tell your cousin about the death of Dr. van de Hove, but I don't know his address. Will you be so kind to say it to him?

I thank you for the idea of the jewelry. It is so hopeless that there are so few things that are allowed to send over the boundary. I went last week to a warehouse to buy something for your birthday, but I could not find the right things. The things I thought you should like were refused to send. Now you must do it with my best wishes I sent you last week. I will think about a present for you that is allowed, that you will like, and which does not make too big a packet.

I go to school again, and I did not have the first weeks many pleasures. But now I am accustomed again, and it is hard working again till it is summer.

What a lovely picture from you! I am so glad with such a "savant femme" as a friend.

Aad does not study at this moment. He is gone for a year in the service of the reign stationed in Breda (a city in the south of the country). He and eleven other students from Delft are going to become reserve officers. Is in America such a universal service, too?

Aad likes to be in Breda. It is very funny there. Because he and his friends from Delft studied chemistry, they must become gas officers. It is terrible to think when there should be a war that he shall have to bring his knowledge into practice.

How do you find Juliana and her fiance! I thank you so much for the pictures and prozas (clippings) of your newspapers. Aad and I read them from A till Z, and we had many pleasures about it.

The stamp I do at this envelope is the last one of a series given at the remembrance of Erasmus, the greatest Dutch Humanist, who lived in the time of the Renaissance. So keep it and give it to your cousin or otherwise, when he will not have it, send it back. Till next time, my dearest. Have you had a pretty birthday? Tell me about it. Greetings of Aad.

Your pal, Hanna

+ + + + + + +

65

Dearest Ruth,

Our princess has found the man of her heart and all the Dutch folk is so glad. We are dancing in the streets, and we cheer for the beloved Princess. The new prince is a "sympathic" man, and he has found the way to our hearts, too. There they are. You see, too, the weapon (standard) of Juliana.

Love, Hanna

+ + + + + + +

Sunday, 20 December, 1936

Dearest Ruth,

Now I must at first tell you that I have received the present of the handkerchiefs. I went to the general post office, and there I heard that all parcels from a strange country were held there because there had come a new law on the sending of parcels from strange countries. Fortunately I could bring my parcel with me to home. Mother said that it is a scandal that you send so much presents to me and that you spoil me too much. But it is such a pretty feeling to have such a lovely friend far away who sends such thick letters with convivial words and beautiful thoughts and who sends you presents, too. So I thank you very much again.

I heard you have seen in your newspapers that Princess Juliana is bethrothed and that she marries at 7 January in The Hague. She and her man, Prince Bernhard, go to church in a golden carriage with eight horses. It is a fairy tale to see. All the people in The Hague have done their best to make the streets beautiful with greenery and flowers. At night all the streets are illuminated and church and official buildings are standing in flood light. It is very beautiful everywhere. The weeks before the wedding from 19 Dec. to 7 Jan. are spent to "feter" the young couple. Everywhere feasts are arranged by all circles of the people.

On 4 Jan. the physical culture circle gives a sport day at their honour. At first over 500 young people, boys and girls together, must do an exercise together which must last more or less 18 minutes. It is in the winter now, and we are afraid that it shall be rather cold on 4 Jan. Therefore, because all must be done on a great sport place in the open air, we are all in ice clothes. With this exercise I am busy, too.

Then there is a football and basketball team from Lippe-Biesterfield (Germany, the country of the Prince) playing against such a team from The Hague. A ski show is at the end. It shall be a pretty day, and I will enjoy myself to it.

Everywhere in the country yesterday the national colours are hung out, and all people wear an orange flower or knot. Orange, because Juliana's name is Juliana of Orange-Nansson and the home colours standard of the family is orange.

We all are glad because these two marry. When Aad writes you, he will tell you surely about the soldiers and the marriage day for he has to go to The Hague that day with thousands of other comrades to honor the High Couple. When you should like, I will send some newspaper pieces who are interesting as to the bridal.

Much love and a kiss for the beautiful present. (The "broderie" on it I like so much.)

Love, Hanna

When you get this letter, it is some days in the New Year. To this I wish you a very happy 1937. I hope you will have 365 pretty days and none of sorrow. So, I hope your whole family will have God bless you. I don't know exactly how it is to you in America, but in Europe we all go with an anxious heart into the year 1937 for everywhere the countries do not trust each other. Weaponed to the teeth they watch each other to trample down each other at the most little thing. Weaponed peace, a horrible thing! Then at Spain where brothers kill each other only for the sake of communism or fascism.

Ruth, when you pray to God, ask him, too, to beware of Europe and to be merciful that such a terrible thing as the war of 1914 does not repeat. What should it be, when such good friends as you and I are, should be enemies because our reigns had resolved that Holland and America should be enemies? That is a contradiction, n'est a pas? It is impossible!

Chapter Five

The headlines in Ruth's local papers concentrated on the Great Ohio River Flood which caused much distress to farmers, damaged hundreds of homes and towns, and caused transportation difficulties in the spring of 1937. Being near the convergence of the Ohio and Mississippi Rivers, Southern Illinoisans are either directly affected or help however they can by sandbagging, sending aid, rescuing those stranded, or contributing directly to the Red Cross food preparation sites. Hanna is concerned for Ruth's safety, but Herrin is far enough inland that it is more inconvenienced than threatened.

Aad took time to answer Ruth's questions and compared American and European universities. While both strive for higher education, those in the United States seem to offer a wider spectrum of requirements for the "well-rounded" student before a major is selected. European classes focus on very concentrated, in-depth studies of one subject. In the United States "late-bloomers" may pursue degrees at any age or stage in their lives. In Europe, one is tested early and either shunted toward technical training or academic pursuits with little chance to change course later. Both styles have their advantages and disadvantages. Many American students delay commitments or change their minds so that their college years are extended and more expensive. Overseas the stress on young college hopefuls is tremendous—both on them and their families as they approach exams. There are others waiting for the limited positions at the universities and only the best are accepted with few second chances.

Aad's regiment was assigned to accompany walkers on a four-day walk-a-thon, and Hanna accompanied him on a bicycle across Holland to assist in being a provider. While this was not a war situation, it provided experience for what might be needed in a future march for survival or resistance. Women's auxiliaries had precedents. During frontier days in the U.S. West, women loaded muskets, prepared the food, nursed the wounded, and did the laundry. Although criticized by some parts of society, Florence Nightingale and later Clara Barton proved the importance of women's support groups in the Crimean and U. S. Civil Wars. Eventually these women opened the doors to the establishment in the United States of the Women's Army Corps (WAC's), the Women's Air Force (WAF's), and the Women Accepted for Volunteer Emergency

Service (the Navy's WAVES.) These uniformed women served both stateside and overseas, but not in combat.

The whole country was excited over the upcoming wedding of their beloved Princess Juliana and her Prince Bernhard. She had been trained with a few select girls in the palace school to reign. Married at the age of 28, she would not become queen for eleven more years. During the stressful war period she would be evacuated to Canada to await her third child. It was not until 1948 that Queen Wilhelmina abdicated. Princess Juliana was "inaugurated", not crowned, since technically the crown belongs to the Dutch people.

Jan., 1937

Dearest Ruth,

I received your letters with the enthusiastic description about your studies at the University. We learned many about it and we have a perfect view about studying in America. How much difference with our studies in Holland, is it not? We never have a job before we are ready with studying at a school or at a university. When anyone is being able to study so hard for a doctor's _____, he writes a book about his study object. He must have it printed and he is obliged to give each professor an example. As to this book it is decided whether he becomes the bull. To us there are not so many people who receive this. It's only a rarity when someone in the family is so clever in his studies.

Ruth, I have a deep respect for your studying person. I believe you are so perfect a girl, as well inside as outside, for as well as your face and figure as your brains are so well developed. I believe to stand a good piece behind you.

We have some American boys here in Holland at the occasion of the World Jamboree of the Boy Scouts. Friday we will have a look there, and when it is possible, I shall do my best to find a Scout from Illinois to have a chat with.

Last week I had some days of pleasure. You must know in our country there is an annual sport feast consisting of four days of walking 40 km. Everyone who likes this can have this. At the 27 Juli all the participants start from Nijmegen, a little village in the eastern part of Holland, and they walk a route of 40 km (24 miles) along hills and meadows, along rivers, etc. Beautiful is this part of Holland. They start about 5:00 in the morning. They may repose enroute, and in the afternoon you see them come back. The

69

second day again is 40 km but now along another way. For four days this continues, and all who bring the walk to the end receive a remembrance on these days. The night of the fourth day, there is a feast in the one great hall Nijmegen has. There is dancing and singing and many pleasures. Everybody can do this walking feast. Girls and women, soldiers, students, old men, young men—all sorts and standings.

This year the regiment of Aad, 13 soldiers went to Nijmegen. Aad had to go with them on the bicycle as provider. On the way he had to care for them. For many boys had troubles with their footskin, etc. Now I went on the bicycle, too, with Aad, and for four days long we enjoyed the fine neighborhood of Nijmegen. We had many pleasures on the way. With the regiment walked four other girls. They liked to go with soldiers for when they walked alone, her footsteps became so small, and they were soon tired.

The last night was the most beautiful of all the days. Everyone was tired, but they all had a radiant humour. During the walking days there were many strangers in our country for it is a very rare event. There is no haste. It is not the fact who can walk 40 km in the most possible little time, but it is only the fact if you can four days long walk 40 km. I have made up my mind to walk the following year, too.

Now Ruth, pleasant study and enjoy this time. I received last week your gratulations and the beautiful card. Many thanks for it. That you thought about me, you get a big kiss for this.

Your Hanna

+ + + + + + +

1 Feb., 1937
(Letter from Aad)

Dear Ruth,

Let me just apologize for not answering your letter from Dec. 30. I'll explain how that was. In my country it was in the beginning of the New Year, very busy about the wedding of our Princess. I myself did belong to the 10,000 soldiers alongside the route through The Hague on the wedding day. I'll tell you how we passed the day before, and the day after with our boys. The day before we had light service.

70

In the afternoon we had a big meal together. After that we went to bed from 8:00 till 12:00 in the afternoon (P.M.) At twelve we rose, had a light meal, and at 2:00 a.m. we gathered with all our boys (100) the strength of a company, and we started for the station in the pitch darkness. There at 2:40 the train started for The Hague where we arrived at 4:00 a.m. We marched to a school where we stayed till 8:45 when we were gathered to take our place alongside the route. There we stood from 9:00 till 2:00 p.m. when we could go back to the same school. The royal family passed us very close so that we could see them very good. Only we stood with presented rifle and couldn't move our body or head. We only could roll with the eyes. But all by all we all saw the Princess and the Prince very good.

In the afternoon we went back to our Ganisin Breda. Already then I had an ache in my throat. The week following we were very busy in Breda. But the Sunday after when I was home, I stayed with an attack of influensa and ache in my throat. And now I'm still at home. Thus already two weeks, but I believe this week will be the last. I have been seriously ill, and for a week I didn't sleep nor eat.

But now another topic. You asked in the last line if I had any brothers or sisters. I am to deny; so is Hanna. We two are quite alone at home with our parents.

I want to know if you suffered from the flood in your country. We read about it in the. . . (Incomplete letter from Aad)

+ + + + + + +

22 Feb., '37

Dearest Ruth,

I thank you for the many letters you send me with such short intervals. I liked reading them, and I can assure you I would to write back to each of your letters, but I had no time. It is this summer for the second time I will do my examinations for the physical culture, and I am working as hard as possible to come through. Without this examination, it is hardly impossible to find any job. And you know in Holland everyone has to learn so much and so heavy. The country will hold the reputation of a well civilized and well learned people. Efficiency as in America to only learn the things you will need in your following life, they don't know at ours. The last time there is come a party who wants to reform the education and instruction, they take the part of Dewey and Kerschensteiver and all other men of the doing school. But most of the teachers and the minister of education will not hear of it.

How is it with the instruction at your school? Do you follow the methods of Dewey and Gankhurst, from whom we hear last time so much here, or is it in your school as to us—learn by heart and learn so much as possible? Tell me anything about it.

I gave myself three days vacation. I was so tired of traveling each day to The Hague and back that I could not follow the lessons at last. Now I am sleeping till 12:00 noon, and in the afternoon I am making an underskirt for myself. So I hope I will go to school with new spirit again after such a recovery. Now I have found the time, too, to call on some of my dearest friends, and this afternoon, Ruth Sullivan is on turn.

Aad is recovered again, and he went to Breda in his training camp. He wrote you a letter. Have you got it? I fear he is writing a better English than I am writing.

It is viz his job to read as _____ heaps of detective novels who are written in English. We have no detective writers in Holland. Now by reading these stories, he learns much English expressions. You must write in your following letter if you read his letters more easily. When it is so, I will do much more my utmost to write without faults.

I read in the papers of the heavy disaster in your country. I was so glad that your family and you had no direct trouble about it. Do you remember how anxious I was when last year the sand storm (Dust Bowl) broke out? But Illinois is so extensive that it seems when one part of the country has a disaster that another part can be saved from it. So when I heard now of the flood I was not so anxious as last year that you were in the trouble, too, but though I was glad when I got your letter in which was the truth, black on white written that God saved you.

I thank you for the fotos and the description. Aad,too, found it very interesting to hear precisely how it happened all. We hear the events, but not the details. And because you live there is naturally that we will hear the details too.

Now, Ruth, I am glad to have had a little chat with you.
Much greetings and a kiss from Hanna

+ + + + + +

22 Juni, '37

Dearest Ruth,

I have succeeded in my examination! It is because you wrote you were with your thoughts to me last time. It were two days of extreme hard working, but now it is done, and I have vacances for a few weeks. Then I must see that I find a job. This is not so easy as last time here in Holland, but I will do my utmost. Father and Mother have taken care long enough for me now.

I liked your last letters very much, but I could not find the time, and the real pleasure to write you back. An examination to us is a very important thing. Without a paper, you succeeded in the examination, you don't get a job. Therefore, everybody of my family was glad when the examination was over. It was in Amsterdam, the capital city of the country, and we are living in Rotterdam.

When I came home there were many bouquets of flowers, and we had a little party. But I was too tired to have much pleasure. That was a pity. Everybody I know came the following day to felicitate when they had read in the paper I had succeeded.

I love your last letter. What a brilliant bridal (ceremony) of your brother!

Kisses from Hanna

+ + + + + + +

15 Sept., '37

Dearest Ruth,

What a pretty birthday I had last month and what a beautiful presents. You understand I am sitting down now to write with your pen in my hand and then the letter opener. What a pretty weapon (emblem) Illinois has.

But now it is your turn to have birthday and to be spoiled by family and friends. And I am glad I am one of your friends, and so I have sought seriously for a present for you. And I found something that was charming. I hope you do find it charming, too. When you get the clock, you will do your best to hang the pieces of the clock as I wrote you. I hope you understood all, and you

73

understood the manner of winding up. Never draw the pineapple #1, but always draw the chain #2. When you don't understand, go to a clock maker. It is the same clock as the well known Schwartzwalder clock. It is a clock of the old-fashioned type with a chain and weight. A clock from grandfathers' time. I will try to send it in the ____ as you have to hang it on the wall. But you know "les donanes" (postal workers or censors) very often pack out (open) the parcels, and then they disorder the contents. So I will tell you how you must do. The wings of the mill, the black ones are spinning round when the clock is going. It is a good clock. It must walk well.

Kisses from Hanna

Chapter Six

By 1938 Hitler had manipulated the German labor forces under his control. Unions had been destroyed except for the Arbeitsfront which was government controlled. Freedom of movement, negotiations for wages, and choices of employment were lost. Catholics had been persecuted and threatened into submission. Political adversaries had been eliminated in false arrests, mock trials (if any), and imprisonment. Torture in concentration camps was introduced by Goering and later Himmler, the head of the German police, the Gestapo, and the dreaded SS troops. Goebbels was in charge of propaganda, and it was too late when the Germans woke up to their own danger.

Jews lost all rights of citizenship. They couldn't work, couldn't leave the country without relinquishing all their property, and couldn't have the privileges of trials, police protection, or franchise. Great talent was lost when many Jews including Albert Einstein in 1933 fled their homeland.

Many "undesirables" from political enemies to the handicapped were sterilized. And perhaps the most horrendous of all was the indoctrination of the youth to become Nazi robots for Hitler's purposes. Trained to obey without conscience, they reported on friends and even turned in members of their own families in the belief they would be honored as loyal Hitler Youth. All this took place inside Germany to its own citizens before the invasions of other European countries. These neighbors had looked on nervously but dared not challenge; had prepared for the worst, but hoped for the best.

20 Jan., 1938

Dearest Ruth:

Your Christmas parcel was a beauty. It was a few weeks too late, but there is something wrong with the post in Holland last time. So it was not your fault. What a fine album and photographs from you in it. I am so glad with it, and I made up my mind to keep it especially for photos from America. What a (lot of) presents I got from you in the course of the years we are corresponding together.

It is not so good that I did not write you so much last time, but it was because I had no time. I got a job as physical education teacher at a school in Hillegersberg. This is one of the suburbs of Rotterdam. I am very busy at the moment, and I do find it a difficulty to teach girls from 12-18 years. I must work hard to get their sympathy. But Aad did write you a letter, is it not. He said he should do.

Here in Holland we are waiting the whole day on the coming of a new prince or princess. When there is one, we have a national holiday. Everybody wears orange colours, the colour of the house of Orange-tasson. The streets are illuminated and full of orange balloons and flags.

(This letter was incomplete.)

+ + + + + + +

18 April, '38 — Rotterdam

Dearest Ruth:

Thank you very much for your last letter with the pretty Easter greeting. I enjoyed the verse lines on it. It was as if they were made for us. I just had the feeling you called on me at that moment. I must write you now anything about my work the last time.

I wrote you about my first job I got at a school in a neighbourtown "+/–" half an hour on the bicycle from my home. I am there to give lessons in physical education. Girls from 12 - 18 years divided in four classes and every week 2 hours. This makes 8 hours a week.

Then I am giving lessons in the night hours every day from 8-10 o'clock. Sometimes to girls and women and 2 hours a week for ladies above the forty years.

Then the factures (factories) in our town have resolved to let their girls one hour a week free to take a physical education lesson. Four teachers are pointed to give these lessons. I'm one of the four. So you see, I got rather good job and I am come round easily enough. It is hard working, especially the night hours, but it is lovely and grateful work. Now I told much about myself. My parents are glad I am ready now to care for myself. They had 23 years long to give their care and their money to bring me so far, and now there is the crown on their work. How is it with your car? I should like, too, to go with you in the car and to have a jolly day together. But there are some things we desire our whole life, and we get never. So it will be with the car riding. Although I do have the thought that we will see each other after some years deep in my heart.

I have 12 days holiday now, and I rise these days very good. We have a little boy of 3 years to us 6 weeks long. It is a child of a friend of Aad's from Delft. Now we go every day to the park, and we play and so the day goes on very hard! Lovely holidays, Ruth, and much pleasure with your car.

Big kiss from Hanna

+ + + + + + +

6 Juli, '38 — Rotterdam

Dearest Ruth,

It is rather long ago that I wrote you and had a pretty chat with you. But as I got your letter last week, I was ashamed about myself so I sat directly down to write you back. I worked very hard last year, and I do find being a teacher very difficult. The work is so alive that you must have all your physical and psychical strengths, and at the end of the year you need a fine vacance. Do you feel it as I or do you find your task more easily? I have to divide my time in lessons to older women (40 years), young women (20 years) and children of from 10-18 years. So I must appreciate them all. I like teaching physical culture, but now and then I am so tired that I liked vacances much better.

In August I have vacances from 15-25 August. Aad has passed his exam. Now he has to learn for one more year, and then he must do the exam for technical sciences. By this exam he will have his degree, and then he will be able to have a job.

We have the vacances together. We have made up our mind to go together to Luxemburg in the centre of Europe and to have their beautiful walks in the mountains.

We did never go together in a foreign country. I think we will enjoy ourselves very much.

In Holland there is a travelling society. They make trips and voyages for you when you are a member and often 20 or 30 members went to a foreign country together with a leader of the society. Last time I read in the papers that they had a trip to America. The price was 400 guilders (for us $50 dollars). The trip was 6 weeks long. New York and Chicago and the Mississippi and the Niagara were visited. When I had had f 400, I had gone with the voyage but I did not have. I must work some 5 months to earn the f 400. But I swore I will spare all my money to come to you after a few years. I like to come to you so much that I will do my best to reach this ideal, and you? You are earning so much money that you do buy a car, and so on. Should you like to come to Holland? How long had you to work to pay the passage? The Holland America line boat comes here in Rotterdam so that you should be here in our house in half an hour. We should let you see the most beautiful places of our country, and we should see us from face to face. Do think about it, Ruth.

Much pleasure with your new studies at the university.

With a kiss and till seeing us

Your Hanna

+ + + + + + +

It was in this period that Aad was able financially to return to the University for his final year studying to become a chemical engineer. There was concern about his having to return to the army with the threat from Germany. January, 1939 would see the end of his class work and exams, but he still had a semester of practicum to complete.

Aunt Clazien, whom Hanna admired for her energy and wide interests beyond her nursing skills, had a train accident while touring in Germany and was from then on permanently injured. This was not only a physical handicap, but seemed also to affect her attitude and disposition making her difficult to live with.

The Dutch were trying hard to maintain their neutrality while feeling somewhat ambivalent in their attitude toward Germany. Hanna admitted that there were German sympathizers among the Dutch as well as German nationals living in The Netherlands. She asked for prayer.

Sept., 1938 — Rotterdam

Dearest Ruth:

Here I am to bring you my best wishes for your birthday. I am sending you a little gift. You know that we have celebrated the 40 years reign of our good Queen Wilhelmina.

All the cities and villages did their utmost to give themselves a fine view. Rotterdam with the harbour has spent over a million guilders for fireworks and illuminations, etc. They went back in history. The ships of one of our most famous admirals were built after ancient gravures (paintings) and laid them down in the harbour. Floodlight shown from the sides of the harbour, and we had at evening a magnificent view on it. Such an ancient ship I send you. It is from the 17th century, and it was all so (just as) you see. There is in the packet a little wonder statue to set the ship up so you can use it as an ornament. I hope the packet will reach you for now we are in such a bad international case to us in Europe. We are afraid each hour of the day that war will break out. But we will pray to God that He will spare us for (from) such a disastre.

We heard yesterday the words of Chamberlain through the radio. But it seems that whatever he will do for peace, it will not have any success.

Aad is in his last study year now. We hope that he can work through and that it will not be his duty to part as soldier to the bounderies of our country, for you know, we are the neighbors of Germany, and Germany in war is for us to be mobile.

I hope our letters will come to their address now. Do you write soon to me?

Your Hanna

Chapter Seven

Saturday, 21 Jan., 1939

Dearest Ruth:

I am ashamed that I could not find the time to write you, but now I will sit down for half an hour to have a chat with you. Thanks for your nice letter. I enjoy to hear that it goes very well with you.

The last year it was not a very pretty one for us. Aunt Clazien who is loved by us all had (7 August) after her voyage to Heidelberg (Germany) where she was with her vacances in accident. At first it seemed that she was able to recover, but now she can't raise her left arm. She is not able to raise and to stretch her arm and you know, she is a nurse and so she can't do her work. In the old days, she was rather jolly, and she had much pleasure in her work. Although she was fifty years old, she could behave herself as thirty. But now she has grown as a old woman. Her hair has become in half a year so grey, and her nerves are ill by the shock. She was to our house 4 months long but now she is to another sister to change. That is good for her the doctor says. So you can understand we were the whole day through busy to care for her. Especially my mother had a difficult time. So it is good for her, too, that Aunt Clazien parted to another family.

With Aad it goes very good. He had his last exam in Januari. Then he must work practical till June, and then he is ready with the study, and he has his grade as chemical engineer. With me it is good. I like to give physical education lessons, and the girls and women like it to have my lessons. With St. Nicholas/Santa Claus I got a tea set from my parents, and a large foto of Aad himself from Aad. A little piece of it I did in the letter. It is rough and only his face, not his hair, and it is but a little one. But now you can see how the lines are of his face. Later on we will send you a foto of us together. I send you a box of post paper (old Dutch) and hope you will get it. I hope you will use it to write all jolly things that you will have little trouble to write. So long—

A kiss from Your Hanna

+ + + + + + +

In April, Italian troops seized Albania, the small country along the west side of Yugoslavia. This predominantly agricul-

tural area, ruled by a dictator, King Zog I, struggled along a mountainous coastline to feed its people. The potential mining of minerals and petroleum products probably was the reason for the invasion of this country with one of the lowest standards of living in all of Europe.

11 Mai, '39 — Rotterdam

Dearest Ruth,

Thank you for your last letter I got some weeks ago. I did not write you for a long time. I had a job on a high school in Rotterdam and had besides my own work 28 hours physical education to give to the girls of that school. So I made +/– 50 hours a week. I had no time to do anything else as physical exercises for much of the good things. But it is for +/– 6 weeks. Then the lady in whose place I am on the high school is recovered again from a stomach illness, and she can do her work herself.

I believe you are amusing yourself very much in your new living place to see on the photos you sent. You can see I did read the talk Roosevelt had, and I did see it very important. But the words Hitler said, and the manner he talked about Roosevelt's words were very disappointing. We heard him over the radio. I fear that a war can't be very long away and the only thing I hope is that Holland will not be in it. Our country is well armed and half the army is on the bounderies to be prepared on everything. It is not a pretty time here, and it is not to be proud or to be an European.

Aad is in his last study year, and he hopes to get a job in our East Indies. He says "so quick as possible out of Europe, that is the best thing." You know Rotterdam is a town of industries. Many factures are in our town, and many girls are working there. It is a work not very much healthy to be 8 1/2 hours a day in a facture, and now there is to us in society who will care for these girls the nights when they are out of the work. They have them lessons in making their own dress, in physical excersises, etc. With 5 lady teachers we are giving the last lessons. Last Saturday we had a party. Every groupe (30 girls a groupe) have to do an excersise on the stage, and parents and friends had been invited to look. After the presentation there was a ball. We had much fun. The girls I had learned an excersise were very pretty. They gave me flowers. How is it with Reathel? Can she live so alone without parents? I had so much compassion with her.

81

The book you sent me is very good for me. I don't write each day, but all important things who happen. I write down on it, and it gives me much pretty hours.

Your pal, Hanna

+ + + + + + +

In October of 1939, Aad and Hanna were hoping that the army would release Aad to go to the Dutch East Indies to work in a sugar factory. They awaited the news with great anticipation.

About a month later (November 22, 1939), Hanna wrote about the feelings of many of her people with regard to the war situation, and discussed the reasons for the conflict in Europe at this time.

In defiance of Germany and Poland's nonaggression pact (expiration date—1944), Hitler aimed his propaganda at his large neighbor citing false abuses to German citizens and fake names and figures. He also raised fears that England and France were poised to invade and "offered his protection". Therefore, on Sept. 1, 1939 the Nazi war machines, which tremendously outnumbered Poland's stockpile, attacked with no declaration of war. To ameliorate Russian fears of a future attack on it, there had been a hasty agreement between those two countries for the USSR not to intervene. Russia seemed to acquiesce to Germany's abrupt invasion of Poland with its rich resources of iron, coal, oil, and agricultural products. However, Russia may have been "buying time" since it probably knew about Germany's earlier attempt to get Poland to join it against the USSR. Hitler's double-dealing would eventually be his undoing, but at the moment, he held all the power and the initiative. Within five weeks the German Army had rolled across the flat plains, demolished cities, bombed League of Nations arsenals, and had taken prisoner, killed, or wounded over 800,000. Still the Polish resistance had been very costly to Germany and also somewhat to Russia which had belatedly joined in the attack from the east. England and France couldn't mobilize quickly enough to come to Poland's rescue, but these five weeks bought them time to prepare against future personal attacks.

Under the leadership of General Sikorski, Polish troops recruited escapees from internment camps and inhabitants living in other countries to help defend France and other countries during the remainder of the war.

Soon after, the republics of Lithuania, Latvia, and Estonia cast their lots with the USSR and forfeited their independence for what they hoped would be temporary protection.

11 September, 1939 — Rotterdam

Dearest Ruth,

Since you wrote your last letter at 31 July with the birthday card, I appreciated so much. Things change in Europe and in our country. We are, as you know, of course, in war and though our country is not yet in, we must do our utmost to be strong and ready at all circumstances. It is not easy for a little country as Holland, not to be driven in the terrible stream that war is. But our queen said in her talk to us that the army and navy should be called to watch the boundaries at the East side (Germany) and the West side (England) to see to remain ourselves.

All the young men from 12-35 years are called at 28 August to come. So Aad had to come and now he is as a soldier at the West side of the country. Fortunately our country is not so large, so I go to see him every Sunday.

Since 20 June we had a very lovely time. Aad had his exam as a chemical engineer and he passed through it very easily. Then he went to see for a job and after a week he could get a contract from a Dutch society who has sugar plantations in the Dutch East Indies. We made up our minds to get married in December and that January we should go together to the Indies. That was 15 August just before my birthday. At 20 August we had our holiday and we went to Swiss. You asked me sometime ago if there was no objection for 2 people of the other sex to go together and travel. To us it is very common. We saw a few weeks ago in the movies Yes, My Darling Daughter with Priscilla Lane and there was the story of a boy and girl who want to have some days together and the family that had some objections. Did you see it? We did not love the story for it is not up to date at us.

We go together with four and nobody sees it as bad. When there is somebody who wants to do bad things, he has not to travel. There are much other occasions for such a purpose, it is not?

We enjoyed Swiss very well all the high with snow covered mountains. We walked hours and hours. We went with the mountain train and we enjoyed each other's company.

But then two days before we should part, we heard of the difficult position between the countries in Europe and we resolved to start the way back at once. So we came 2 days earlier in Holland than we should. The way back we were in the train with many English people who broke off their traveling too, to go home. They were afraid to become in war with Germany.

Through France we had to travel in a very dark compartment. It was forbidden to have a light. That was meant as a precaution for attacks from the air. But we came to Holland safe and well and the other day was our off day: the mobilization of army and navy to watch our boundaries.

So we don't go to the Indies and this is our personal sorrow you understand for we two enjoyed it to go. But when we think of all the people who have to suffer from the war, as the French, the German, the Poles, we are not allowed to complain ourselves.

Now I am a teacher again and working. That is the best remedy for all sorrows. This is what you wrote, too, when you went to school again after the bad days after your father's dead, is it not?

Ruth, I hope your family will recover from the blow they got. I hope this letter who is not joyous, can let you see how bad circumstances we are. We don't complain of course not. When we need, our whole country will stand as one man after our queen to fight for our independence, but it is all so very sad and miserable that men must fight again each other.

I hope this letter will reach you. The post does not go so very well now. I will think on your birthday now and hope you will be very happy then and afterwards.

As a present I thought to buy you a little fotograph album with the photographs of me and my family and some friends I do love. I hope it will reach your home and do think on us. When you will write Aad, his address is: A. J. Muijser, Vaandrig staf I gRT, Veldleger, Holland. Veldleger is army at the field in Congrary with army at the coast.

Your Hanna

+ + + + + + +

When Nazi Germany invaded Poland with Russia's coopera-tion and trust, Great Britain and France declared war on Germany while the United States amended its neutrality policy to permit shipment of arms on a cash-and-carry basis. President Roosevelt

was trying to encourage Congress and the nation to build up
defenses and prepare to support our European friends. Many young
sympathizers went to Canada and joined the Royal Air Force.

September 21, 1939 — Rotterdam

Dearest Ruth:

Your parcel I got yesterday. I'm so glad with it. It was just
what I liked to have. For you know I have to save in it my things
worth to have: my birth act, my act of having had the middle high
school, my act as a teacher of physical education, my passport to
travel in foreign countries, and my savings bank book, some
letters of Aad I will have, receipts, and so on.

It is such a luxury to have such a fine box to have all those
things in. I hope you reached my parcel, too.

Aad had 2 days vacances from the army service. He came
home and we had 2 fine days. Now he parted again. He is
fortunately not so far away. He is 1 1/2 hours with the train in
Haarlem. Every Sunday I go to him. You see, in our country, life
is not so terrible as in some other parts of Europe.

But we must see that our men go in the army to defend
(guard) our neutrality. They have not to fight yet, and we pray
they will not have to do in the future.

It is a lucky thing that our letters and parcels reach each
other across the ocean in this time. I'm grateful to have such a
faithful friend in America.

With lots of love and a kiss for the beautiful friend,

Hanna

+ + + + + + +

October 27, 1939 — Rotterdam

Dearest Ruth,

I got your letter which spoke about the war circumstances. Yes,
indeed, though we are, as King Leopold of Belgium said in his talk to
America, living at an isle of peace in the corner of Europe where
Hell had burst out the last month. It is a terrible thing now to live
in Europe and one can be ashamed to be an European. Our
country is armed from teeth to tooth, all our men between 18-35
are under the weapons and are ready to defend our country

against all possible issues. But our folks, they want not to fight. I think I should not over live, when we came in the war. Suppose all people we love to see in terrible circumstances to lose your father, your husband, your beloved! To see that the cities are crumbled and that unarmed citizens must suffer under the fire of aeroplanes. But fortunately our reign does her utmost to sail through all dangerous spots with her ship of reign and to hold us outside the conflict. But all those Germans and Frances and Englishmen. They have to suffer because their reigns can't speak to each other and can't understand each other.

Aad and I we hope that Aad can go to the East Indies. It is possible that the sugar cultures at Java (where we should go) go on, though it is war. In December the decision falls if he is so allowed to go. I will give you some words as soon as I can.

How it is with you? Did you have my parcel I sent you at your birthday? Did you have a pleasant birthday? I hope so. Do console your mother as good as you can. I have much pity with her. She must feel lonesome. The living in Holland goes on ordinary. There are difficulties with some parts of the industries, but so good as possible, the places of the men who parted to defend the country, are replaced by others, especially women. Life goes on and so it is better. It is astonishing how little time we were ready for our new manner of life. Some girlfriends of me, who are teachers physical education too, have now to teach boys.

Other friends have got other jobs than they did usually. And the soldiers have it good too. Where in the country they are, the people receive them cheerfully and we all do our utmost to give them some pleasure.

I hope you will soon answer me with a jolly letter.

Love, Your Hanna

+ + + + + + +

Thursday, 22 November, 1939

My dearest Ruth,

I got your letter of 13 October. It had not been opened in the way to Holland and I liked to hear that you got the map with the photos.

You spoke about your sympathy with England and France and you asked of what sort our feelings are.

Look here, we as a neutral country, we don't have feelings of antipathy or sympathy for a country in war.

But beside this, it is possible, that some people in Holland are feeling symphatically with Germany or with France and England. But most of Dutch people I can say and so I am feeling for don't know who is right.

Of course, Germany took Warsaw and he showed no pity with the population. But on the other side, in 1918 in Versailles, England, France, and America had no pity with Germany. They took from him all he wanted to live, and your President Wilson who made the fourteen points, and did not know as an American that in Europe there are folks, many of folks, who must live in their own way. That the German people is not like the English people. That the French people is not like the Dutch or Norwegian people. They all have their different ways of living of doing their different characters, their different habits.

In 1918 they put Germany in the ground, but it was to see that it should climb again, as soon as it should have a leader, a man who knew to make the people enthusiastic for an ideal, the ideal to make Germany as strong as long ago and with what means. Never mind! This is the dramatic side of this war. Who is right? Of course, England can't admit that Germany takes all he wants, but on the other side, a country with a sentimentally folk as Germany shall fight and take the war, when an ideal must be fought.

We, in Holland, we desire to remain out of the war for we think it a terrible thing. I don't know if this letter will reach you. They are so many ships who have an accident. Last week, our Simon Bolivar, a ship with much Dutchmen who went to the West Indies. But I hope it will reach you. We in Holland who are so near the war country, we can make us perhaps a more right ideas, how the situation is. We have pity with all folks in war, for the life for all those is terrible. The countries lost much of money, and the civilization of ages goes away. Please, pray for the end of the war.

A kiss of your Hanna

Chapter Eight

One day Ruth received a letter saying that Aad had received permission to leave the army and had a new job in a sugar refinery in Java, part of the Dutch East Indies—half the world away from the Netherlands. Hanna and Aad were married Jan. 25, 1940. Hanna wrote about the difficulties of leaving their native country and the separation from their families and friends. However, they were so happy because they would be away from the European war. Following frantic preparations to purchase and ship all they felt they would need, they sailed in February from Genoa, Italy through the Suez Canal and across the Indian Ocean to Java by boat.

Java is included as one of the Greater Sunda Islands and is one of the most populated islands of Indonesia. It was the center of much of the nation's economy in the 1940's.

Java and its surrounding islands had been discovered by the Portuguese explorer Vasco da Gama in 1497 while he was trying to find a shorter sea route to India. Later in the 17th century, British and Dutch East India Companies established claims there. The Dutch forced the British to leave and encouraged tea, coffee, rubber, sugar, indigo, and other crops to be planted on plantations. These were purchased at set prices to get profits for the East India Company. Later, other territory was acquired by political maneuvering or direct conquest by the Dutch government when the Company was disbanded.

As early as 1908 the native Indonesians began to form nationalistic organizations because they were not getting to share in the wealth of the productions. The standard of living was low. These conditions later had a profound influence on Hanna's life.

The Muslim religion was introduced along with Hinduism and Buddhism.

Dutch investors, colonists, and traders had long been involved with this part of Asia so it was not too unusual for a young Dutch couple to agree to spend the next five years "halfway across the world." In the light of the threats from Germany, it seemed the expedient thing to do as well as adventuresome.

When Hanna and Aad got there, they began informing Ruth about their new home which was another unique experience for all of them. The people were Polynesian and served the white people. Their house was on stilts for relief from the heat and for protection from insects. A siesta was a custom observed by all workers and students. They had native servants and experienced for the first time a state of luxury. However, adjustments to a tropical climate also incurred occasional health problems.

An east-west chain of mountains extends across Java and includes fertile plains, volcanoes, limestone ridges, and highland plateaus. In many of her letters, Hanna speaks of vacations in the mountains where she and Aad spent many happy days in a cooler climate.

Aad explained about the sugar processing factory where he worked. He was over-qualified with his degree in chemistry for the work he did there, but that seemed to be the norm for the Dutch workers.

They were so happy and felt so safe in their new home. She wrote, "Everything is so beautiful and calm here that it is hard to believe that back in Europe a war is in progress. Please pray that Holland will be spared."

January, 1940 — Rotterdam

Dearest Ruth,

I received your letter in which was your Christmas greetings. What a beautiful card and your name printed! I hope you received my letter, too. I hope you understand my view on international circumstances I told you.

Now we had a pleasant Christmas for this I tell you. The day before Christmas, Aad received a letter from the ministers of colonies and war that he was permitted to leave the army here in Holland to go to the Dutch East Indies to do his work there in the sugar manufacturies. Aad was at home at Christmas and told the news. For us two it was a very good news, but for our parents it is very hard to let us go so far away.

Now you understand, Aad has to go 7 Febr. to Genoa and then with a boat of the Rotterdamche Loyal to the Indies, at first Batavia and then Saerabaja. We plan to marry 25 January then we are living from 25 Jan.-7 Feb. in the house of my parents and then we are beginning our life together.

We in Holland with our colonies we are accustomed that sometimes people of our family or friends go away. But although it is a great change, we shall not be as strangers in the Indies. At first we can speak our own language, except with the black people who are speaking Malanese.

You understand that the three weeks before our marriage we shall be very busy to buy all sorts of things we need in the tropics, to have passage on our boat "The Dempo", greet my pupils, a.s.o. Ruth, now you know again how we are.

The five years diary your present some time ago will not have much unfilled pages, you can be sure.

It is 1 January '40 today and my parents, Aad, Aunt Clazien and I we wish you all good for 1940. We know you had much sorrow this year, but you must have sorrow to know to appreciate the beautiful things in life. We in Europe wish the war to be only a rumor. We hope that after this sorrow shall come a long time of peace. Aad and I going in a new future, leaving our native country, it is all very difficult. We don't know when we are coming back for a weeks after staying there 5 years what Europe has become. But be sure Ruth, you and your family the best wishes for the future and 'till we are writing each other again.

Your pal, Hanna

Hanna and Aad Muijser's wedding—Jan. 1940

My dearest friend,

Ruth, I don't know how long it is I wrote you a letter. I am ashamed very much about myself but I know that you will forgive me.

I wrote you the last time that Aad had finished his studies as a chemical engineer, that he was to take a job at an sugar manufacturing in the East Indies. That war broke out and he was to be under arms too, with almost all young men of our country to care for Holland on the boundaries. We thought all our ideas to go to the East Indies had gone, but the day before Christmas, Aad got a telegram from the minister of colonies, that he was free to take the job in the Indies and that he was allowed to leave army in Holland. Now Ruth, you can feel with us our pleasure about it. Our fathers and mothers did not deal our pleasure any how, for they had to say farewell for 5 years. For every 5 years we got one year with vacations in Europe.

The days between Christmas and our leaving at 5 February were more than full. We had to marry at once (25 January). I had no time to write you but I sent you a card and the wedding foto. We had to buy in some days our clothes for the Indies. Your parcel with the red towels was packed too in the chests and box we took with us, and so all our possessions were packed. All your presents I got in the eight years of our friendship are now in the Dutch Indies and the most beautiful of it is now the personal folio map you send me. For in this map I am keeping now all the letters I got from home, from all my friends and family in Holland and my friend in America.

We had a beautiful voyage from Holland to the Indies. At first with the train from Rotterdam-Genoa to avoid the mines in the North Sea. Then with the Dutch mailboat to the Indies Port Said, Suez, Singapore, Batavia.

With the train to So . . . , the East coast of the isle Java and from there 2 hours with the train to the sugar manufact.

We are very happy together. The dream of many years is now a reality, and sometimes I can't imagine that it is a reality. That Aad and I have married indeed and are now far from home in the colonies. It is very warm here, a tropic temperature. But we have a large house, with stone floors and high walls. Inside the house it is always fresh and cool.

In the contrary to a Dutch household where the housewife generally cooks and works herself, sometimes with a domestic or servant, (only very rich people have more) in the Indies. We have four servants, a man servant, a wash servant, a cook and a gardener. I only have to look on. But this is a good thing for I liked never the household, you know. I like much better other things. I have made up my mind to begin here too with giving lessons in physical culture to the ladies in the neighborhood.

It is a very little place here. Except the 40 European employees of the factory, it is all native people. The language Malenese is not difficult to learn, but at the moment we are not yet very clever with it. Next time, Ruth mine, I will tell you more about our living here.

Love, Aad and Hanna

Hanna and Aad's home in a Javanese compound
Thinggiran, Java

Sugar factory where   Wood carving Hanna
Aad worked in Java   sent to Ruth

Prior to May 10, 1940, the little country of Holland had declared its neutrality, including the years of World War I. They had eluded conflict and hardships inflicted upon other nearby countries. However, the German army under the command of Adolph Hitler was invading surrounding countries, ravishing and ransacking everything in its path.

Although Queen Wilhelmina had declared Holland's neutral position and protested against any violence of Netherlands' territories, Germany ignored the Queen's promise to her people that "the neutrality of our country will be respected as long as we ourselves maintain neutrality."

It had been apparent, due to periods of crises prior to World War II, that Holland should not be caught "asleep", but should *prepare for such an invasion that now threatened this peaceful country. Therefore, Queen Wilhelmina commanded military forces to do their duty and build their defenses to delay the invading Nazi army.*

She appealed to the British and French governments for help. They assured her they would give all the assistance they could muster. But after only five days, the Germans had subdued the Dutch troops. Holland was not spared.

Despite shooting off red flares of surrender to ward off destruction to the city, the rape of Rotterdam began at noon. From 12:00 to 2:30 on May 10, 1940, thirty German planes bombed this city as well as several others. General Winkleman, having seen the advancing army capturing the countryside from east to west in less than a week, had hoped to prevent mass destruction in Rotterdam, The Hague, and Amsterdam by not resisting, but the Germans used this unnecessary obliteration of the harbors and civilian areas to intimidate France which was to be its next conquest. In all, 26,000 buildings were destroyed including hospitals, churches, schools and homes; 25,000 people were killed and buried in the rubble; and ships in the harbor were in flames. Broken water and sewer lines paralyzed the cities. (It was predicted it would take 15 years to rebuild.) The city where Hanna and Aad's parents lived was almost leveled.

The German troops occupied the territory, took whatever they wanted, and made the young men go to Germany to work in factories or fight.

America, too, was appalled by these attacks on neutral countries and considered the Nazi invasion a threat to its security.

When Rotterdam was bombed, the Dutch learned about it in Java, but communication was cut off. So Hanna and Aad could not write their parents nor learn about their welfare, and their parents could not contact them either.

Both parties had the same idea to use Ruth as their go-between since the USA was not at war, and communication was possible through the States.

That summer Ruth was attending classes in Champaign, Illinois, and, believe it or not, she received letters from both Hanna and Aad and their parents on the same day desperately begging her to get word to the other of their circumstances.

Hanna and Aad's parents knew their children would be frantic with worry and wanted to get word to them that they had all survived the devastation. Hanna and Aad also sent several poignant pleas to Ruth for help.

They knew Ruth would respond to their requests as soon as she could because they were so desperate. However, it took two weeks for a letter to reach Europe by ship and five weeks to reach Java. Ruth thought how awful it would be for them to wait another five weeks to know whether their parents were dead or alive. So, she cut her classes that afternoon and went downtown to Western Union. She asked about the procedure for sending a cablegram. Although Ruth had sent and received telegrams occasionally, that was the first cablegram she had ever sent. One had to pay per word including the address, and Hanna's address was very long. Ruth remembers it cost her $5.85 (of the $100 she had for the summer's schooling), and back then that was a lot of money. The message to Java was just two words, "Families safe." Then she sent one to Holland which simply said, "Hanna knows." That one incident made them her friends forever. They would always keep in touch.

16 May, 1940 — Thinggiran (Java)
(Six days after invasion of Holland)

Dearest Ruth.

You have heard the terrible news. That our poor country has made through, that they had to fight against Germany and that they lost. Towns were bombed, soldiers were shot dead. Aad and I are in the Indies and we are impatient about the fate of our parents and other family. We hear naturally nothing about them. The communication between Holland and Dutch Indies has been broken. Are they dead or alive? We don't know.

Now, as your country is not still in war with Germany, it is possible that a letter sent from America can come in Holland. Therefore we pray you to send the letter in your letter to Holland. It is possible that we hear in this way anything about our parents.

O, Ruth, this is the most great sorrow we ever have in our life, and we ever could have. It was a bad thing the moment you wrote me your father died. But you knew that and how it was. You could do anything to relief his last moments but not to know anything, it is not to carry (bear).

You are my friend Ruth. I know you will do what you can to help us. Send the letter soon and we only ask in it how the parents do. We cannot say anything in it for fear German post does not send it through. There are two letters. Will you do it, Ruth? I can't write a pretty chat to you now. I regret very, but it is a sorrow now, and about our good country and about the fate of our family that we can't think about anything other. Pray for our country and our family please. With a kiss from me and greetings from Aad.

Your Hanna

+ + + + + + +

On June 12 and July 1, 1940, Hanna again pleaded with Ruth to try to get word about her family, and expressed her feelings of despair in not knowing the fate of her loved ones. Her first letter was still enroute to the U.S.A.

12 Juni 1940 — Sugar Manufactory Thinggiran
(One month after attack)

Dearest Ruth,

Again I come to you as you are the only friend we have now and we can write to. All the sorrows we have I told you already. And again I come to ask you will try to send a card to my familie and Aad's. The first time I asked you I put in a letter, but Aad says it will be better to put in a card. Then the censor can read easily what has been wrote on it.

Oh Ruth, how Hitler could do it to take us! A peace loved country and ruin it all. Have you read the ruin Rotterdam, our good town has been made. It is to cry and to be without hope. We can't think about nothing other and I feel I bore you too with my letter. But it is impossible to take my thoughts together and to have a pretty chat with you. Perhaps later on. I hope you will write us soon a letter. It should be the only letter we get nowadays. For all our family and friends in Holland, we don't get a word from as you know. We fear, most of them are dead or wounded. It is all so terrible. O Ruth, can you help us? Write soon. Many kisses. Aad gives you his greetings.

Your Hanna

+ + + + + + +

Juli 1, 1940
Sugar Manufactory Thinggiran —Kediri Java

My dearest Ruth,
    Since the day Aad and I were married so much things have happened, happy ones and sad ones, that it is to me as if the 5 months were one week.
    We went with the boat to the East Indies. I wrote you many times about our impressions but I don't know you ever got my letters by the political circumstances. When we had arrived in the Indies, I wrote you again a letter. This letter was to be going with the boat. But now I have seen planes go from the Dutch Indies to America and I am in a hurry to write you such an air letter. In my last letter I asked you to try to come in connection with our parents in Holland. You have hear too, that our good town Rotterdam has suffered so much and we two so far away. And it is impossible to telegraph or to write. O, you don't know what it is to have your whole family in Rotterdam and not to know where they are and how they are. You are our only friend now. To you only we can write and all our hope is fixed on you, that you should be able to send a telegram or a letter to my parents that we are safe and how they are. We will send you by a letter all the money. You should pay about it. You have to write only how much. Ruth, try if you can to hear something about our dear parents. We should bless you and thank you our whole life long. At first I was so sad about war that has come to our country Holland too that I could think about nothing else. But Aad saw I had to do my best to think about other things and now I try to do as he and it goes better now. The Indies are not in the war and it is so quiet here that one cannot think about happen to terrible things in Holland and in other countries too. Aad has a busy work in the sugar. It is very hot here, but we have a great and cool house and four servants to do the household, so that we can make it ourselves very well. I am sending you a photo about a Javanese boy with two cows. The cows are used for everything here. They too draw the lorries with the sugar reed to the manufactory.
    It is evening now at eight and I am setting here to write to you. It is a cool evening and when I look outside the open window, I am seeing the tropic night. The ski is full of stars. They seem not so

97

far to be as in our own country. It is a beautiful sight and in nights as this one, when I am sitting here alone, I must think about my parents and other family who have to suffer so much. Maybe, they are dead, without our knowing and then I am praying that God send you as a friend to me some years ago, maybe to help us now. Could it be that you wired to my parents: "Hanna and Aad safe." And the address is you know. de Bruijn Velseniuststraat 4, Rotterdam. And the same wire to my parents-in-law Muijser Schieweg 251a.

It could be that one of the houses were burnt down or bombed and then we have a chance more. Write how much money you spend, if wiring is possible (but you are neutral, is it not) and we send you the money. Many kisses from me and dear greetings from Aad.

Your Hanna

Send our parents please your address too. Maybe they have lost it.

+ + + + + + +

After three months on July 31, 1940, Hanna received Ruth's telegram telling her that their families in Holland were safe!

The next letter from Hanna was much happier. She wrote, "An hour ago we received your cablegram saying our families were safe. Oh, how we do thank you that you were so kind!" She also expressed her views on the war in Europe and the reasons for them.

From that time on every letter Ruth received from Java, she sent on to Holland, and every letter from Europe, she sent to Java. Ruth began to receive lots of letters because everybody Aad and Hanna knew began to write to her. Hanna wrote more frequently than she ever had, perhaps in fear that Ruth would not answer the letters and they would lose their sole means of communication. Ruth heard from Hanna's parents and Aad's parents. Hanna's mother even began to study English so she could write Ruth. Soon Ruth was also corresponding with Hanna's aunts and uncles, some of her girl friends, and Aad's Uncle John who wrote long, very interesting letters. And later she began to get letters from people she didn't even know who had family in Java and who needed her to forward their mail. Uncle John had two sons, one of whom also wrote Ruth. Aad Broekman was a dance band leader who wrote about his concerts and his girl singer. He mentioned how much

98

they all enjoyed American music but that it took a long time for them to be able to get the music. Ruth started sending them sheet music which put their orchestra ahead of the other local musicians.

They realized that it cost a lot of money for her to correspond with all these people. Today it costs 60 cents per half ounce airmail, but back then it cost <u>a whole nickel</u> to send a letter by boat. Hanna and Aad's parents sent her international coupons which could be purchased at any post office and exchanged for stamps in any other post office in the world.

Aad's letter thanked Ruth for all her trouble after receiving a packet of family letters. He said, "It is obvious that mankind is not so rotten as we might perceive it to be when we think of the kindnesses you've done." His aunt wrote in Dutch, "Ruth is a darling. Please thank her for the telegram she sent. There are still people who believe in honesty, kindness, and freedom, and that is our hope for the world."

Juli, 1940 — Thinggiran 31
(Ten weeks later)

Dearest Ruth,

An hour ago we received your telegram (wire) saying, "Family safe"! O, how we do thank you, that you were so kind, to write us this telegram. Never in our life we have been so glad as we are now. To hear that our parents are not dead, that they are safe! Ruth, we give you a big kiss for giving us this good news through.

When we began to correspond, dearest, we did not thought about these horrible things in Holland to be happened. And we did not know that we should become such good friends, and I did not know however that it should be you who would send us the news which we were longing for such a great deal of time, the news we were so glad to hear, as no other news ever before. Ruth, again we give you a big kiss for this.

You must write how much you paid for it. For we will ask you this: Will you be so kind to wire back once more to my parents? What do you think? "family received telegram" or "Aad and Hanna well too". We would be so grateful to you when they will hear we two are well too.

We decided to send you a post cheque containing the costs and expense you had. You write it in $, we can pay it here in guilders. This can be arranged. We think it will be 30 guilders

99

but we don't know. It can be more, it can be less. Do you write please? Can you pay the money for a wire back in advance too? We hope you will do it. We are so anxious to know how you got the news from Holland. Did my parents send you a wire asking to wire us? Or did you inquire about them yourself and wired us later on? Is it possible to send letters from Holland to America and from America to Holland? Or is only a wire possible? O, what an asking!

I should like so much to have you here and to embrace you. I am so excited about this telegram. I received it an hour ago at 10 o'clock in the morning and Aad slept for he has done work in the plant last night through. I ran toward him with the paper and now we are sitting here in the room and I must write at you at once. I received your letter, too, you wrote Juni 15. A month it lasted before we got your letter and it had been opened by the censor.

We enjoyed your letter very much. And you have another job again and a raise in salary. Congratulations, Ruth! Your foto we did not receive about Christmastime. We are so sorry for that. But we enjoy that you received our wedding foto. The view you have about the war is typical American, Aad says. "A cause, that is not ours" you wrote. We, here in the Indies, we changed our mind as you can understand, after the invasion in Holland. Before this we could understand that the Germans led by their chief Hitler, desired to get more rights in Europe. But when the invasions in Poland, in Norway came, we understood that, although it was a specimen of escaping more perils, Hitler was a person who did not spare respect or consider anything or anyone. And when the invasion in Holland came, and we heard about the many soldiers dead and mutilated and missing, the civil population bombed and murdered, a feeling of hatred came in all our hearts and a strong feeling is here to fight for winning our freedom again.

I believe we all think it is not a fight between folks, but a fight about ideas. The idea, the principle of the democrats against the principle of the state where one person or a few persons have all the power. It is not as in past wars in Europe, that the folks stood against each other with a heart full of hate. It is the idea.

And so it happened that both in Norway, as in Holland, Belgium and France it was possible that a rather great groupe of persons existed who admired the principle of the autocratic state, who admired the Hitler, the Mussolini, the Stalin principle. They founded a party and they resolved to help Germany in case of an invasion. And so it happened that when Hitler had his invasion that he found a "fifth colonne" who helped the enemy. All for their principle. They were it who made it possible that Holland was conquered in five days, they too were it who helped that France could fall in so short a time. Even here in the Indies, there are enough people, real Dutchman, who admire the principle of an autocratic of a dictatorial state, weak persons who ask for a strong leader, who want to feel above them a strong man to which they can cheer and which they can trust blindfolded, who thinks for them, who excites them. The real Dutch thought of a democratic state they have abandoned. They forget that we Dutch men founded with a eighty years fight our democratic thoughts, that our country was the first one in Europe with a democratic government, that our glorious Prince Willem I gave his good and his blood for this cause. That was in the last part of the 16th century. But it must be a strong folk who is able to bear the rights of a personal freedom and besides, to bear the duties of it. But we know here in the Indies how to do with the weak elements who too want a Hitler. The government has arrested them all. They can do here no harm, we hope. We know that you Americans love the democrat idea and therefore, we think that our cause is yours, too. It goes all over the world.

In the first days the war came in Holland too, I was so out of my balance that I could not think or write or do anything. A feeling of desperate sadness was upon every one here. I believe I wrote you some desperate letters. I am now ashamed about it and I wished I had not written them. I had to know that some day my dear Ruth should send us informations. But you must forgive me writing this letters, I was not myself in these days.

We have here a beautiful life. Java is a beautiful country and people are so interesting and lovely. There is so much to see in a tropical country, when you have never been there. We are in the lower part of Java the sugar is always in the lower part. And it is very hot. From 1-4 in the afternoon we always are in bed. Then you can't walk outside the door. But the evenings are cool and as I told you, the houses are great and cool and twice a day we bath. I am sending you two fotos.

I am thinking about a birthday present for you and we are sending you a weaving, made by native people here. It comes from

Soemba, an isle near Java. You can use it as table-cloth or as a wall cloth. We use here such weavings on the walls as a garment for we don't have wallpaper in our rooms. We are sending it soon. Perhaps you have it on your birthday. When you have a foto more of yourself, please send it, when you can spare it. Many kisses, many good wishes, also for your dear mother for whom we are so sorry.

Your Hanna

Letter cancellation during Nazi occupation

UNION POSTALE UNIVERSELLE	COUPON-RÉPONSE INTERNATIONAL	CN 01 (ancien C 22)

Ce coupon est échangeable dans tous les pays de l'Union postale universelle contre un ou plusieurs timbres-poste représentant l'affranchissement minimal d'un envoi prioritaire ou d'une lettre ordinaire expédiée à l'étranger par voie aérienne.

Empreinte de contrôle du bureau d'origine (facultative)	Prix de vente (indication facultative)	Timbre du bureau qui effectue l'échange
	$ 1.05	

Sample of an international coupon used to
repay Ruth for her postal expenses

Hanna, Aad, and other family members wrote to express their appreciation to Ruth, their wonderful friend in America. By relaying messages and sending cards to Ruth in America, Hanna and her family were able to keep in touch with one another throughout trying times.

Every Dutch and Javanese letter was censored. The letters Ruth received had very few words cut out because the Dutch were careful not to write about Germany nor any war conditions, but mainly about their families. These Dutch envelopes were stamped with the Nazi swastika. It was always obvious that the envelopes had been opened and resealed. Therefore, before Ruth sent them on to Java, she enclosed them in a different envelope so that it appeared that Hanna and Aad were receiving mail from the States. For a year and a half that was the way they heard from each other. From the time Rotterdam was bombed in May, 1940 until the Pearl Harbor bombing in Dec. 1941, life in the United States was fairly normal as it was in Java. Even Holland had settled down under the German occupation forces. The Dutch parents didn't burden Aad and Hanna with all their difficulties and couldn't have even if they had wanted to due to censorship.

Under Nazi rule, listening to foreign radio stations was forbidden. Newspapers were also taken over by the Germans. (TV had been invented, but did not even exist yet for the general public.)

Aad wrote Ruth and asked her to forward letters to their parents in Rotterdam.

Sept., 1940 — Thinggiran 6

Dearest Ruth,

This letter is to gratulate you with your birthday 14 October and I hope that the letter will reach you. I hope you have a happy birthday and so Aad hopes too. We wish you all the happiness that is possible. That you and your country will be spared all the time. After your telegram I wrote you a letter. We were so excited that I believe it was a letter full of nonsense, but we were so glad to hear about our parents and to hear it from you that we should have kissed you, had you been here. But all our gratitude we had to send in a letter and this was very difficult.

After the telegram we did not hear anything more from you and you can believe that more than ever we are longing for a letter from you. You are the only friend now with whom we can

103

correspondent. O, Ruth, I am so grateful that Fate brought us together some eight years ago. We never had the opportunity to see each other in the eyes, but though I know you are a faithful friend. A friend on whom we can trust in times of difficulty and sorrow.

Now it is nearly four months ago that our native country has been invaded by the German soldiers and you know at first I was hopelessly out of my nerves, and Aad too though he was stronger in our sorrow than I. But now I know my parents escaped a horrible death I am more quiet again and my hope is fixed upon you. Can be my parents write you something. You can tell us again. Might be that you will be so kind to write a letter to our parents and to tell them that we are well here.

The sugar campaign is here in full speed now. The manufact works day and night through and Aad has to work 8 hours and to sleep and eat his meals 8 hours. He has no time at all for other things. This work lasts 5 months, then we have the stop. The machines and the further manufact then has to be cleaned before the following campaign. The employers can have their month's vacances but there is only work at day and not at night. But these 5 months all is in a hurry. I hope you got the letter I sent you after receiving the telegram. There were a few fotos in it. How are you? Do we hear some anything about you. Many greetings from Aad and a big birthday kiss.

From your Hanna.

Do send something in your letter the costs you did have with the telegram. This Aad is asking. We do not will that you spend any money on this. We are so glad you sent the telegram.

Hanna

address parents: A. de Bruijn
Velseniusrshast 4 Rotterdam

+ + + + + + +

15 September, 1940 — Thinggiran

Dearest Ruth,

I received your birthday card. What a lovely thing. Thanks very much. And then half a week ago your letter came you wrote 24 July.

104

It was a letter that did us so very good you know. It was full of sympathy and now I know you are not only the pretty looking cheerful Ruth, a handsome teacher and a very good letter writer, a little brave person who stands her part in life, but though I knew it, now it is clear, you are so very kind hearted too. You have so many things to say to someone in trouble. We thank you for this letter. I did say it before, I am ashamed I wrote you such a letter full of sorrow some time ago, but I had to have someone to say my troubles to and I knew you would understand me.

And Thursday, 15 Sept. we got a new letter (air mailed from you) with the note of my mother in it and now we understand that you with your kind hearted nature went to wire us so that we sooner heard the good news. You did not mind the high prices of wire, you followed your heart, is it not, dear? We thank you and kiss you for this. Please write down the costs and we send you a cheque. We have done you so much troubles, we don't like you are spending your money on us the money you are earning by working hard. Besides, we are pretty well-off this time. Aad is earning now 1300 a month, he has a jolly good job here. On the post offices here you can get cards 17 1/2 cent. When I include such a card in a letter, you can change it in Amerika for a stamp for Holland. This is a way in which we in the Indies can correspond with relations in Holland with the help of relations in America, without the relations in America having to spend money with stamps. I am to buy such cards. But now I am asking you to mail this included letter to Holland without my sending you a stamp card, for I did not buy them yet and the airmail is to start tomorrow morning. Dear God bless you for your lovely character.

Many kisses, your Hanna

+ + + + + + +

19 Sept., 1940 — Rotterdam
Schieweg 251a
(Letter from James C. Muijser, Aad's father)

Dear Ruth,

Today we received your letter of August 11 for which we sincerely thank you. All the same time there arrived a post card of July 24, by Aad and Hanna, from which we saw that they were both doing well. We are very pleased by this good news from them.

Together with that letter we have posted another letter to Aad and Hanna.

It is all right with us in Holland.

Again we offer our hearty thanks for all the correspondence we are receiving from you and we hope that this letter may reach you in good health. Believe us.

Yours, Jam. C. Muijser

+ + + + + + +

September 20, 1940 — Rotterdam
(Letter from Aunt Clazien)

Dear Ruth:

We were very pleased to get Aad's and Hanna's telegram and thank you very much for it.

We were so glad to hear that they are both all right and that they received our message.

We here too are keeping well. My old aunt who has 90 years of age is staying with me in my own home and is pleased to do so.

If you are writing to Hanna, will you please give her our love? I would like to thank you again for your kindness and with kind regards I am Hanna's Aunt Clazien.

C. Rens.
Oudedijk 207c
Rotterdam, Holland

+ + + + + + +

October, 1940 — Thinggiran 12

Dearest Ruth,

This day we received your letter from 8 September in which you enclosed the letter our parents had written you. What a great day this is for us. We should put you in a golden frame when we could. Thanks much dearest, you know what a lovely thing you did when you made the communication between our parents and us. What a lovely letter you did write. We are always glad when the post brings us a letter from America. Last week we received the birthday card and the foto. We were so glad about it and we thank you much. We admire the foto and you are so pretty on it. All the years we are corresponding I did not know exactly your age, but I thought, in one of our first letters you wrote it I believe you are a few years older than I. I am 26 now. But on the foto you resemble more like a schoolgirl yourself than a lady who teaches the schoolgirls. You are so pretty small and thin and your face looks so young and fresh. I am not small, but large. That is the body of near all Dutch women. I do not like it myself but I have to do with it. We hope you will soon write about the money you were spending on the two telegrams. O, I can imagine how my parents were glad you wired them a cablegram that their message had reached us. Here a cablegram for America costs 10 words twenty guilders, so in our money we can see what the costs are but we do not send you the money before we know exactly how much it was for it can be that the Dutch money is very cheap now in America. Then we should have to pay more. Let us know soon, dear. It is better we send the money than that our parents should send for they can spend their money better for food and coals now.

You asked about the weather here. Very warm and very dry half the year and very warm and very rainy the other half year. We are near the evener here (the O line) and we are living in the low place. On the mountains it is rather cool. But for us the mountains are only our holiday places. Greet your mother from us. It is hard to live so lonely, is it not?

Many greetings and kisses for you, Hanna

+ + + + + + +

16 October, 1940 — Thinggiran

Dearest Ruth,

We received the fotos of our parents and you can imagine how glad we are were in getting them. We are at home again after Aad's military service month. It is so hot here. We are awaiting the first rains of the W. Monsoon. In a week the natives are to celebrate Lebaran. This is the day which the Catholic religion names Easter, the end of the Lent.

The days before a month in which the natives abstain from food at day is called Pocasa. They only take food at night one time a day. (This is the Muslim Ramadan.)

With "Lebaran" they all have new clothes, even shoes. And they are walking in the streets and calling on relatives. The factory can't work two days. All the natives have a holiday. The servants have holiday too. I am to cook and wash clothes myself for 2 days.

In a month all the sugar canes are used and the very busy time in the factory is done. It is 4 months now that Aad is working so hard and he is longing for the end of the campaign. I received the fotos of my mother in the swimming pool. I was so glad with it.

Ruth, I hope this letter will reach you, for I wish to ask you to send another wire to my father and mother at December 7 when my father is celebrating the day at which it is 40 years ago he took his job on the railways. You may write in Dutch: "GELUK WENSEN. DANKBARE KINDEREN" which means in English "Best wishes, grateful children".

Maybe you will write a letter to them too. I should like it when you should. Can you imagine what my parents' feelings and thoughts will be at this day? They will probably remember the day, 40 years ago, 1900 when my father as a young fellow took the job on the railway when our country was in peace and freedom and when he saw his life lying before him. And when he at Dec. 7 will have a look after him he will see happiness and sorrow had been in this life. He had to bear it with my mother and he had to enjoy it with my mother. But the last few years, there was much more sorrow than happiness. At first, when Aad and I went to the Indies we all know it was a terrible thing to them. And afterwards the invasion in our country. The war and its terrible accidents but I hope it will not last very long. There will be happier days for them. My father himself is always saying: "after the rain there is always coming sunshine again." I must close dearest Ruth. Aad is sending his heartily greetings and I myself am sending a big kiss.

Hanna

+ + + + + + +

26 Oct. 1940
(Letter from Aad)

Dear Ruth,

Just today we received your letter from 26 September with the enclosed letters of our relatives. How glad we were to get now a self written letter so that we knew they themselves wrote the letter. My mother-in-law wrote in Dutch and among other things she wrote "Ruth is a darling to telegraph us". I just want now to emphasize that whole-heartedly. For those last months have shown that you enjoy helping other people in distress. And how that not withstanding you never saw us, or heard us.

It gives us the right to say that mankind is not yet so rotten as we sometimes believe it to be. That there are still people which believe in good will among inhabitants of different nations, which believe in freedom of thoughts, in honesty, in friendship, in love. But I stop that subject. You, in America , are now in the midst of the elections, and when you receive this letter it has been long made out who will be president for the next four years.

We are very interested in it, for although both candidates do their utmost to help the Allies, the German Huns won't like Roosevelt to be the President and that makes us hope he will be it; that only because of his outstanding political behaviour. We here know nothing about the "Home Office" programs of the candidates.

Again we enclose some letters for our parents. We hope that you will send it to my parents:

>Fam: C. Muijser
>Schieweg 151A
>Rotterdam

I close this letter now. Hanna sends you many kisses over the ocean.

Aad

+ + + + + + +

Letters from the de Bruijn family acknowledged receipt of Ruth's letter and expressed the wish for Ruth to continue sending letters to Hanna and Aad in Java.

October 28, 1940 — Rotterdam

Dear Ruth,

This morning we received your letter of October 28. We are very glad to hear again that our Hanna and Aad are well. We ourselves are also well and healthy.

We have sent Hanna 1 packet and a chest by steamer and two postal parcels. Would you be kind enough to write us occasionally whether Hanna received them? In March we sent you

109

a bridal picture of Hanna and Aad. Have you received it? A picture of you did not reach us; so it has clearly been lost. Would you send this picture to Hanna?

We appreciate it so much that you write us regularly and are very glad to hear continually good news from you.

Hoping that it will soon be peace we end with our best wishes and heart greetings.

Your N de Bruijn

+ + + + + + +

19 November, 1940 — Dinsdag

Dear Ruth,

I don't know when this letter will reach you. I want to wish you already now a very happy new year. I hope that it will bring you much prosperity and a good health. May America be spared for a war, for I think and know by experience that there is no greater evil. We hope that you will be so kind as to help us in the coming year too and we thank you for it. We know that you are making many expensives and we should like to pay them back to you, but as yet it is not permitted to send money, although we think that your help can't be payed back. Will you give the other part of the letter to our children to let them read it? How we should like to go to them to see how they are living. But you never can tell what will happen still. We had had the plan to go to them in January, but in the first years that will not be possible. But when they are happy that is the principal thing. Ruth we send you our best wishes and much love.

Your affectionate
Mr. en Mrs. de Bruijn

+ + + + + + +

13 December, 1940 — Semarang
(Aad's location)

Dearest Ruth,

I did not hear much from you after your letter in the beginning of November which I answered. We wonder if you got the parcel with the weaving and if you get the money letter I send by air mail 7/2. Write soon please dearest Ruth.

Last week I got a letter from Aunt Clazien. Many thanks that you sent it through. We did not hope that she was alive and see a letter with pompous talking from her. Here in the Indies, many people have sad news about dead family, but I can't imagine hardly that our parents and my petty aunt are safe and well.

Aad is in military service now for a month and I went with him to Semarang, We are in a hotel. It is very dull. The whole day I must spend with reading, writing letters and knitting. I should like to be in my own house again. When the month is over, we have our holidays a month, too. Then we go in a little house high in the mountains. We are choosing a place of 3000 feet. There it is cold enough to recover from all the warmth here beneath.

Ruth, Januari 18 is my father's birthday. May I ask you to send him a wireless with "birthday greetings from Hanna and Aad"? After this I could as the last time, send you the money you spend about it. Will you do us this pleasure? Many greetings, a good New Year and, if I am not too late, a happy Christmas.

Write us usually to Minggiran. Letters will be sent to us.

Aad and Hanna

+ + + + + + +

20 December, 1940 — Rotterdam
(A postcard from Mr. and Mrs. de Bruijn)

Dear Ruth,

Many thanks for your kind letter in which you write that our children are doing well and that Hanna has gained so much in weight, as however she will not become too thick. How pretty that she needs (sews) her own clothes. Here she had not so much time for it. Kindly tell her that.

I am learning English and about some time I hope to write the letters myself. Could you teach me? I should be an old student. After all, learning is pleasant and one forgets all one's worries.

Send with heart greetings for our children and the best of luck to you. Also the compliments of Aad's parents.

Mr. and Mrs. de Bruijn.

111

+ + + + + + +

(no date) — Minggiran

Dearest Ruth,

As you know by Aad's writing you, we received your letter from 28 August and the letter with my mother's own handwriting paper. You can imagine how glad we were. So you have succeeded in making contact between us and our parents. In the last letter was also one from a mother of a girl friend of mine who came to the Indies two years ago. I sent at once the letter through and you can imagine how glad she was too. She wrote back to me "I opened your letter and how great was my amasement and gladness when I saw in it a paper with my mommy's own handwriting." She asked me if it was possible to write back. I answered that perhaps you should be so kind to send her letter through when she put in the envelope papers with a stamp.

I did not hear if these papers can be changed for stamps. I hope so. Will you let me know? It should be a very nice way to send letters to our parents. Without you have to pay the stamps. Stamps, especially for air mail are very precious now a day, is it not? Here in the fact(ory) is an employer who loves stamps and every time there is a letter from you he asks for the stamp and especially the transpacific stamps he does find very interesting. Now Ruth, when there are American stamps who are beautiful and for you not heavy to get, please send some of them to us. We can make this friend of us very happy with them.

With happiness we heard of your passing through this final examination. How proud we are of you. We can imagine that you know a pretty heap of English literature. It was a beautiful studying, was it not? And your papers with these red lines on the side. Was this prescribed or was it your own choice? Very neat it looks.

The news of the last two days that Greece is stopping the marching through of the Italians has filled us with new hope. This is the first country that with success is fighting against one of the totalitarian states. Roosevelt has been chosen again in America. Are you glad about it too? Did you choose Roosevelt too, or Wilkie, or did you not choose? When we lived in Holland everybody, man or woman when twenty five years had to choose. The difficulty was that also people who did not know anything about politics

112

had to go, too. But here in the Indies, there is not a reign chosen by the population but chose by the chief of the reign. The governor general who is chose on his turn by the queen. Yet there is a population council who has members of Dutch, Javanese, China members. They may have critic on the reign, etc.

It is a very beautiful country here. You asked . . . (the rest of the letter couldn't be read.)

Hanna

Chapter Nine

Others in Holland appealed to Ruth as a means of communicating with loved ones outside Holland.

Hanna spoke concerning America's aid to England and wondered if the U.S. would eventually become actively involved in the war in Europe. In May and June of 1941, Aad and Hanna's parents wrote from Holland that they had not received word from Hanna and Aad in several months. A reply from Ruth was anxiously awaited to determine if she had had news from them in Java.

Ruth received a response from Hanna regarding the concern of her parents. She sent letters to be forwarded to Holland and told of the possibility of war. She had received a degree as a nurse-helper of the Red Cross to prepare herself for duty in case of war.

No particular name was given for a serious illness that sent both Aad and Hanna to the hospital and later several weeks for recovery. It was probably a tropical disease like malaria or hepatitis.

Jan. 4, 1941 — Rotterdam Schieweg 251A

Dear Ruth,

A lady unknown to me sent me the enclosed letter destined for her husband:

Mr. Anton Podrimek

c/o Tratariasche Radio Fereeniging

Batavia C India

asking me whether I might see a way to dispatch it. I, therefore, appeal to you with the hope you will be so kind to pass the letter to the address for which I thank you very much.

With greeting, Gremain,
Yours, as usual
T. Muijser de Brockman

+ + + + + + +

4 Januari, 1941

Dearest Ruth,

Your letter of 29 October we got some days ago. We enjoyed your story about your birthday. What a pity that our birthday present was not in time. We hope you will get it soon. We are in our vacances now. With another family from Minggiran with which we are very good friends about some months, we hired a little bungalow, a little vacances house in the mountains. They have two little boys, of one and three years and we enjoy our time very much. Aad and I often make trips in the neighborhood. This day we took a horse each and we went away for a trip of four hours high up in the mountains. We had, once above, a fine view upon the little Javanese and the more great European towns beneath. It was very fine. It is also much more colder above than in the hot places beneath where we are the remainder of the year. Our house is on 3000 ft. high. And from the house we have a fine view on the mountains in the neighborhood. 28 Januari we leave this place to go to Minggiran again, to the work for Aad and the warmth of 30° C.

We have here in the tropic only two seasons, the dry time of 6 months without rains and the wet time of 6 months with every day very fast rains. Now the rain time begins and every afternoon the rain is coming. After half a year dry weather, everyone is greeting the rains with enthusiasm.

We hope our parents will send you once more a letter to send through to the Indies. We are also so very glad with a letter from them. This you can imagine.

The letter from Aunt Clazien we got. This I wrote you already some time ago, I believe.

Many greetings from Aad, a big kiss from me.

Your Hanna

+ + + + + + +

1 April, 1941 — Rotterdam
(Letter from Hanna's parents)

My dear Ruth,

Many thanks for your sending Hanna's letter. We just received it on the first Christmas day, so it was the most beautiful present we could wish. Aad's parents have also been reading it.

Our child was writing so cheerfully that it comforted us too, so that we are still hoping to see one another back again. We are very happy that she received the packets and the table cloth I made myself. You can tell her now that I have ready such lovely little things for tea trays and little tables. I have also made a large cloth of 150 cm diameter. If I just knew how to send them to her.

Will you ask her if she received the biscuits I put into the packet?

Our daughter is becoming a real gardener with her kitchen garden. We also have had such a garden only for pleasure and she must have learned a great deal by watching.

I am learning the English language of Hanna's friend, Jo Meskamp. She is always translating and writing the letters for us. Now, dear Ruth, send our greetings to Hanna and Aad, also of Jo and for you much love of

Mr. and Mrs. de Bruijn

+ + + + + + +

28 April, 1941

Dearest Ruth,

In my last letter I wrote you about our illness. We were after the high fevers very weak and now we are in a hotel in the mountains for a month to recover from our weakness. We don't do anything the whole day but eating, sleeping, lazing and reading. I don't tell anything about our illness to my parents but sincerely hope you will do your utmost to send this letter through soon. I am afraid my parents should be quiet when they hear about us again. We received your letters and read them in the hospital, but I could not read and only yesterday afternoon I read them all, also the letters your pupils sent me. I enjoyed it all very much. And the letters of our parents you sent through were cheerful enough to make us glad they all are healthy, have their common work and try to make the best of it.

You asked if we have papers and radios. Yes, we have and in the war time we always are listening to the news we can receive from the radio. We often are listening to the London radio. Yesterday we heard America will continue to increase the help to England. Lots of people in America think they will have war at the end, too, isn't it? What do you think about it?

Did you already receive the bracelet we did send to you? I have not sent a few photos I promised you, but as soon as we are at home again at the beginning of May, I will do this at first.

What a brave person your mother is! It will be difficult to her to conceal her sorrow about your daddy. She was glad to have you all at home at Christmas, was not she? I thank you so much, you sent the telegram to my father. I think it was the present he loved best. I am so glad with the photo of my best friend Jo. Did she write you? She has had a very difficult time, but she has her husband again. Do write her, if you should like to do this. Dear Ruth, do send a letter soon. We are so glad with your letters.

Much love from Aad, too.

Hanna

P. S. Will you send this enclosed letter to Aad's parents?

+ + + + + + +

May 13, 1941 — Schieweg 25la, Rotterdam
(Letter from James Muijser, Aad's father)

Dear Ruth,

Since months ago we did not receive news from America, why is this? We hope there is nothing serious? Are you doing well? With us, in Rotterdam, everything is going straight on. Will you please assist us and write whether the address of the family A. Muijser is still the same? Since the 20th January last we did not hear from them. That last letter was dated November 26, 1940, a long time ago as you will see. We do not understand why they are reporting so little about themselves. We are regretting it so much; we are so anxiously waiting for a letter from them and there arrives nothing. Perhaps you did hear from them in the meantime.

We wrote to them on various occasions during this year, but we hope those letters reached their destination.

Did you receive the letter with the photo for Hanna of Puss? It is a fine, pretty animal. We call him Hans.

We are sending this letter by airmail and enclose a few international exchange marks, in order that in replying you may likewise avail yourself of the air route. We hope you received the marks we sent you already before, and are waiting to hear from you at an early date.

With kindest greetings, I am, as ever.

Yours, Jam. C. Muijser

117

+ + + + + + +

June 1, 1941 — Rotterdam
(Letter from Hanna's parents)

Dear Ruth,

Many thanks for your letter which we received on May the 29th. Though we regret to have no news of Hanna, we are very grateful to you that you have written to us. How nice that you receive presents from time to time and that you liked the bracelet. We too should like it very much if we could send something to you for all that you do for us; not as a kind of recompense, but only for warm sympathy. Here too spring is very beautiful. In our garden the lilacs, snowballs, and hortensias are flowering. It gives joy in our life, in spite of all we have to live through. My English lessons are going on well. I can read and write already some little things, speaking only rather difficult, but in persevering we can reach much. I always send a coupon for answer in my letters to you. I hope it reaches you. In case of need you will do a great pleasure to us if you send a telegram. I can't telegraph you from here. I wish you very delightful holidays after your hard working.

Many hearty greetings of
Mr. and Mrs. de Bruijn

P.S. Also the compliments of Aad's parents.

+ + + + + + +

30 Juni, 1941 — Minggiran

Dearest Ruth, ·

I got your letter from May 14, the one you sent by sea mail, and in which you wrote about my parents. But now I hope they will have letters enough. I hope you will think about the telegram for my mother and my mother-in-law at their birthdays. I thank you by sending through their letters and that of my friend Jo V.

I am sending you two fotos and hope you will enjoy it. Will you please send the other four to my mother-in-law? They will be glad about it and no doubt give two of them to my own parents.

It is all quiet here in the country though we are preparing ourselves very much. I got a degree as nurse-help of the Red

118

Cross. In case of war, I will help with the nursery of wounded soldiers. It is the best thing a woman can do in times of war. Don't you think?

Had you your vacanses and did you enjoy the rides in your new car? A family here bought such a new Chevrolet too. The colour is red with grey. Beautiful too.

I bought a little dog, a white curled poodle. He is a pet 8 weeks old but so intelligent. He is walking the whole day near me and is sleeping under my bed. We are great friends and Aad says he comes in the second place in my heart now. I am glad you got the bracelet. It had been a pity if it had been lost.

Now I will ask you to send enclosed letter and photos to my mother-in-law this time and to date them. In a fortnight I am writing you again and my parents too, when you like to send all these letters through. When you do think it too much you will say, don't you? Heartily greetings from Aad but especially from me.

Your pal, Hanna

+ + + + + + +

The threat of Java being invaded by Japan seemed imminent. Hanna wrote that Japan had invaded IndoChina and was advancing toward Java. The Dutch felt confident they could resist this invasion because they were forewarned this time. Nothing is mentioned about trying to leave or return home, but the countdown for Java and the United States had started.

30 Juli, 1941 — Minggiran

Dearest Ruth,
   We are in the dry half of the year and it never rains. We are beginning the day at six o'clock with 82 Fahrenheit in the shadow. But our house is fortunately very cool, high ceiled rooms and floors of stone. We are so glad with a letter of you that it makes nowadays the most pleasant event in life, especially when there is included a letter from our parents. I send you a few photos last time and hope you got them. Did you enjoy your vacances? We did not yet hear about it.

I never heard anything from your friend on the Phillipines but it is not so near to us and I think he is not allowed to leave the islands. Aad is not allowed too to leave Java in these

119

dangerous times. Suppose we had to fight one day and the government had his soldiers and officers not at home!

August 17 we leave Minggiran for a month stay at Bandoing in the West of Java. Aad has to do there a month military service and I go with him. Fortunately he is allowed because he is an officer to live in a hotel during his stay and we will have a little time to go and see the beautiful surroundings I hope.

I sent a letter to my parents. Will you send it through? We will be very grateful. You asked about our having a radio and a paper. Of course we have them too. We always are regularly listening San Fransisco, Sydney, Singapore, London and our own broadcasting corporations. We catch the news of the world through the radio and the papers. Just now we heard that Japan is penetrating into Indo China. He is coming nearer and nearer to this country, on which he is casting desirable views too. But he may look as desirable as he can to our materials and our fertile grounds, we will not indulge this time. We learned a difficult lesson from our country men in Holland and this is: Don't be weak or indulgent or friendly to such neighbours as the Nazis and their friends, for you can't hold with them your freedom and prosperity. And, learning this lesson nearly every man and woman here is preparing himself to be strong and stubborn and memorable, if the day should come, this is war for now. I hope you will write soon and about the way you passed your vacances.

Many greetings from Aad and kisses from me.

Hanna

+ + + + + + +

Hanna described the Javanese people. She also expressed the hope that America would join the Allies to win the war in Europe and of the Roosevelt-Churchill meeting in the Atlantic Ocean.

Hanna and Aad were now in Solo, in the center of Java and one of the two capitals, where Aad was serving a month of military duty. She described the house of the reigning monarch and some of the culture in this city.

One of Hanna's friends from Holland sent Ruth a letter to forward to Hanna. Brief notes from C. Muyser and Hanna's parents indicate that Ruth continued to be the liaison for these families.

Dear Ruth,

   Yesterday I received your card with the cat. What a lovely card. Such ones you can't have here. It was just in time for tomorrow it is my birthday, the 27th. We received the letters from home with this one from my friend Jo. Thanks! I hope you will send my mother-in-law a wire too at September 14. She will be so glad about it. Let me please know in your next letter what were the prices of it?

   We have yet a very quiet life here. Aad is very busy with the fact. Now I will tell you something about the population here. In contrary with our native country, where we all were Dutchmen, and but a small part of strangers were living, we have here very much different people. The inhabitants, the Javanese, are the greater part. Most can't read nor write. They are very poor, living in little villages in very small houses. They are for the greater part agriculture men. These in the neighborhood you see are rice and sugarcanes. They are also used as mean labourers in factories and as servants in our houses. Nowadays the Dutch government has many schools in every place, how little it may be. But it is very difficult to send every one to school. The wife which has had an intellectual education can earn their money at offices and some of them whose parents had money to send them to Holland to go to an university especially the sons of the Javanese princes or noblemen, come back from Holland with a degree and are allowed to have a job as a doctor, lawyer, etc. The Chinese, very poor, very rich, and all midlings of this. They are earning their money with commerce and stores. The Europeans and Judo Europeans—the Judo Europeans have in their complexion something from their Javanese ancestors and something from their Dutch ancestors. They are considered by the government as equivalent to the Dutch. They all are born in the Indies, have had their school education, some higher school and some of them when their parents can afford were sent to Holland to learn at a high school or to have their degree at an university. They can have all sorts of jobs, as a doctor, lawyer, clerk, teachers. But though they are equivalent to the Dutchmen most concerns like better to have as their cheap labourers a Dutchman imported from Europe and with a European education. Therefore, most Dutchmen, living here and having children were sending always their children at the age of twelve to Holland to have their education in the native country. Besides, a degree as doctor or lawyer you could not get here.

But wartime stopped the importation of studied men. There is a deficit now. The government is busy now to have universities and all sorts of study establishments here too. But you can imagine what a giant work this is, to found all these schools and universities and what a lot of men are drawing from facts a.s.o. to become a teacher at high schools or a professor at an university. You can imagine how great a deficit of studied men is now. Besides there is the military service asking many men.

We heard through the radio and in the papers from the Roosevelt-Churchill meeting in the Atlantic Ocean. We hope America will help the Allies to win the war soon. Then there can be made an end to all the sorrows of millions of people. Do you hear about the bombers of the RAF? They also bomb our native country. Every time we hear about bombing Holland too I must think again about my parents. What a courage to be glad (and we know they are) when they see the airplanes of Brittan—although they don't know they will not be bombed themselves by a mistake of the crew of the plane. We also hear about suspensions in America in war industries. Is this too a sort of Nazi work behind the scenes or are the labourours only planning to increase their salary by this. And then the great fire in New York, where many ships were burnt!

I must finish this letter now and hope you will send enclosed letter to my parents-in-law.

Dearest Ruth, goodbye to you. Many thanks for the birthday card. It was the only one I got and you know, I was so glad with it. Aad is sending his greetings and I myself a kiss.

Hanna

+ + + + + + +

9 September, '41 — Solo

Dearest Ruth,

As you see, we are at Solo now. Aad has to do his military duty during a month here in the centre of Java and I went with him. I took my little white dog with me. He is such a lovely thing and very clever.

Yesterday I got your letter with the foto of my parents. We thank you most heartily for sending it. I was weeping a very long time when I got my parents foto. Can you understand this? What a lot of trouble my people went through and it is to see in their faces too, you know. I hope you will send through this included letter to them. It will give much joy to them.

We are here in the centre of Java now, in one of the two capitals, where native monarchs are reigning themselves. The other capital is Kjakyatarta. The house of this monarch, the Saisoetoeran is full of orient beautifullness. The house is surrounded by four walls. He has +40 wives, living together in a women part of the house. But he has one wife, the principal one, a high born princess, who goes with him to parties a.s.o. a lady educated in European schools. She wears the native clothes and she is very handsome to see. As she got her education in Europe, she objects against all these other wives. But this habit can't be throw away at once. Everywhere in the neighborhood you have the places of old ancient Javanese culture. It is all very interesting.

It is very hot here, but at 30 miles from here you can reach Taman Manjjar, a place high in the mountains at 4000 feet there is coolness enough. We will go there for a day when Aad has a vacation day.

I will end this letter by sending you our best wishes at your birthday October 14. Aad and I hope your next year will be so happy to you as possible.

We bought you a wooden statue of a native and hope it will reach you once.

A lot of love from us two
Aad and Hanna

+ + + + + + +

18 September, '41 — Solo

Dearest Ruth,

Yesterday we received your letter 15 Aug. with the letter from my parents. They wrote as you did that they did not receive a wire on my mother's birthday What a pity you did not get the letter in which I asked you to send. When this letter is in time, you could perhaps receive our best wishes for your birthday just in time.

You asked if I got the pillow cases. Yes my dear I did already a long time ago. They were beautiful. I never had pink ones on my bed, always white. But I use them and think them very pretty. Do you have too colours in your bed?

We are very happy in Solo where Aad, as I wrote you before, has to do his military service during a month. I went with him and we are living in a hotel now. I go swimming every morning and we often play tennis. The hotel is very comfortable. Very nice people living there, to which we can have a chat or a bridge in the evening. Do you play bridge? We like it very much. Aad is a very good player. Tomorrow is Aad's birthday. Very sad for him to have this day without his family. But we know they think about us on this day.

Last week we heard Roosevelt's talk through the radio. We were very glad about these strong words. A pity, he did not speak about the Pacific. Yes, I am sorry too for your friends in the camp, but it is better preparing yourself. I will have a list with the dates of the letters I got from you too. Then we can see what letters come through.

I am glad you got the money. I hope you will send the included letter to my parents-in-law.

I was so glad to have a word from you. It was a long time ago. Next time I will send you a letter to my own parents.

Bye, much love from us

Aad and Hanna

+ + + + + + +

4 November, '41 — Minggiran

Dearest Ruth,

You had your birthday Oct. 14 and I hope you got the letter and the present we sent to you. The present consists of a wooden figure, a Balinese native. I hope you will be glad with it, when you got it.

Did I tell you that I passed my nursery's examination of the Red Cross? It is using to be able to help a real nurse in time of war. The examination has 2 parts, a theoretical one and a practical one, a fortnight in a hospital to learn how to take care of men and women who are ill. The practical part was very difficult, but very interesting. I was so tired at night after working the whole day. But I passed. I am very glad for in time of war, when Aad has to go to fight, I can go away too to help where it must. I am also registered as I am a teacher for the women service. When war should come, I can be ordered to take the place of a teacher who must go to defend our country.

We got letters from home with a foto, the second one from Aad's parents. Thanks very much, dearest Ruth! I hope you will soon write to us. We are happy when a letter from our friend Ruth comes. Are you healthy and do you enjoy your job? These are principal things for happiness, is it not?

Many greetings from Aad and me. I sent a letter to my parents, please do send it through.

A big kiss from Hanna

+ + + + + + +

This was the last letter from Hanna until the war was over in 1945. It was written shortly before the Japanese bombed Pearl Harbor on December 7, 1941, the beginning of war in the Pacific.

Dec. 4, '41 — Minggiran

Dearest Ruth,

Once more I am sending you a letter which I am asking you to send through to my parents. How are you? It is a long time we heard something from you. Are you very busy? Here we are listening the whole day the radio, anxious to hear something about some agreement between the Japanese and Americans. We hope, they will come to an agreement, but we fear the worst.

When the factory here was ready with the busy time, and all the sugar canes had been changed in sugar, Aad got three days vacation which we passed with our friends here, a family with two little children of 3 and 5 years old, in a little mountain hotel, 3000 feet high, a home with a car from here. We had there a beautiful weekend. We made an excursion in a tropic wood and had a lot of orchids to take with us. Besides, there was a tennis court. We made a lot of fun. The nights were very cool. This did us a lot of good. We are now at home again. I am knitting a good deal of my time, stockings for the marine in Midain. All the women here have a war job, or are preparing theirselves for a war job. Are you in America doing the same or not yet? Do you know already something about nursery and first help to accidents?

We hope we will soon hear from you, your family, your friends, your job and your thoughts.

Do write what the costs of the cables were. Do you still enjoy your car?

Love from Hanna and Aad, too

+ + + + + + +

World War II had been raging in Europe for over two years when suddenly on December 7, 1941 the United States was plunged into the war with the attack on Pearl Harbor in Hawaii. All hopes of diplomatic negotiations being conducted in Washington D.C. ceased that Sunday morning when the radio announced the terrible devastation wrought on American ships and personnel. The deceit of the Japanese diplomats and military strategists caught America off guard. As President Roosevelt declared war on Japan, factories began converting to military causes, the draft was initiated, blackouts were required on the coasts, and security suspicions concerning Japanese-Americans pulled them away from their homes and jobs and interned them inland for the duration of the war.

England's Prime Minister Churchill informed Parliament that Britain was also at war with Japan. On December 11 Germany and Italy joined Japan in its declaration of war against the United States. Congress recognized the state of war with the three nations composing the Axis.

By December 22, 1941 the Japanese had landed in the Philippines. General MacArthur retreated and arrived in Australia on March 15th with his famous quote "I shall return!" From there the slow, tedious effort to drive the Japanese northward began.

The Japanese had swept through the Pacific like a typhoon, overrunning and conquering everything in their path. Java prepared the best it could for an invasion, but in March 2, 1942, the Japanese landed 85,000 troops on Java. It took a week for the Japanese to overrun Java, the jewel of the Dutch East Indies. Despite heroic defense by both the Dutch, Javanese, and weary Allies, on March 7, 1942, the radio in Bandung signed off with the words, "We are shutting down now. Good-by 'til better times. God save the Queen!" [1]

[1] Miller, Francis T. *History of World War II*, Iowa City, Iowa: Riverside Book and Bible House, 1945. p. 450.

126

This very densely populated island of Java contained rubber plantations, cinchona bark for the quinine drug, teak wood, oil and tin, plus fertile fields. Japan had destroyed as many airstrips as possible along its path to hamper air support.

Hanna and Aad had not escaped the devastation of war after all, and there would be a long silence before their families could learn whether or not they had survived. Americans no longer could send routine mail through the Pacific war zones, and Hanna and Aad, who had fled Europe to avoid a war, found themselves in the middle of the Japanese one. For three and a half long years there was no correspondence among any of them. They had no way of knowing what was occurring in each other's lives. It gave Ruth an empty feeling after receiving almost daily letters for so long. She knew she would hear from Aad and Hanna the minute the war was ended if they were still alive, but no one knew how long that would be.

Meanwhile, in the United States the war had become very personal. Rationing books were required to buy shoes, gasoline, and certain commodities. This insured fairness for limited items and allowed those working in essential industries such as mining and military supply factories to have sufficient tires and gasoline to get to their jobs. Pleasure trips for vacations and visits were abruptly limited as well as unpatriotic. Victory gardens provided provisions for the family which had to make its money stretch farther. The breadwinner might have been drafted, and everyone was encouraged to buy government bonds to finance the war. School children accumulated the required $18.75 for a $25.00 bond by purchasing 10 cents or 25 cents stamps weekly at school

The difficult-to-import rubber was needed for military purposes so civilian uses such as elastic for underwear, rubber bands and balls, heels on shoes, and tires were made of poorer quality synthetics or discontinued completely. Vulcanizing tires used an outer strip to patch an old "slick." Due to German U-boats roaming our coasts, tropical imports such as chocolate disappeared and sugar and coffee were in short supply.

Saccharin made from coal was a poor substitute. Nylon was a recent invention, and women had quickly learned to appreciate nylon hose. But with the need for nylon parachutes, women had to revert to the sagging rayon and cotton blends. Nylons were so revered that they became a form of exchange for other products if one were lucky enough to secure a pair and were willing to part with it. Butter was substituted with a white oil-based "oleo-margarine" which had to be mixed with yellow coloring to avoid its looking like lard. It was illegal to sell it already colored because the dairy industry protected its butter.

Blue stars on white banners began appearing in windows of homes from which a son or daughter had been sent to the service. Later a gold star in the window meant that the loved one would not be returning home. Too often more than one gold star at a home told of their supreme sacrifice and heartache.

Weekly newscasts could be seen at the local movie theater since there was no TV. Desperate parents, wives, and girl friends searched the scenes in hopes of seeing someone they knew. People listened daily to their radios and read the newspapers for updates on the campaigns, battle sites, and casualties. Letters from overseas were censored, but by pre-arrangement, coded messages were sent back to families alerting them in what location and state of health the loved one was. (Mentioning fictional names such as asking about the Rabbi Oliver and Mortimer Eller told them Rome was the site.)

This became the time of Rosie, the Riveter, made famous by a song. Housewives and mothers filled all sorts of positions from taxi, bus and truck drivers to factory workers to replace the men recruited for combat. Hospitals found themselves poorly staffed with fewer, older physicians. Schools sought substitutes from all walks of life and lowered their requirements for certification by necessity to cover their classes.

Gratefully, the United States proper was never damaged by bombs or actual combat as were the United Kingdom, European countries, USSR, Northern Africa and Pacific war zones. Alaska and the coasts were always on alert for sudden attacks especially from submarines. Hawaii, of course, had been the most vulnerable and suffered tremendous losses and damage.

Later reports from the Netherlands indicated that while they had been captured and had surrendered, they were still "at war." Part of the Dutch navy had escaped to defend its country's colonies throughout the war in both hemispheres. The government was based in London where eleven Dutch cabinet members and the monarchy had been welcomed by King George VI. In May, 1940 when the Germans were within 15 miles of Rotterdam and 30 miles from The Hague, Queen Wilhelmina and her daughter, Princess Juliana with her consort, Prince Bernhard and their two daughters Beatrix and Irene fled to London on a British warship. Prince Bernhard returned to the battlefield narrowly escaping German mine layers. Princess Juliana later moved to Ottawa, Canada where her third daughter was born.

Next, the Germans began looting Holland of its bullion, oil, tin, copper wire used for communication and transportation, railway cars, precious gems, and art work. The Dutch people were deprived of most of their natural resources and manufactured products such as clothing, textiles, and leather goods which were shipped to Germany for their personal use. Thousands of cattle had been lost when damaged dikes caused flooding, and tons of oil had been destroyed probably accidentally by the bombing. The Germans could have benefitted by that. Fortunately, someone had had the foresight to ship 117,000,000 pounds of bullion and millions of pounds of diamonds abroad, mostly to the United States for safekeeping until the end of the war.

Resistance continued on the homefront in any way possible to frustrate the conquerors. Underground newspapers tried to keep the people informed since Nazi newscasts were often misleading and erroneous. Germans administered the government by using Dutch quislings, Nazi sympathizers, and tried to infiltrate groups to learn of Dutch activists. Doubts about whom one could trust must have been very troublesome because a neighbor might have been intimidated or bribed in a promise of help for his family. Nevertheless, the Dutch rescued Allied fliers, blew up oil depots, and systematically sabotaged anything they could to handicap the enemy. They hid Jews who had realized too late their need to escape. Hitler's troops were rounding them up for concentration camps (and annihilism). With the harbors destroyed and factories converted to German war suppliers, life became a struggle just to survive. Many died of hunger or illness due to poor diet and conditions. The happy prosperous country Hanna and Aad had known was practically nonexistant.

During the long silence when they could not correspond, Ruth knew her life, as a whole, was much calmer and more peaceful when compared to those living in Europe and the Pacific. Ruth had no immediate family members in service as many did.

In the early 1940's all teachers were called to register every man between the ages of 18-45. School was dismissed one day all across the United States, and all men between those ages were registered in that one day.

129

During those years Ruth taught her classes at Herrin High School from September to May and worked in Chicago at Encyclopedia Britannica during the summer months. There was a shortage of manpower and nearly everybody worked. There was a united effort, and everyone did his part. Approximately one-third of the teachers in Ruth's school were young men who were called into service. Temporary teachers were hired, as each service man was guaranteed his job at his return. All teachers did whatever job was needed to keep the school running normally. Ruth reported that she even kept score at big track meets and also helped transport basketball and football teams to out-of-town games.

Students were organized into teams to sell war bonds. There was a great competition among students to rise from sergeant to lieutenant to general, etc. by selling more bonds. Pictures of each of these groups were in the yearbook at the end of the year.

The Herrin Woman's Club to which Ruth belonged designated every other meeting to make dressings to be sent to the front for wounded soldiers. Also, the club divided the town into sections, and each member was assigned one part to canvas to sell war bonds. Practically everyone in town was solicited, and people were generous in buying as many as they could afford.

Ruth always was more interested in the progress of the war than she might have been had it not been for her anxiety concerning the fate of Hanna and Aad in Java and of their families in Holland. She was also well aware of the persecution of the Jews in Germany, as Jewish families in Herrin sponsored a Jewish family from Germany. The family lived in the rooming house where Ruth resided until they could get settled in a regular home. Ruth became rather well acquainted with them and some of their experiences in Germany.

The United States was not prepared for war, but munition plants sprang up almost overnight including the Ordill area south of Herrin. There was a great influx of workers. The government built a housing project called Egyptian Heights in Herrin for these workers. After the war, these houses were sold to individuals and are still used for private residences.

Prices were frozen on all rental properties to prevent owners from taking advantage of the housing shortage. Each landlord had to post the rental fee on the walls of apartments, rooms, and rental houses, and those prices couldn't be raised until controls were lifted following the war.

But the biggest inconvenience was the shortages and rationing of supplies—meat, sugar, gasoline, nylon, shoes, and many other items. Food stamps were issued in booklets to each person, and one had to present stamps before buying these items, and then only a very small quantity. Before Ruth could take her mother to St. Louis to the doctor, she had to go to the OPA (Office of Price Administration) in her town and plead her case to buy a few extra gallons of gasoline. New nylon hose were unavailable. If a pair of hose had a run, Ruth took them to a lady in town who could mend them (using a special needle to catch each stitch.) After the war when she heard that nylon hose could be purchased, one pair per person, she stood in line to buy them. It was impossible to buy a new car until the war was over and a few new cars became available.

People carried on at the home front. They often griped and complained about shortages and many inconveniences. But when Ruth finally got the news of the suffering endured by her friends in Java and Holland, everything seemed to fall into perspective, and Ruth realized how fortunate she and the United States had been after all.

Chapter Ten

VE Day (Victory in Europe) was May 7, 1945, and VJ Day (Victory in Japan) was August 14, 1945. The Allies had won the war, and Germany and the Axis had been defeated. This resulted in Germany's territory being quartered and governed by four nations: Great Britain, USSR, France, and the United States. The American President Franklin D. Roosevelt, who died in April of that year, had not lived long enough to see the complete end of the war, but there was no doubt he knew it was imminent. Hitler also was dead having allegedly committed suicide just before the capitulation of his Third Reich.

The surrender of Japan on the battleship Missouri in the Pacific was witnessed and signed by a Dutch diplomat among the others from China, UK, USSR, Australia, Canada, France, New Zealand, and the US on September 2, 1945. Those in Holland had been living in devastating conditions and Mrs. de Bruijn spoke about a great number of the population who had starved for a lack of food.

There had been no news from Hanna and Aad from Java since December, 1941.

May 28, 1945 — Rotterdam
(Letter from Hanna's Mother)

My dear Ruth,

How do you do? Now there is an occasion to write to America. I want to send a little letter to you. I am still in a good health, notwithstanding all that has happened here. My dear husband has died after a short illness on the 15th of May, 1943. I am very, very sad of it. I could not yet send a message to Hanna. Please, can you write me when there is any communication with the Dutch East Indies?

How glorious that America has won the war and that Germany has been destroyed! We also are so grateful for all the food we are receiving for the greatest part of the population was starving. We know now what it is to be hungry.

I send you my best greetings and much love

Mrs. N. de Bruijn-Rens.

+ + + + + + +

The following letter from Hanna's Uncle John Broekman detailed what life in Holland was like during the war years with Germany. Japan's surrender in the Pacific had just been announced.

August 15, 1945
Hogerbeets-straat 14c.

Dear Miss Sullivan,

Mrs. de Bruijn told me that you had written her, and in addition to what she reported about the situation in Holland, I am glad to say that the Broekman family, too, is doing well again. We suffered much, but everybody finally pulled through, and apart from a radio and a bicycle stolen by the Huns, no material losses were suffered. Brassware, tinware, and so on, hidden at the time, have now taken their old place in the home.

The two sons, Aard and John (Jan), managed to keep out of Germany. They had an anxious time, and in December last they lived in a boiler room of a factory behind a wooden bulk-head for nearly three weeks. We had to go out in the dark to bring them food, with the risk of being discovered and arrested, but we escaped the spying eyes of the enemy. Also on other occasions they were obliged to "dive" for some time, until the danger had passed.

When the liberation came, the boys at once took an active part in the Netherlands Home forces, mopping up Dutch Quislings and other Nazi satellites. Now they are in the Canadian Army, entertaining the soldiers with their dance band. Probably John, the younger one, will return to Rotterdam by the end of this month to resume his studies. He is to become an architect. Aard, the elder one, has no definite plans; he studied Spanish, but now intends to cross to Canada or the States for business. He made friends with various Canadians.

My wife (Aunt Minnie) has fully recovered. In May last she weighed 88 lbs, being a living skeleton, but now it is 118 lbs, and her health is perfect. She has always been rather small and slim, so there is no need for a further increase.

As for myself, I collapsed in December last, and had to remain in my bed for about a month. It was a narrow escape from death—an exhausted body and a blood temperature of 35.2 C I weighed 112 lbs (now it is 158 lbs). In February I decided to leave Rotterdam for the Northern provinces where living conditions were still reasonable. Being over 50 years, I was not to be sent to

Germany, so I could take the risk of travelling. After a few adventures and wanderings, I found a home in a Friesian farm where I remained until the Canadians drove the Germans out. This happened on April 15. Then I acted as an interpreter with the Canadian Army, but when Western Holland was declared open to travellers again, the desire to see my family again became too much. On foot, by "lifting" on trucks and cars (hitch-hiking), I at last reached Rotterdam, where fortunately everyone was found safe. I must add that we had not been able to exchange letters for over three months.

Aad Muijser's grandmother and grandfather (my parents) have been on the verge of starving, and even now they have not yet fully recovered. Probably they will never do. Anyhow, we may thank Heaven that on this side things have turned out well after all. At the same time, however, we must remember the many thousands which have been murdered here, or who died far away from their homes, doing slave work for our oppressors. We shall never forget how the Nazis treated us, and are of the opinion that nothing can make good our sufferings and losses. We are grateful to the United States—the death of President Roosevelt caused general regret all over the country—and the other Allies for their help. Now that the end of the Pacific is in near sight, we hope also that the "stop firing" signal may soon be given, and no further loss of American and European lives caused. I do not speak of the Japs; they should be wiped out altogether and the news of the first atom bomb falling on Hiroshima was welcomed here with as much enthusiasm as the final capitulation of Germany at the time.

Dear Miss Sullivan, although the details of this letter may not so much interest you, I am giving them in order that you may have some information to pass to the Indies should occasion offer. Indeed, my wife and myself doubt whether Hanna and Aad Muijser will have succeeded in passing through that hell, for we know the Japs are even more cruel than the Germans, but we may not lose courage, and as long as there is no news, we may still hope for favourable information to come. So it is with all of us.

I hope that when this letter will reach you, you will be in good health, and thanking you for your kindness in former times, and maybe also in the future, I am

Yours sincerely,
J. Broekman (Uncle John)

Please excuse the quality and form of the paper sheets; we have really no better at present, and are glad if we can obtain a sheet here and there.

ADDED NOTE: Just now the news of Japan's definite capitulation came in. The radios, many have reappeared after having been hidden for years at the risk of their owners being shot for "black listening", play the National Anthem of our allies. U.S. flags are flown in abundance.

+ + + + + +

Hanna's mother wrote of her concern for her daughter and son-in-law. She also reported on the suffering in Holland as a result of the German invasion.
Ruth had kept some letters from Hanna throughout the war which she could not forward due to certain restrictions. Air mail was becoming common place now that the war was over, and this thankfully, speeded up communication.

30 Augustus, 1945 — Rotterdam
(Letter from Hanna's Mother)

My dear Ruth,
I received Hanna's letters which you have sent to me and also the first letter which you had not sent by air mail. The airmail letter was here within 10 days and the other ones took 30 days. I am very happy with Hanna's letters and the photos. I am very grateful to you because you kept them so long. I should like so very much to do a favour to you, if I just knew how. Can't you give me a tip? Now that Japan has been defeated, I soon hope to hear something out of the Dutch East Indies. How my husband would have been happy if he could have lived to see all this. I have enclosed a letter for Hanna in which I have told her about the death of her father. As I think that the communication with the Indies will soon be restablished with America, then with Holland, you will perhaps be so kind as to send it to Hanna as soon as it will be possible. I am happy to know that your mother and sisters are all right and that your brother has not fallen a victim to war either. Kindly remember me to them please. I am

135

very lonely and I am still very sad often. I hope that Hanna and Aad are still alive, but I can do nothing but wait.

Many thanks for your picture postcard. What a high building! In Holland we can't imagine how such houses must be. I should like to see once something of America. In the newspapers we have read about the crushed aeroplane. Now I can understand the whole thing much better. The fotos I have enclosed show how the Germans have made havoc here in 1940. Aad's parents and his whole family are all right excepted the father of Mr. Muijser, Aad's grandfather who died. Hanna's Aunt Clazien is still well too. Just like we all she was extremely lean during the last months, but now we all have fattened again. We have finally now plenty of food. Wheat only is very scarceful. How we lived through the German occupation time is impossible to tell to you in a short letter. I can fill Romans (volumes or novels). Already books and tragedies have been written. Terrible things have happened to innocent people, they have been shot, old and young men were starving with hunger. We have suffered a terrible cold during the winter. Women and children have made large expeditions even to the eastern parts of the country, walking on bad shoes or cycling on cycles without tires, to fetch food. But always there was the strong knowing of the unbroken will to resist to all Germans tricks and lies. The beautiful "going slow" campaign, the care for the young men who had escaped the Germans chains, and then the secret pleasure when we had again been a little bit more clever than those German supermen and much, much more. My dear Ruth, I can't tell you how I am always enjoying your letters. I am very grateful to you, you really do as if you were my second daughter. Let us hope that all things in Indies will come to a good end. I send many greetings to you and much love.

Mrs. N. de Bruijn (Hanna's mother)

+ + + + + + +

A letter from J. Broekman told about conditions in Holland shortly after the end of the war. News that Adrian (Aad) Muijser had been liberated from prison camp in Singapore was thrilling and encouraging, but still no news of Hanna. However, a letter written by Jam. Muijser to Ruth on the same day (October 2, 1945) told about receiving the long awaited word from Aad who had previous news that Hanna was in a prison camp somewhere in

136

Middle Java. This was also very exciting and offered guarded relief.

October 2, 1945 — Rotterdam
(Letter from Uncle John Broekman)

Dear Miss Sullivan,

I am in my office, and just a quarter ago my son Adrian rang me up, telling that Adrian (Aad) Muijser has been liberated in a prisoners' camp in Singapore, and that about Hanna there is no definite news, but that in March, 1945 she was still in Java, and in rather satisfactory health. So we may hope for further good reports to come within short.

You cannot imagine what this means to my parents, hearing that their grandson has survived. My mother, now 75 years old, has suffered much under the uncertainty, and I believe that the news will bring her back to health, both mentally and physically. Also to my father (Adrian was named after him) it will be a relief; his grandson was his pride, having studied under difficult circumstances, and passed his final examination not only cum laude, but also four and a half years after entering the University. As a rule, it takes some six years to become a chemical engineer.

Adrian's parents, too, may be congratulated. His father, although externally he remained the gay man he ever before was, had his sad days now and then, and his mother, who during the hunger period in Holland suffered much, up to now had not fully recovered. She remained nervous and—as we Dutch call it—she was "skin over bones".

Now there is hope again, and if Hanna likewise proves to be safe, the family ring will be closed again. If only all families, in your country as well as in Europe, might be so fortunate! ! !

I received your letter of the 17th September, and I must say you are asking me a big quantity of work to do telling about conditions here. I understand your fellow teachers and students are anxious to receive what newspaper men call "good stuff" about Holland, and they will not be dissatisfied. I am preparing a long letter, not about a small, low land with wind mills and inhabited by men and women walking on wooden shoes, but one of the industry, farming, shipping and aviation, worth of maintaining its old place among the other nations of the old and the new world.

So long! I hope to write you again, and meantime I remain,
Yours sincerely
J. Broekman

+ + + + + + +

October 2 , 1945 — Rotterdam
(Letter from Aad's father)

Dear Ruth,
This morning we received a letter from Singapore written by Aad himself. He has been interned in a camp there since January 1943 as a prisoner of war.
From Hanna he had news dated March 8, 1945. She is in a camp in Middle Java; this information we think rather encouraging. You will understand what a relief it is to us after all those months of fear, hope, and uncertainty. We feel of course quite happy. We have experienced terrible years, and winter 1944-45 we shall never forget, but thanks to God all this has passed and we are living in peace again. We feel quite indebted to the United States, Canada, and England for the help they brought us.
How are yourself and your family doing, all well? I hope you did not suffer much from the war.
I stop and we wish you all you may desire, and expect soon to hear something from you, too.
Yours with heartiest greetings
Jam. Muijser

+ + + + + + +

Oct. 4, 1945 — Rotterdam-C (Blijorp)
Hogerseetsstraat 14c.
(Letter from John Broekman about the war)

Dear Miss Sullivan,
Your letter of the 17th September reached us within ten days, and we are very pleased to learn that you are doing well.
I feel you are very interested to receive some more information about Holland, and I may say, that generally speaking matters are going well here. Certainly, there is still much to be

138

desired, but if one compares the situation of three months ago with the present, there is every reason to feel satisfied. Railway traffic has gradually been resumed—as far as circumstances permit. Between Rotterdam and Amsterdam there are now 12 trains a day in either direction. Before the war they numbered about 60 a day in either direction. So it is with the other railway communications. Fortunately, we have an extensive river and canal system, and although it is slow travelling by boat, it materially helps to relieve the situation. It should not be forgotten that the Germans carried away 80% of our locomotives, and 85% of our electric and diesel trains, which formed the backbone of our passenger traffic, as all main lines—double track—had been electrified during the last couple of years. Besides these, 85% of the box and flat cars, coal cars, and what further is necessary for handling merchandise. Add to this the blowing up of practically all bridges across the rivers and the complete destruction of the electric overhead material—wires, poles, transformer stations, and so on—and one will get an idea of the difficulties we have to cope with. There are, likewise, no motor buses worth speaking of.

In Rotterdam 30% of the streetcars were stolen, and another 30% badly damaged, so only seven lines are now running out of 27 in 1940. We had four buses left, and instead of 16 lines mainly running to the outskirts and surrounding places, only one has been restored as yet. But never mind; we have learned to walk, in spite of lack of shoes. Bicycles, too, are an exception. In 1939, there were about 230,000 bicycles in Rotterdam for a population of 640,000. Automobiles and motor trucks have gone the same way, but thanks to what our Allies turned over to us from their army car park, there is already a considerable improvement in this respect.

Clothing and shoes are scarce, practically not obtainable. We need special permits to obtain them, and it costs hours of waiting in the distribution offices. It is expected that within a year everybody in Holland will be enabled to buy a pair of shoes again. Underwear is all worn out, and this is indeed the great winter problem. My wife had a well filled linen cupboard, so we have still something left, and now we hope we may gradually succeed in filling up the gaps—and there are many. So it is with suits; each of the family has one or two that can still be worn, and because my sons and myself are of about the same size, we can make interchanges if necessary. It is said clothing will, likewise, be distributed on a larger scale during the next half year (perhaps a suit or a coat a head.) Generally speaking, our family is still much better off than the majority of the Dutch people, not to speak of those who lost everything by fire or bombing or German robbing. It is doubtful whether they will ever again reach their former standard of living. I have a friend, sub-manager of a bank in Arnhem; during 1944, his house with everything in it was burnt down, and after that the safe of the bank where his money and other valuable possessions had been deposited, was dynamited by the Germans and contents stolen.

During the next months many people whose homes even escaped destruction and for the rest may still be called well-to-do, will be compelled to go outdoors without suitable underwear, in worn out or too thin overcoats, to women often without stockings, and all with shoes—if they have—cracked and open in the sides, so that the water and melted snow will easily penetrate and cause wet and cold feet.

You will perhaps feel somewhat annoyed because I am talking so much about such subjects. However, I continue, not because I wish to complain or tell you interesting things, but simply in order to give you Americans a good idea of what life here really is. Can you fancy that, for instance, if a housewife loses or breaks a sewing needle, she cannot anywhere buy another, and must ask a friend or relative to lend her one? And that there is no sewing yarn or mending cotton or wool to be had? And that a man cannot drive a nail into a wall or into a shoe, simply because nails are unobtainable to everybody, but distributed in very limited quantities among carpenters, shoe makers, and those who want them for their respective jobs. Things of first necessity in modern life, such as brushes, combs—take what you wish—are not obtainable, and we must wait until they come again.

We use wooden tooth brushes, with fibre substitute; just think what a horrid thing from a hygienic point of view. Cannot United States factories provide us with a few millions of tooth brushes on short notice in order to avoid that within a few years there will be no Dutchman with sound teeth? What a good job will dentists then have!

Now as to rationing: At present each adult in Holland is receiving about every fortnight (metric weights converted in U.S. weight system, for easy comparison):

7 oz. flour

8 oz. groats

4 oz. jam or marmalade

7 oz. cheese (half American, which is excellent; the balance
        Dutch, with a much lower percentage of fat.)

4 oz. salt

12 lbs. bread

1 lb. sugar

4 oz. margarine

1 box matches, being about 60 sticks

1 gal. milk (we had, in pre-war years 3/4 gallons a day)

8 oz. meat (there has been no fresh or frozen meat since
        several months, and to substitute it, we receive
        the same weight in the shape of canned fish,
        canned meat hash or stew, canned meat and
        vegetables, or something of that kind, out of
        American and British army supplies.)

18 lbs. potatoes

4 oz. soap for washing (no toilet soap)

1 lb. pulses (peas, beans, for instance)

4 oz. butter

4 oz. vegetable fat

The Minister of Agriculture announced an increase in the meal ration next month. Refrigerator vessels are to bring large quantities of frozen meat from Argentina.

Men of 18 years and over receive during that period:

40 cigarettes, or alternately 10 cigars or

3 oz. of tobacco.

For children there is an extra allotment in the shape of 8 oz. rice or baby food, plus 1/2 lb. of sugar.

Tea, coffee, cocoa and chocolate are not available, but will probably follow in the second half of this month, and in limited quantities. Oil for baking purposes will also be put at our disposal in the near future. Eggs—the few that are produced go straight to hospitals. Fish: 1/2 to 1 lb. per head about every three weeks.

You see there is enough food already, but a little variation would be welcome.

Fuel: Gasoline: 3/4 gal. per head about every month

Gas: 800 cubic feet per month for a family of four. If
        that quantity is exceeded, the pipe line is cut off.

Electricity: 17 K.W of electricity for a family of four as a
maximum per month.
Coal is rationed at about 800 lbs (!) for a family of four
for the whole winter. In normal times we used
about two long tons during that period, and it was
first quality of anthracite. We have base burning
hearth stoves, no central heating.

At present fruit—apples, pears and grapes—are rather
abundant, and so are vegetables. In winter, until April next, there
will certainly not be sufficient for reasonable needs. Oranges and all
other Southern fruits are absolutely lacking. In pre-war times
Holland was an excellent market for imported fruits, and California,
Oregon, and Ontario apples, Californian pears, oranges and lemons,
Texas and Florida grapefruits, Central American and Mexican bana-
nas were not an uncommon sight in our grocers' shops.

Taking everything together, we may look into the future
with confidence. Rotterdam, despite its blown up docks, sheds, dry
docks, shipyards and cranes, can nevertheless handle what
merchandise is entering, at a rate of 800,000 tons per month, and
the capacity is rapidly increasing. There is an exportation of
flower bulbs—the only thing we have available now—to the
United States and Great Britain. The Holland-American Line,
where I am now again working as an assistant freight traffic
manager, handled already some 30,000 cases; other vessels have
accounted for a large number, too, both to your country and to
Canada. Apart from this, few articles are exported, but in Spring,
1946 a variety of commodities will find their way to overseas
markets again. Of course, it will last some years until the former
extensive export figures will be reached.

Inward there is a heavy movement, and it is astonishing to see
the huge quantities of food stuffs, machinery, hardware, agricultural
implements, coal, gasoline, petrol, etc. that are discharged, quickly
finding their way to the interior. Do Americans know that there are
Dutch Rhine vessels capable of carrying 3000 tons of iron ore, coal, or
grain, and that in 1939 the inward and outward traffic handled via
our port amounted to over 40 million tons?

Here and there in the center of the city, where during the
war over 40,000 houses, besides a number of railway stations,
schools, churches (including the well-known St. Lawrence, with a
square tower forming a landmark visible at a long distance)
banks, hospitals and musea were destroyed, the hammering noise

142

of pile drivers is again heard, concrete mixers are turning, bridges newly built or repaired, and the pavement restored. We have now the opportunity to build up a new Rotterdam, and we shall do it. avenues will cross what in former times was the old center. Of the large buildings plans have been worked out for a large maritime center, a new opera house, several theatres, cinemas, hotels, and department stores. Broad, the Town Hall, Post Office, and the Exchange Building escaped destruction. They all were partly damaged by air droppings, but the fires could be stopped, and now the traces of what happened have been practically removed.

Small neighbouring communities have been annexed, so that there is again ample space for house construction, and it is hoped now gradually an end can be made to the forced dwelling of two or more families under one roof, frequently leading to less desirable or less hygienic situations. The intention is to cover the suburbs with garden villages, connecting them with the City center by a net of street cars and motor buses via roads enabling a regular and swift movement even in rush hours.

The Dutch mercantile fleet suffered enormously. The Holland America Liner, including the Red Star Line, came out of the war with nine vessels out of 31. It may still pay to have five vessels repaired, so that next spring we may count with a total of perhaps 14 vessels, including the well known New Amsterdam, 36,000 tons gross register, and 52,000 tons displacement. This steamer has just been requisitioned by the Dutch Government to carry troops to India. Among the vessels we lost were four passenger steamers of between 16,000 and 30,500 tons gross register each. In May, 1940 I saw two of them catch fire and disappear in a hell of flames and clouds of smoke until, after a few days, only the burnt out hulls were left. I shall not repeat what I then said; God may forgive me, but I could not help.

The shipyards in Holland, which strange to observe, have rather been spared by the Germans, will get a busy time for a number of years, and be able to turn out many new vessels of all types if they have the material. Now they are doing repair work, as far as the position permits, for the larger part of them have no machinery or tools. We have been building every kind of craft, from a coastal or a tramp steamer to a large tanker, and from a submarine or torpedo boat to an ocean vesel of 40,000 or 50,000 tons. The New Amsterdam is of practically 100% Dutch make, and so is the Oranje of the Nederland Company of Amsterdam, the pride of the Dutch East Indies services, displacing 36,000 tons, and with a speed of 25 1/2 knots the fastest large motor vessel in the world. She is now a hospital ship.

As to aviation, the Royal Dutch Airmail Lines have resumed various services, and as soon as there are again somewhat normal conditions in the Indies, they will start again their Amsterdam-Batavia line, which in 1939 was the longest route flown on this side of the globe. There were three planes a week in either direction, with a duration of six days for the trip. Thanks to more modern craft, it will be reduced to four or even three days if circumstances permit. It is just announced it will be a daily service. By the way, the Holland America Line, besides building new ships, has scheduled a regular Airline between Holland and the States.

Perhaps you will be thinking, "That Dutchman in Rotterdam is exaggerating." No, on the contrary, I am quite in earnest, but it has often struck me how many Americans are ignorant of what Holland really is. I have for many years been in shipping between Rotterdam, Mexico, Cuba, and Gulf ports, such as Galveston, Houston, New Orleans, Tampa, Penscola, etc. There is one thing which many Dutchmen like myself are expecting from you Americans, and that is: Please do not continue looking upon Holland as a low-lying country covered with wind mills, and inhabited by women and men in wide petticoats and trousers, walking on wooden shoes. I never wore wooden shoes in my life, and even farmers rather seldom use them. Only in dirty work wooden shoes are worn, if not rubber boots are available. Now a rubber boot is hardly to be had here.

We are an industrious and industrial people, whose factories may stand a comparison with those of any other country, supplying products of high standard for both home consumption and export. Only the factories have for the larger part been ruined, needing rebuilding and refitting, and for that we have to rely upon the goodwill of our Allies. That they give us credits, and the opportunity to obtain machinery, cement, structural material, and tools, and we will then show the world that in a few years most of our former prosperity will have returned. Please do not go to Holland for Volendam and Marken only, which are mere shows with a people making it their profession to pose for photographs and selling curiosities which before the war they imported wholesale from Germany, Czechoslovakia, and even Japan. I make an excep-

144

tion to a small number of artisans, pottery makers, producing an article of a special style and fashion, much in vogue here.

Instead you should enter Holland right from the sea by the New Waterway. That waterway looks like a natural river, but, in fact, it is an artificial Rhine mouth, excavated some 75 years ago with enormous difficulties and at an enormous expenditure. You may then pass the many oil tankers of the Shell, Standard Oil, and Texas Companies (now for the larger part seriously damaged and in course of repair), the docks and shipyards, and see many other things connected with shipping. In Rotterdam there is a grain elevator with a capacity of 120,000 tons. After visiting Rotterdam, one may go to The Hague, in 1939 taking 15 minutes by electric train, running every quarter of an hour, thence to Haarlem and Amsterdam, which city once, as the famous poet Vondel said, "wore the crown of Europe." There is Rembrandt's Nachtwacht (Night Watch) escaped from Hun robbing by hiding it in a mountain cave near Maastricht in Limburg. The colonial Museum, the "Grachten" lined by old patrician houses, where the trees reflect in the quietly flowing water; the large banking buildings and so on. Then, by the way, go to Marken and Volendam, it is only a few miles, and takes a few hours. See the great locks at Ijmuiden—now blown up—once exceeding in dimensions locks at Miraflores and gatun Locks of the Panama Canal. The Alkmaar cheese market deserves a visit, and the long dyke across the Zuyderzee, 20 miles, and capable of withstanding the severest storms. Then, at the same time, you have a look into the new Polders, spotted with the most modern type of farm houses and barns, lying at 10 to 15 yards below mean sea level, and kept dry by powerful motor pumps. One of those polders was inundated by the Germans, but the other, and larger one, escaped that fate. Thanks to the aid of some Polish young men, forced to serve in the German army, the engineers ordered by the German commander to blow up the sluices, could at the last moment be overpowered and millions damage prevented.

After that Frieland and the Groningen province are worth a few days' spending. There are the best farming grounds of Holland, producing also the famous pedigree cattle exported all over the world, and of which fine specimina may be seen every Friday on the market at ILeeuwarden. A motor trip through Groningen province is paying in every respect for its scenery on pastures and fields, covered with a variety of agricultural products.

South, Eindhoven, Tilburg, Maastrict and the mine district, where scenery is generally lacking—except for a number of old churches such as Saint John's Cathedral at 'S Hertogenbosch (Bois-le-Duc)—give a real idea of what industrial Holland is. In Eindhoven there are the Philips Works, as a rule employing over 30,000, often even 40,000 people, and making radios, electric lamps, scientific and optical instruments, electric tools, plastic articles, and so on. Hengelo, Enschede and Almelo are the textile cities in the East, where in normal times the spinning machines and looms are ticking day and night, and thousands of bales of cotton, for a large part arrived from the States (Texas, Louisana, Alabama, Georgia) are converted into endless reels of cloth for dressing as well as for many other purposes, household and industrial. Now the outturn is only a fraction of what is even necessary for the country proper.

On account of bad hygienic conditions and the lack of disinfectants and medicines contagious diseases, especially typhoid fever, were expected to break out this summer, but there were only a number of diphtheria and scarlet fever cases. What is worse—tuberculosis has increased in an alarmant way, and statistics show the number of patients to be about 400% more than there were in 1939. In our country the death rate by that scourge of manhood had in the course of time gradually been reduced to almost the lowest level in Europe; now there are not sufficient sanatoria to deal with even a fraction of the patients. We are grateful to Sweden and Switzerland for having sent us a number of barracks; now we hope that within a reasonable time it will be possible to fence also this menace to within small limits.

Outdoor swimming, this summer, was too dangerous on account of the water having been infected, causing various cases of Weil's disease (Leptispirosis—fever, jaundice, possibly fatal). The covered swimming pools in Rotterdam had all been damaged or destructed, and now that two of them are again available, there is no fuel to heat the water to the required temperature.

The death rate in Holland, in general, is not alarming now; the birth rate only 48% of that of 1939. Holland already had a low birth rate; its steady increase in population may only be attributed to excellent sanitary conditions existing here.

Now I switch over to some questions you put before me.

The feelings of sympathy shown by your fellow teachers and students towards our people were indeed a revelation to us. We had not expected that details given by a layman like myself would have roused so much interest. It is a pity that so few American soldiers are seen in Holland; they would then have been in a position to obtain a first-hand and personal insight into our present local conditions. The Canadians, thousands of whom lie buried in our soil, mainly in Walcheren, came into straight contact with the people, and although to many of them after fighting, women formed the only attraction, there remained quite a number who liked being introduced into our homes, and now that they have returned to their own country, are regularly exchanging letters with their Dutch acquaintances. During their stay in Holland many Canadians voluntarily assisted in reconstruction work. A number of trained engineers was daily busy in Rotterdam Telephone Central, refitting lines and installations. The Central had been destroyed in 1940, and only a few auxiliary stations were still functioning.

We Dutchmen, like the Americans, dislike war. Perhaps our people have in former times been too lenient and hospitable towards the Germans. There lived thousands of them in Rotterdam, occupying places in shipping and industry, acting as bankers, shipchandlers, merchants, shop owners, etc.

This may have given Hitler an impression that we were weak. But how he was disillusioned! Whatever the enemy undertook to oppress us, there were always means found to lead him by the nose. Illegal papers continued circulizing, black (censored, forbidden) radio listening remained common, when there were razzias (raids) to pick up young people, it was as a rule the police that warned them.

I might fill a booklet telling stories of quite humorous occurrences, but also of thrilling and tragical events. Young men and girls of the underground forces showed examples of courage and spirits, also of contempt for death that would have crowned the best soldier.

What the Germans after all achieved, was exactly what they had tried to avoid by all means; the unification of the Dutch nation. In concentration and hostage camps men and women of all classes and political views came to speak with each other and exchange opinions, finding after all that the separations between them were not so great as they looked, often only trifling, and they smoothed the way for the development of new ideas in government and social life after this war.

147

As a consequence, the new Government may reckon with a good working majority for their future plans, to the benefit of the nation as a whole.

We feel disappointed at the situation created in India (Indonesia) by the attitude taken by the Allied forces towards the Soekarno (Sukarno) group in Java, allowing them to act as successors to the old regime. The Javanese have an old civilisation and many of them are highly educated people, fine to deal with, but the masses as a whole must still be instructed in politics like most Oriental people. Such instruction takes time.

I certainly despise oppression, but there was not in the Indies during the last half century. We still have a mission to fulfill there; we must gradually improve the standard of living here, and, in fact, we have done already much in that direction. And what if the natives should be left to the mercy of Governors of their own? What if some potentate, hitherto kept in check by the "Company"—the Government's name among the natives—came to seize power, in order to exploit his subjects in a way far worse than it ever was under European government? The majority of well-thinking people, both in India (Indonesia) and the home country, are of the opinion that self-government of India (Indonesia) must come along lines carefully set out in advance, and the reins be loosened as circumstances permit. Away with red tape and bureaucracy, but too much hurry will certainly cause damage—probably irreparable damage. I am sure that only a return of the Dutch government in India (Indonesia), be it on more liberal and modern principles, can offer a guarantee for a regular prosperity and progress of the Indian native, now that the Japanese have made such a mess of everything. The natives should be enable to obtain again sufficient food, cattle, clothing, medical assistance and what they may further need, and have they an organisation themselves capable of tackling all the problems entailed therewith?? Certainly no!

The British, I guess, had better look after their own colonial questions. In the Punjab and Central Indian provinces thousands of people are dying from starvation often in normal times, and the British themselves admit they cannot help, because an adequate organisation or means to bring food where it is necessary simply do not exist. Did you ever hear in the last 40 or 50 years of such a situation in Java, Sumatra, or in the Outer Dutch Eastern colonies? Look at the people exploited in the Jute Mills and Iron

Works in Calcutta, the Cotton mills of Bombay, and Cocoa fibre industry on the Coromandel Coast, you Briton, and then.....shut your mouths, and lower your eyes.

In former times, the sole aim of Holland, as of any other white colonizing nation, was reaping the benefits of the natives' labour. This system has since long been abandoned by Holland, and there is hardly an Indishman (by which we indicate a white who has lived in the tropics for a longer period) who will think of taking again recourse to the ancient methods of treating the coolies.

Our family is doing well. The Canadians left Holland and several of them came to Rotterdam to say us farewell. Adrian, the elder son, joined another band, with a good reputation, and has regular employment. Some time ago they played in an evening party where also General Forster, Commander in Chief of the Canadian forces in Holland, was present. Adrian plays string bass; I understand the band further comprises a few saxes, trombone, trumpet, guitars and a drum set, but I am not very well versed in such business. Their lady crooner is excellent.

Johnny, the younger one, is not so ambitious in music. He is a guitarist and, as a rule, plays on his Spanish instrument—he has a Gibson, too, at his disposal. He likes modern as well as classic music, and sings all kinds of French and English songs, cowboy melodies being his favorites. As every other young man of his class, he speaks French, German, and English, and three months with the Canadians made him a fluent speaker of the latter language.

Rhythm in Holland is not so fast as in the States. There are practically no Negro bands here. Dances comprise of foxtrots, rumbas, tangoes, and how you may call them. Indeed, I do not believe there is much difference between the music actually in vogue on either side of the Atlantic; maybe we take things in a more quiet way. However, are not boys and girls in every civilized white country about the same in their behaviors? (I except the youth of the totalitarian nations which must again be educated to normality.) Would a Dutchman enjoy life less than an American?

My elder son always is after the newest hits, and if he cannot obtain the written music, he listens to the radio until he is able to make his arrangements. He has a good feeling for composition. Sorry to say, written music of new hits reach us as a rule only after they have already become rather trite on your side.

We can imagine what V-J night was in Chicago. The Michigan metropolis, with its 4 1/2 million inhabitants, forms the centre of

149

the Middle West, still rapidly growing, and when the Lachine shallows will have been removed, and the Welland Canal widened, it will become the terminus of an important number of transatlantic lines. Sorry that navigation will only be possible during a limited time of the year (due to the freezing of the Great Lakes.)

I suppose that you, as a teacher of English Literature in a large school, will enjoy your job very much. School life in the U.S.A. is so vivid; the students of each school or university look at each other as members of a community, as a team that must show superiority over other schools or universities. So things as a school band, orchestra or chorus are exceptions here, and except for the Universities, who have their regular rowing races and cricket and football (soccer) tournaments, the physical education is mainly in the hands of clubs. Of course, every school has its gymnasium; if that should not be the case, we might be ashamed!

Unlike in your country, the possession of a car is a kind of luxury, and middle classes, as we are, must abstain from having one, on account of the price and high cost of upkeep.

My wife and myself are only occasionally visiting the movies. Music we like very much, and we regularly attend the evenings when the Rotterdam Philharmonic Orchestra plays. This orchestra has a renown of its own, and has made successful tours to Belgium, France, etc. French and Russian compositions (Moussorgski, Glinka, Rimsky-Korsakov, Tchaikovski, for instance) form a large part of their programs, and many an artist of world fame we have heard here in Rotterdam. Now that all concert halls and theatres have been burnt down, we are listening to our concerts in a church, where, of course, the acoustic is far from ideal, but we have no better.

Now my letter comes to an end. We are making headway, and that gives reason to satisfaction. When this letter will reach you, perhaps the mist hanging over India (Indonesia) will have further cleared up, and the sun of hope returned in our hearts.

Now that Adrian (Aad) Muijser is safe, our expectations as to Hanna being well, too, are increasing, and her mother expects to receive a letter every moment. Poor woman, she lost already so much by the death of her husband.

With best wishes, and to write you again with a short time, I am,

Yours sincerely,
J. Broekman

+ + + + + + +

AT LAST! NEWS ABOUT HANNA!

Ruth received the first news of Hanna from John Broekman which told of her survival of the war camp. Although life in the camp had been difficult and Hanna endured many hardships, her relatives were more positive than ever before that she would return safely. However, there were new concerns about the dangers which existed in "liberated" Java. A nationalist movement was taking advantage of the missing and weakened Dutch control, and widespread rebellion was threatening the Europeans.

October 18. 1945 — Rotterdam
Hogerbeetsstraat 14c (Blijdorp)
(Letter from Uncle John Broekman)

Dear Miss Sullivan,

It is with pleasure that I can now report you having received a letter from Hanna. It was dated Banjoe Biroe (Middle Java) September 23rd, and she wrote that she was in good health. She has had much to endure in the camp, where more than 4000 women and children had been crammed together, but in spite of the bad hygienic conditions prevailing there, she did not fall ill. She had to work very hard, but by taking a job in the kitchen could escape starvation. for the rest she did not say much about her adventures. She only added that all her possessions and furniture had been stolen, and that nothing is left of all the nice things she had gathered in their home in Minggiran.

You will understand how glad her mother and other relatives were when the news came in. We now sincerely hope that she will have been in a position to reach Batavia or Sourabaja, for the radio yesterday evening reported alarming things about women and children having been driven out of camps in Middle Java into the mountain region, where there is practically no food. If she should be in Banjoe Biroe at present, she will again be in great danger, now on the part of the Javanese. Though those people are as a rule quiet and rather modest, they possess little self control and rush to extremes if stirred up by reckless agitation.

For these reasons, we hope that things in Java may soon improve. Of course, there will be no question what the end of the

151

Soekarno (Sukarno) adventure will be, but native fanatism may cause the death of thousands of Europeans if the allied forces do not handle the situation tactfully. The fact that, without listening to the advices given by the Dutch Indian experts, the British Forces allowed the formation of a "Government" by a few native leaders, who now appear to have no control whatever over the masses, shows how those Allies have misunderstood the situation. We fear there will now be much bloodshed on both sides, and this is the more to be regretted, because it will cause an aliention between the white and the brown people. It will take years to wipe it out, and result in many assassinations and similar crimes by "bigotics" long after the country as a whole will have been pacified again.

I think it better not to continue writing on this subject. The most important thing is that there is now positive news about both Hanna and Aad. May they also overcome the difficulties that may still be lying before them!

With greetings from the various relatives, including Mrs. de Bruijn and Aad's parents, I remain, as before, yours sincerely,

J. Broekman

CLASS OF SERVICE

This is a full-rate Telegram or Cablegram unless its deferred character is indicated by a suitable symbol above or preceding the address.

WESTERN UNION (25)

1201

A. N. WILLIAMS
PRESIDENT

SYMBOLS

DL = Day Letter
NL = Night Letter
LC = Deferred Cable
NLT = Cable Night Letter
Ship Radiogram

The filing time shown in the date line on telegrams and day letters is STANDARD TIME at point of origin. Time of receipt is STANDARD TIME at point of destination

```
      AB27
      A.CDU349 INTL=CD ROTTERDAM VIA RCA 17 18 1050  OCT 18  PM  1  00
      RUTH SULLIVAN=
         311 NORTH 14ST HERRIN (ILL!)=

CONGRATULATED ON YOUR BIRTHDAY HANNA AND AAD ARE ALLRIGHT=
      MVS DEBRUYN.
```

Long awaited telegram sent two months after
VJ Day and liberation affirming Hanna and Aad's survival

Sequence and dating were confused at this point showing the breakdown of communications and lengthy delivery periods. Aad

152

had escaped the horrendous Bataan Death March forced on the prisoners from Corregidor and had been fortunate enough to know the progress of the Allied defense by way of a radio he and others had assembled while being held captive in Singapore. However, Hanna had spent those devastatingly long months without knowledge of advancing help and hope. That must have been even harder than the lack of food and cruel conditions.

To further add to Hanna's danger and distress was the fact that even after she was rescued from the Japanese internment camp, the Javanese seized this time of confusion as an opportunity to turn on their Dutch colonizers and, led by Sukarno and his Nationalist party, engaged in bitter fighting for the next four years for their independence. Hanna and the other prisoners were caught in this rebellion as well, forcing additional stress and delays in their repatriation. Aad's letter gave more details.

29 Sept., '45 — Singapore
(Letter from Aad)

Dear Ruth,

You will be very wondered to hear something from me from this part of the world. This is just to inform you of me still being alive. I have been prisoner of war for 3 1/2 years now and you will no doubt hear of what that meant. But I must confess that I have been pretty lucky. I was taken prisoner in Bandoe in April '42. After a lot of moving over the island, I left the island of Java 4 Jan '43 for Singapore. We were bound for Japan as technicians, but for some reasons the ships did not want the officers. So most of the officers stayed in Singapore and apart from the amount of food which gradually diminished until a bare minimum was reached just before the capitulation.

Later on I'll give you more particulars about my adventures and about others. For no doubt you are anxious to hear something. So far I did not hear anything neither from Holland nor from Java. The last message from Holland as far as I remember was Nov. '41 and was dated March '41.

Have you further messages?

But now Hanna. She was free at first (in 1942), but later on all European women were put into camps in different towns of Java. The treatment was different in all these camps depending upon the Jap commander. Some were very, very bad; women with

153

children were forced to work on the "savah" (field) for 7 hours day after day! And that in the tropics! But about my Hanna. I know nothing so far. The last message I got was dated 8 Mar. '45. It was a plain postcard with sentences so it does not mean anything. I got this card on her birthday the 19th of August. But now we are very anxious to hear something from Java.

_____is still very bad especially with the Middle of Java. We are here in a more spacious camp waiting for an opportunity to return. But shipment is very limited as you no doubt heard so it will be quite a time before we can go back. Well, Ruth, I hope this letter reaches you in due course. I am so anxious to hear something about your war experiences. As soon as I know something about Hanna, I'll write you immediately. My address is at the back, but I'll repeat it—2nd Lt. A. J. W. Muijser RNT, No 2 R.A.P.W.I., HQ S.E.A.L., Wilhelmina Camp, Singapore.

Greetings and Love,

Aad

+ + + + + + +

The first message Ruth received from Hanna was written on Nov. 28, 1945 on a small 2" X 3" folded piece of yellowed wrapping paper, hand sewn for closing, and stamped with a "Prisoner of War" mark. It arrived in Ruth's mailbox from Batavia with no postage required.

Dearest Ruth,
I am just evacuated from Middle Java to Batavia. I haven't anything in the world but my body and two frocks. Fortunately Aad has gone through prisoner of warship without any harm. But he is in Singapore, and I have not any hope that we will see each other soon again. My father dead. My mother lonely in Holland, and I here. When I had known this five or six years ago, I should have said, "I can't stand it. It will be my death", but it shows how much a human being can stand! We are treated in the Japanese camp as beasts. But this you will know by the papers and the disappointment after the war that the natives being so much changed that they will not work again for us. I see the future as desolate, so difficult. I hope you will write me a letter again as you used to do.

Lots of love, your Hanna

Hanna's letter, in her own handwriting, from Batavia after her release from prison.

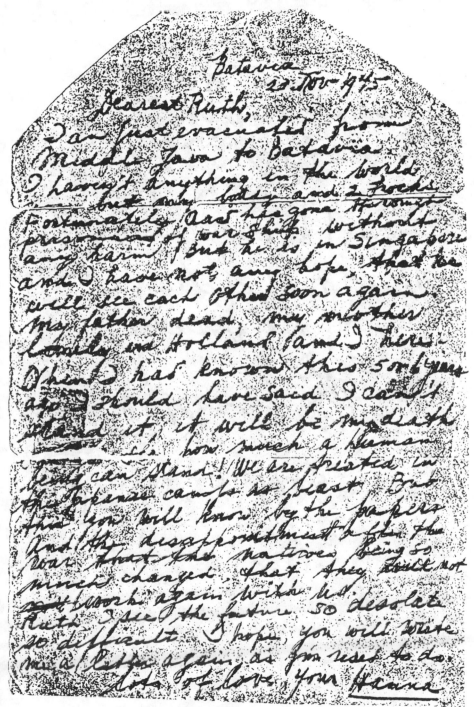

*Envelope containing first post-war letter from Hanna marked
"Prisoner of War" from Java, Batavia*

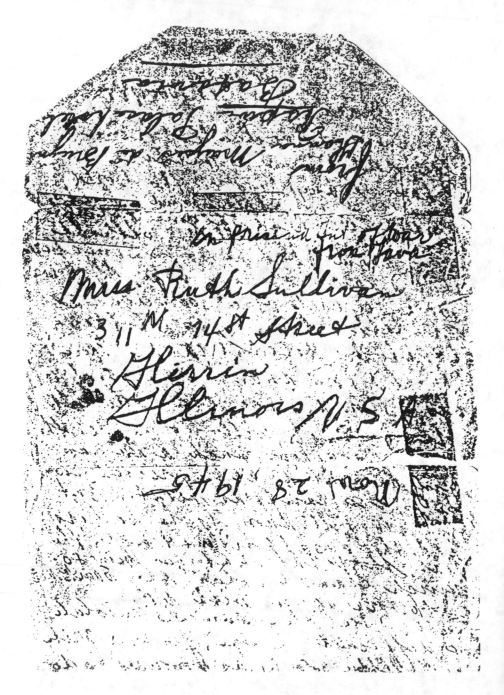

Hanna later admitted to Ruth privately that she had had doubts whether Aad would want her back. The poor diet had affected her appearance so much. She had lost hair and teeth, and she was very thin. One of three friends she'd been imprisoned with had died of cholera, but she and another had survived.

Letter undated — Java (NOJ) , Camp C.P. 10

Dearest Ruth,

I am alive and kicking and my husband Aad too. When the war here was over March '42 and the Japs had to come and although they have tried to murder us by keeping us in jails and giving us too little food, that most of us did not die, but were hungry all the time. The children did not grow any more, the women did not have their monthly periods any longer. The men were brought in different camps and the men who did belong to the army, as Aad did, were brought over the sea to Malaysia, Japanese a.s.o. I got a letter from Aad that he has spent 2 1/2 years in Singapore.

How did you do in all these 3 years? Did the war do any wrong to you? I did not hear anything from my parents. I hope I will soon have an answer to my inquiries. Most of the elder people in our camp starved. The women had to care for their children and the women had a hard time. But now it is over. As soon as I know that you are to reach, I will send more news about our wartime. I hope you did not forget me in all these years.

Lots of love, Hanna

+ + + + + + +

23 October, 1945 — Rotterdam
(Letter from Hanna's mother)

Dear Ruth,

How I was happy with the pictures you have sent to me. I have put them on my writing table. I thank you so much for Hanna's letters, too. I have brought the one for the family Muijser immediately to them. As to the English language; I was busy studying. When my husband fell ill and died, I was no more able to do it. Now that I have good news out of the Indies, I want to start again. As you will know already by my telegram and a letter from the family Muijser, Hanna and Aad are both alive. Hanna has stood a great deal of trouble. She has been interned in a camp in the center of Java. But she has come through in a good health. I only got a little letter with her address which is:

Mrs. A. J. W. Muijser de Bruijn
Camp Banjoe-Biroe
Care of central information and post office
Batavia N.O.T.

As yet we can't write from the Netherlands—no post for the Indies is accepted. Perhaps you will be so kind as to try to get through something I can to tell you, how I am grateful that I have been allowed to hold my child. It is a pity that the situation in the Indies has changed so much. When I hear more, I will write a long letter to you.

Much love of yours, Mrs. N. de Bruijn Rens

+ + + + + + +

Ruth received an invitation from Hanna's mother to come to Holland.

Wednesday 5th, 1945 (November) — Rotterdam

Dear Ruth,

Many thanks for your two letters, which I can answer now only. It is hardly to believe that my two children are still alive. How happy my husband would have been. First I got a letter from Aad and then Hanna wired that she was on her way to Singapore. I was so glad and sent you a telegram saying that they were together. A short time afterwards there came another piece of news that the boat was ordered back and that my child had been put ashore in Batavia. She is now staying at an hotel and is quite well. She has lost everything only her table silver she has been able to save. When I get news again I'll write you. From me Hanna has not yet heard anything, for her letters are still addressed to both of us, so she does not yet know anything of her father's death.

Since the airmail with the Indies has been re-established by now she will know. That gives new sadness after all the misery she has gone through in the concentration camp. I hope they will soon come to Holland. There is work enough over here for engineers.

I say Ruth, should not you like to come and spend your holidays with us next year? We'll receive you with open arms and

158

then we can compensate you for all you did for me and my husband. To the Muijsers family I told that you had got their letter and that you intended to write them if you had time.

Well Ruth, many kind regards and best wishes from
Mrs. N. de Bruijn Rens.

+ + + + + + +

28 November, '45 — Singapore
(Letter from Aad three months after end of war.)

Dear Ruth,

Just a short letter to inform you that I received your letter. I'll give you the latest news about us.

Hanna is now in Batavia. Her address is Palace Hotel. But I shouldn't advise you to write to her for any day can she come over to Singapore, either to join me here or to go to Holland probably with me too. For I think we all shall go back to Holland in the course of the next month.

I asked for repatriotism for her. That is a long story actually, but I will try to make it as short as possible.

I wormed myself into a job here i.e. I succeeded in making some Japanese radio transmitters which were in the camp here work again and this transmitter is working now traffic between Batavia and Mingaque. We were told that when you had a job here that your family was allowed to join you in due course. But that was prevented by the British who feared too great an influx in Singapore. And so I'm still waiting for Hanna here. The war is now over already 3 months and still nothing doing.

Besides that, trouble started in Java as you know. That is entirely due to the part that the Allies (whoever they were) were too late in bringing troops or us to Java. The first month our people were hailed and cheered by the Javaneses, but when nothing happened the bad elements got the upper hand and succeeded by bullying, murder, etc. to turn the population against us Europeans. To my personal opinion we lost Java in that first month. What shall happen now is completely enigmatic. I think the best thing for me to do is go back to Holland and try to get a job there but maybe you know of a job for me. Your language has no difficulties for me any more. I've been in Singapore since Jan. '43 and I have not been idle. I gave lectures in English on chemical subjects and so on so that I have no difficulty any more in speaking English.

This letter goes to Illinois with a Dutch plane and I take this opportunity to get it away. I told you that the chance of getting Hanna here is pretty remote so that I applied for repatriotism for her and for myself. I don't care about my job here for when they can't get Hanna here, which is my only wish, I don't care to leave them without any substitute.

Well, the letter is full now.

Cheerio from Aad

+ + + + + + +

Hanna and Aad had not yet been reunited.

23 December, 1945 — Rotterdam
(Letter from Aunt Clazien)

Dear Ruth,

With Christmas and New Year approaching, I beg to offer you my sincere wishes for the future. May 1946 bring you good luck, health and prosperity and every respect.

We are doing well and with things gradually improving we have no reason to complain. Much is still lacking here, specially clothing, but some foodstuffs hitherto rationed have already been given free to trade.

Sorry to say, Hanna and Aad have not yet been reunited. Aad is still anxiously waiting in Singapore, and notwithstanding all effort, the British in Batavia do not allow Hanna to leave there.

What a situation for a woman like her! Three and a half years the Dutch in India (the Indies) have suffered under the Japanese yoke and now their sufferings are continued. We must call our Allies. Aad, who is now in charge of the Wilhelminacamp Radio Station, has only one wish: his wife, and so is the case with Hanna. May their desires soon become a reality.

My brother John Broekman said he had written you a few letters without having received a reply.

Expecting you will soon be in a position to write us, and with best wishes and greetings I remain

Yours truly, Miss C. Muijser

Chapter Eleven

HANNA AND AAD REUNITED AT LAST!

Hanna wrote Ruth about her imprisonment and the hardships that she suffered. Also the Javanese natives used this opportunity of confusion over control to push for their independence that they had sought for many years. Under Dutch colonization they had been second class citizens, and they now, ready or not, seized this situation for self-government.

Aad had difficulty getting her admitted to Singapore and allowed to reenter The Netherlands partly because she had been born in Germany (but reared in Rotterdam by Dutch parents.)

January 9, 1946

Dearest Ruth,

At last I am able to write you now. Being here in Singapore from Java, reunited with Aad at last, I am getting restful again after all these emotions of the last few months and now I am able to tell you in a quiet way what has been going on since we could not write each other any more.

When the Nips got hold of Java, a lot of people still were on their factories and so did I succeed to live on our factory for quite a time, but the Nips became more and more rigorous in their treatment of Europeans and at last we were interned in the beginning of '43. Then trouble and misery started. We were taken out of our houses, had to leave everything with the exception of some luggage and we were interned in camps without articles of furniture, crowded together for insufficient food. That was very bad. The worst was the hunger. You can't imagine day after day insufficient food. People are so completely disinterested in life that their only happiness seems to concern a plate of rice. Of course the Nips were very impolite and rude and brutal against us. But you heard enough about that, I think.

When at last liberation came was that for us very sudden. We knew nothing. We had not seen a paper for 3 1/2 years. We did not hear any radio. In our loneliness we were so afraid sometimes that the Nip would win. After the capitulation, we were allowed out of the jail for small trips and so we could buy food from the natives or swap for old clothes. For food was plenty,

161

but clothes were practically non existing. Everybody in rags. The natives were very glad that the Nips should disappear and our people should come back. However, our people were long in coming. The internees, also the male internees, who were still on Java in camps were ordered to stay in the camps until the British should liberate us and disarm the Japanese. However, nothing happened and after a fortnight, the natives' mood changed completely. You know the result.

If only the Americans could have taken over instead of the British. In that case, I am sure, we should be on our factory again. In that case no women and children should have been butchered in Antaruwa, Temarany and Toerabaja by encited natives. In that case there should have been no chance for the Japanese to give their weapons to the natives and the latter would have got no help by Nips or Germans. Of course Java should have had self-government, but by evolution, not by revolution

I myself was just in time out of camp Banjoe Birve. We went away in trucks flanked by armed Ghurhas (a kind of British Indies soldiers). It was just a feeling of participating in a wild west film with a lot of trouble. I first went to Batavia by boat and from there to Singapore again by boat. How glad I was to meet Aad there! He was brought there already 3 years ago by the Nips from Java. Lucky for him, that he had not to work on that railway in Siam or in the mines of Japan.

My health suffered a bit after all these happenings, but I sincerely hope, that it will be all right now after being reunited. We lost everything and now we are living in a room, rented from a Chinese family and waiting for things to come. Oh, I had rather go back to Holland, but that is not so easy. Besides that, I should be forced to leave Aad which would be very difficult for Aad is again in the army as a reserve lieutenant.

It is a difficult situation here in S'pore. Thousands of POW'S and evacuated women from Java lodged in various camps. This is not so easy as concerned the food situation. The British who were living here before the war are not yet back, so that the town is crowded with Dutch. And the shops are crowded too for all these women from Java who lost everything want to replace some of their property. Most of them lost everything, no frock, no shoes, no plates, no soap, no pins, no needles. In short, nothing.

There are lot of men here who until now heard nothing about their family in Java and a lot of women who got notice that their husband died somewhere. We Dutch, we truly got our part of the war and I can't see the end yet. Please write soon Ruth. I hear from my mother that you wrote such splendid letters to her. I thank you very much for that. How lonely she is after my father's death. I still remember when you lost your father and wrote to me about that. Now the same happened to me. But I did not know that my father died. That I think the worst of all, Ruth. Aad gives you his heartiest greeting. From me a big kiss and lots of love.

Your friend, Hanna

+ + + + + + +

Hanna and Aad were finally able to return to Holland and told of the reunion with their family and friends after being away for six years, with much of the time spent in a concentration camp. Food, clothing, and housing were scarce. Hanna was living with her mother, while Aad awaited permission from the military for his release. Fear continued that he would be held in the army to defend the Dutch colony in the Indies against the insurrection of the natives led by Sukarno. War-weary troops were again mobilized in Holland and sent to the trouble spot, but eventually they turned the running of the Javanese government over to the natives. At first it was Communist ruled and later controlled by military power so the dream of an independent, prosperous democracy never materialized.

In April of 1946, Aad and Hanna were together again in Holland. He was teaching chemistry in a high school in Rotterdam. Hanna described the living conditions and the ruins of the city after the war. Her own health had been affected as a result of being detained as a prisoner in Java and suffering from hunger and sorrow.

10th Feb., 1946

Dearest Ruth,

I am so glad to write you that Aad and I are on our way to Holland, on our way home. You can imagine how our thoughts were in Holland the last few months. I was so happy to go to Singapore and now we are going home. It is as if there never was such a horrible time we spent in prison. Now we are able to forget this. Our ship is named the Alcantara. It is an Italian ship, captured by a Dutch battleship in war time. Now it is in the poole and used as evacuation ship. The ship is overcrowded. 2000 men, women, and children. There are many women who lost their husbands during the last years in Thailand or Burma. They are travelling alone with their children to go back to their family in Holland. They are, you can imagine, in a very sad mood.

Also there are many women travelling alone because their husbands can't leave Java. They must work there for the government. But Aad, as his job is on the sugar factory which cannot work now, because of the extremists going round, murdering and stealing all things up country, was allowed to go to Holland from six months. There he can regain his health. My health has suffered too from being imprisoned for 3 years. I am so tired and nervous all day. I am longing to go home for a rest. We like to live at my mother's home. I think we can get there the rest we need.

We have lost everything we possessed, our house in Manjgiran with the furniture, our clothes, all things we possessed, the Japs took off from us. After the Jap capitulation when we thought that the bad time was over, we had to begin a much more time under the Javanese extremists. Fortunately I escaped from them when I could go to my husband in S'pore, but many of my friends are still living there in camps under much more circumstances than ever.

Really Ruth, no well thinking man can allow this. The extremist leaders are devils in human statue. It is a very fine thing to say everybody has the right of self determination and the natives have the right of freedom and they are right to send away the Dutch and reign themselves, but this is right for men as you and your folks in Amerika and we in Europe. For you and we are able to do it. We can think, write, and read. But the population in Java is not able to do it. Ninety-five percent can't read nor write, is only working as a peasant, working in the rice fields and sugar factories and the bad rubber plants. Their brains are not yet developed enough, really not. And the 5% who are the intellectuals who have studied at the costs of our government, who were allowed to study in Holland, it is a very corrupt little plot when they should govern Java. The population will be poorer and more unhappy than they were under the reign of our Queen Wilhelmina. Really Ruth, this is the truth.

Many lots of love from Aad and me.

Your Hanna

+ + + + + + +

164

Dearest Ruth.

Now we are home again after all those months of waiting, fear, and voyaging. From Singapore we at once could repatriate with the "Alcantara" a British troopship with very few accommodations for men, women and children, nervous and tired and not able to do all those works as cleaning and washing plates and clothes. It was a voyage of 28 days before we saw Southampton, the southeast coast of England, and then we repatriated with another ship the "Sibajak" to Holland.

In Amsterdam we got a very heartily welcome. We had a strong feeling to be home again. Aad could not go home immediately. While he was an officer before the war, he had to go to the military office at first to be examined as to his health. We don't know but we think that when he has recovered after a few months he will be directed to the East again, for you know, that already 90,000 men are mobilized again in our country. The government don't want to lose Indonesia. The people is not very enthusiastic as you can understand—to leave house and family and work again.

I could go home immediately and when I came with a car in our street my mother opened already the door and we could kiss again each other. It was very sad that my father could not enjoy this moment. At night everybody came to see me, my parents-in-law, my aunts and uncles and friends. I had to tell my adventures and they liked to tell theirs. For we all had been in the war as you know.

I did not know, neither enjoy my old Rotterdam. The streets where I played as a child were ruined, and it is a wonder that the house of my mother and parents-in-law was not bombed. The following day Aad arrived. We are living now at my mother's. A house of our own we can't get. Furniture is not to be sold, curtains, shoes and dresses, you can't get it. With many difficulties my mother got a special permission to buy a bed for us and we got an extra ration coal this month because we are from the Indies.

The impression we have, coming back in our country, is that of a very, very poor country where nothing is to buy, except some food as potatoes, bread, very few butter and meat with a large shortage of houses, dresses, and everything of ruined towns and villages. When Aad and I leaved Holland 6 years ago, this country was very rich. Everybody could buy everything. Houses stood to let, the furniture was cheap and the dresses too. But there was a terrible number of employments less (unemployment). However, they got money enough for living from our government, this was a very sad situation. And now, nothing to buy and a large lack on workers. Nobody wants to be a servant. Everybody wants to have office of his own.

I should like to have a sewer to alter a frock for me, but I have to wait very long and to buy a large sum of money. Very few workers and already 90,000 new mobilized again. My mother showed me your books from school. She is very proud about it and she asked me to thank you most heartily. And the calendar! It is hanging on the wall opposite me. It is so charming. We are all so grateful that you held so long you could the threads between Aad and me and the family in Rotterdam in your dear hands. We should like to show you how grateful we are, but there is nothing we are able to do now, for everybody here is so poor.

Aad and I are very tired, but our health is rather good. We have a lack on blood but with rest and food, it will come good, the doctor says. We are very fortunate for many of our friends are coming home ill or without husband or wife.

My best friend, with whom I shared the camp life was reunited 4 days with her husband in Batavia when he was called back again in the Dutch navy. She was very upset about it. Now she is coming to Holland too with her two children. I enjoy thinking about us seeing again. I fear that Aad will be mobilized again after his health has recovered. Maybe in this time, the quarrel with Indonesia is over.

In your last letter you asked my mother if you could help her with anything. She says she don't like you spend money for her, but she badly needs a pair of stockings. We have enough food. The quality is not so good. Last week everybody in Holland got 1 egg and this week we hope to get an orange.

Dear Ruth, many greeting from Holland, from my mother, Aunt Clazien, Uncle Jan, and my husband and specially from me.

Your old pal, Hanna

+ + + + + + +

Unbelievably, despite their desolate conditions, they encouraged Ruth to come to them and were willing to share what little they had.

Dear Ruth,

I got your letter from 22 April in which you told us about your steeple chaser for hosiery. We laughed a lot reading your letter and we did see you standing in the line trying to get some stockings. But if you knew how glad my mother is to have some day a pair of stockings who are really new after so many years! She says, "Oh, is Ruth sending 3 pairs of stockings, but she must not do that. She did already so much for us and now standing in a line and giving her money in our favour!" But she is very glad.

We are glad to be here in Holland again. It is very pleasant to live here with our trees. Aad's health is rather well and now he is a chemistry teacher at one of the High Schools of our town. He hopes to remain here and not to be send back again to the Indies. When you are walking through the town we see the ruines of the houses, shops and cars on which we were accustomed before the war. But everywhere workmen are busy to clear away the remainings and they hope to build again when there are bricks and wood.

Many people don't have more than one or two rooms to live in. There are houses in which a family is living consisting of 20 or more persons. Before the war such a house belonged, for example, to a family consisting of a father, mother and 2 or 3 children. People who are marrying can't get a house. They are glad when they can get 2 rooms in their parent's house or in the house of a relation. They can't buy furniture, for you can't buy any. The life is very difficult especially in a great ruined place as Rotterdam. But we have food enough, although rationed. Nobody has hunger and we are grateful for this.

We are enjoying the very fine spring weather. What a difference with the weather in Java. Always warm. Always the trees very, very green and 1/2 year rain and the other half year longing for rain. Here you feel you are coming back to life again as the trees who are producing their new leaves.

My teeth are ruined so much by underfeeding that the doctor must extract 3. Four must be plumbed. I'm going to get some false teeth. We are enjoying your very interesting letters in which you are telling us about your school work. Yesterday we got the letter you sent to the Julianacamp, Singapore, including another letter in which my mother's letter about the death of my father. What a pity that I did not get this letter in the time you planned for it. It is now almost 3 years that my father died.

We are surprised what you are doing in your holidays. Can't you spare some time and money and come to Holland? All our family and friends would receive you most heartily, for everybody knows what a fine woman you are and how you were interesting in our conditions during the war.

With much love from us all.

Your Hanna

+ + + + + + +

June 5, 1946 — Rotterdam

Dearest Ruth:

Some time ago I received your letter with the photos and stamps. I gave the fotos to Uncle John and Aunt Clazien and they were very glad with it. Now I hope we will receive your photos soon. I don't like to go to the photografer and to have my face on a paper. For all those years of sorrow and hunger did not as much good to it.

Specially my teeth are in a terrible condition. But the dental surgeon says he can make it well again. Every week I am going to him. When I am the Hanna of some years ago again as much as possible, I shall go to the fotographer and send you a snapshot.

Aad is still teaching. I told him to write you about his studies, students, etc. as you asked.

The vacation from the school is beginning in the half of Juli. We made up our mind to go to the country then during a month. We decided to go to Hilversum, a little village +70 miles from here amidst the forests. I enjoy to go for I am bored to death to look at all the ruines in our town. When you go everywhere these ruines.

We did not get your hoses. I hope they will come soon. Perhaps the strikes are the cause. To us there are many strikes just as in America. This is the chief cause why we can't get sugar in Holland any longer. This is a pity for tea and coffee and porridge without sugar is not a pleasure. But on the other side we are glad not to be hungry.

My mother is away for some weeks. She is working in a nearby village as chief of the household in a country house where +/– 25 old men and women are living. She has to cook, to play cards, to read from the Bible, to help them washing their bodies etc. with the help of a cook and 3 servants. She is earning some money with this job and she has plenty to eat too. For in the country it is more easy to get food than in a town. And all things, when available are so terribly expensive. And she has after my father's death but little money to spend. She enjoys this job too.

Now I am in the house alone. When Aad is teaching I am cooking, cleaning, washing etc., a real housewife. Sometimes I am longing to do my old job, physical education of the young girls and women of a high school, but I don't believe I am already fit enough to do this job. Dearest Ruth, write soon please.

Kisses of your Hanna. Good wishes from Aad

+ + + + + + +

Aard Broekman, Aad's cousin and son of John Broekman, wrote about meeting a sailor from Herrin, Illinois (Ruth's hometown) who had been one of Ruth's students. What a small world! Mr. J. Broekman also commented and "enlightened" Ruth about conditions in Holland after the war.

4 August, 1946 — Rotterdam (Blijdrop)

Dear Miss Sullivan,

A few days ago we received your magazine and music--and in the first place I want to thank you for this attention. With much interest I read the article about our country. Most striking was the photo of our Princess Juliana lighting a cigarette. We never saw this picture, for here in Holland there are a lot of people (and with them our Queen) who do not approve this frivolity, like they used to call a lady smoking a cigarette. This is one of the reasons why pictures like this are never published in the newspapers.

Several friends asked me to read the magazine because here in Holland everybody is interested in American life. When reading the advertisement they remind me of our prewar weeklies. In our interior market firms do not need to recommend their articles in the newspapers for the demand is still much greater than the offer. Articles of an inferior quality are now being sold in a moment because there's still a lack of necessities of life.

Your music has been appreciated very much. Here we cannot yet buy American hits. Therefore, we try to copy them from the radio. Especially the A.F.N. Radio Munich, a station broadcasting for the American troops in Germany gives us much pleasure. They always relay programs of American orchestras from New York, etc. My favorites are The King Cole Trio, The Pied Pipers, Charly Spivak and Woody Herman. The hits you sent me are just getting popular in England and I do not doubt they will be in Holland too. Especially "Oh, What It Seemed To Be" will become a great success here. This week I made the orchestration from your copy and next week I'll bring it in our rehearsals. We have a nine piece orchestra consisting of trumpet, 3 tenor saxophones, piano, drums, guitar and bass as instrumentalists, and a girl as vocalist. Till the 1st Novenber we have a contract in Schiedam where we play in a very modern dancing.

This week our port was visited by a cruiser and some destroyers of the U.S. Navy. I spoke to several American boys and to prove you the world is very small I'll relate you the following story.

On board the cruiser I met a very sympathic boy, who told me he was a student in Chicago. The last day of their stay in Rotterdam he told me he had to go to one of his friends on board a destroyer. I waited for him and when he came back he showed me the address of his friend. When I said the word Herrin I thought of you and I succeeded to come on board, where I made the acquaintance of him. It was Mr. C. D. May, 1405 W. Monroe who told me he had been one of your pupils. We have been talking some time and he promised me to bring you our greetings. It was a pity he could not leave the ship, otherwise I had invited him to go to our house to have a talk to my parents. He told me that you had said you had a Dutch correspondence girlfriend in Holland; he even knew Hanna and Aad stayed in the Indies. I could not introduce him to Aad and Hanna, because they are on holidays in Hilversum. Aad has got a job in Rotterdam as teacher in chemistry at a secondary school. As you will understand—they are very happy to have some certainty for the future.

I suppose you are now enjoying your holidays too, but I do not hope the weather in America is as bad as it is here in Holland, for here it is always raining and rather cold for this season. Although it is August, it seems as if we have October now. At any rate we all wish you some nice weeks of rest before starting your new lessons.

Miss Sullivan I repeat my thanks for the souvenirs you sent to us.

Greetings from my parents and a handshake from Aard.

170

Aad teaching after returning to The Netherlands

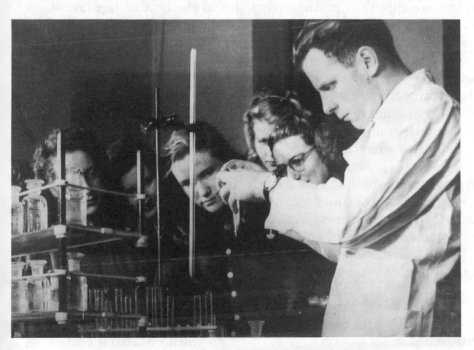

Aad with students in a chemistry class
Rotterdam, Holland

Aad wrote that he and Hanna were expecting a baby in December.

13th August, 1946 — Hilversum
(Letter from Aad)

Dear Ruth,

You will be wondered at our absence for such a long time, but there are quite a lot of reasons for that actually.

In the first place I had a very busy time at the end of the school's term for I took over the 5th class i.e. the class who has to pass its final exam. I took over one subject i.e. Physics. And so I had to do Rotterdam (Blijdorp) the oral exams in physics and to correct the paper work too. Besides that I had the 2nd, 3rd, and 4th classes for physics and the 5th year chemistry. So you see I had quite a crowded month. The second half of the year we went down to Hilversum which is a holiday resort in our country.

Hanna has an old school friend living there who went to the seaside during the month of August and she lent us her house. So we are nicely installed there now till the end of August. And then we will go back to R'dam but not to the old address but to Schieweg 251a, my parents' address. We are going to live there in future so you perhaps know my father has a job at Middelburg, the capital of Walcheren. He works there with the administration of the rebuilding and replanting organization. So they are leaving their house and we are trying to wangle it thus that we can have their house when they shift. So that gave us a lot of trouble too last month. I even started a letter about school life and my experiences here, but I mislaid it and so far I couldn't find it. In September I'm continuing my teacher's job but as far as I know so far only chemistry now. However that is liable to change at the last moment.

But now something about our holiday resort here. Hilversum is in between Amsterdam and Utrecht. I hope you have a map which shows it. It lies on the edge of a very interesting part of country. For in the glacial period the big "gletchers" came down from Norway and Sweden straight south. And they ended on a latitude just about Amsterdam and so you find at the end of all these glaciers the big end moraines forming the center of our country north of the big rivers. This stretches east till East

172

Prussia. Everywhere in between you will find a broad belt of hilly country, very meager soil consisting of sand and gravel brought there by the glaciers. The vegetation is when mud cultivated mostly heather and woods, mostly firs.

For two weeks we had bicycles, borrowed them in fact but we were free to roam about a bit. But now we have to give the bicycles back again so that we have to go by train or bus. For it is nearly impossible to get tires here. They are not manufactured here in sufficient gravity yet. (lack of material) and we haven't got the foreign value to buy them, so there we are.

By the way we got your fotographs at last. But the stockings didn't show up. It seems that a lot of parcels got lost somehow so you would better send it by registered post if you send anything.

I started this letter telling you that we had a frightfully busy time just now and that for more than one reason. But the most important reason (at least to us) is that we expect an addition to the family in the near future i.e. December. So you understand that quite a lot is to be done just now. For we in Holland are very short of clothing, wool, etc. But we will manage somehow. In the meantime I hope you enjoyed this letter and I promise to tell you another time about a teacher's life here in Holland. How did you spend your vacation? Tell us something about it. Well, for the moment I wish you everything good from here.

Kisses from Hanna.

Aad

+ + + + + + +

25 Aug., '46 — Hilversum

Dearest Ruth:

Thank you very much for your sending letter and the money for my birthday at 1 Aug. The letter came at Aug. 18.

Aad has already told you that we are spending our vacances in a lovely country village in the middle of our country. Although one has to do a voyage of 3 hours from Rotterdam by train and not a beautiful train but sometimes one without windows, without seats, etc. while they are trains left behind by the Germans when they drew back. My whole family was present at Aug. 19. My aunts, my parents-in-law, a good girlfriend with her husband and another girl friend with whom I spend my camp life in the East

Indies. We had a very pleasant day. The first birthday in Holland after seven years. We had enough to eat, sugar to take in the tea, even chocolates. I thought many times about this day a year ago when I still was in prison, hungry, without neat clothes, without a token of life from Aad since three years, neither from my parents, no notice about the state of war, no knowledge about America winning the war. When I thought about all that I was very grateful with this day, although life is still very difficult. With the money one gets with one's job, one can't buy anything but food. The food is so expensive that you have to spend most of your money for it. Most people have no money to buy clothes or furniture. The houses are very scarce while many are disturbed. Fortunately we have a chance to live in my parents-in-law's house, when they move to Walcheren. Aad and I, we will try, to build a new life again after all those horrible war years. We are going to have a baby, too in December. Though we are married for more than six years now and though I am 32 now, we are so glad about it. There will be many difficulties with clothes, perambulator, a.s.o. for all those things are very scarce, but my mother and aunts will no doubt help me to make from old clothes some little new ones for the baby.

The stockings you send have not yet reached us, Perhaps they are coming sometimes it lasts very long before parcels from America reach their destination. I am very glad with your dollars. I will send you notice when we bought something.

Many kisses from Hanna

+ + + + + + +

8 October, '46

Dearest Ruth,

I hope this letter will reach you at October 14 when it is your birthday. To wish you a happy day and many good wishes for the future.

I am so glad to be able to write to you. Last year I tried to write to you at your birthday, but you know, that just a year ago we went out of the hands of the Japs into the hands of the horrible Javanese.

We read about your holidays in the Rocky Mountains. We envied you very much, although we had a lovely holiday too.

174

And now you are on your new term at school again? Ruth, I am sorry, but there is no present for you this year. You can't imagine how strange it is not to be able to buy things of beauty for a friend's birthday, but in our country is not yet the most urgent. So you can understand that we can't afford to send you a birthday present. We hope that next year we are able to send you one.

I told you already that we are going to have a baby. The great event will be in the beginning of December. A strange time for having a baby, is it not? The little bed and blanket, the clothes, it is all very difficult to get and besides it is very expensive.

Fortunately Aad is able to work and to earn enough money to buy all these things. Many of our friends from Javanese prisons are not so lucky. They are suffering from bad health and not able to work and depending from their family.

Ruth, do write us soon one of your interesting and nice letters, we enjoy them so much. Aad does wish you a happy birthday too and so does our whole family.

Lots of love and a birthday kiss
Hanna

+ + + + + + +

18 November, 1946 — Rotterdam

Dearest Ruth,
Yesterday I got your parcel with the baby clothes and blankets. You can't imagine how glad I was when I opened it. Especially the blue cloth with the pink little buds, I think the most beautiful! I don't know, Ruth, how I ever can give a suitable compensation for everything you did for us. The best thing should be to offer you hospitality whenever you should make up your mind to make a trip to Holland.

We, too, got your letters with the photos and the money. So you see, that besides the stockings, everything comes here all right. How lovely the photos are. We think you had indeed a marvelous vacation, Ruth. (incomplete)

+ + + + + + +

Apparently Hanna interrupted her letter writing to concentrate on delivering their first child—a miracle child

175

considering the recent harsh conditions under which her parents had struggled to survive. She was Wilhelmina Hendrika, a delightful daughter who is referred to later in this book as Ineke. She would grow up to send her own letters to her "Aunt Ruth."

12 December, 1946

Dearest Ruth,

I wanted to write to you and when I opened my papers, I saw I began a letter to you at Nov. 18. But then I did not finish, for I feeled sick. I was ten days ill, and then our baby came. I expected her to come after 18 Dec., but her birthday now is Nov. 28. After the birth I was recovered soon, and now I am at work again. We are so glad and happy. I did not know that a little baby could give such a happiness. I wish you could come and see her, Ruth. She has blue eyes and fair hair. She is a darling.

We got your second parcel with the Herrin School yearbook and the stockings. How to thank you?? The book is so interesting. Aad brought it with him to his school and all the other teachers liked to read it. I am so proud of you, dearest.

The baby has the names of the oldest ladies of our family. "Wilhelmina" is the name of an old aunt of me and "Hendrika" is the name of Aad's grandmother. We call her "Ina" (eena). The beautiful blue cloth is used every day many times. For our Ina is sleeping in the bedroom where it is cold. When she gets her drink, I take her with me to the sitting room where the fire is burning. I have to walk through the corridor, and I am wrapping her in the cloth. The blankets I am using in the pram, and most of the clothes are too wide. I will use them later on.

In our country everybody is thinking these days about Indonesia—must we let it free or not? Personally Aad and I are thinking that the Indonesian people have a right to govern themselves, and when they don't like the Dutch, that we are obliged to retire. But all the conservative elements among the people (and all the rich because they have their parts in the rich plants of Java) say that Holland has his duty to cultivate the Indonesians, that we are more clever, that the Indonesians can't do without our brains. We hope that these people are in minority and that the Indonesians get their self-government without fighting.

The translation of the card is: Mr. and Mrs. A. J. W. Muijser de Bruijn are glad to tell you about the birth of their daughter Wilhelmina Hendrika.

Love, Hanna

+ + + + + + +

20 Dec., 1946
Rotterdam-C (Blijdorp), Hogerbeetsstraat 14c
(Letter from Aad Broekman)

Dear Ruth,

Supposing you will receive this letter after Christmas I hope you had pleasant days. At the same time I want on behalf of my parents too to wish you a happy 1947. Fortunately the past year brought an improvement all over the world and it is to be hoped that the coming year this progress will continue. Although there's still a lot of work to be done in every respect before the world has arrived at its prewar standard of life. But in comparison with the past 5 years here in Holland there are no reasons for complaining. There is only one thing that gives us some trouble and this is our struggle in our foreign colonies (The Dutch East Indies). A lot of young people were sent to it in order to establish our authority (lost by the Japanese as our government tells). However most of the soldiers did not like to go there. They were all glad they survived the very difficult years of occupation in Holland and now being liberated they have to part from their relatives and again run the risk of losing their lives. But also in this respect there is a little bright spot, for our government did just sign an agreement with the new established Indian Republic which will probably result in an armistice.

Ruth, please will you write me something about the reason of the coal strike in the U. S. A. for here the newspapers write very little about the reasons and only write about the results. If we must believe this newspaper John Lewis is something like a dictator, who wants to force everything for getting his demands. (Lewis was the union leader seeking safety codes, improved wages and pension plans.) I can't hardly believe this and I suppose there will be several reasons that will be moderate.

I hope to hear from you soon. Lots of luck for the coming year.

Yours sincerely, Aad Broekman

Chapter Twelve

The rejection of a 1947 article in Time *regarding what had happened during the war years in 1941-1943 was obvious in Aad's letter to Ruth. The betrayal felt against the Allies for unfulfilled promises of airplanes and divisions of military was vividly described.*

A bit of "bitterness" is noted toward some Americans who, in Aad's opinion, were "making propaganda for Indonesia because of their bad colonial attitude". He referred to the United States' treatment of American Indians and "colored people" in the southern states, and suggested that we, in America, should clean up our own mess before condemning others.

7th March, 1947 — Rotterdam
(Letter from Aad)

Dear Ruth,

In the first place many, many thanks from both of us for the packet you sent us. It was really too much, the nylons, the baby things. We were dumbfounded when we opened the packet! To our opinions all these gifts place us in a very bad situation, for in the near future it will be utterly impossible for us to compensate in any way the many gifts you showered on us. For you know, our country is not in a position to produce or buy things we need here. We'll have to work hard, very hard, to get industry giving again and we, i. e. the country as a whole, is very, very poor because of the war. The 5 years occupation cost us billions of guilders (1 guilder +/– 2/5$). So you'll have to do with our many, many thanks and we'll hope to be able to do something for you in future.

But now something else. Some days ago we too got that copy of Time in which we found that article on Sucharno! We found many good things in it but a lot of it is sheer nonsense and was written by a man who was very badly informed about the matter he discussed.

The Sucharno speech is sheer nonsense. This is just something to boost morale a bit. When we think back to Java, the villages we saw there where the peasants (illiterate) live together with their cows, their fowls, etc. and we have a big laugh when Sacharno exclaims "a car for everybody"!

We know that in December, 1941 we were promised 2 Australian and 2 American divisions to garrison Java. We had about 1000 planes in Australia to be sent to Java for the defense. These planes were paid for in advance, in gold. But they didn't come. They were kept in Australia by the Allies. The same with the promised divisions. Java was sacrificed for the Allied cause and with it the whole white population. For we were forbidden to evacuate as the British did. It was forbidden to send women and children to Australia by the government. The correspondent told that the governor general (The GG as we shorten it) fled to Australia. This is a lie. What he did was send Dr. Hvanilink to Australia (the latter was Lieutenant GG) to arrange matters for a later reoccupation. But Tjarda van Starhenburgh Stachanwer stayed in Bandoeng and shared internment with all of us. The same did his wife and daughter.

When I arrived in Singapore in January, 1943 in the back of a Jap transport with 1000 other prisoners of war, the GG just had arrived there and we saw him there, thin but in good spirits. He had been subjected to the same treatment as we had been and he refused other food than the kind we got. He had a shaven head just like the criminals we looked like and was brought to Singapore in a like fashion as we were. So it is very disappointing to see in a leading weekly such gross nonsense as we saw here.

(Ruth wrote Time magazine and sent a copy of Aad's criticism. They replied, admitted their mistake, and were sorry. She sent their letter to Aad.)

A lot of your people are making propaganda for Indonesia because of our bad colonial attitude. But as the article says: we augmented the population from 35 to 82 millions in a dozen years but what did your people do to the native Indians in America itself? We can speak then of a diminishment (not to use a harsher expression) in that case.

And what to say about the treatment of colored people in the southern states? I think that instead of having a bad opinion about us, some of your countrymen better improve conditions in "God's Own Country" itself as I so often saw it described.

Well Ruth, I'll end now. I have been writing 1 1/2 hours at a stretch this Friday night. Tomorrow I'll send this letter by airmail. We, Hanna, Ineke, and I, give you our best wishes and hope to get a reply from you soon.

Love from all of us.

Aad

+ + + + + + +

22 March, 1947 — Rotterdam

Dearest Ruth,

I have got the time now to write you for it is Sunday night. We had tea and now I sit down with my thin paper that we use especially when we write to you. At first I must thank you for your last parcel. Aad wrote you already how glad we were. It becomes a monotonous story always and always to thank you for your good gifts. We should like to make you so happy with a parcel as you make us. But for this we must have as little patience till we can buy here some pretty or beautiful things.

The frock you send for our baby suits her so good. When she wears it, she looks so pretty that I have to kiss her. We named her Ineke, an abbreviation of Wilhelmina. I am a real house mother now—in the morning sweeping dinner room and sleeping room, a.s.o. cooking the meals and washing up, washing all our things and baby's. Then my many plants before the window and the cat. They all must have my care, and I am spending the whole day with these things.

After Easter I shall try to get some young girl to help me a few hours a day, for when summer is there, I must have some time in the afternoon to go with Ineke in the pram outdoors. But servants are very difficult to get, and they ask much money. When we were in the Indies seven years ago, you could have four or five servants, who did all house work for you with a salary of a few guilders. But now this will change in the Indies, too. Javanese people don't want to work hard for Europeans for a little money any longer, and they are right.

Now I am afraid to annoy you with my chattering about household difficulties. Do you send us some one of your interesting letters, Ruth? So long.

Regards from Aad. Kisses from Ineke and me.

Your Hanna

+ + + + + + +

On November 15, 1947, Aad sent apologies for not having written for six months. Their little daughter, Ineke, had been seriously ill with encephalitis for several weeks, hence the lack of interest in letter writing.

On December 8, 1947, Hanna wrote of her struggle with post war nerves. Her daughter, Ineke, born November 28, 1946 was now one year old and Hanna was awaiting the birth of a second child.

15th November 1947 — Rotterdam
(Letter from Aad)

Dear Ruth,

I hope you will accept my apologies for not writing so long. But I'm sorry to have to tell you that we had a very bad time last month. As usual here our little daughter was inoculated against pocks. (vaccinated) before the age of 1. This because of the danger of encephalitis after vaccination which occurs sometimes.

However within a week Meke, as we call her, had a very severe attack of convulsions and some days afterwards another attack which lasted about 14 hours. She was brought to the hospital, and the neurologist found it to be encephalitis. Her condition was very, very near to hopeless. This was 25th September, but gradually she recovered and now she has recovered to about the same standard as she was before her illness. She can stand with aid of a box, etc. and she is as lively as ever. So we hope and trust that the worst is over now and she will be as usual within a short time. So you will understand that during these very, very anxious weeks we had neither time nor interest in writing. But now, when situation levels much better, I take the time to write to you and to thank you very much indeed for all the nice and useful present you showered on us. I mean the toys and the tablecloth. We got it in good order. Meke is always playing with the blue and white toy you sent. She is always playing with it morning and night and she enjoys it very much.

In the summer holidays we, i.e. Hanna and I went with a group of children to Belgium in exchange for a group of Belgium children who visited our country some months before. The weather was superb, actually it was too hot. But anyhow we had no rain at all during the 22 days we were there. We were at Rochefurt in the Aidennes. In Richefurt which was still very much damaged because it was just at that spot that the Christmas offensive of Von Runnsled was broken up in December, 1944. But the surroundings are marvelous. We visited the famous "grott de Han"—you know, the dripping stone type. Most of the children never saw much surroundings for before the war they were too young and during the war there was no opportunity for it.

The organization was not what it ought to be but because of the very fine weather this did not hinder so much. We, i.e. Hanna and I, did not make any photos because as you know we lost our set in India and a teacher's salary is not a very big one nowadays.

Besides such an apparatus, at least a decent one, is very expensive here. So we have to depend on other people's photos. But we hope to find some good ones amongst them to send to you.

The last part of August we spent in Middelburg with our parents. I sent you a folder on the recovery of Walcheren. It was written in English with photos added. I hope it will be a help to you to understand the plight these people were in and are in now. For we had a very dry summer this year. As long as we have any written statistic about the weather and that is more than 250 years no summer was so dry as this one and that is very bad for the recovery of the salt soaked soil of Walcheren (a polder that was flooded with sea water). You know it needs rain, and rain to get the salt out of the soil. But nothing came this summer so that situation is worse this year than last year.

We have to apologize again for not noticing your birthday. But that day just was in our darkest hour and we just lived and did nothing but think of our little darling. But we hope to make good again for Christmas.

Ruth, dear, I have given you now an account of all our deeds, good and evil, of the last months. I must close now for it is about bedtime now. We all here, Hanna, Meke (sleeping quietly) and I thank you very much for the gifts and we hope to hear soon from you again.

Yours, Aad

+ + + + + + +

December 8, 1947 — Rotterdam

Dearest Ruth:
I am ashamed for not writing you in such a long time. But now I am sitting down at the table with your letter of November 12 before me and I will try to answer you. Aad has to work this

evening and he has gone away to school and is not back before 11 o'clock. I have put our little Meke in her bed and it is very quiet now in the house. Aad did write you already about the difficult months we had with the illness of our little darling. But now she is going quite right, She has had her first birthday Nov. 28 and on the occasion of this day we went with her to the photographer who took this picture of her. You see, she has not any curl in her hair, a high forehead and very large and pretty eyes. We did receive all your gifts, especially the toy Ribby mew-mew has become little Ineke's darling. She is always playing with it. You are so very kind for us, Ruth, and your letters are so interesting, especially that about your voyage to California, that I am always glad when there arrives a letter from you.

However, I am still so nervous. We did have so much sorrows and difficulties the last year that I always have a feeling of to be tired so much. In such a mood I cannot answer letters, I cannot go out in the fresh air with Ineke then I can't come to nothing. Did you ever have such moments in your life, Ruth? Many men and women in our country suffer from these post war nerves. It are the results of years of lack on food and the feeling of being chased by Germans or Japs. I must conquer it and I believe that gradually it becomes better and better.

When I was a child and in high school myself we too read Macbeth in the English literature lesson. I do remember it and when we had read it and translated in Dutch we went to the theatre with all the class and the English teacher where Macbeth was on the scene. We had a magnificent evening then. I was seventeen then and now I am 33. You see, I hope your pupils will enjoy Shakespeare as we enjoyed him.

I should like to be taken by you in your new car. You had before the war a green Chevrolet too, is it not? Green is your colour then? In our country it costs so much to live. Almost all the money Aad is earning I must give to buy food, clothing. When I bought a overcoat, black with a little fur collar I was glad to have it, for in a great warehouse this was the only coat they had in my measure (42) and I must give 350, precisely a month's salary of Aad.

Fur coats are rather expensive. Stockings, underwear, shoes, it is all so expensive that we can't hardly buy the things we do need.

The food is scarce and expensive too. Sugar, butter, bread, cheese are distributed (rations). Every week one person get 250 gram butter (2 sticks), 300 gram sugar (1 1/4 cup), 2000 g . bread, 50 g. cheese (2 1/2 slices), coffee, and tea 100 grams a month, soap 100 g. a fortnight (every two weeks). (An ounce equals 28 grams. One slice of cheese weighs 21 grams. One slice of bread, 28g.) Baby, she double ration, meat 400 g. a week (four hamburger patties). Though it is not so much, one has not a hungry feeling. Potatoes so much as you want you can buy. Fruits and vegetables, too. There are not enough houses. The new married couples have not a house of their own and are living in their parents' house. But when you compare circumstances here and in France, we are happy to live here. We hope that Marshall with his plan to help Europe will give us some of our prosperity back.

I'm awaiting a second child, Ruth. I am so glad to have a new baby that I can hardly believe it. After all those years we were married and did not see each other, you can't imagine how happy I am!

From Aad you have his kindest regards

Hanna

Chapter Thirteen

The Marshall Plan mentioned in these letters was first proposed by Gen. George Marshall, then Secretary of State under President Truman. It resulted in $13 billion in food, machinery, and products being sent to postwar Western European countries, Greece, and Turkey from 1948 to 1952 from the United States alone. (Eighteen other nations also made contributions toward the gargantuan effort.) Also called the European Recovery Act, it is credited with stymying the spread of Communism by easing the plight of the war ravaged survivors who might otherwise have been tempted to fall for the Marxist line.

It was gratifying in each succeeding letter to learn that conditions were slightly improved over the last few weeks or months. That held out hope to them that their lives might return to normal with hard work and patience plus the gifts and low term loans offered them. Exporting products for cash sales, while delaying the production of their own needs, was thought the better method in the long run to earn capital for rebuilding.

John Broekman described the economic situation in Holland continuing two years after the war and presented his philosophy on world economics. He foresaw the need for a united Europe which is slowly coming to pass 50 years later.

Hanna wrote about her family which now included a son, Hans. Living conditions had improved and things were getting back to prewar status.

Aad continued to cite the unrest in Indonesia, that is, the stifling of nationalism. He blamed the Japanese for continuing hostilities there.

Aad and Hanna were able to purchase some furniture from some friends who had moved from Rotterdam. Their home was quite comfortable now with four rooms on one level and a bedroom and storeroom downstairs.

January 15, 1948 — Rotterdam
Hogerbeetsstraat 14c (Blifdorp)
(Letter from Uncle John Broekman)

Dear Miss Sullivan,

Your card and letter were duly received about ten days ago. We thank you for what you wrote us, and in turn my family and myself are wishing you and your relatives happiness, health, and prosperity during 1948. May your country flourish and grow in wealth, and not suffer from strikes and riots.

Shipping in our port is going excellently. In 1947 the movement both in ships and cargoes was nearly 60% over that in 1946, and for 1948, when the Rhine navigation will be reviving as is expected under the new transportation scheme of the Occupying Forces in Germany, still better results are to be seen. Whatever there enters, the port can handle it at present and the dispatch of steamers is as quick and efficient as before 1940, in spite of all that is said from time to time by journalists or other men who have an interest in other ports, such as Hamburg/Bremen. Reconstruction will be finished by the middle of 1949, if nothing unforeseen happens.

As for my wife and myself, there is not much to report. Life goes on, and my wife has still trouble in getting what there is necessary for the household. Especially food and textiles remain scarce. Other articles are obtainable at prices a few hundred percent over the 1940 level, against an average increase of wages to 150-180% of these, which were then paid. You feel that many people have been hard hit, and an improvement of the situation is not seen.

During 1947 bread, meat, fat, milk, and cheese rations were reduced to some extent, and various articles which in the beginning of last year were free, are now again on the points list or included in existing rations. Eggs can be obtained one every three weeks. Textiles are shown in the shops in large quantities, but as nobody has sufficient "points" those who can profit of it are few. Prices are exceedingly high; one sees Czechoslovakian shirts and underwear, Spanish underwear and socks, and Spanish clothing. Dutch goods are lacking for a large part and what is offering is below the average grade. We produce excellent cotton and woolens of good quality, also rayon silks, which are going to foreign countries, mostly Argentina, Brasil, and other food exporting countries.

Shoes are allotted one pair every 18 months on points. Foreign shoes are freely obtainable at prices nearly 400% above prewar level. Under such circumstances it is but natural that a black market is still flourishing, and that also we now and then are violating the law. One has simply the choice of getting or getting not.

186

Coal is rationed at 12 units for the season. A unit is about 150 lb. of anthracite or soft coal (bituminous) or 280 lbs. of coke. One must accept what is allotted. Fortunately, there has up to now been no cold weather. It has been raining frequently and this helps dissolving the salt which penetrated into the soil of Walcheren and many other regions that were inundated by sea water during the war. On the other hand we are wanting frost to kill the vermins in the soil and prevent the trees from sprouting, as otherwise night frosts in April and May may spoil the young fruits. Please do not forget that on account of lack of foreign currency, we must try to come out with what our own soil produces, and Holland is nearly the most densely populated country of Europe. We had a good apple and pear crop in 1947, but oranges and lemons are a luxury. Importation of dried and canned fruits is forbidden.

You asked whether young people can find a home of their own. That is practically impossible except for the better classes who have connections. Young couples are compelled to live with other people, mostly with parents, so that real home life is an exception. If one of my sons should leave home, our remaining family would be too small for the number of rooms that we occupy, and two rooms will be embargoed and allotted to somebody who solicits at the Home Registration Office. To prevent foreign people of penetrating into the homes, mostly one tries to arrange for some relative or good friend to take the vacant space. This is allowed, but should one not do so, he runs the risk of seeing some day an entirely unknown person presenting an official document entitling to occupy the space, which must be placed at his disposal sufficiently furnished if required. The occupant must pay a rent for it, but the amount of same is low as compared with the value of the furniture, which is calculated on 1940 basis.

You will imagine that under such circumstances everybody is hoping for home building on a large scale, and then in the near future. Sorry to say, prospects are very poor, as the supply depends upon the material that can be placed at the disposal of constructors. In 1947 only a small number of homes were built, and for 1948 the government stopped the allotment of wood, cement, steel and brick for homes, turning the whole production over to utility building, which means factories, bank buildings, offices, bridges, and similar objects. Such are considered of more urgent need. Everything

187

is dominated by the necessity of exporting and so obtain money for food, fertilizers, iron and steel, lumber, etc.

You see, we are in a vicious circle and if I should have to give a plain answer to the question, "Are conditions in Holland improving?", I must say, "I guess, but I cannot confirm." The official statistics show an enormous increase of exports and the mercantile papers are very optimistic for 1948 in this respect, at the same time adding that prospects for an improvement of the standard of living in the near future remains poor, and that even in 1952, when the Marshall scheme should be fully executed, we will have to reckon with conditions that remain a good deal below 1940.

Indonesia remains the main problem. You know what my opinion is about the question as a whole, but you will at the same time have to admit that with a war stricken country, it is a Herculean task maintaining an army both in Europe and Asia of about 150,000 men, who in normal times might have done excellent work in relieving the labour shortage here. Not only do they produce nothing; they cost enormous sums of money, not to speak of the many hands which are necessary here to provide them with supplies of all kinds. Nevertheless, we must pull through, and we hope that the news which is received here about the Indonesian problem, may soon turn for the better. It should not be forgotten that before the World War, Indonesia was the most powerful producing center of colonial products of all kinds, and also for the United States, it is essential that our former colonies are soon providing them with tobacco, rubber, vegetable oils, copra, chinchone bark, spices, and so on. Should Indonesia be pacified, it may be relied upon that in f.i. 1950, it will supply as much as in 1939, and perhaps more, because the so-called outer possessions or small islands in the Eastern part of the Archipelago, which at that time were practically of no value for Indonesia's economy now are intensely pioneered and already exporting in fair quantities.

I understand the Americans will be fully aware of the dangers connected with the possibility of Europe having to stop buying foreign goods and submit to a period of hardship and famine solely because of the lack of hard currency. Should this happen, the production of a large number of articles in the world will be far in excess of the needs, and price falls and idleness will be the consequence. Between World Wars I and II this happened and history is there to show what will happen if such essential facts are neglected.

It is for this reason that I hope the American Government will not be handicapped too much by criticism of certain Deputees or Senators who—although they may be clever and most honest men—do not possess the broad view over the complicated economical and governmental system that is called Europe. The United States are a vast region extending from Atlantic to Pacific without customs barriers and a factory in Vermont or Massachusetts has only to reckon with inland carriage cost when selling to Arizona or Oregon. In Europe, however, there are entirely different standards of life, currencies, import duties, restrictions as a result of the war, etc., all obstacles to pass over. It may be easy to say to Europe, "Do away with import duties" but the result will be chaos all over. And how is it with protective duties in the United States? I guess that an enormous number of factory and other people would violently protest if your own Government should abolish import duties and, for example, Holland with her extremely low production cost starting to spoil the market by offering prices that are far below every American production cost. And this is easily possible and no dumping.

Please do not think I am a protectionist. On the contrary, I believe in free trade as most conducive to good living conditions all over the world be it that at present there must exist guided economics in a large part of it. The large differences in wages prevent industries in several countries from protecting themselves against price cutting by competition out of low standard regions. To reach the ideal, Europe wants time. Benelux (Belguim, Netherlands, and Luxembourg) is a good example of three partners uniting to defend interests they have in common, and maybe other countries will join within a reasonable period. To obtain results in this respect, proper and careful action is necessary, and many obstacles should be removed.

I hope you will excuse me for writing things so openly. Maybe many a person will disagree with me, and if he can prove that I am wrong, I am glad to admit. For the rest, Dear Miss Sullivan, I will gladly help you if you want news regarding some object for you Club Program in March, and then I expect you will write me.

With best wishes, believe me.

Yours sincerely, J. Broekman

189

+ + + + + + +

3 Februari, 1948 — Rotterdam

Dearest Ruth,

A magnificent doll for Ineke (N-ne-k stress on the first syllable) and the handkerchiefs and shawl for us. This was your Christmas parcel which we got a fortnight ago. It was marvelous, and we should thank you for it very heartily. Ineke and I, with a big kiss. When she saw the doll, she began to reach for it with both hands. We named her "Ruth", but as Ineke cannot yet speak except "wa, fa, me, be", the name is only used by Aad and me now.

Do you like children very much, Ruth? We did not speak about this subject in all the time we are writing each other now. I liked children, but now I have one of my own, it is as if I am feeling a love so strong, as I never felt in my life. It is a love without any feeling of sece (self) or egoism.

This afternoon our Queen Wilhelmina spoke to the Allies of the Second World War about Indonesia. Did you hear her? She is an old woman now and very idealistic. She thinks, with goodwill of both the Dutch and the Indonesians all will come right, and they and we can live with each other in peace and prosperity. Freedom for the Indonesians! But people who were in Java, as Aad and I were, and saw how dumb 90 per cent of the people are (as they can't read nor write) know that it is a too difficult task to bring this people so far that they can govern themselves in the way that there is rest and safety for the common man. We are sure that it will end in murder and chaos. We saw it with our own eyes two years ago, and now it is not much more better. Every month a ship goes to Java with our soldiers, young men, away from their studies or work to serve two years in the army overseas to protect Dutch and good willing Javanese against the extremistic elements. And in many a family is fear about the fate of their men for often occurs, that a soldier is assassinated by one of the extremistic Indonesians.

Yesterday we went to the last film of Walt Disney named "Fantasia" to the music of the great Beethoven, Schubert, Stravinsky, a.s.o. He created fantastic stories. It was all drawing (cartooning). We appreciated it very much and could not imagine how Walt Disney came to such an idea.

Aad gives you many greetings. From me much love,
Your Hanna

190

7th October, '48 — Rotterdam
(Letter from Aad)

Dear Ruth,

I know we are very busy since Hans did his appearance here. During the holidays, i.e. July and August, we stayed at home, and we were only one week at Middelburg, (You know, Walcheren) and the rest we played quite a bit of tennis. The last week of August and the beginning of September saw the Jubilee of our Queen Wilhelmina and the start of the new reign of Queen Juliana. I presume you know quite a bit of it in the papers or on the movies. Therefore, we refrained of sending you clipping. Our papers are still very thin due to lack of paper and the quality is bad, too. Of course, we heard everything over the radio which was moving, especially the abdication (of the King of England and Wally Simpson).

I'm crowded with work. Besides that I'm playing hockey (tennis nearly finished) and quite a bit of bridge, which means a lot of work.

Our little son is growing excellently. He is laughing always especially when you go to his little bed, and we are all very fond of him. Ineke is very fond of her little brother. She is also quite O.K. She walks like mercury and starts talking a bit, which is quite amusing as you will know yourself.

But something else first. On behalf of the whole family many happy returns of the day to you. We sent a little present on your birthday, but we had forgotten the export regulations so we got it back to get export paper. For that reason your birthday present will be late. Of course, we are very sorry, but it can't be helped. I only tell you that it is made in Holland. For the rest you have to guess. By the way many thanks for the booklets and descriptive letters of your holiday in Washington.

Until next time, many greeting from all of us.

Hans, Ineke, Hanna, and Aad

+ + + + + + +

Hanna and Hans   Ineke and Hans

3 December, 1948 — Rotterdam

Dearest Ruth,

I hope you got your birthday present, and I hope you can use it on one of your frocks. It is so difficult to send a parcel to anyone in another country. You must have a special permit and a special reason to do it. Generally one can buy several things now a day which were not to be had one or two years ago. One can buy stockings and shoes so much as one needs. Sugar, soap, bread, milk, you can buy so much as you want. Clothing is more difficult and all you buy is very expensive.

Fortunately, Aad has a job, in which he earns enough to feed us and then there is a bit of money left to buy a good book, to go to the theatre now and then or to buy a new frock for the children. We filled out our home with quite a little bit of furniture. We got it from friends who were going to emigrate to South Africa. They did like to go, as quite a lot of people here because there is a big over population here and went because they want to change after the war. They want to see something new, something fresh, and they are afraid to be mixed here in a new war.

Our friends sold out everything they possessed, and we bought quite a lot. We have a quite comfortable home now. On the ground floor we have two rooms which are coupled to each other by a set of two glass doors. One room is Aad's study. The other is the room in which we live, in which the children play, where I am sewing. We are eating also there. When the children at night in bed, we go to sit in Aad's study, and we are very comfortable then with a book, a cup of tea, and sometimes the radio. On the same floor we have got the kitchen, a small bathroom and a room where the children are sleeping. Downstairs there is one bedroom and a store room, actually a cellar. We are very glad with this house. There are so many people who don't have a house and are forced to live in one house together with their parents with all the difficulties which are the result of living together, especially when there are little children or babies. Which holiday are you going to come and see us—our country, our cities, our health, our tulip fields, our wind mills, our plagues (scars of war) and last, but not least, us and the children? You would be very welcome here.

Lots of love, Hanna

Many greetings from Aad and from the children a kiss for Auntie Ruth.

+ + + + + + +

Hanna and Aad continued being troubled over the seemingly endless conflict within Indonesia. Also closer to home, the Cold War between the Communist Blok and the Western Capitalist countries kept up a high stress level. Would there be a Third World War among the supporters of these two ideologies with the added threat of nuclear power being available now?

Dec. 31st, 1948 — Rotterdam
Schieweg 251 A
(Letter from Aad)

Dear Ruth,

As the postmark shows you, we are spending some days in Middelburg (southwest part near the coast) with my parents. We came there Thursday, 23rd of December, and we are staying until 3rd or 4th of January

The Christmas days were cold, about 5 degrees (Celcius) below zero (freezing—about 25 degrees F.), but as is usual in our country in one day the weather changes, and now it is 5 degrees above (about 40 degrees F.), and a storm is blowing from the valley with quite a bit of rain. But within the room it is quite comfortable. The fire is going full blast, and the radio is playing soft music, so what!

We are very surprised. The Dutch in general and especially those who have been in Indonesia, over the attitude taken by quite a lot of countries (also by yours) in the Indonesian trouble. The point is that most people who make a lot of din about it know nothing about it. They think that we are trying to stifle sane nationalism, but that is nonsense. The so-called Zepveblik is an outgrowth of the Japanese occupation. In fact, quite a lot of Japanese deserters keep the hostilities going for that is the only way of keeping themselves out of the Allies' court-martials.

The tourists are all common bands of robbers, looters, etc. who play havoc among the civil population, i.e. the natives themselves. The Republic government has nothing to tell about them. They obey no orders, they do what they like. And the republic had no power whatsoever to take efficient counter measures. So it is quite necessary that action was taken against them. And the course of it shows very clear that the whole so-called T.N.T. (the Army) fell apart in small bands. I feel that quite a lot of Republic government officials will be quite happy that the time of unrest is over now. But another time more about it.

From all of us, Hans, Ineke, Hanna and me—all the best wishes for the now coming year.

Yours, Aad

+ + + + + + +

26 Jan., '49

Dearest Ruth,

Thanks for the Christmas cards you sent us. I hope you got ours too. A happy New Year, that is what we want you to have. Though the world is still in disorder, and we, as West European people, fear to be ground to dust in future between East and West—between Russia and America, our life is more easy the last year. We can buy the things we want although they are very

194

expensive. We can buy enough food, eggs, flour, etc. Nobody has to be hungry, fortunately.

We can buy a frock and stockings again. Nylon stockings very expensive 10 guilders. (You must know, Aad earns about 350 guilders a month, as a teacher high school. A labourer about 50 guilders a week (about 200 guilders a month when he is schooled.)

I bought a silk frock last week—a blue one with great flowers— 30 guilders, a pair of shoes—20 guilders, and the stockings of 10 guilders. I enjoy to be dressed in new things now.

Our children are very healthy now. Ineke begins to speak now. The toys you send on her second birthday we did not receive yet. Perhaps they are coming in a few days.

My mother knitted a frock for her of blue wool. She enjoyed to knit for her granddaughter. Till now she was not in the opportunity, for having no wool. Only young mothers had a permit to buy some. But now all those things are for everybody to buy.

Much love from Ineke, Hans, Aad and me.

Hanna

Aad and Hanna on a bicycling tour—Summer, 1949

Chapter Fourteen

It had been 10 years since Hanna and Aad were married and had moved to Indonesia. Hanna reminiscenced about those years and some of the things that had happened to them.

During this period, letters from Hanna to Ruth were not as frequent, but it was obvious that their friendship had not waned. Packages were still being sent, and sentiments of humble gratitude remained foremost in Hanna's thoughts.

In 1958, Hanna's mother passed away. Hanna urged Ruth to travel to Holland.

January 25, 1950 — Rotterdam

Dearest Ruth,

You are a darling to send us all these beautiful presents we received at January 2. We had a fine Christmas at home with the children this year. We bought a Christmas tree and several glittering bells, birds, etc. to hang them in the tree. The children were so glad we had electric lights in it too. When the children were in bed at night, Aad and I had a little dinner which I had prepared. Do you eat a Christmas rabbit or chicken? We do. We finished with pineapple and later on coffee.

On 31 December we went to Middelburg to my parents-in-law with our Ineke. She is 3 1/2 now and old enough to go with us in the train for 3 hours. We left Hans at home and we asked Aunt Clazien to come and look after him for a few days. She likes to do such things and she enjoyed herself very much with little children, although she herself has already sixty years.

We had five days in Middelburg awaiting the new year 1950 and my parents-in-law were very glad to have us in their house and Ineke very glad to stay there so her grandfather and grandmother and her other grandfather and grandmother (great-grandparents) who are both still alive.

When we came back at Jan. 2, there was your parcel. The first thing we did was to open it. We were very glad with all these beautiful things, myself with the tablecloth. I use it daily. When the work is done at night and the children to bed and we have some tea, I put it on the table in the living room. Aad with his pen. He is anxious to know what to do when it is empty? He is very proud of it and shows it to everyone. The colour is bright green and often people say "Aad, what do you have there, a pen, a pencil? And he very proud. "O, a pen I got from America from a sweet friend." We have such pens too in the shops here. I myself got one. I am writing with it but the colours are only brown and black and they don't write so easily as yours.

How are you, Ruth? Glad to work in your new school building? I am so busy with the household and the two little children that I am tired at night. In the morning I say to myself, tonight you must have a chat with Ruth, but then I am often too tired to write the difficult English words. It should be much more easy if you lived here. I should take my bicycle and go to you for a chat and a cup of tea. Tomorrow it is 10 years ago Aad and I married and went to the Indies. We did find so much troubles, but so much pleasures too on our way in these 10 years that I wonder it were only 10. When we went away we were both 25 years. Now we are 35, but when I think about the time, I was 25, I think, I was only a child that never had some trouble serious enough to make you ill or nervous and I thought that I would have my life just as I wanted it. Now I have learned that troubles and sorrow come that you can't do nothing against it and that you can learn much through it. In these 10 years we have lost everything we had, except our life and each other's love, and we have learned that we lost but a little. Now we are very happy to have a house again and our two children. We are busy now. When we have some money, a thing in the household, a beautiful chair, a new bookcase for Aad, a painting on the wall. Gradually, we shall have a real home again.

Clothes we can buy here as much as we want. They are very expensive, but they are good. Shoes, stockings, as much as you want.

The children are so glad with your presents. The great car with the little cars is the whole day in the little hands of Hans. He loves it very, very much. I am sending some snapshots Aad took this year. We will take some from the children when they are playing with your toys.

Ruth, do send us some news from you.

Lots of love from all four of us, but especially from me.

Your friend Hanna

+ + + + + + +

After five postwar years and the birth of two children, Hanna and Aad settled down to a more normal existence. Summer and

winter vacations seemed to be very important—both from the
standpoint of rest and relaxation, and also to escape the frustra-
tions of long tedious rainy weather and the stress of living in a
heavily populated country. Perhaps having had such severe trauma
in their early married life, "taking time to smell the roses" was even
more essential to their family.

June 15, 1950 — Rotterdam

Dear Ruth,

We are sorry that you have gone through such a misery of serious illness. This is the first time we heard from you about an operation. I myself never was operated and I can't imagine what it is to have an narcose (narcotic). Aad has been operated once when we lived in Indonesia and he was very nervous before it. We are so happy you have finished it all, and we hope you feel better now.

I am glad you liked the book Roll Back the Sea. We ourselves read it in Dutch. Of course, it has been written by one of our best writers, and though it is a novel, the circumstances in which the novelist's persons live are just as they were in war and post war time.

It is a pity for you that you can't offer yourself such a trip as you did last year in your vacances. We enjoyed your letters, your fotos and your picture cards very much. You wrote about your trip in such an amusing and pretty manner that it seemed as if we travelled there to the mountains and the strange and far away cities and villages. But better to have your rest now. Don't ask too much from your self, Ruth, that is not good, I believe.

Aad's school is ending July 15. We go with the children to a little watering place named Hoek of Holland. There is a beach where the children can play the whole day in the sand. We can bathe, read a book for which we could not find the time and I hope, that I can knit some underwear for the children to wear when it is winter again. We stay there a fortnight. The voyage is not far, one hour with the train from Rotterdam. When we come back, we go to Middelburg to my parents-in-law for a fortnight. They are happy when we are there. They amuse themselves with the children, just as you do with your little niece.

The foto I am sending has been made by Aad. Ineke is holding the doll you send her 2 years ago. The doll is an invalide now; her head is broke and repaired, you see she burst on the foto, but it is Ineke's most beloved darling. She is sleeping, eating, dressing with her and her name is Ruth.

Dear Ruth, kisses from me and the children, greetings from Aad and best wishes.

Your Hanna

Ineke and Hanna
(Ineke holding American doll named Ruth)

January 23, 1956

Dearest Ruth:

You spoiled us as ever with the big Christmas parcel. We got it 3 days ago. You see, the post office is so busy with Christmas and New Year, especially in a bay town as Rotterdam is, that most of the gift parcels from overseas are staying for a long time in the offices. But the joy of the children was not a bit less. They enjoyed immensely unpacking the parcel.

Now it is bad weather here, rain and rain. We had our vacation with Christmas in Austria at 4000 feet in the White mountains in a very lovely little village near Innsbruck. We were on skis the whole day in the fresh snowy air and we enjoyed ourselves very much. At 6 January we came home again.

Did you ever any winter sport? We never did, but it was so wonderful that we should like to go again next year.

Dear Ruth, many thanks for that lovely parcel and lots of love from all.

Your friend, Hanna

+ + + + + + +

12 September, 1956 — Rotterdam

Dearest Ruth,

Such an interesting letter was this of July 29 in which you took us with you traveling from your home to Reathel in California. We went with you in the train, we gave our luggages to these Redcaps too. We ate dinner with you and stood with you at 4:30 in the morning at the train window enjoying the scenery of the mountains. No doubt, you have a gift for writing.

We were glad to hear that you spent your vacances in such a pleasant and wonderful interesting way. To have seen Mexico! Yes, I can imagine how the trip with the ski lift was. I myself went often in it when we were skiing in Austria last winter. It is a wonderful view from such a little chair, is not it?

We spend our vacances from 1-30 August on Renesse again— that little cute watering place on one of the Zeeland Islands. It is so quiet there, our hotel lying behind the first row of dunes. When the children awake in the morning, they went to the beach to play in the sand, looking for shells a.s.o. We possess a rubber boat, an emergency raft, which can be blown up, and there was no more fun as to go with it in the sea, when the gulfs were high.

Four days before we went to Renesse, I broke my leg at the tennis court. Fortunately it was not a complicated fracture, and I was allowed to have gipsun at which I could walk. I had no pain. Unfortunately I could not go swimming which I like so much. I did everything on my leisure most of the day in an easy chair at the beach with a book or a needle work. It was years and years ago that I sat with a needle work on my lap, it was in the first year of our marriage when I came in the former East Indies and had but a few things to do. But I do like such work. This one is a white linen tablecloth and I make it full of crosses in red, brown, and gold yellow.

I believe I am growing too old to play tennis any longer. I am 42 now but my doctor says it is just an accident and even children break their bones very often when they are falling. But I don't know whether I will play tennis again who this time the broke bone is cured again. Tomorrow morning the gipsum is take away.

This year it is 350 years ago that the famous painter Rembrandt was born. In Amsterdam was an exposition of his works brought together from all parts of the world. The exposition was famous and unique and drew a lot of visitors from all part of the world too. From Sept. 1 till October 15, the exposition is in Rotterdam in one of our museums and of course we go visiting with the children.

The newspapers are full of the difficulties coloured people have to live in the U. S. especially in Kentucky.

(The rest of this letter regarding the Civil Right's movement is missing)

+ + + + + + +

Monday, 22 October, 1956

Dearest Ruth,

Although I really know since how many years that your birthday is October 14, I forget it this time. Thousands of excuses! I can say that I was so busy or any other reason, but that does not help me. I forget it, that is all and I am so sorry about it and a bit ashamed, too.

When I had a look at the calendar last Saturday with the purpose to see what day Ineke's birthday was, I at once was aware that it was too late to write you at the occasion of yours. I said to the children who had the afternoon free from school "Come on to the city, we go and see in the shops if there is a nice thing to send to Auntie Ruth that she can see we love her so much." Both of the children admired the shawl. I am sending you now by air mail so we bought it.

Ineke is now in the 4th year at school. Hans in the 3rd. They are already nearly 10 and 8 years old. Ineke has many difficulties in school with learning. Hans not at all. They have a good health.

Dearest, till the next time, many regards from us all.

Your Hanna

+ + + + + + +

2 Jan., 1957

Dearest Ruth,

Luckily, on Monday 24 Dec. your parcel arrived. Everybody was at home. The vacances had just begun and the parcel was in the middle of the table and the four of us among it. The children had so much pleasure and were so excited about all those beautiful things that came out of this box of Pandora. Much thanks. You gave us a delightful afternoon and besides we are so glad with the playthings and especially with the earrings and hair pins. Such things are not yet here. Besides, most women here do not wear earrings. I did not have any, but now I have plenty at once (ha, ha) Aad and Hans very glad too. All the things you mentioned in your letters were there. I had to pay some money to the post, not much—2 guilders.

What lovely letter papers you send me! Here is one, only for all the things I have to tell you, dearest Ruth, it is too small. This is the last of those papers you receive. Next time, it is as usually on air mail paper and these beautiful papers I take when writing to my friends here in Holland to let them see how lovely things I received from my dearest friend from America. Do you feel quite right again after the accident with your car? The broke rib was painful I think? The picture of the new car is very beautiful. We hope you will have many pleasant hours in it. We wish you a very happy 1957 too with many joys and few sorrows.

How is your new home? Does it agree with you? Do you like it? Have you time enough for cooking for yourself and have you someone who is cleaning the house? Or do you do it all by yourself? We should like to receive a picture of your living room and, especially of your kitchen. I hear Americans have kitchens with all modern facilities. Have you too?

Kisses from the children, from Aad and me lots of love.

Your Hanna

+ + + + + + +

July 26, 1957 — Rotterdam

Dearest Ruth,

In answering your letter from May this year in which you told us that the school year was almost over, we wonder whether you went to California to take Reathel back with you to Herrin. Another school year is here almost over too. Aad is very tired and he too is glad with his 6 weeks vacances. The year was over Juli 20 and the new year starts Sept.3.

The children had a good year. Hans is going now in his fourth year, Ineke goes to the fifth class They both are swimming fine and they begin to play tennis too. They are very healthy fortunately. In the neighbourhood of Rotterdam, in the centre of rich pastures, in a landscape of mills, cows, pasture, flowers and water, there flows the "Rotte", a little river where on her boards (banks) Rotterdam was formed a few centuries ago. About 20 miles from Rotterdam there is its origin in the pasture and after a few miles the little river becomes broader and broader and there is a lake. Further on the lake grows smaller again and the river goes to Rotterdam. But the lake is beautiful and there we go very often in summer especially when we have some hot days as we had a few weeks ago. Earlier we went by bicycle and we did not go so often because it was 1 1/2 hour by bicycle but now we bought 2 small motor cycles. Ineke and Hans on the duo sit and now it takes us 3/4 hour. We can have there a swim, we can lay in the grass with a book, the children can play there, it is a very lovely place.

We bought a little spoon for you, the flowers are daffodils which are so very beautiful here in the springtime. When you enjoy it, we can send you for instance an occasion of your birthday more of such spoons with all sorts of other spring flowers, tulips or hyacinths. You must write us when you should like to have more.

Aug. 4 we leave Rotterdam for Renesse, a little place on a little island in the province Zeeland. We are there during August in a little hotel, 20 beds, so not too noisy and we hope to have warm weather to enjoy the beach, the water, the dunes, the flowers, the birds and the silence. For life in a great city makes you very tired. The traffic, the people crowded in the streets and the fast way of living of everybody. It is good to be a few weeks out of this all.

Lots of love from Aad and the children.

Hanna

+ + + + + + +

203

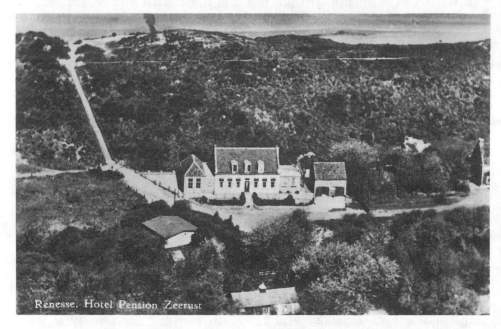

Summer vacation resort visited many times by the family
(Note the sea behind the dunes.)

Canal transportation (1995 photo)

17 January, '58

Dearest Ruth,

Yesterday we get your Christmas parcel. It had been a long time underway as you wrote in Ineke's birthday letter that you bought already the presents. It was again a fine surprise when the post man came on 12:15, just when the children came from school to eat their lunch. We all four were so anxious to see what was in the box you sent. And there were all the parcels so carefully packed and with its lovely contents. The bracelet, the ear clips, the red and green writing sets, the play games, the ballpoint, the shawl, especially so lovely. The comb set and the stockings we all thank you very heartily. It was a fine day, the American parcel day. The bracelet was on Ineke's arm the same afternoon she went to school and so it was with the writing set. Hans was not in such a hurry. He said "I'm not such a show-fellow" (ha, ha). I hope you received the Christmas card we sent you from Tirol (middle Europe, Austria). We went with the children during the Christmas vacances with the train to Tirol to a little village 1300 mi. above the sea level to do winter sports, a bit of ski walking enjoying the sunshine a.s.o. It was a very fine holiday. We enjoyed ourselves very much and the fortnight we were there was far too short. Jan. 5 we were at home again. The sun had a bit burned our skin and we were feeling very happy and healthy. In our country, life in wintertime is very difficult. November and December are very wet and foggy, (we live here especially in the west part under the sea level as you know) and almost everybody is catching a cold.

In Januari we have a chance that the temp becomes under zero and that the sun sometimes is shining, but very often also in Jannari the clouds are hanging low and the sun is behind them. Februari and March are often cold and stormy (and snowy) and we all are glad when April comes, however the man in the streets says: little April love gives us sometimes a white hat (snow) so many people who can afford love to go a few weeks in more healthy climate, as it is in the mountains in the middle of Europa.

Lots of love from Aad and me,
Kisses from the children

+ + + + + + +

205

Ineke and Hans skating on a canal with
their grandmother, Oma de Bruijn

23 Sept., '58 — Rotterdam

Dearest Ruth,

    I must write you to send you a sad message. My mother died last week, Wednesday Sept 17.

    When she came back from vacances at August from the North of Sweden, she was so tired, but had no pain. The doctor ordered her to the hospital for photos and other treatments, but they did not know what illness she had. In a fortnight she went down from a very stark and joyous woman to a weak poor creature, and there was no hope for us to hold her with us. She died, as she lived, quiet, without difficulties.

    The children especially have a great loss. She was a grandmother, one in a thousand. She went with them swimming and wandering. They both liked to go to "Oma's", though she was 74 years old. The most sad work of the moment is to go to her house and to make the house empty for a couple of new married people to live in the house. I think to do it next week.

I thank you for your birthday greeting from August 19. It was the time at which my mother's illness began. We think that it was a certain shape of cancer, but we are not sure so are not the doctors.

We all are very quiet about her death. She had a very beautiful life without sadness or illness or sorrows, exceptions during the war years when Aad and I were in Indonesia and she lost my father, whom she adored.

After the war, when we were home again and she had the joy who gave our children her, she often said she was very happy. That is a great relief for us.

With many greetings and lots of love,
Your Hanna

+ + + + + + +

25 November, '58 — Rotterdam

Dearest Ruth,

I thank you very much for your words of sympathy after my mother's death. I read some of your letters again this evening. A cold evening after a very still cloudy and foggy day. Aad is busy with his pupils' papers now and then he is sighing, for like you, he believes that most of the pupils are more dumb and uninteresting than a few years ago. Generally, he has classes of 20-25 pupils to learn them chemistry and physics, but he is glad when he can give 5 of them a high grade. The marks are from 1-10:

10 excellent	5 doubtful
9 very good	4 unsufficient
8 good	3 bad
7-6 sufficient	2 very bad

Sometimes he is giving a 10, most of the marks are between 7 and 4. Especially the girls have difficulties with Aad's lessons, some boys sees in him a specimen of a mental father and visit us sometimes in the evening to speak about some things they will not or cannot discuss at home with their own family.

You read about the Brussels Fair and you did see fotos of the Royal Dance with our princesses as guests. I did not see the Fair because of my mother's illness, but in the first days of October,

207

friends of us, a doctor's family with a car invited us to go with them in the car to Brussel. We should go at 2 p.m. in the afternoon and be back very late in the evening. Aad said we must go, it should be good for me. Aunt Clazien used the same words. She should cook dinner for the children and herself and so we went. It was a magnificent Fair so great and vast. And in the evening everywhere flash lights and fountains with all colours of the rainbow.

Where to eat? In Hungary or in Russia or in Belgium or in France? We had a roasted chicken in a Belgium eating house and it was perfect. At 10 o'clock we returned and as it is a 150 km with some formalities at the boundary, we were at 12:30 at home. I was glad we went there though. The time was too short to see much of the foreign houses. Aad went 3 or 4 times. The house of science was very important for him. You did not drive far away in your vacances, well?

I think your mother is glad that you are so often near her. I hope she will live many years for when your mother is dead, you realize so well what an important place she had in your life.

The children and I are able now to think about my mother and to remember how happy the last 10 years of her life were. She often occupied herself with them, went swimming with them and went to the zoo which is in our neighborhood. She was very quiet the last years, lived in her house and once a year she made a great trip to North Africa, Italy, and last summer to Lapland. Traveling that was her hobby. She could tell very much about her voyages and it was all very interesting.

Aad Broekman is very well. He does fiddle his bass in his empty hours, but he is very busy with his job as the assistant of a great cargo line. He married an English girl, but I wrote it to you six years ago, I guess. They have 2 little daughters now. We see each other now and then and spend the evening with playing bridge.

We are enjoying the numbers of Life magazine you sent us. We read in the papers that in the U.S.A. the small cars are bought now, and you wrote it in your letter too. In our country there are not so much big cars, only very rich people, doctors, specialists, businessmen etc. have one. Half of the teachers in Aad's school have a small car, a German or an English (Morris or Austin) or a French one. The price of a new small car is +/- 4000. Aad is learning car driving now and when he has done his examination, perhaps that we are going to think about such a small car for to make trips during the holidays. It seems delightful. But at a monthly salary of 1000 it is a great luxury. Our bicycles with motor we are using daily are now our faithful friends for covering the distance in town and neighborhood. The children are sitting comfortably behind our backs.

We had Gerda Hoss visiting us a few days ago. She came quite unexpected and at first I did not know who she was. We had a very cheerful conversation. Ineke and Hans were speechless and looked steady to her face, listened the words from her mouth. A person who had seen Auntie Ruth so very near! You are a sort of fancy person so far away you know and never to see. But now they know that you are of flesh and blood for Gerda brought a ring, a very charming one the whole family admired then. Many thanks, Ruth!

We asked Gerda all about you, if your foto was well and how you talked and lived. It was a wonderful evening. I asked Gerda why you did not make a trip to Europe during all these years. I do write you what she said: "I think, she would like to go, but she needs someone who says to her, 'Come on, Ruth. Here is your ticket and now you go to Europe and to Hanna.' " Now, Ruth, go and find anyone, who says these words to you. Your mother or sister perhaps. Or Reba, your loving niece who is so young and perhaps very enthusiastic for such a voyage. Gerda is now graduated from High School as you wrote. That is with a congratulation, I guess. Will you do her our greetings.

Many lots of love from your Hanna

+ + + + + + +

Dec., 19, 1959

Dearest Ruth:

Thanks for your letter Oct. 22nd. Ineke's birthday card which she enjoyed very much because she is learning English now since she went in September to another school. She was so proud with her American aunt and took the card with her to school. Thanks for the Life's. We read then from beginning to end. To us such dream kitchens are only for millionaire, but not for the middle classes to which a teacher at high school belongs.

We bought our car second handed an Opel, a German car from 1955. We are very fond of it and often have a drive. I'm going to learn to drive. Next Thursday we are going with the children and the car to Austria to a little village in the mountains where we will enjoy sun and snow. At Jan. 7 we will be back. We hope you have a merry Christmas.

Many greetings, especially to your mother too. Love,

Aad, the children and me—Hanna

They must have changed their minds about driving to Austria. Perhaps packing four people and their belongings proved too crowded for an Opel, or the weather may have been a deterrent.

February 6, 1959

Dearest Ruth:

We got your Christmas box the day before we went away to the Austrian Alps for having a winter holiday. We were packing our bags when your box came. The children were at home and Aad too and we all forget our bags to pack at first see what the box contained. It was all very nice and so carefully packed. Many thanks, Ruth. I did not pay much here. It is always fun when your box comes from the postman.

All things you mentioned in your letter from 21 Dec. were in the box. No such curtains we don't use. I did never seen them here, but perhaps it is as with many things you sent us in the past: after a few months or after a year they appear in our magazine too. The plates with the red flowers and the paper napkins we took in our bag and we used them at Christmas in the farmer's house in a very little village high in the mountains in Austria. They were very cosy. We went away Dec. 23 by train in the afternoon. We dined and sleeped in the train, while he was carrying us through Germany along the Rhine. The next day 10 o'clock we were in Austria and went the last miles by bus 1 1/2 hour climbing in the mountains till we were in Gerlos, the name of the little village. There was snow. We went skiing, walking and lying in the sun. We lived in a farmer's house two bedrooms, a sitting room and the use of the kitchen. So we were not in a hotel but I cooked the meals. Now the children are older and help a hand it is less expensive than to be in an hotel with 4 persons.

The children and Aad and I too enjoyed ourselves very much. After 14 days we went back to our own country where it rained and the sun days and days behind the clouds was. We got a great deal of health there in Austria. Aad took a lot of photografs. I am sending you some of them. So Ruth, I did thank you for your Christmas gifts. I decided to do this in Januari, but always postponed it. Sorry.

Many love you, Hanna

Hanna vacationing in Austrian Alps

Chapter Fifteen

December, 1960–December, 1964

Life in the 60's brought many changes to the Muijser family. In February, 1960, Aad changed jobs and moved to a position at the University of Delft to teach chemistry to young students who had already completed one year of study. It was apparent that teachers' salaries in Holland were much like those in America. That is, educators were frequently underpaid when compared to those in other more highly regarded professions. Burdensome income taxes to pay for increased social programs such as free schools, health care, and defense measures took a toll on incomes, and the idea of becoming affluent was a mere Dutch fantasy.

Contents of the letters reveal the close, personal relationship between Ruth and Hanna. Details of vacations, exchange of photographs and gifts, views on political events, and news of extended families indicate that they became like sisters to one another. The concern that Ruth showed over the years for Hanna and her family contributed to a continuing correspondence and a desire that they would someday be able to meet in person, to gaze into each others eyes, to hug one another, and feel the reality of their long established friendship which was divided by miles of land and ocean. From young girls in high school to womanhood, their devotion and commitment never failed nor faltered.

News of America continued to be of great interest in Holland. The election of John F. Kennedy as president of the United States and the defeat of Richard Nixon were headline news. Hanna expressed hope that peace would again reign in their country and that the United States and Russia would be able to settle their differences without another war. The fear of war remained in the hearts of the people in Holland, and they had not forgotten the terrible devastation brought about by the Germans under the command of Adolph Hitler. They longed for "rest and peace."

However, on April 17, 1961, a Cuban rebel invasion called the Bay of Pigs that was planned in the United States to unseat the Communist dictator Fidel Castro was a failure. Encouraged by that, the Russians steathily brought in missiles capable of reaching many U.S. cities. In October, 1962, President Kennedy ordered a blockade and called out 14,000 Reservists before the Soviet Premier Nikita Khrushchev backed down and agreed to dismantle the *missiles. There were very tense weeks when Americans prepared their homes against radiation debris fallout. They built bomb shelters, stored food and water for a two weeks' duration (the length of time believed to be the most critical against radiation sickness), sealed their windows and doors, and did whatever else seemed crucial to protect their families.*

Earlier in 1961 the continuing conflict over the portion of Berlin that was controlled by the French, British, and Americans versus the USSR's desire to regulate the entire former capital kept tensions high in Europe as well. In August of 1961 the East Germans built the infamous Berlin Wall to prevent their citizens from fleeing to the West. One must remember the Dutch were not fond of either the East or West Berliners, recalling the cruelty that came from that capital.

On November 22, 1963 President John F. Kennedy was assassinated in Dallas, Texas, and Lyndon B. Johnson became president. Meanwhile at the same time in The Netherlands, Hanna and Aad had moved to Enschede, on the east side of the country near the German border, 250 miles from Rotterdam. Aad was asked to teach at a new university still in the planning stages. The idea of a campus with student and faculty housing was a new concept in Holland and a challenge. Hanna wondered if the idea for such a facility would be a good and an acceptable one.

12 Januari, 1960

Dearest Ruth,

Thank you very much. The Christmas parcel arrived two days ago. The reason why it was so late, though you had send it so long before Christmas, was that there was a "not working" in most cities of America by all sort of labourers. But we get our parcel and it was, as usually, especially, for the childrens a great party, to unbind the parcel. Though they are eleven and thirteen, every year they are so glad when they come home from school and they hear me crying "there is a parcel from Aunt Ruth from America". But, Ruth, what did you spoil us! For every member of the family a dress. How could you guess the real measure? The shirt for Hans is very good, and it suits him so good. The rose blouse for Ineke is also very good. The blue one a bit narrow. The shirt for Aad is good, hope it will not become smaller when I have washed it. And then the night gown for me. With great fear I saw

213

but there showed the number 40 inside it and my measure for dresses is 44. Well, said Aad, so I am obliged to go and search another woman who can wear it. Fortunately, when I folded it out, we saw that it was large enough. The American measures are not the same as ours. It suits me very good, it is warm and cosy and I am so glad with it. To us all textiles are very expensive, a shirt for Aad as you send is +/– 15 guilders. The night gown +/– 18 guilders. The shirt of Hans +/– 10 guilders. The blouses I don't know. There are here not in the shops.

Many greetings, much happiness in the new year
Your Hanna

+ + + + + + +

December 6, 1960

Dearest Ruth:

Many thanks for the card. You were sending to Ineke on her 14th birthday. The years are running fast, I agreed this with you. Yesterday we got the "Lifes" (Life magazines) and we enjoy them very much.

We have had so much rain this summer and this autumn, more than in a hundred years. Our country already so deep under the sea level at many points is very wet now. Great pieces of land are flooded. Fortunately, we live at a piece of Rotterdam which is rather high, so that our house is dry. But there are houses enough where the cellars are flooded, very inconvenient. My aunt Clazien is living in a house in a suburb of Rotterdam lying 20 feet beneath the sea level and it is all very wet there. Fortunately it is nearly Christmas holidays and then we go to Austria for a fortnight to the sun and the snow on the mountains.

You are right, we enjoy our car very much. I don't drive myself. I am used to my bicycle and I am afraid to begin learning car driving. I do find it difficult to drive in the traffic and I assure you that the traffic in Rotterdam is very busy.

Our papers were full of the news of the new chosen president of America. I hope that Mr. Kennedy is the best choice American people could do. We read that the number of votes given to Kennedy was only a little bit more than the number given to Mr. Nixon.

I am reading a book written by Betty MacDonald "Onions in the Stew." Have you read it? The place of action is one of the Islands between the cities Seattle and Tacoma in the Puget Sound in the neighborhood of Vancouver. I should like to go there. It seems so quiet and so lovely. Sometimes we are sick of living in a country so overpopulated as ours. Eleven million people in such a small area. When we go in summer to the beach and the weather is fine, the beach is overcrowded and you have to seek for a quiet place for a swim or for lying in the sun. How is that in Illinois. Are you with many people, or have you space enough?

Ineke had a party on her birthday. We had seven girls here the whole afternoon and they amused themselves with playing the piano and accordion, community singing and games. We had long drinks and apple pies. It was all very nice. Of course, Hans is now in high school too. He has no difficulties in learning. He does all his subjects good. He is in a group of 14 boys and 8 girls.

Ineke is now in her second grade on a school only for girls. The geometry and algebra are not so important there. The modern languages as German, English, French are very important for that school. She is also learning to sew a bit, to sing, and physical training and drawing too. She is very diligent and some-times very tired.

Aad goes to change his job on the school for a job on the University of Delft. He is charged at February 7 to give lessons in analytic chemistry to the young students who have studied already one year. He enjoys his new job very much. He has been teacher in chemistry now 14 years on the same school and you understand, that there will be a big farewell party on Januari 30. The new job gives a little more salary too although one never shall be rich here in Holland by teaching or education young people! But this is the same thing as in America, I believe. The salary as a teacher is 15,000 guilders a year. The income taxes are very high (+/– 3,000 guilders (20%). The salary at February 1 becomes 17,000 guilders, but the taxes are increasing very quick. A family without children is paying more and a bachelor is paying most. The income taxes are very high after the war and this is due to all the social laws for sick and old people, the free schools, and the defense measures we have to take as a partner in the N.A.T.O.

So long Ruth, Merry Christmas, and Happy New Year.

Your Hanna

+ + + + + + +

215

Dear Aunt Ruth:

I am thirteen years old now and since September I am at a following school. I am learning English now. My mother said I was allowed to write a letter to you.

We were very glad with our Christmas presents you gave us. With the rose dress I play table tennis every Tuesday. The purple one is a bit too small. I should like to give it a girlfriend, may I?

In the Christmas holiday we went to the winter sports. We always went by train, but this year we have gone by car. Daddy drove the first day 9 hours and then we slept at a hotel in Germany. The following day Daddy drove 8 hours and we were in the mountain village Gerlos. Where did you go in the holidays?

Many greetings from mother and Daddy and Hans.

Ineke Muijser

Gerlos, in Tirol, Austria—scene of winter vacations

Ineke and Aad in Gerlos, Austria

8 Sept., 1961

Dearest Ruth:

Before me is lying your letter from August 6. We received it,
being at the seashore for summer vacation. We went there Juli 20
and we went back to Rotterdam August 26. Four weeks we hired
a part of a farm to live in it. It was very beautiful there, cornfields
round the house and the dunes were at a distance of a mile behind
the cornfields. When you went through a narrow path up to the
dunes, you saw the sea before you, very wide and imposing. The
weather was not so good during these weeks. It rained often and

the wind blew often too fast. But there were also days on which the sun shined very warm and we could lay on the beach or play and swim. On the days with stormy weather we always took a walk along the beach. We enjoyed the high waves and the cloudy skys.

I hope the gentleman K and K from America and Russia will agree with each other so that we can have at last rest and peace. We are such a small country we can only help America with our good intentions, with a few battle ships and a handful soldiers a.s.o. But we all know what a war means and we all fear it immensely. And you must not forget we don't like the West Berlin Germans. They bombed and overwhelmed our country in 1940 and nobody here has forgotten it. Now I must stop. There is only space for many greetings and much love from my husband and children and me.

Your Hanna

+ + + + + + +

10 Dec., '61 — Rotterdam

Dearest Ruth

How are you? Ineke has got your birthday card and of course she will answer soon.

She has had busy days. At first her 15th birthday with all the friends and her grandparents and aunts having dinner with us. And then a week later, we have the feast of Santa Claus with giving each other a present, hidden in a fancy parcel with a poem. That is meant to tease each other with some character strain or fault. The whole evening there is much laughter and fun.

I am so glad your Delft Blue has arrived in good shape and I am glad that you like it.

22 Dec. we start with the car to go to Austria again for the winter sports. We start in the early hours at 5 o'clock in the morning. It is the only day in winter we rise so early. Usually we rise at half past seven, breakfast at eight, and then the children go to school at half past eight and Aad leaves for Delft. He has a fine job there, just what he likes and what he always wanted to do. Working with students, boys between 18-20 years who chose chemistry as their profession.

I hope America and Russia will not begin to fight for the domination in the world. Nobody in our country believes that there will be any good in it. We had already a war and nobody enjoys to repeat it.

Our government though has advised us all to have some food in the house to have something in case of danger. But in our country nobody is very nervous. There a very few communists, but nobody hates them. As a rule many jokes are said about politics. One of them: one German is a fine boy, one Russian is a fine boy, 10 Germans are an army, 10 Russians is a band of murderers. Do you like it?

Very much greetings.

Much love from Hanna

+ + + + + + +

24 January, 1962 — Rotterdam

Dearest Ruth,

Just a week ago your box arrived. It was very late this time. You remember that last year your box came the day before we went to Austria? Then we were packing our bags and unfastening your box. We had much fun.

But this time the postman knocked at the door with a box from which the wraps were loosened and he was very sorry, it was too late, but the custom people were the reason for it and I had to pay 74 1/2 guilders. We happened to be home all of us and the children jumped from their seats, so glad they were, the long attended box had arrived at last. The bracelet and the deep blue with golden ends waist ornament lay alone in the box unwrapped, but fortunately nothing had happened, though we don't know how. To whom you had sent it? Ruth, many thanks for all the beautiful things you send us, The underwear suits me perfectly, the blouses for Aad and Hans are good of measure, and the blouse for Ineke is a very pretty one. We say in Holland, "een schatje" and I don't know how to translate. It suits so lovely to Ineke. She has a deep blue skirt to which it goes very good, a skirt with many little buttons. I believe Aad will make a foto of her and her skirt and blouse.

I gave the jewelry to my mother-in-law. We showed her all the things you gave us and I know she is fond of all such jewelry

219

and she wore a black frock on which it suited so perfectly. I hope you don't care. I gave it to her in an unguarded moment!

Hans had his pulse bracelet and the charm round his neck. In Holland these things are not yet seen for boys, but in a few weeks or months, I am sure one will see these things here too. He is very proud of them.

I believe I mentioned all the things that were in the box except the ballpoint which are very fine too. I am writing now to you with the one with the rose on top. It took a week before I had the time to write you. I am always so busy after the Christmas holidays that I am too tired to write in the evening. I hope you will forgive me. Did you have a pleasant vacances? You write in your Christmas card that you should spend the days with your family in Mt. Vernon and Decatur. Did you amuse yourself and did you get a lot of Christmas cards?

We had a fine holiday high in the mountains in Austria in that little village in a farmer's house. We enjoyed every day of snow, blue sky, and sunshine. The children did every day their exercises on the skis or they went for a day's trip in the mountains and Aad and I were very quiet, we walked hours and hours in the sunshine. Now and then we stood on the skis too, but we were very careful. You must not forget we are middle-aged people now! (ha!)

With love, lots of love from us all

Your Hanna

+ + + + + + +

26 March, 1962 — Rotterdam

Dearest Ruth:

I wonder, how you are? I hope everything is OK. since you wrote us in the beginning of the year.

We had a cold winter, heavy storms and rains not to send a dog outdoors. Sometimes the temperature was below zero and there was ice in the canals and lakes, but it was not enough for skating. Hans and Ineke are going very well on their schools fortunately and Aad is very happy with his job, which he is now doing since one year.

The brother of your President Kennedy visited our country during a day. He was received by the queen and all he said to the

Dutch people was that we were too emotional in the New Guinea sale. We all hope that we can getting rid of New Guinea without spoiling blood but this seems to be very difficult. There are many young men who don't like to go to New Guinea to fight, but when they are in the military service (which lasts for every young men 2 years) they have to go, when they are ordered to do so.

We are spending the evenings in this cold spring very quietly at home. The children making their homework and we reading or writing as I now do to you.

I am longing for a better weather so that we have a bit of tennis again and perhaps on Sundays a walk in the dunes.

How is your mother's health? I wonder what her age is now. She must have the age of the very strong ones. I think Aad and the children are sending you heartily greetings and from me lots of love.

This letter has been written with the ball pen with the flower in top.

Your friend Hanna

+ + + + + + +

Juli 12, '62

Dearest Ruth.

Your portrait has arrived here and has its place on the mantelpiece in our living room.

Your face is very lovely and friendly and I see you are wearing your hair in another style than you did in the portrait some years ago. I guess it is shorter now and it lets your forehead free. Of course one can see that you are not longer a young girl, but nobody here believes me when I say that you must have passed the age of fifty years.

When I am looking at your face on the portrait, a great desire is coming to me to see you, to speak to you, and to touch you. I should like to see the paper friend changed into a living flesh and blood friend!

Many thanks for the portrait. Many good wishes and greetings from Aad and the children and me.

Your friend, Hanna

+ + + + + + +

221

18 December, '62 — Rotterdam

Dearest Ruth,

Your box has arrived December 8. It was a great day for all of us. All these beautiful parcels with magnificent glittery silky papers. It was all very fine. Many, many thanks for all those presents. The white blouse for Ineke was too small. We gave it away so one of her friends who was very glad with it. And one of the shirts for Hans was too small again. We did the same with it with the same result. We enjoy the plastic teacups very much. Here in Holland we have plastics too, but they are less beautiful. The napkins are very fine. I used them at Ineke's birthday dinner. She had 16 years at Nov. 28 and she was very happy and lovely. At lunch we had four friends of hers from school and we ate salmon salad with slices of bread and fruit: apples, oranges, pears and coffee. We went away the four of us at six o'clock to have dinner in restaurant in the city. Ineke loved to go to a Chinese restaurant. It was very funny. We were back at home at 8 o'clock to receive the grandparents (72 and 69) and the two old aunts (80 and 75). We had tea with sweets. Later on some bowl (that is fruits cut in slices and white wine). Grandpapa don't like this stuff. He likes better a gin (the famous Dutch brand is Boll & Genever) which comes from Schiedam, the city where my parents-in-law live now, 6 miles from Rotterdam.

At eleven o'clock they all went home and Ineke had had a fine birthday. She will answer you on your birthday letter and she likes to wait until the vacances in Austria. She asked me when she saw me writing to mention it to you.

Then on Dec. 5 we had our family dinner as you remembered very well in your letter, Dec. 3. We had soup and after that I put on the table delicious chickens. I had done all my best to have them good and with a good sauce. We had potatoes friters with it and mashed apples. Then we ate pineapple slices with cream.

Later on in the evening we gave each other presents but as you know, every present must be a surprise with a poem, a teasing poem. We had much pleasure.

Your box came Dec. 8, so that it was a pity, but I could not have opened it at Dec. 5 with the family. Now I am thinking about giving my mother-in-law the blue furs to have smart feet, to give to my father-in-law the candelabras and to my aunts the plastic flower saucer. The towels are so fine too. I am using them.

I can understand that you had to pay much for these 2 boxes. We ourselves had to pay 10 guilders to receive it for taxes. I inquired how it was made and they answered that you had written on your box that it was $10 worth and a certain % we have to pay as taxes. I believe 7%. I am asking whether you had to pay for your birthday calendar or not?

We enjoyed your boxes so much Ruth. These 10 guilders did not disturb our pleasure. I hope you believe this.

Friday 21 Dec. we go for our trip to Austria. We start at 7 o'clock in the morning and we drive through Germany to Munchen where we spend the night. The morning of Dec. 22 we have our trip through the mountains to Gerlos.

The children enjoy it very much and we too. It is here all rain and wind and we are longing for some sunshine.

Best wishes, lots of love.

Hanna

+ + + + + + +

20 Dec., 1962 — Gerlos

Dearest Ruth:

We have fine vacances again in our mountain village in Tirol (Austria). The name is, as you know, Gerlos. We are 15 C below zero, but no wind and a bright sunshine every day.

The children are away at 10 in the morning to go for a trip in the mountains on skis. There are ski teachers who lead the way, so that they are rather safe. We ourselves don't go so far and so high. We stay in the neighborhood of the village for a walk or a little bit of skiing.

Yesterday we met our youngest princess Marghi, who is staying here with some girlfriends and an elderly lady. They are living here just as we, in a farmer's house, very sober.

I thank you for your last letter with the fotographs of our queen mother, who reigned over our country during 50 years and who died a few weeks ago.

We have Christmas and New Year here in the snowy world, far from all vast cities and in a serene quietness. It will give us new strength to live in Rotterdam again. We are staying here during a fortnight, but the days are flowing so rapid, it is a pity.

We all wish you a happy New Year, good health, and great pleasure in your job at school.

Lots of love, Hanna

+ + + + + + +

Sept. 5, 1963

Dearest Ruth.

I am sorry that I could not find time enough to write you sooner about our moving to Enschede, 250 miles from Rotterdam.

In Juli Aad became suddenly asking to teach at a university in the east of the country near the boundary with Germany. The university has not been built yet. The first stone has been laid by the Prime Minister. Aad is very enthusiastic. The university shall be founded, as you do in America, with a campus where the students live. In Delft, the boys coming from High School must see they succeed in getting a room somewhere in the town. That brings very much difficulties and it is very precious too. The students living at their parents within 20 miles from Delft are lucky, they can stay at home and travel every day to the laboratories and so on.

We used the vacances for moving, for Aad and Ineke can begin here in Enschede a new course at a new school. The schools are here the same as in Rotterdam. Hans with his 15 years goes in his 4th year at High School and Ineke with her 16 years does the 3th year once again here. She has never enough time to do all her work and she herself is suffering about it.

Aad is 3 or 4 days a week in Delft working, till a new man had been found for his job. He is working 2 days a week here to organise the studies. The first students are planned here to come September '64.

What about the money Aad earns is the job here the same, but the work is new and interesting. We live now in a house with one large living room and kitchen and upstairs 3 bed rooms and bath room. A small garden behind the house and a little building in the yards for the bicycles and so on. It is an easy house to clean and very cosy but it is a little bit too small for us. For Hans and Aad have their hobby to play with radios. They built one and then when it is no good they built another. That never finishes and we

224

have no ceiling or hobby room. That is a pity for Hans' bedroom is full now with all those radio articles.

When the university is settled, some houses are build for teachers. I did see the planning for those houses, 5 or 6 rooms. But perhaps it is not so pleasant to live with our family on the ground of the campus. Perhaps is the intimacy of the family disturbed by living so near to the students. What do you think about this?

Enschede is the first university now with the idea of a campus and a little bit study accompany by the teachers. It is an experience and nobody knows how the Dutch young men will take this idea. After our moving we went for a fortnight to Gerlos, the village where we use to be in wintertime. In summer it was beautiful too there. Much flowers, orchids especially and we had warm weather. I was so busy when we came back. I am sorry that I did not write you sooner. Many thanks for your letters in which we learned how you spend your vacances. Heartily greetings to your mother. We are glad she does rather well.

A big kiss from your friend Hanna.

+ + + + + + +

Hanna was 55 years old in 1969. She had witnessed the space walk of U. S. astronauts on the moon.

Although correspondence slowed down, Hanna and Ruth continued to write to one another. Hanna disclosed that the wedding of Princess Irene, daughter of Queen Juliana, was unacceptable to many of the people in Holland. This was due to the fact that Princess Irene became a Catholic and married an heir to the Spanish throne, whose political ideology was termed as Fascist.

26 Mai, '64

Dearest Ruth,

Your letter 11 Jan. lies here before me and I am ashamed that I did not answer in such a long time. Many thanks for this letter. Indeed we have been married for 24 years and it seems only some years ago. The date is 25 Januari so the gratulations were on time. I wonder why you wrote on this day. Is it in USA usual to celebrate 2 dozens of years? To us we don't celebrate 2 dozens of years, but at the next Januari when we have been married 25 years 1/4 of a century, all the members of our family and all friends will be invited for a dinner.

We changed our life when we went away from Rotterdam to live in Enschede, the east part of the country. Aad has to help to build a new university and he is very busy with it. At September the students will come the first year 240 and every year more till 4000. He likes his work very much, preparing all sorts of things.

We made acquaintance with many people, married and unmarried, old and young. And the neighborhood is unlike the west part of the country. Here is not too much water, we have woods plenty, but no hills. We live at 5 miles from the boundary with Germany. The children are at ease here. Ineke has in her class a girl from U. S. A. She was in Enschede one year and goes back to Washington at half Juli. The girls have intended to make a band recorder tape on which every girl of the class says some words and to give this tape as a present.

The teacher of English language will speak longer and she will speak about our Princess Irene who became a Catholic and married one of the Spanish heir of the throne in Spain. He is a Fascist and therefore the Dutch people did not agree with this marriage. Was anything of this case in your papers? What do you think the American girl will have on this tape about this case? Ineke asked me to write you and to ask if you would be so kind as to answer on this question. The question is: What to say about Irene on this tape that would interest the American girl and her American friends when she is back in U.S.A.?

We hope you can find the time to write us about this or is the question not so important as we thought it here in Holland?

With many greetings and lots of love,

Your Hanna

+ + + + + + +

5 Nov., '64

Dear Ruth,

We received your box with the wedding presents. It was awfully magnificent especially the tray which is never seen here in our shops. Snacks on the first floor and snacks on the second floor! This letter is to thank you very, very much for this box. You know, we celebrate our 25 wedding at 25 Jannari 1965, so we wait to use the tray till this day.

We bought a house this year. On the ground floor a room to live in, a hall, and a kitchen. On the first floor 3 bedrooms and a bath room and above these rooms under the roof a large space to put the things you don't use.

In all the troubles with the building of the house and moving from Deldstrant to the new home, we have forgotten your birthday. Thousands of excuses Ruth, but yesterday Aad, doing a little job in the house, at once said "Do you mind it was Ruth's birthday a fortnight ago?" Now I am busy to write you and to apologize. This morning I go down town. There is a shop who sells linen clothes. The measures are 80 cm/30 cm and on this cloth are printed all sorts of designs as you can find them in this part of the country, the east part, on the dons or above the dons of the old farms. I will send you it as soon as possible as a late birthday present.

To move from one house to another, that is a very difficult case. We all are tired. Hans & Ineke have helped so much that I was afraid their schoolwork should not be so good as it could be. But this week we think to come ready with it.

You wrote about houses and apartments. This time we have a home we call it two under one roof. How do you call that?

Much love from everyone. A big kiss from me.

Hanna

P. S. The remarks you gave in your letter of June 5 about Princess Irene have helped Ineke and her classmates very well. The tape was not ready before the summer holidays and in September it was sent to U.S.A. The teacher and the girls hope the American girl will enjoy it. Now at Ineke and Hans' school there is an American teacher who teaches history. He uses a very easy and simple English so that the pupils can understand him. In Ineke's class he teaches now at this moment American history, secession war or slave war. Very interesting. We in Holland learn at school naturally about this war, but now a real American tells about these important years. Ineke enjoys it very much.

Your point of view about Irene was very good. She married against her parent's wishes with a Catholic reactionair prince who hopes to conquer the Spanish throne and then to put the clock three ages back. We think Irene was very, very fond of him, in love from top to toe and willing to do everything for this man, moving her religion, leaving her country and her life of charming princess, loved by everybody.

It may be she was a little bit jealous on her sister Beatrix the future queen and that she has believed the dreams of the family Bourbon Parma she should be queen of Spain in the future. The government with the prime minister has done well. We don't like a fascist marrying a daughter of the House of Orange which was always fighting the ages through for freedom. And Juliana was a real queen. Her duty above her love for her child. Of course, she had tears in her voice and on her cheeks sometimes, but we did admire her and we had no pity. That is the meaning of most of the inhabitants of this small country. It was the conversation in all families. You can imagine.

Love, Hanna

Chapter Sixteen

In 1965, Hanna and Aad celebrated their 25th wedding anniversary, and Hans started to college where Aad taught.

30 March, '65 — Enschede

Dearest Ruth:

Before me on my writing desk are laying all the cards your people sent to us on the occasion of our silver wedding celebration. Our deepest thanks for all those magnificent cards, especially to your mother who wrote a few words on it too. All those people who wanted to send us a sign of friendship. We are so grateful!

It is almost two months ago this celebration and of course I was obliged to write you earlier, but every day I postponed and you know then it goes from bad to worse.

We went by car on this 25th January at 4 a.m. to Rotterdam (3 hours) and there we received in a hotel, our guests and Aad's parents, Aunt Clazien, Aunt Ida, and Aad's Uncle John and Aunt Mien. We had at first short and long drinks with some delicious shrimp to eat with and after an hour we were going to have a fine dinner at a magnificently laid table. Waiters who brought all sorts of excellent food and Hans, he is almost 17, rising from his seat with the wine glass in his hand to gratulate us, and he said he thought his sister and he were lucky with us as parents. Some other children were not so lucky. It was all very pleasant.

Ineke had a red frock which suited her very well and I had a cocktail dress of blue which suited me too. They said at 11 o'clock all was over and the family went home and we spent the night in Rotterdam and the next morning we went back to Enschede.

Ineke and Hans had behaved theirselves very well and they were very cheerful to the grandparents and aunts and uncles. All these persons are older than 70 years and at their age one likes good food and drinks.

In Enschede we went the next day with the children to a performance of a play to celebrate our wedding. It was King Lear of Shakespeare in a Dutch translation and we enjoyed ourselves very much. From the family we got presents during the dinner, a fine table, a lamp, a silver spoon for me and a drinking glass with silver foot for Aad. Besides we had your presents. I had your table cloth sent to Rotterdam and the hotel had used it to cover the dinner table. It was quite a surprise. A big kiss Ruth from all of us for what you sent to us and for the way you enjoyed yourself about our silver wedding. Greetings and thanks for all your people.

Aad, Hanna, and children

+ + + + + + +

11 Oct., '65

Dearest Ruth:

At September, Hans went to the university and he went away from home to live on the campus. He does it very well. He has got a nice room with bed, writing desk, bookcase, two cupboards in a building of 4 floors. On every floor 12 rooms with a kitchen in which the 12 young men are eating their breakfast and lunch. Dinner is served in the Mensa (a building where all 400 young men are having their dinner and sometimes spend their evening).

Aad is also working there as a teacher, but he has done his utmost not to teach his own son. As it is a quarter of a hour by bicycle, Hans comes home now and then and at Sunday he comes home for dinner.

At my birthday we had a nice day. Hans and Ineke were away to a holiday camp where they sailed on a lake during a week. Aad and I had a nice drive to a little town in Germany +/− 30 miles. There we had a walk and later on a dinner. Then we went back to Enschede and there we went to the cinema where we saw "My Fair Lady" about which you had already spoken. It was very beautiful with Audrey Hephurn. We knew the book since the time we were on high school and now Ineke has read it too at school. A few years ago a musical has been made of it, but at the movies it is much more beautiful.

Now you know again anything about us and we wish you a very happy birthday.

Aad, Ineke, Hans, and your Hanna

+ + + + + + +

In November, 1965, after two and a half years of long and arduous work at the new university in Enschede, Aad fell ill and

230

was advised to go to Gerlos, in the mountains of Austria, for rest and recovery.

After spending about a month at their favorite vacation retreat, Aad had recovered from a severe bout with nerves and had decided to leave the new university and again pursue teaching chemistry and physics at another school similar to the one where he had taught five years earlier. Fortunately, he and Hanna were able to maintain the new home in Enschede that they had built, and life was again pleasant and happy.

Gerlos 11 Jan., 1966

Dearest Ruth!
    I will write you from Gerlos, the place where we since 8 years are spending our Christmas holidays with the children. I took with me your letter from December 18 in which you wished us to have merry Christmas. I thought here I have enough time to answer you. Two days before we went to Gerlos with our car your box came and as always we enjoyed all the things which came out of it. The boxes for sugar, coffee, a.s.o. so brightly coloured, for Aad the standard with pens, for Ineke two lovely presents. The jacket for Hans did not fit as you feared, but Ineke wears it and it suits her. It is shorter than we are accustomed, but perhaps that is the new fashion in the U.S.A. Ruth. We think and we did see that you have wrapped all these things with love and tenderness and we were so glad to receive them. Many and many thanks for it from everybody. The presents for my parents-in-law and aunt. I did send them to Rotterdam and Scheidan, but I did not yet hear about them.
    Aad has worked too fast the last two years with the building of the new university in Enschede. He fell ill just before Ineke's birthday 28 Nov. He had an inflammation of the kidney basin and he was so badly ill and so tired.
    We had a miserable time, but the doctor advised us to go to Gerlos. Aad should recover there sooner and he advised to stay there a month. So we did. The children went back to Enschede by train Jan. 4 and we stay here till Jan. 18. Aad is recovering, but it does not go very fast. I think he can work again on the beginning of February, but more calmly as he did.

I hope your nephew is not called to join the army in Vietnam. I did not know that there were sent boys who are not volunteers.

We are nearly in the half of January but Aad and I wish you to have a very happy 1966. Excuse me that we did not send you such a wishing earlier, but we had sad and busy days.

It is very beautiful here in Gerlos. High mountains all around us and a quiet, lovely, snowy village. We are sending you many greetings.

Much love,
Hanna and Aad

+ + + + + + +

5 September, 1966

Dearest Ruth,

I at first must apologize for my being so long as to write so few letters during the last year. But you must know that we had a sad year. Aad having been so ill. He worked far too fast with the foundation of a new university in the East part of our country, and you know, he had a nervous breakdown on November last year. This is a disease in which nobody can help you. It was our daughter, Ineke, who could make quiet him and it was she who could make him laugh again after a few months.

We went 20 December to Austria. The mountain air in winter should do him good. The children went skiing while we make walkings. We came back in the half of January and then Aad decided to leave alone the university and to become a teacher of chemistry and physics again on a college school. The same job he gave up 5 years ago. But we did not move. Fortunately, the college school in Enschede needed a teacher, so we could remain in our new built (2 years ago) house. To change a job and to change a house that was a thing that Aad could not do at the same time. Besides, we love to live here in Enschede with her beautiful surroundings and a less dense population as in the western part of the country (1000 people per square kilometer, 2500 on a square mile.

The last letter you wrote was on the occasion of my birthday (52) and I was very glad I get your letter. We were from 10 Juli-22 August on the Isle of Schonwen, southwest part on the beach. Aad thought that we should spend a summer on the beach, that he should be as before. He was right. It was a quiet time for all of us. We enjoyed the sound of the sea, the golden sand, and the quiet way of life.

Ineke passed her examination as she wrote you, and she likes to take a course as an analyst. Hans has left home. He lives on lodgings in a university town (Groningen) in the northern part of the country. There he will study physics. The past year he studied here on the campus university, but he did not like too much the study and the campus life. Besides, his girlfriend went to Groningen to study laws and he is so in love with her that we did not have the courage to force him to stay here. She is a very nice girl, simple and good mannered and we all love her too. But Groningen is 145 kilometer away from here and I think that is very far.

Now we are three at home and with Aad recovered again, quiet in his new job, we are very happy again.

Love from all of us.

Your Hanna

+ + + + + + +

8 Dec., '66 — Enschede

Dearest Ruth,

I have forgotten your birthday on October 14. I am very sorry, but you must believe me when I say that we had so much sorrow about my father-in-law who had a stroke, as you know. He was paralysed and could not speak and the doctor said it was not possible that the situation could change. The illness of his brains was too serious during three hours and I don't know if my father-in-law knew what was going on. He held my hand all the time.

When he was in the nursing home a few weeks, he grew so ill that they feared the end of his life was coming. Now he is unconscious about what is going on and we are waiting day by day.

For my mother-in-law it is a terrible time. She waits and waits. She is 73 and living alone in her apartment of 3 rooms, a kitchen, and a hall. Fortunately she has a neighbour woman who is very good for her a woman of 56 who is caring for her husband and her boy of 15. Her daughter 23 married last year. She looks after my mother-in-law now and then, drinks a cup of coffee with her at eleven in the morning.

Last week I bought for you a pair of wooden shoes. I think your feet are not so large and I bought a size who will maybe suit you. The farms wives here wear the wood shoes with thick stockings. But you may use them too as a box to put flowers in. You must consider it this time as a Christmas gift, will you? This was not a very amusing or interesting letter, but when you are waiting for the death of a beloved person, you have a difficult time. And Aad loved his father very much. He had a very sad year. His illness, changing his job. But now his health is much more better and he does his work with pleasure. He has some spare time again. But it was a disappointment that his work on the university here was too much for him. He could not work 70 or 80 hours a week.

Ineke was 20 years old this week and though her beloved grandfather was so ill, she had a little party with a glass of wine and all sorts of cheese going with it.

I will write you again dear Ruth.

Much love,
Your Hanna

+ + + + + + +

December 14, 1966

Dearest Ruth,

My father-in-law died last Thursday. It was a very sad day for all of us, but especially for Aad's mother. Between her only son and her only grandson, on she went to the ceremony of the burial. In Holland one can choose a burial, the corpse is then buried in the earth or a crematie (I don't know the American word). Then the corpse is burned to ashes. We chose the last manner.

My mother-in-law was very brave and she wants to live in her 3 rooms apartment alone, but we don't like this so very much as she can't see very good so short a time after the cataracts operation.

We received your Christmas parcel very early and since we are not going to Austria this year, I decided to wait till Christmas to open it. But Ineke and Hans were so anxious to know what the parcel behold (18 and 20 years old) that at last we opened it.

You know so very well what we like to have sent from America. We all had a very nice hour with unpacking. I believe Ineke spoke you already about all things we found. I must thank you especially for the leatherware for Aad, the belt and tie for Hans, and the presents for myself. I am not going to use the beautiful Lincoln paper when I am writing to you. I spare it for my friends in Holland. Now we are living in the East of the country. I often write to my former friends in Rotterdam. Dear Ruth, now you know again all things about us. Aad's health is very good now. Now and then he can't sleep, but these sleepless nights are rare during the last three months.

With many thanks, wishing you all the best for Christmas and New Year.

Many greetings from Aad, Ineke, Hans, and lots of love from myself.

Your Hanna

+ + + + + + +

25 June, 1967 — Enschede

Dearest Ruth,

Many thanks for the letters you wrote to us during the last months and too, that I did not answers till now. It is Sunday now and warm summer weather and I feel that I must write you now.

We have recovered us from the death of my father-in-law. My mother-in-law is living alone now in her 3 room apartment in Schiedam and now and then, almost every first weekend of month, we are driving at Saturday afternoon to Scheidam (3 hours driving) and Sunday evening we return home.

You know that Aad worked far too fast in helping to start this new university here in the east of the country with a campus. When his health was recovered, he went back as a teacher in chemistry in High School. Aad's life is now quiet again, boys of 15-20 obey him very well and he has enough time again for a bit of tennis or badminton or bridge. Hans is studying in Groningen. He does it very well. At Juli 10 we are going, the four of us, for a trip by car through France. We did not go there earlier. It will be difficult with the language, but we shall have to come through.

We had some weeks of intense tension because of Israel. We (I mean all the Dutch people) admired their quietness and strength.

235

We do hope that the States and Russia shall be able to beware the peace in the Middle East.

Hans has become a young man of 19 years with much criticism about the existing situation in our country. He said that he shall write you about it and about the provos in our cities, young people who want to change existing situations, even the royal family should be sent away, they say. Ruth, now you know again much about us and you are informed that our life is rather quiet and happy again. How are you? I was allowed to read Hans' birthday letter. So nice of you! Did you meet your nephew who came from Korea?

Lots of love from all of us and best wishes,

Your Hanna

+ + + + + + +

At this time, Hans was a 20 year old student at Groningen. He described the traditional initiation rites and customs of certain fraternities. The "Provo Movement" was developing in Holland and had moved from a conservative view of life to one of dissidence with the establishment. Many of the ideas contradicted the beliefs of parents and the causes for which they had fought.

In the United States, the same type of change was occurring. The "hippie culture" resulted in radical thinking, rebellion, and non-traditional lifestyles. "Free spirits" chose non-conformity in dress, the use of illegal drugs, defiance of law and order and criticism of the Vietnamese War coupled with draft dodging. "Flower children" espoused love and the protection of natural resources over development of land to provide jobs, homes, and shopping centers. Older generations in both Europe and the United States found the impact of these "provos" or "hippies" on their society disconcerting to say the least.

16 July, 1967 — Gillestre (France)
(Letter from Hans about college life.)

Dear Aunt Ruth,

Thank you very much for your letter on my birthday. It is a long time you have heard anything from me. I studied one year at the campus technical university in Enschede and this course (1966-1967) at the University of Groningen. Although I passed my examination at the campus I feel much better at home in Groningen (situated in the northern part of our country). I study now physics and mathematics instead of electronics at the campus. Also, in Groningen students are more integrated in normal society. Another factor may be the far better ratio of boys-girls because of the possibility to study all kinds of things: literature, Russian, Dutch, English, Spanish, psychology, ceriology, medical science, biology, pure mathematics, chemistry, and so on. Till 1955 students in Holland were very conservative and even reactionary. But since the coming of the student trade union and labor, the provo movement, things have changed considerably. Before the war, students and now still a large minority were members of the student corpora. They are very proud of their (in my eyes) anecleonists traditions. When in September new students are coming and they want to become a member of the "corps", they are in a way brainwashed to think like a good corps member. To accomplish this, their hair is completely cut off, and they have to do everything the third and higher year members want them to do during three weeks. They get very little sleep, 5-6 hours a day, much lectures about the traditions and the importance of the corpse. At night they have to talk with the members of the corpse. and then they are humiliated and often forced to drink too much. As a corpse member you are supposed to consider this very funny and very good for the character of the future corpse member.

Democracy is poor in this society. In most cases, it is the case of the biggest mouth. I forgot telling you the corpse is for boys only. For girls there is an analagous of the corpse, but it is more human.

The student society I am a member of is only ten years or so old and it's more like me. Introduction of the freshmen is on an equally basis and they are not supposed to behave and think in a special way. They are not forced to wear white collar and tie like you are in the "corpse". The trend nowadays is to abandon the drink societies of the 19th century and to rearrange in societies with a special purpose, sportclubs, debating clubs about the atomic bomb, exitentialism of Sartre, buddhism, humanism, the Vietnamiese war, the right and wrongs, the possibilities to and of, sexual problems, student marriages, of course also study societies. Such a structure would be much more up to date, but I doubt it will soon become a reality.

In Amsterdam matters are changing now, although for American eyes it will be rather left. Last year a majority of the students in Amsterdam worked for the student trade union. They have very left ideas. They think they must have a voice in their study programs, they want to integrate students in society rather than keep them a privileged group. They wish to be part of the government instead of their parents lending it from the government. So they consider their study as a job and want to be paid for it. They consider the paying as an investment for the state. In Holland a student pays the equivalent of $50 a year for lectures: the government pays the professors, lecturers, and all the rest which is needed for an university. That is $5000 dollars for each physics student and $2500 for English language and literature. The remaining slightly more than $1000 dollars a year for living can better be supplied by the government because the government can then better force the students to work.

Politically the students trade union is left. Generally speaking they are against the use of A.B.C. weapons if not totally against war. They think also peace is more important for the Vietnamees people now than the system, communist or dictatorship of a very small group and maybe in the long run, democracy. In Europe most young people think neither the Viet-Cong nor the U. S. army will ever win the war because Viet-Cong will keep the countryside where the poor farmers live and the U.S. army will keep the cities.

The provo movement has the same set of ideas, but are mostly non-students. They are very non conformitie. They wear long hair, all kinds of vestment except the common kind. In general, boys and girls wear the same and look out the same. The elderly people aren't yet used to it. The provos are against looking at the television for whole nights as so many people do. They try to be more creative in their spare time. In Holland most elderly people don't understand anything from the long haired provos and consider them dangerous idiots. I don't think there is an analogy in the States, maybe the New Left?

Best Wishes to you from Hans Muijser.

+ + + + + + +

14 August, 1967

Dearest Ruth,

We spent the last five weeks in France and in that part of France where the mountains are very high, 3000 m. and more.

We started at Juli 8 from Enschede. We were glad that Ineke (21) and Hans (19) liked to go with us. Many young people here in this country like to spent their vacances with friends of their own age, and perhaps they are right, for when one is young and the parents are older, it often comes to a disappointment when the vacances are spent together. Fortunately, Aad and I are fit and healthy now. We go swimming, play tennis, walk hours at a stretch. Ineke and Hans see us more as friends as we are still able to enjoy the manner of spending the vacances they enjoy.

We rode by car in two days to Gillestre, in the southwest of France. It was lying in a valley near a stream. We hired there an apartment, a kitchen-living room and 3 bedrooms. The apartment was part of a large building, property of a French family. We learned there a lot of French conversation. We enjoyed the French manner of life. We went in the morning to a little cafe to eat a breakfast of coffee and little, delicious breads. Most French people do that. They often are eating outdoors. The climate is warmer than in our country. The people are living outdoors more than we.

We often made trips in the mountains and climbed very high. We even found the flower edelweiss. Do you know that flower? At one of our trips we rode by car to a little village high in the mountains, 20-40 meters. And there nature was so beautiful. The flowers so numerous, the snowy tops of the mountains so near to us that we decided to stay another week in this place. We found a little hotel near the village and at August 1, we started our last week of vacance. I believe it was the loveliest week of our vacances.

The couple who ran the hotel was a young one (35). She cooked deliciously, all those French sauces, meals, cheeses, fruits, and he was a mountain guide. Every day he went to the most beautiful places in the mountains and the guests who wanted, he took with him. Ineke and Hans enjoyed every day. They hung on cords between the rocks, they walked an 3000 m where they saw marmots (a sort of rabbit) and lakes. Aad and I sometimes went with the guide too. On days when he announced a tour, less fatigant! Ha!

239

We did never see such a beautiful region. We liked the French people. They can enjoy life with a glass of wine. They are laughing! And they make themselves ridiculous in their papers.

The voyage of Gaulle to Canada was critized in their papers with caricatures and satires.

Now we are back at home and Aad has to begin his school at August 22. Now he is a teacher again. He has the freedom he needs to be happy and he likes the contact with the pupils.

The letter you wrote on January 6 came into my hands this morning. I read it again and Ineke too. It is a pleasure to read your letters. We can exactly know how you are living, with your work, your family. I can understand that you debated a long time before you accepted your job of Chairman. When you like to be associated with your pupils, it will be difficult for you to have fewer classes; but to earn more money is always agreeable. Ha!

The Christmas presents for my aunts and mother-in-law were a top in the life of these old three women. A present from America! Ruth I must thank you that you are so nice for my family. Uncle Jan and Aunt Mene celebrated their 50th anniversary of their wedding.

Love from everybody, but specially from me.

Hanna

+ + + + + + +

14 Februari, 1968 — Enschede

Dearest Ruth,

We enjoyed your Christmas presents very much. I guess that in your country people go back to the romantic period just as in our country. All sorts of old fashioned things as crystal wine glasses with incrusted roses, Queen Anne style chairs and tables, velvet curtains. It is all very wanted and in plastics it can be exactly imitated. The miniatures you sent we did not see here yet. They are very nice.

The white shirt and chain for Ineke suits her so well. As I wrote you before, she likes to wear it under a frock without sleeves and collar in a white/black tweed. The white dress suits her very much, as every woman. She is 21 now and 1.72 m, just the same length as I have. She weighs 62 kilogram, so she is rather tall. Her hair is chestnut colour, her eyes gray-blue, and she has a white and rose skin. She is wearing spectacles and she is rather serious in her behaviour. She likes reading and her hobby is to photograph flowers and to make colour slides of the flowers that are in the meadows and the woods.

Hans is almost 20 and he enjoys himself much better in life. He is serious too, but he has better conduct with other young people. He studies very strong and he becomes high marks. He hates the idea to go in military service and for the war in Vietnam he has no good word.

We saw a few hours ago President Johnson in television. He spoke about the first president of America and himself. His wife stood beside him. Her face was very sad. I don't know what to say about Vietnam. Aad says America has a duty to fight against communism and we must stay firmly besides U.S.A.

I can't agree with the idea that young men of America and young, old people of Vietnam are killed for political reasons.

With many lots of love from all of us

Your Hanna

+ + + + + + +

Hanna referred to the Kennedy clan and its image. Two sons had been assassinated, John while president and Robert while a candidate. Later Ted, a younger brother and also a presidential hopeful, caused a scandal when he left the scene of an accident in which a young woman companion had been killed.

2 Sept., '69 — Enschede

Dearest Ruth,

One day before my birthday I got your letter. Many thanks! I am ashamed that I did not inform you about us during such a long time. But perhaps you can excuse me when I tell you that we have gone through so much trouble.

In the second week of Juli, my dear Aunt Clazien got a stroke. She was at once unconcious. Aunt Ida, who lives in the same building where old people are cared for had so much sorrow. She could not understand why Clazien slept all the time. She is 87. The nurses and I tried to convince her that Clazien did not sleep, but that she was unconscious and that she must realize that Clazien should die in a week or so. At last she understood.

241

Death came earlier than the doctor thought. At July 18 Aunt Clazien died very quietly.

The vacances had begun and we had promised Hans and Ineke that they could lend our car to go to Great Britain and Scotland. They had organised with 6 friends (plus themselves) to travel in two cars (2 other parents gave their car too). They had cheap passenger cards for the boat to cross the chanal from Hoek va Holland to Harwich and they should start at 23 July. This was the day at which Aunt Clazien should be buried. We said that they must go with their friends, that Aunt Clazi should have been the last person to forbid this. At the burial I laid flowers from Hans and Ineke on the chest. It was all very sad. Friends of Aunt Clazi's spoke at the burial many words of love and friendship and later on we had coffee and everybody went home.

Hans and Ineke had a fine holiday. I believe Ineke sent you a card from Scotland. They were away 4 weeks. In England they had to drive left instead of right in our country. The lakes of Scotland were splendid and the weather too. They made a camp at a farmer's ground and they cooked for themselves.

Hans is still studying at the University of Groningen. Besides the learning he gives his time to all the new ideas in the world. We are content about him and we believe he does it well.

Ineke has finished her course as a laboratory assistant. But though she did not intend to do so, she will learn about her work a lot more. Aad and I are glad she has the courage to do so. When you will learn, you must do it, when you are young. She is now in a course (+ 2 years) in which she learns more about laboratory activities, especially about bacterees, seeds.

This course starts in Groningen and we had to look for a family who wanted to have Ineke in her home. We had success. She lives now in Groningen with a family with whom she has breakfast and dinner. She has a room in which she can sleep and work. She lives unlike Hans, who has only a room to sleep and work. He is eating with the other students in a mensa. We thought that it was for Ineke better to live with a family. We were afraid she should be so lonely. She is 22 now. Hans is more able to have social contacts.

Now the vacances are over and we have not relaxed much. We, Aad and I are together at home and married life is now as when we started. I am 55 now and not too old to start with a job. For only cleaning and cooking, that is not a way of living. I can stand during the rest of my days. So I am starting at the end of September with lessons in physical culture for women 40-60. I begin with 4 lessons a week and the ladies are divided in clubs of 14 or 16 persons. I hope I will have success.

We did see of course the men on the moon. We did not go to bed that night. It was 3 o'clock in the morning, we saw the first step. I can't imagine such things. Aad and Hans do, and I believe that Hans' studies correlate to go with such difficult problems. Sometimes with such new things, I feel myself very old. Do you have such feelings too? What a troubles with your Edward Kennedy! The image of the Kennedy clan, faithful, serious men and women has fully disappeared, is it not?

Many good wishes from the family and much love from me.

Hanna

+ + + + + + +

10 October, 1968 — Enschede

Dearest Ruth,

In 4 days you will have your birthday and Aad, Ineke, Hans, and I send you our greetings and best wishes for a happy birthday.

It is a pity that your mother is so weak. We think that you and your family are very good for her and are spending a lot of your time and vacances to let her not alone. I looked again at the pictures you send me last Christmas on which you wore the red dress. I think it should have been a very happy Christmas for your mother to have her children in the house.

My mother-in-law is lonely too. She has her 3 room apartment and passes the day with a little bit cleaning and cooking. Besides she fortunately has a hobby. Everywhere in the rooms you find plants and flowers. Even in the middle of the winter she has plants which carry flowers.

After the death of Aad's father we did not go to our beloved Gerlos at Christmas. We went to Rotterdam to pass Christmas with her. You see, everywhere in the world the same troubles with old people you love and for whom you feel a certain responsibility.

Aad is going well in his school. His health is excellent again. He has to work 28 hours a week (chemistry and physics) plus the work that goes with graduation papers a.s.o. He likes better to teach boys and girls of 17-18 years than 14-16 years.

Hans is in his 3th year in Groningen University now and he is working very hard. I believe he wrote you about the modern youth movement?

We had strange vacances. Aad's school was finished at Juli l and Hans had finished too and came home. Hans wished to go to Yugo-Slavic. He started with a shelter tent and a rucksack. He went by train through Europe. Ineke went with us for a trip with the car in Germany. We saw beautiful countries, mountains, old villages and cities, Munchen, Trier. When we came back 20 Juli, Ineke started for a sailing camp with 9 young men and girls. She sailed a week, she had much wind and rain, but she amused herself. In the beginning of August we went with the four of us to the little island situated an hour sailing from the North coast of our country. It was named Schier monnit ooj (mouth) (eye). Cars are forbidden there. Everybody hires a bike. The hotels are very simple and you must amuse yourself with walking, swimming, sun bathing (when the sun is there!) enjoying the dunes and the wild flowers. We were there during a week and we had 7 happy days with the children.

We send you as a birthday present a calender on which old famous churches. I hope you will enjoy it and you will have a happy birthday, dear Ruth.

What a troubles in the world in the U.S.A. and in Mexico. Our newspapers are full of talks about the president elections in the U.S.A. I think the responsibility of the new chosen president too heavy. What about the war in Vietnam? What about the Black Power Movement? What about the criminality in the big cities? Sometimes we think that we, here in Holland, are living on a little island of peace. But every day the waves of war can take us, too. 800 km from here are the Russians with their tanks in Tsho-Slowakge, on the boundary with Germany.

Much love from all of us, Hanna

+ + + + + + +

October 14, 1969 — Enschede

Dearest Ruth.

The first birthday after your mother's death. The saddest day you can imagine. But I am sure that although your mourning

244

is still so steep that your family and friends come to you on this day with their good wishes and so do we.

Aad and Ineke and Hans and myself, we do wish that you, your brother and sisters will find the courage and strength to go on with the work you have to do in this world. I am sending you as a birthday present an old fashioned sugar spoon. There is a little story about this spoon.

My grandmother received as a wedding present +/– 90 years ago 12 silver teaspoons and a matching sugar spoon. When she died my mother got the teaspoons and my Aunt Clazien got the sugar spoon (among other things which belonged to my grandmother).

My mother, who wanted to possess a sugar spoon matched to the teaspoons, had made by a silver factory a sugar spoon precisely as the original one. After my mother's death, I used every day the spoons. When Aunt Clazien died, I got the original sugar spoon, and I made up my mind to send you the sugar spoon I myself used during 12 years. When you and I use the spoon every day we know that we both use the same spoon, a silver one with the same decorations. Only the one I am sending you is a copy. We wish, dear Ruth, that you will use it many years in good health!

Lots of love, Hanna

+ + + + + + +

16 October, '69 — Enschede

Dearest Ruth,

My thoughts are with you all the time since we got your letter with the sad news of the death of your dear mother. We want to let you know how we understand your feelings of sorrow and loneliness and we wish we could go to you to console you a little bit. In such moments it is a pity that we live so far away from each other. I myself lost my parents. My father died in the last year of the war as you know and my mother survived him 13 years. It is 12 years ago that she died. But growing older myself, I often think about my parents and I believe that the manner of life they had has indoctrinated me. All sorts of things they used to approve concerning education, social life, morality, I do approve too, generally speaking.

Aad lost his father as you know and his mother is very lonely now. About 200 km (200/126 miles) away from us. At Aad's birthday 10 Sept. (the day on which your mother sank to death) she was here and stayed with us about 10 days.

Aad and I were the only child of our parents, and I think you are lucky with your brother and sisters and their families. You belong to a number of relatives, to which you can always go and who have the same background, and they have the same feelings of sorrow about your dear mother, so you can speak about her with these relatives.

Dearest Ruth, we all wish you a lot of strength in the days that will come in the first year after you lost your mother. This first year in which memories come each day. And especially when you are busy with the difficult job of disposing of her belongings. It is good that you are teaching again. In the teaching hours you can't worry about other things than the young people you have to learn and educate.

Love from us all, especially from me a kiss.

Hanna

Chapter Seventeen

10 October, '70 — Enschede

Dearest Ruth,

Again your birthday! You was right when you said: they come sooner and sooner. Again we wish you a happy birthday with your family, your sisters and brother, nieces and nephews.

At September 1st I went to the hospital for a toncilectomie. I had to go for the last year I was tired, and I had every day a temperature that was a little bit too high. The toncilectomie is painful, when one is 56 years old as I am and there is a recovery who lasts + 3 months. After a week I was back from hospital and at home and then Ineke fell ill, a serious flu, with headache. Aad had to cook a.s.o. for two women and he had his work at school. Ineke was after a week again recovered, but she was so weak and she could not go to school. It lasted 4 weeks, till she was recovered to be able to work. (I am still tired when I try to work a little bit). She dismissed herself from the job on the factory and went to school again. She thought she did not know enough about chemistry to go a step further in her job of assistant in the laboratory.

AT LAST WE MUST SEE EACH OTHER ONE TIME IN OUR LIFE DEAREST RUTH!

Hanna

Hanna and Aad's home in Enschede

Dear Ruth,

Your letter arrived here at the moment we were changing our home Louis Braillestraut for a house, that suits us far better. The new address is: Bolhaanslaan 73, Enschede

It is a house built 40 years again and very cosy. It has a thatched roof and a beautiful garden. Now I want to live 20 years more to enjoy all things in this house.

When you don't mind telling about your salary I will tell you that Aad receives for 26 hours a week teaching chemistry and physics to young persons 14-18 (sometimes 20 years) about 30,000 guilders a year. He has to pay much taxes which are needed for our defence, care for ill and old persons. There is no poverty in our country because all ill, old, and invalid persons receive enough money from the government to live. Families with children become in our country for each child till the age at which it earns his own money, a certain gift per month. So Aad gets with 2 children every month then the taxes are paid + 2000 guilders.

Aad teaches every Friday evening 7-10 on a special school where teachers want to know more. There he earns some money extra. He earns enough to have with us in a middle class way. We are not hungry, have enough dresses, can afford 2+ months year a vacation, live in a house in a well situated neighborhood. We earn less than a doctor or a judge or an owner of a plant or a colonel of the army, but Aad has much more time to spend at home where he can prepare his lessons. etc. As you growing older, he does not have much activities outside school. I am recovered from my operation which was a little bit horrible.

Ineke goes to school. She is trying to do her utmost to join the class. We hope she has success.

At December 19 we all go to Austria, Ineke, Hans, Aad and I. Ineke and Hans to ski, Aad and me to wander. We remain in Gerlos (Zellerthal Tirol) till 2 January. Ineke's birthday is Saturday, she has 24 years then. Now you know again everything about us. We are sending you a lot of greetings and love.

Hanna

+ + + + + + +

Dearest Ruth,

It is a long time that I did not write to you. When we were in Austria, we send you a card of the surroundings of the village and we hope you received it in good health.

We went by car 900 km and Aad, Ineke, and Hans drove each 2 hours and changed. We drove 14 hours. We went from Enschede at 5 o'clock in the morning and we were at 7 o'clock in the evening in Gerlos in the snow. We were a bit tired, but after half an hour we went out to eat in the village and at 10 o'clock we went to bed and slept immediately.

Ineke and Hans went skiing 10 days and Aad and I made excursions by foot or by car. We enjoyed ourselves very much. We were glad that Ineke and Hans accompanied us. They are 24 and 22 and both have had good vacances, they told us.

We did not live in the same house as we used to. Now we were in a large wooden farmer's house at the end of the village. We had large warm sleepy rooms and a sitting room where we had breakfast, arranged by the farmer's wife. For lunch we bought some bread and made tea in the farmer's kitchen and dinner we cooked ourselves in their kitchen. We cooked very simple. Sometimes we went to eat in the village 2 or 3 times a week as you did, writing in your Christmas letter. We, too, have in our shops deep freezed food. It is indeed very easy to prepare.

Hans is still in Groningen. I believe he is very clever, he still lives in his living boat with 3 other students. They have there all the freedom and privacy they desire. Ineke is again at school. In the job she had last year she was not so happy. She thought she knew too little and wanted to learn a little bit more. So we are living in this house with the three of us. Now and then Hans comes a weekend or Aad's mother comes a week or friends from Rotterdam are invited. We hope to hear from you again.

Much love and greetings from us all
Hanna

+ + + + + + +

September, '71

Dearest Ruth,

Many thanks for your birthday letter. I am always very glad getting a letter from you.

You wrote that teaching is becoming strenuous when you are a bit older. So is Aad shrinking, too. He has the same experience. He is 56 now and he hopes that at 60 he will be able to finish his job. People are asking for it, but we don't know. Perhaps he has to work till 65.

One of the ideals I had during my life is to see you and to talk with you. Perhaps, when you are free from work that you come to Holland and stay a few weeks to us, sitting in our room, eating our food, enjoying the environs, the surroundings with us.

Dear Ruth, many greetings from all of us.

Hanna

Chapter Eighteen

Hanna continued to plea with Ruth to come for a visit. Only once did Hanna mention the consideration of their going to America. Perhaps with Hans still at the University and Ineke newly employed, Hanna felt it would be much easier for Ruth to travel to them and meet all the family and friends she knew through correspondence.

Hanna grieved for countries struggling for their democratic type of government and felt fortunate to be living under a constitutional monarchy. Having survived the effects of the most brutal tyranny on two continents caused her to be most appreciative of democracy, although she recognized its weaknesses. She would probably have agreed with the saying, "Democracy is a poor form of government, but it's the best we have." In 1973 the Labour Party gained control, and Socialism crept into many areas of Dutch life with mixed consequences.

Dec., '71

Dearest Ruth,

Here we are to wish you many happy days in the new year 1972. We hope you had a fine Christmas. We were not in the mountains in Austria this year. We would go to my mother-in-law but the day before Christmas Ineke fell ill with high fever (influenza) and we had to ring up that we could not come. It was a pity for her, but she said very bravely I will wait till a weekend in the new year when Ineke can come too.

Hans is at home now. He stays a fortnight and with peniciline, Ineke's fever disappeared fortunately.

WHEN DO YOU COME TO HOLLAND? IT IS TIME THAT WE SEE AND KISS EACH OTHER BEFORE WE GROW TOO OLD TO MAKE THE TRIP OVER THE OCEAN!

Many greetings from us all,
Hanna

+ + + + + + +

251

October, '73

Dearest Ruth,

Many thanks for the beautiful fotocard you sent us about your new home. I think you will be very happy in such marvellous furniture chairs, cupboards and bed. Do you have a colour television? We have since a few weeks.

At 14 Oct. it is your birthday and we tried to catch something that will serve in your home. We found in a shop where the owner imports all things of beautiful objects from Poland this handmade wall cloth. We think it suits to your grey velvet chair or maybe it may hang on the wall next to your bed? We hope the colours will do in one of your rooms.

We had a fine holiday in South England. Ineke is now ready with her studies. She is working in Enschede at a laboratory. The white coat suits her very well. Hans is still in Groningen. He is in his last year (we and he hope) of his study. He now studies his last subject, a very difficult one in physics. He is 25 now and Ineke 26. Yesterday we heard about the war in Israel. We hope the Jews will win on defending their right to live in an own country. and what to say about Chile? It is far away from our bedside, but how many countries in Europe and in other parts of the world are reigned by a dictator nowadays? We love the democratic although we know that in a democracy it is possible too that faults are made.

We wish you to have a very happy birthday. Lots of love from all of us.

Hanna

+ + + + + + +

April, 1974

Dear Ruth,

It is already a long time ago that I wrote a letter to you. We looked again yesterday to the fotos you send us when you moved to your new apartment. I believe you are so happy there.

The Easter holidays came with beautiful weather. The sun shining all day, spring flowers in the gardens and in the meadows and woods. Especially here in the East of the country where not so much people are living on a little space. Nature is still around us.

252

Our neighbours from Rotterdam came up to us. We had invited them to stay with us with Easter and three days long we walked with them in the fields and woods. They breathed the fresh air.

Hans was with his girlfriend Liesbeth invited by her parents. He is now almost at the end of his studies, but he should like to stay at the university as a member of the staff. We don't know if there is any chance for it, we hope it for him. At first is he obliged to go a year in military service when he is ready with his study, but perhaps when he can get a place as science worker at his university, they will let him free. Experimental physics, that is what he is studying. It has to do with biology and physics. He is working with flies, how the brains are working, for me too difficult to understand (ha). Ineke is now working since a year in her job in the laboratory of a small paint manufactory. She is living in our house and we managed very well with the three of us. Aad is happy with his job as a teacher of chemistry. The final examinations are these days beginning. We are near our 60th birthday and we are very healthy, but feeling that we are not so strong as in our forties. Are you in good health? Are you still thinking of retiring?

    Lots of love and greetings
                  Aad, Ineke, Hanna

P.S. What a strange world we are living in! Israel, the Arabs, Chile, the oil, the multi nationals. Nixon with his affairs, the United Nations, and our defence organisation, the NATO. We are glad to live in that small part of Europe where there is still no war and where we are living in a democracy where nobody is hungry or cold. This is a rather egotistic thought, isn't it?

+ + + + + + +

Sept., '74

Dear Ruth,
    Your birthday parcel I received a few days before my birthday. XXXXXX, the six crosses I have now behind me (meaning her 60th birthday). 10 August was a beautiful day. In the morning I had coffee with a few lady friends in our garden and in the evening Ineke, Aad, and I had dinner in a China restaurant.

    At eight o'clock a few friends came in to spent the evening with us with a glass of wine and cheerful talk. Hans and his girlfriend Liesbeth came the weekend afterwards so I had two birthdays. I can feel I am not 30 and not 40 and not 50 any longer. When I am tired after playing tennis or after a long walk of 3 or 4 hours, it lasts nowadays much longer to recuperate. Do you have the same experience?

We had a nice vacances in Scotland, a little bit rough climate. The evenings were long. At 10 o'clock it was possible to fotograph. We climbed hills and rocks, enjoyed lakes and islands, and old castles. We saw the men wearing a skirt with flies backwards. Ineke bought one. In Holland also women wear such a skirt. In Scotland no woman likes to do that, it is men's clothes.

Hans and Liesbeth have finished their studies. Hans is going further with his research on biological physics, only now he earns a rather high salary. He can stay at the university four years conducting young students and working on his own research and writing a book for his doctor's degree.

Liesbeth is looking for a job. She is a psychologe and wants to help a psychiatrist (a doctor for nervous illness). But it is difficult for her to get a place. There are much young people in Holland who can't find a job after their studies. How is this in America? We are glad Ineke works in a laboratory and earns her living. How do you do now you are retired? I should like to see your home. On the fotos it looks so cosy! <u>Always longing to see you with my own eyes once in our life</u>!

Lots of love.

Hanna

+ + + + + + +

October, '74

Dearest Ruth:

A thousand excuses for my forgetting your birthday! I have not a single reason why I did forget the 14th of October. Maybe I'm getting old (ha!) Although my health is very good, I have sometimes painful muscles in my back. You know that I had some groups of women between 40-70 years I gave an hour a week physical education. I did exercises with them. I had 5 groups of 15 women and it was a pleasure for me to do it 5 times a week in the afternoons. Now I had to say that I could not do it any longer because of my backache. I knew a younger collegue who wished to do this work. I did not have a single thought that all these women should be sorry for my retiring. They were sorry and invited me and gave me a goodby present, a viewer for colour slides. We can imagine that you, after your 45 years teaching was honoured by Herrin High School and received so many presents.

We enjoyed the pictures you sent us and the contents are really worth the stamps!

We are making since 10 years colour slides, but I have a book in which I collect all the pictures I get from friends or from Hans and Liesbeth and from you. The pictures you sent in the occasion of your retiring are in this book now too. They are very beautiful.

Yesterday we bought a present for you, a calender with views of Holland. It is a bit late for a birthday present. We call it "using mustard after dinner".

We enjoyed your last letter and my friends are fighting for the stamps.

Dear Ruth, when do you come to visit us? Aad says, "When Ruth does not come to Holland, why don't you go to her?" Planes are cheaper than in the days when we were young. I'm 60 now.

Lots of love, much greetings from Aad, Ineke and me,

Hanna

+ + + + + +

Both Ruth and Hanna had retired from teaching, and Aad had greatly reduced his hours. The Dutch worried about excessive unemployment in their country which had affected Ineke who lost her job in a lab and would be on reduced "welfare" for two and a half years before an improvement in the work force allowed her again to be employed.

However, on an even more personal note for Ruth and Hanna, the bittersweet ending to this relationship was just beginning with this letter.

16th July, 1975 — Enschede
(Aad's letter about Hanna's illness)

Dear Ruth,

I write now in a hurry for we have had a very bad fortnight. We went to Scotland for our summer holidays and being there Hanna discovered a lump in her left breast. The G. P. in Villin (on

255

Lock Tay) after some days sent her through to a hospital in Stirling (the former royal capitol of Scotland). The local surgeon advised us to try to return to Holland to have it attended to. So said, so done. This was Wednesday 9th. We immediately went through to Edinborough airodome and within the hour she could get a plane to Amsterdam and from there a plane to Enschede.

Last Monday she went to hospital after a lot of x-rays, blood analysis, etc. and yesterday the surgeon took a look inside and found his suspicions confirmed. It is malignant. Instead of taking everything away, a new technique in such a case is irradiation, with cobalt treatment and that will start on Monday next (21st July).

We, i.e., Ineke, Hans and I, had a long talk with the surgeon who is an acquaintance from the tennis lot. He explained everything to us and later to Hanna as well about this case and about the treatment they are going to give. The chances of total recovery are between 40 and 50% and it seems to be very important that Hanna herself believes in recovery.

Well, sorry to have to write much bad news, but this is something nobody can do anything about. <u>We all hope to hear something from you as soon as possible or rather to see you!</u>

Yours, Aad

Greetings from Hanna, Ineke, and Hans

+ + + + + + +

Sept. 24, 1975

Dearest Ruth,

Your letters you wrote me after the day you had a message from Aad that I came back from Scotland holiday with a breast cancer were a precious present for me. I read them over and over, and I felt that though we never saw each other from face to face we knew each other's heart and soul so very well.

Many people wrote me, many people visited me. Some knew perfectly well, as you, what to write or say, others were afraid or began to cry when they saw me. You know I was too late for an amputation and so the doctors decided to use cobalt rays during 5 weeks. They hope the cobalt rays will kill the cancer cells and in 40% of the cases it will help. I went through the daily portion of rays. I did not become ill or very nervous. My skin was not burnt

256

until the end of the 5 weeks, and now it is waiting till end September. Fotos will be made of breast and thorac.

I am healthy, walking, playing bridge, cooking and all. But the fear of having such a death bringing thing in your body is horrible. In the first time, I was thinking every minute about that and what it would be to be dead at sixty one or sixty two, but now I am rather accustomed to all those things and I am enjoying (I try to enjoy) the things that are coming to me as fine autumn weather.

Your sending me cards of cheer, the happy days when Hans and Liesbeth are coming here for a weekend, and the presence all days of Aad and Ineke. I read in one of your letters that perhaps you are coming to Holland. Last year, when I invited you to come before we two are old and perhaps ill. Now I am repeating the same words to you. Hans and Liesbeth are married now, after living together since two years. I am convinced that the marriage will be a happy one for they have had the chance to know each other very well. The marriage was a simple one. Only the family (fathers and mothers, sister Ineke, three brothers and wives and 2 children and my mother-in-law at 82) were invited to come to Groningen and to go with them to the town hall. No church, no professional fotografer. Ineke and Aad took some fotos which we will send to you later on. In the afternoon we went to a country seat, rebuilt as a restaurant. The weather was fine. We sat outside for a while and later on we had dinner inside. A barbeque. It was very, very lovely. Nobody became tired. At ten o'clock we went home and at twelve we went upstairs to go to bed. My mother-in-law was very happy. The next day we brought her home. Then 19 August came my birthday. I feared that day, but it went all very well. Hans and Liesbeth came during the weekend and now I am in my 61st year.

Much love from me and my family, and thanks for all your love.

Hanna

+ + + + + + +

12 November, '75

Dearest Ruth,

Again the postman with a parcel from a far away country, from Illinois.

I must thank you with all my heart for your thoughts about me and all the good wishes you sent me during these 4 months of unbelievable sorrow and despair.

I have learned now to live with the idea that I have this cancer in my body and that it is possible that it will creep out of my breast into other parts of my body. But there are many points of light. The cobalt rays help sometimes to stop the evil. Aad and Ineke who are living with me are patient and help me with their courage. Hans and Liesbeth are coming sometimes. They were here this week-end. The weather was fine and we made a trip by car through the woods and where the colours of the trees were very fine. We stopped the car and had a fine walk during 2 hours. I am fully fine and I hope it will last a long time. I enjoy your letters and I am so glad you enjoy your retiring so much.

Now I am sending you at last some fotographs. The coloured one was made on the wedding day of Hans and Liesbeth. I liked to send you a foto of Hans and Liesbeth, but they asked me to do not for they like to send you one by theirselves.

Again, many thanks for your friendship and love. Greetings from Aad and Ineke.

Love from me, Hanna

+ + + + + + +

26 January, 1976

Dearest Ruth,

Many thanks for your greetings on the occasion of our 36th marriage day. We spent the day with Hans and Liesbeth and Ineke. At four o'clock in the afternoon there was a piano recital in a 12th siecle (small church some 30 kilometers from Enschede in a small village) and later on at six, we had dinner with the five of us in a cosy restaurant in Hengelo, a small town some 10 kilometers from Enschede. Hans and Liesbeth went back to Groningen by train at eight. We had a nice day. It is not our custom to celebrate this day. Other years Aad brings a bunch of flowers for me or I am cooking his favorite meal. But now, because it was on a Sunday and because Hans and Liesbeth visited us, we made a nice day of it.

The doctors are not so very content about my health. They are trying to stop these cancers with new medicines, Hormone preparations young women can't use them, but fortunately I passed sixty years. I am feeling very well, walking, shopping, cooking. At Friday morning I go to the swimming pool to help elder people to learn swimming.

We should like it very, very much when you should come to Holland. We have a small room for guests. Of course you are always welcome whenever you want to come. We think however, that Holland is beautiful between Easter and Whitsuntide, when it is full springtime. At Easter and Whitsuntide the roads are very crowded with cars full of people going for a trip. When you prefer to come, when Aad has vacances from school, you may come between 3-8 of June. But before June he has time for you too, for with 60 years, the job of teacher is far more easy 16 hours a week instead of 26, so he has time enough to accompany us when you like to see some parts of Holland. Come to Holland whenever you like it. You are always welcome. I hope I will be healthy a few months or a few years, nobody knows, no doctor knows. Thank you for your letters. With all my heart, and we are sending you greetings and love.

Aad, Ineke, Hanna

+ + + + + + +

At last Ruth decided to go to Holland to see Hanna for the first time! For 43 years the two women had corresponded, and during that time their friendship had developed into a strong bond of love and concern for one another.

The discovery of Hanna's cancer was probably the factor that caused Ruth to make the decision to travel to Holland knowing it would, perhaps, be the only chance for them to "gaze into each others' eyes" and to give Hanna the loving support that such a true friend could offer.

From Aad's following letter, plans were made to show Ruth a good time on her visit. Hanna's heart was "full of joy" and she was looking forward to Ruth's visit.

15th Feb., 1976 — Enchede

Dearest Ruth,

We should like it very much if you and your sister would stay in our home these 4 days. We have a not too large room with two beds for our guests on the second floor. The only inconvenience is that bathroom etc. are one story down.

The Nederlands Lucht (Dutch Airline Company) takes care of the airline Amsterdam-Enschede. These planes specially for business people do not fly on weekends and holidays and as our Queen has her birthday in 30th April (holiday!). You had better come on Thursday 29th April. If that is impossible, you must take the train to Enschede from Amsterdam. There is a train starting in Amsterdam and ending in Enschede every hour from the Central Station in Amsterdam (2 hours!) From the airodome to the station with a bus takes half an hour. Airplane Amsterdam-Enschede 20 min. The NLM told us that you can get tickets probably much easier and cheaper in America. From Enschede we should like to make some trips through our country e.g.

1. Vicinity old Saxon farmhouses and water mills in our part of the country near our home. By car!
2. By car over the town of Zwolle and the village of Giethourn to the Trierian lakes and over the Zuyder Sea dyke.
3. To the islands of Zeeland (Sea land) where we find old towns (16th century), the sea, the dunes, the delta winds.
4. Visiting Rotterdam, the biggest harbour in the world, the windmills.

We can also make a road tour and stay somewhere in a hotel for a night. It isn't expensive. We believe 30 guilders for bed and breakfast ($10) We can arrange that. We hope that Hanna will be fit enough to go with us. She is fit now, very fit, I must say. Thus, we can show you our beautiful parts of the country.

Should her health be less good, then we can arrange a simple hotel here. Ineke and I can, in that case, accompany you both on our trip.

This is written in haste.

Many, many greetings from the three of us.

Aad

P.S. March 31, '76 Tel. No. when you ring from outside our town from Amsterdam for instance 023-351358.

+ + + + + + +

No date

Dearest Ruth,

My heart is full of joy when I am thinking about your wonderful coming to Holland. I received the booklet "The Joy of Friendship" and I admired it. The postage you used was enough. I have not to pay anything.

We will meet you on "that wonderful day you come to Enschede" at the railway station and bring you in our home (5 min. driving).

I am very well. I am housekeeping, shopping, going every Friday morning to the swimming pool to teach older people who has not the opportunity in their youth to learn swimming. We often play cards, bridge, 3 women and I, so my days are busy and so I have not much time to think about my illness. But I know of course that this illness is not a dream, but reality and that every day I am in good health is very precious. I hope that when you come my condition is still good.

Ineke and Aad are as enthusiastic as I to meet you and your sister, and we shall do our utmost to give you some cheerful days. So, much thanks dear, that you come to me!
Lots of love, Hanna

I enjoyed your story about our correspondence and showing all the things we send you in the course of the years!

+ + + + + + +

Wednesday, 21 April, '76

Dearest Ruth and Euvera,

We received the two letters and are enjoying our meeting each other as well as you. This letter is to wish you a wonderful voyage and a happy landing on the airport of Amsterdam named Schiphol. When you go by bus KLM to the Central Station of Amsterdam, you can catch the train leaving straight to Enschede just 2 minutes before each whole hour. The end station is Enschede. Every half an hour a train starts from Amsterdam, but then you have to change the train in Amersfoort. But with your luggage is it a bit difficult. At the station in Amsterdam you can phone us, as I told you 053-351358. The train takes exactly 2

261

hours. On the day of your arrival that Friday it is the queen's birthday and as we all love her, you will see the flags (red, white, blue) with the orange scarf everywhere. That is not for you (ha!)

We had very beautiful weather last week too. It was almost summer and we put away our winter clothes. But it is possible that when you arrive, it is raining or colder than now. So I hope you don't take winter clothes. I myself will meet you in my grey skirt with a dark blue blazer. I bought the shirt yesterday. I could not wear any longer my skirts of last spring, for the medicine I take (hormone) did make me put on weight and I are tall too, and Aad has the same length as we have (1.72m). Ineke is asking a few days leave. She likes to accompany us and to meet you at our station too. You will see the three of us. Lots of love. We count the days, the hours till your arrival.

Hanna

+++++++

Ruth visited Holland in April, 1976. Ruth and her sister Euvera spent three lovely days meeting family and friends. They visited in the home of Karel and Zus who are mentioned frequently in these later letters.

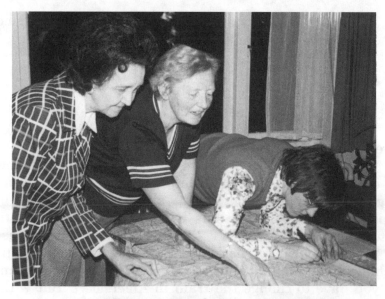

Planning Dutch itinerary
Ruth, Hanna, and Ineke marking a map

Aad photographing Ruth admiring the tulip fields
(Hanna nearby)

Karel and Zus—good friends of Hanna and Aad
(Zus survived imprisonment in Java with Hanna.)

Hanna wrote to Ruth after her return trip home and described her emotions upon seeing Ruth, in person, for the first time.

19th June, 1976 — Enschede

Dear Ruth,

We enjoyed your big letters 23 May and 8 June. My finest memories are too our first meeting in Enschede. The moment you stepped out of the train and we kissed each other, this moment I will never forget so long as I am permitted to live. I am afraid that the 3 days tour through our country was a bit too much for you, but we wanted to let you see some wonderful places, especially Renesse where we spent our vacances during so many years.

I am sending you some pictures which are ready now. In a fortnight perhaps some others are ready.

We get a letter from Euvera and we will send her some pictures too. It was so nice of her to come with you. I love much, dear Ruth and Euvera, and we are happy to have met you two and that you had such a nice trip in good old England.

My health is still good, but every six weeks I must go to the doctor and I don't know each time what is the result of his examination.

Greetings from all of us, especially from me.

Hanna

Ruth and Hanna greeting each other after 44 years

Hanna and Ruth enjoying their time together

Hanna, Euvera, and Ruth at a
lighthouse in Holland

26th Juli, '76

Dearest Ruth,

We enjoyed your last letter very much, the one on the notepaper from Scotland. The heather and the blue grass bells are so beautiful. We found these flowers last year when we spend our vacances in Scotland. We had bed and breakfast in Killin on Loch Tye with the mountain Ben Awes 2 miles away. It was a beautiful scenery there, as you know now you travelled there too. It is more than a year ago we were there and discovered the little red spot on my breast. I had a very quiet year and you saw yourself when you were with us that I am still in good health. But the cancer goes on, very, very slowly and the medicines and the diet are helping to keep my health as good as possible. We have got the slides back of our trip to the Zunderdee dike and Hoorn and the one of the first day we went to Germany Benthem Castle. We enjoyed yesterday evening the slides very much and tomorrow morning we go the fotoshop to bring the slides and to order some fotos for you. But it will take a fortnight we get them back.

Yesterday evening I saw on the projection screen your lovely face and that of Euvera. The tears came in my eyes, for I love you two so much and as you say in your letter "I should love to drop in to you" and I should love you to take me in your car for a drive. But for the moment we must do with a letter and a foto. Wednesday Karel and Zus come to Enschede and Friday we are going to Switzerland 1000 km from here. We hired a little apartment for a fortnight for we have to cook my diet. Ineke is going with us and Zus and Karel remain in our house to take care of the cat. They love to take some bicycle trips in the neighborhood which is different from the scenery in their village.

Greetings from the four of us to Euvera. For you a big kiss from me and Ineke and Aad.

Your Hanna

+ + + + + + +

20 August, 1976

My dearest friend, dear Ruth,

What a surprise to hear your voice from so far away and it was as if we sat again besides each other on the couch and you

266

wished me a happy birthday. I thank you very much. It must have ruined you to speak to us such a long time, but we thought it is always cheaper than to buy a ticket and to fly to Enschede (ha!).

Indeed we had a fine vacance in Switzerland. Ineke was with us with her boyfriend. She is very much in love. We do see her not so often any more. When her work is done, she goes to Frank and most of the time she is not at home at night. She is 29 and he 32 and we do not say a word against it. In our youth it could not occur, that not married you stayed with your boyfriend you know, but nowadays much things are accepted in our country, in Germany, in France, in Great Britain, and I believe in America, too. We don't agree with all those modern philosophy, but we don't like to lose the sympathy of our children.

I had a happy birthday in the morning, two lady friends to drink coffee with sweets. For lunch Ineke's girlfriend Tlon whom you know + a couple which are friends of us, and at 5 o'clock Ineke came from her work. Her boyfriend came too and we all went to a family who invited us for dinner in their home. They wanted me to do nothing but eat and enjoy myself. I was very grateful, you know.

I forget to thank about the money you gave to Aad the last day you were here. I bought cups and saucers for it which were very expensive, but beautiful. Many thanks again.

Lots of love from Aad, Ineke, Hans, and me Hanna

+ + + + + + +

October 11, 1976

Dearest Ruth,

You are spoiling me with so much letters which I enjoy very much. But now I have to answer 2 letters and besides inform you about all things who happen here.

At first I must thank you for the 20 dollar note. It was not necessary to send it for you have during all these years sent so much pictures, especially the ones when you retired and why you moved in that cosy apartment. I knew then where you were living and how you relaxed in that very pretty chair a.s.o. I will send the pictures of the airport and the garden, but they were colour slides and we will bring them to the fotoshop to have pictures. But no more money. It is already too much which you sent!

I read the newspaper cuttings about cancer and I believe the doctors here are thinking in the same way about this awful disease. I thank you for sending. I let it see to my doctor and he appreciated them. I am going on with the diet. It is not too easy when you are invited by friends for dinner. But last weekend we stayed at Karel and Zus (greetings) and she cooked for us all the things I must eat. Fine friends they are!

We walked in the dunes and in Sunday we had a trip to Zandomt on the beach and walked an hour along the beach with the sea roaring in our ears. It was very fine autumn weather and the sun was warm.

I read that you get from friends vegetables and fruits. That is fine and very healthy. Our green grocers sells now vegetables who are picked from the fields where the farmers are not sprayed and the vegetables are growing in a natural way.

This morning I had a look to my birthday calender and I saw that your birthday is 3 days from now. I chose a card of a mill because you and Euvera were so fond of all mills we saw on our trip through our country. In your letters I feel that you two liked this trip. But we thought we let see you too much on three days. But the time was not enough to let you see at ease all these landscapes and buildings we like so much ourselves.

Oktober 16-Oktober 25 has autumn holidays. Usually we are spending these days in our own neighborhood. The trees are colouring their leaves and when the weather is fine, we are walking through the woods every day. But now we made up our mind to go by plane to the south of Portugal (near Spain). At first to Lisbon and then by a smaller plane to the south (named the Algarve). The temperature is there very agreeable. You can have a swim in the Atlantic sea. We stay a week there in an apartment so that I can cook my own meals.

My health is still good, though I believe I am often very tired. But I try to have courage and I try to enjoy the days I still have. My diet doctor was during a month at the University of San Francisco to learn more and to tell there about his ideas. Dear Ruth, we wish you many years more in a good health.

Kisses from Aad and me

+ + + + + + +

268

October 25, 1976

Dearest Ruth,

Saturday evening we came home from our one week vacances in the South of Portugal. It was the first time that Aad travelled by plane, but he just as I enjoyed the flight very much. We had to go by plane and it flew not so high, so that we could see villages and cities, woods and islands, and beaches and mountains.

We hired an apartment because I wanted to cook that strange diet, what no hotel can give you. The weather was fine, we had 2 or 3 hour walks along the beach or in the pine woods behind the beach. We took a swim every day. The water was clear, warm, the sun was shiny every day, temp +/– 75 degrees. Some of the beaches behind the fisher villages were full of rocks that you can't meet in Holland. We had a magnificent holiday. Aad hired a car for he wanted to visit the whole south coast so that we visited Cape St. Vincent, the West Point of Europe.

The population is very poor, though there are a few very rich people. You could see that the man in the street was very proud to have after 40 years of dictators, the right to vote and choose their own government.

They are poor in the mountains, a citrus culture, some vegetables, hens, pigs, cows we did not see in the villages they make out of leather from goats and sheep, coats, a.s.o. They also make out of silver jewelery named filigrain. We bought for your birthday a pair of earrings. We hope you like them. My health was excellent there in the beautiful nature, no doctor in the neighborhood. Tomorrow morning I have again to go to the doctor for the injection, the one who takes care of the growing of the cancer cells. How are you? Did you have a happy birthday? Many greetings from Aad, Ineke, and me and a big kiss.

Hanna

+ + + + + + +

14 Nov., 1976

Dearest Ruth,

Your letters of Nov. 1 and Nov. 3 received. I am glad that the birthday present and the pictures reached you in good health.

We too were very anxious to know whether Ford or Carter should be elected as president and I know you chose Ford.

We don't understand all these troubles and voyages and spending and lengthy and shown their wives and children from the candidate president. We are glad we have our queen and when she retires or dead, it is clear that her daughter follows grown up in the idea that one day she will be queen and the prime minister is chosen because his political party (26, I believe), is the biggest one. The queen asks him to form a cabinet consisting of 12 clever men to reign the country.

My diet I shall write for you. Forbiddin: all what is prepared of white grains, as white bread, macaroni, spaghetti, white rice, pudding, sugar, 2 meat, fish, chicken, coffee, tea, cocoa, yogurt, potatoes, no vegetables in cans, no cabbage, no fried food. A must: every day 1 lite milk, 2 eggs, lemon juice, oranges, grapes, apples, pears, nuts a.s.o. Every day pea soup with vegetables, rice (with the silver edge on it), vegetables cooked or raw, dried fruit, as apricots, raisins, a.s.o., porridge, butter, oil of olives. The diet is full of vitamins in every meal, as you noticed. and good food.

I feel rather well, though the cancer does not stop but have not yet reached important parts of my body. Besides the diet, I get 2 times a month injections. They make that the cancer cells don't grow so fast (in great speed). I go swimming, walking. Sometimes I am very tired, that is the truth, but Aad says, "You are 62 now, mind you."

We think often about the days you were here with Euvera. It was a wonderful time. Did I already tell you that Ineke has no work since Nov. 1? She was dismissed, because the boss had no work for her. Many people in our country have no work. It is as in 1930-1939. It is a pity. Ineke is sad, and we hope she will find some other work. So you know something of us all.

Many greetings, lots of love from all.

Hanna

+ + + + + + +

16 Dec., '76

Dearest Ruth,

Your Christmas parcel came in yesterday and the three of us enjoyed it very much. Thanks are coming from here to you!!! The nightgown is so lovely and such perfectly, and Aad and Ineke are so enthusiastic about the wallets. It is such a pleasure to receive a package from a faraway country and from a very dear friend. We also received your Christmas card and we are sending you our Christmas greetings now and hope you have happy days at Christmas and a very happy New Year.

My health is the same as when you two were here. I am walking, swimming, playing bridge, cooking.

Lots of love, Hanna

+++++++

27 Februari, 1977

Dearest Ruth,

Two letters and Valentine greetings lay waiting on an answer on the cupboard in our room. We read in your letters how cold it was in America. We too saw on T.V. pictures of snow and ice and shortage of gas and electric, but now fortunately you have had the worst and spring is nearby.

How do you think about your new President Carter? Does he know enough about things concerning leadership for such a large country and leadership for millions of people?

We did not have a cold winter. Skating was not possible except on the artificial ice skatings.

My health does not go forward, but not backwards either. I have injections against the cancer cell growing and I have my diet too.

It works with natural products and Dr. Moerman, who invented it, thinks that cancer comes from bad food. I don't know if he is right but I take this food and now after a year I am accustomed to it. Some restaurants make it too. They call themselves "en nouvelle cuisine", French what means, as you know, "the new kitchen".

Greetings from all of us.

Ineke, Frank, Aad, Hans, Liesbeth and your Hanna

+++++++

30 April, 1977

Dearest Ruth,

It is just a year ago that you and Euvera came to Holland to us. You told in your last letter about it and this day, when all the flags are out, red, blue and white with the orange pennant because our queen's birthday and the weather is beautiful, spring is there with all the trees in blossom, I am thinking of you both all the day and remembering how grateful we were that you came flying over the ocean to us.

My health is still good. I am tired when I am doing too much, and, of course, the cancer does not stop but grows, although very slow. The doctors are happy that the diet and the medicines are helping me. The weather is so fine that I go playing tennis tomorrow for the first time this year. I hope I can manage. Dear Ruth, now you know again about us many things. I thank you that you are writing so often. A letter from you makes always a happy day.

Greetings from Aad, much love from Your Hanna

+ + + + + + +

4 June, 1977

Dearest Ruth,

This day I again read your letter of 27 April and 8 May, and I enjoyed as you did the happy days we spent with you and Euvera again.

I admire you that you remembered all those trips. It seems as if you wrote down these things in a diary. There were no faults, besides the little hotel in Renesse what you called Lee Rust (Lea Rest).

At the moment I am staying a few days at Zus and Karel's. I am here alone for Aad has to do school work. But Saturday he is coming, and Sunday afternoon we return home. They are sending you many greetings. Zus and Karel they remember that happy evening in their home with all of us with pleasure.

I am feeling well. The cancer does not grow very rapidly, fortunately the medicine and diet are helping so that the disease is going on very slowly.

This summer when Aad has his vacances at 28 Juni, we go with the car to Liege (Belgium) and then with the motor rail car on the train, we sleeping to Narbonne in the south of France near the frontier of Spain. There we stay with friends of us who have a little house in the mountains. We stay there a fortnight and then we go with our car slowly back to Holland. In the middle of the trip back, we stay a week in a beautiful and cozy hotel in the north of France. I hope our health is good enough to make the trip. I write "our health" for Aad is complaining of backache. He is very tired all the time and a little bit nervous. I think he is worrying about me.

Many greetings, lots of love from Ineke, Aad, and me,

Hanna

+ + + + + + +

9 Aug., '77
Stadsmaten Hospital, Enschede

Dearest Ruth,

Now I am lying in a bed in the hospital. When I wrote you my last card I was healthy and glad that we were spending our holidays in the south of France. But after a week my left arm began to ache so terrible that the doctor advised to return home. So we went by plane and were in one day in Enschede in the hospital. Now the specialist doctor neurology (I can't translate it, but it has to do with the nerves) says that by the cobalt rays two years ago one of the arm nerves has been hurt. He thinks about cutting the nerve so that the pain is over, but afterwards I shall not be able to move the arm without help of my right arm. Fortunately it is my left arm so that I can do much things afterwards. I have such a terrible pain during seven weeks now that I can't stand it any longer.

I enjoy your letters, but I was not able to write you back because the pain and the nervous situation. But now I know the doctor will operate my arm next week. I am calm again and can write you. The cancer is not going further now as the doctor told me. He says my condition is so good he can operate me without any troubles. So I hope he is right.

Dearest Ruth, do think about me next week, probably Thursday 18th, and I know you hope with me that all will come to good end. What luck we saw each other one time in our life. Those days were so beautiful. Nobody can take them from us.

With lots of love,

Your Hanna

+ + + + + + +

Sept. 8, 1977

Dearest Ruth,

Since a week I am home from the hospital. The operation was two hours long, and the doctor has made the operation in my neck. He has cut off the nerve who caused the terrific pain in my arm. The pain is nearly over now, but I can't move my left arm very well. Fortunately I am doing all things with my right arm.

Aad's school has started again, but he works in school 12 hours a week (in general a teacher has to do 26).

He is 62 now, and the doctor said, "You were a prisoner-of-war during four years and with your wife at home in bad condition, you are to do 12 hours."

I am very glad. Teaching at 62 is very difficult. Besides there are so many teachers, especially in Chemistry who do not have a job and are glad when there is a chance to start.

So I hope that you believe that I am recovering now from that bad illness. You see, I can again write to you.

With all best wishes for you from Aad and me and from me a big kiss.

Hanna

+ + + + + + +

Tuesday, 11 Ocktober, '77 — Enschede

Dear Ruth,

Your package at my birthday was lying at home when I left the hospital, and I believe that I forgot to thank you for it. But it was such a sad time then. The operation in the hospital had not helped and I had to do my utmost to recover from all this. Now I have recovered, except, that the pain in my left arm is still there. The doctors don't know how to help me. I hope that once upon a day the pain will be gone.

274

Except the painful arm, I am a good condition. Every day Aad and I take a walk of about an hour and fortunately he has enough time to help me with house keeping. Sometimes we invite some friends to play bridge a few hours. Last week Hans and Liesbeth came here for a weekend and we enjoyed that very much.

A happy holiday for you, dear Ruth, all the best and send our love.

Aad and Hanna

+ + + + + + +

On November 16, 1977, Aad wrote Ruth about Hanna's condition and felt that the end of her life was near.

By December 26, 1977, Hanna was critically ill and bedridden most of the time. Her letter on this day was very brief, but she was steadfast in her desire to continue her correspondence with her dearest friend, Ruth.

On February 3, 1978, writing had become difficult for Hanna, but she showed great courage in her efforts to answer Ruth's letter. As the end of Hanna's life drew near, she thanked Ruth for her friendship and counted it as one of the most important things in her life.

Nov. 16th, '77 — Enschede
(Letter from Aad)

Dear Ruth,

I have bad news. As I told you already in the telephone that she wasn't so good as she told you. But after that her condition has deteriorated very much. She had terrible pain, and as you know, the cutting of a nerve did not help. That was 18th of August. After that pain returned and the 7th of November during a yoga lesson, she felt a snap. The next morning heavy hemorrhage in the left arm, but the pain was already so terrible that she did not know that the bone was broken. That was discovered on Friday 11th when an x-ray was taken. The same photo showed that also the 7th rib had abberations due to cancer.

Today I brought her to the hospital for a general investigation, but as I see it now, I fear this will be the end. And she is living now with terrible pains the whole day through. She herself has no hope more, and she hopes that it won't be long.

275

she is living now with terrible pains the whole day through. She herself has no hope more, and she hopes that it won't be long.

I promised through the telephone to write immediately, but everything went so fast all at once that only now, when I'm alone here in the house I can take the time to write you.

I finish now this letter to put it away in time. Dear Ruth, many greetings from all of us and especially love from Hanna.

Yours, Aad

+ + + + + + +

26 Dec., '77

Dearest Ruth,

Thank you so very much for all your letters.

I am very ill now but now and then I leave my bed when the pain is a little bit to bear.

We wish you and your family a happy New Year. In our country the winter has not yet come. It is a rainy day now with a temperature of 6 degrees celcius. Yesterday Ineke and Frank were here to cook for us, and I sat at the table to eat with them. It was very difficult for me, but I hope they did not remark. After dinner I went to bed again.

Hans and Liesbeth are coming the last day of this year. I hope I have a rather good day then and can come out of my bed a few hours. I am so tired now, dear Ruth, but I wanted to write to you.

A big kiss from your Hanna

+ + + + + + +

3 February, '78

Dear Ruth,

I am enjoying your letters so much especially now the world around me has become so small. The room with the four walls, the pain every day, the bed in our living room on which I go lying down when I am too tired to sit in a chair. Sometimes when the sun is shining, and it is not too cold, Aad and I go for a little walk in the street, 5 to 10 minutes. Then I feel the fresh air for a while. I am sorry to hear that the winter in your country is so very cold again. Here we don't suffer. There is now and then a bit of snow. The temperaturo is mild for the time of the year. No ice in the rivers.

I thank you very much for the Christmas present which was you told me already a bit too late and yesterday there was a parcel again with the blue nightgown and the white bed shoes. You are spoiling me, but I know, that you are sending these presents with all the love you feel for me. Again I thank you very much.

Friday Zus and Karel came to Enschede by car and they were with us to Sunday morning. We enjoyed it very much but I was so tired and so sad that I could not do for them as I always did in former days, no cooking dinner, no walks in our fine surroundings. But we talked much about the time we were still young and how happy we were then together.

Hans and Liesbeth came on Sunday afternoon. They had spent a week at Austria skiing. There was a lot of snow there and they skied the whole day. They were tired in the evening and went early to bed. They went with the train of nine o'clock back to Groningen. Ineke cooked a fine dinner that we ate at six o'clock, I in my bed, the five of them round the table.

We hope that Egypt and Israel will have peace in the future with the help of your President Carter. The papers here are spending their pages about this.

I am getting so much letters, most of them I can't answer while I am so tired. In former days I was fond of writing, especially to you, my dear Ruth, but now it takes a lot of courage to get going to get some words on paper. But as long as I can, I will do my best to answer you. I hope the hard winter will not last too long in your country. Fortunately you have a comfortable and warm apartment.

With love from Aad and me, Hanna
Greetings from Hans and Ineke, Liesbeth and Frank

+ + + + + + +

11 April, 1978

Dear Ruth,
I thank you for so much writing. I enjoy your letters and yesterday, when your letter with the pictures came, I can imagine

277

what hard and strong winter you have had again. Our winter was mild, much rain and wind, but the water in the rivers was not frozen.

Yes, I am terrible ill now. I am lying in my bed the whole day. Fortunately I can still stay at home because Aad, Ineke, Frank and many friends do their utmost to care for me. Every weekend Hans is coming from Groningen to help and tomorrow Zus is coming three days. She is nearly a sister for me. My whole body is painful and I can't move my legs. But my arms I can use. So with much effort I can write to you. I am not afraid for death. I hope it comes soon, but I am very afraid of more pain.

Thank you for all the friendship that I received so many years. It was one of the most important things of my life, my dear Ruth.

Love and kisses from your friend,
Hanna

Dear Ruth,

I'll add some words to this, maybe the last letter Hanna is able to write. The metastasis has reached a part of the spine and now she is lame from the hips down. No hope of recovery. The nerve specialist last Saturday remarked that the process got into the rapids now. You know what the end will be. I (we) hope it will be soon for even with quite a lot of morphine, etc., pain is difficult to suppress. After writing this letter, she was extremely tired and started talking a bit incoherently.

Love, Aad

+ + + + + + +

Hanna's last letter (no date). The scribbling of this letter was difficult to transcribe, but Hanna's struggle to write to Ruth one more time indicated sincere affection and care for her friend of many years.

Probably about July 17, 1978

Dearest Ruth,

Yesterday the nurse entered my room in the hospital with a large basketful of flowers and plants. I was so amazed, I wondered who should sent me such a precious present. Then I looked at the card and saw your name. The tears came in my eyes, so glad I was. The nurse looked for a good place so that I can look at it very easily. I feel that I am very ill, but I will try to write to you and to thank you for all the letters and cards, the covers for the pillows, and so on.

Ineke and Frank are here in the room and offered to write to you, but I think you should be glad with a letter from me. They are holding the paper before me so that I can write, although I see that the letter is not so beautifully written.

With greetings and all my love,

Hanna

+ + + + + + +

Tuesday, July 20, '78— Enschede

Dear Ruth,

Last Saturday a beautiful greeting full of flowers was brought into Hanna's room in the hospital. I don't know what Ineke has written to you, but I'll try to bring you into the picture.

You know that all that pain and lameness has arisen from metastasis from the mammal carcinome. These metastases creep in a bone and more or less destroy it. So that when one part of the spine was attacked, all the nerves further down were cut out or immobilized and so she was lame from the hip down. That happened about Easter. She stayed at home with a nurse who came every morning to wash and treat the wounds of the left breast. The task grew too heavy for Ineke, Frank, and me, and after some serious talk she was admitted to the hospital with more help, more facilities, etc. And there she is now, waiting for the end. Because she has fought against fate with all her willpower, but now her strength is diminishing. As you see, she has written a letter to you, but she couldn't finish it. This morning I'll ask her to sign the letter.

Dear Ruth, there is tragic news, but methinks you expect it. This illness is a killer, whatever the doctors say. We hope that she is allowed to stay in the hospital, for when no care is possible, the hospital people try to get these patients into a nursing home. But we try to avoid another change if possible.

Please give us your telephone number, with district number, etc. I'll try to write more now school is over.

Love, Aad

+ + + + + + +

On July 23, 1978, Hanna finally got relief from the cruel disease. Aad sent Ruth a copy of the funeral services and jotted down the following note at the bottom of the printed program:

After a long and painful illness, this day passed over our dear, caring, brave Hanna Muijser-de-Bruijn. We did love her very much.

Enschede: A. J. W. Muijser, Ineke and Frank; Groningen: Hans and Liesbeth; Schiedam: N. C. Muijser-Broekman (mother-in-law).

Enschede, 23 July, 1978, the cremation will take place Wednesday, 26th July at 12:15 in the crematorium "Enschede" in Usselo, situated at the road Enschede-Haaksbergen. Condolences can be given after the solemn gathering in the crematorium.

I'll write later.

Aad

+ + + + + + +

Five months later.

8th October, 1978 — Enschede

Dear Ruth,

I'm sorry to confess that I have postponed writing to you too long. But I have been so busy clearing away all kinds of things which has been neglected during the last years in our house. For instance, we live at the Balkensslian f3 since 20th October 1970 and the living room has not been whitewashed since that time. And I took the opportunity to have the wallpaper changed and to change the place of bookcases, chairs, etc. This took rather a lot of time.

But now back to July 23th. I rang you at the end of the day to tell you of Hanna's death. I sent you a card. The same card was sent to more than 100 persons. Besides that, we put an announcement in 4 papers, two local papers, and two papers which were circulating all through the country.

On Wednesday 26th, the cremation took place at the specified time. We had no notion how many persons were going to attend because it was in the middle of our summer holidays.

280

People came from everywhere, more than 100 attended the ceremony. Besides that we got packs of letters.

I have been able to say a few words at the cremation in Menery and I shall translate the text as literally as possible for you. The music was Mozart's clarinet-trio (part of it), i.e. the andante and from the same composer the clarinet quintet (Stodtler Quintetr) allegro and larghetto. It was the last concert she attended and she loved the music very, very much.

After the ceremony the people who came from far away or dear friends from near came to Balkensslian f3 where we had some coffee and sandwiches.

One of my cousins took my mother from Schiedam to Enschede and back. She was very strong for her 85 years. Next year, by the way, she is coming to live in Enschede. It will be much better to have her here in the neighborhood.

I answered all the letters myself. I didn't want to send a printed card with "thank you". I thought it would be my duty to respond myself. I always let Hanna write letters for she was very good at letter writing, but now after 60 letters, I know it was just a habit to let her write. I answered especially those friends who were absent in the holiday time.

Dear Ruth, I close now for the moment. Maybe you can think back a moment, but time does not stand still. I must go on and go further. I hope you now have found the way to Europe, you can find Holland easier than years ago(!). I should like to make another trip with you through Holland in spring! Greetings from Ineke, Frank, Hans, and Liesbeth. Till next time.

Your Aad

+ + + + + + +

The following is the English translation of the Dutch text, the words that Aad spoke at Hanna's "funeral".

Before saying forever good-bye to Hanna, I want to talk about her for a short while.

In the beginning of 1940 we were married and went to the then called Dutch East Indies to get away from the unquiet Europe, but that resulted in a long separation via concentration and prisoner-of-war camps of the Japanese.

In 1946 we made a new start. Later we said sometimes that that time which we had with Ineke and Hans in Rotterdam had been the most careless time.

A lot of time spent outdoors in the summer in Renesse, in winter to Gerlos.

When we think back of the many people not returned from Indonesia or returned broken physically or psychologically, then this time was extra. Here in Enschede we had ups and downs, but what Hanna concerned practically no illness. That has been going on till the summer of 1975 in Scotland when we discovered cancer. That is now practically 3 years ago.

The last year she has suffered intensive pains. Why? You all knew her, some of you very well. Some of her outstanding characteristics I want to mention. In the first place her social commitment and that she didn't hide. That was difficulty sometimes, for with some people we were known as say "red rebels". But there is a big difference between that notion and social committance about things in our community.

Sport and games took an important place. Earlier in her life hockey, later tennis and badminton. She was well known for her extreme spiritivity.

Another outstanding characteristic was for all of us her easy and fast way of writing and organizing. We often said, "Just somebody for a travel bureau". That was also very convenient by helping young people who came to us with difficulties or for young colleagues of mine.

In her own teaching she had the idea that it did not amount to much. But she came back from that idea later.

She also did not comprehend earlier how much she wanted for her surroundings (that taken in the widest sense).

But happily it became clear to her later during her illness. When everybody kept coming to visit her, although her brave fight against pain and cancer lasted very long.

I assure you she understood it very well. I now ask all of you to say with us good-bye.

The music we hear has been her own choice. It was the last concert she attended.

I myself now take the opportunity to thank you all in the name of the family for your presence here.

+ + + + + + +

282

Dear Ruth,

With this, methinks, nice card I want to greet you and wish you all nice things for the new year. I don't know how you are going to spend Christmas, but I hope the time will flow as usual and give a pleasant feast.

Concerning myself, I am quite well. Better than I thought I would be after these bad years. I had a difficult time, but that is over now. I always was very fond of playing bridge. I do this a bit more now and that is a wonderful past time.

Maybe you remember that I came to Enschede in 1963 for the new teacher at University here. My boss here was Professor Greiven who died after a few years. His widow has been a friend of us since that time. Now I spend quite a lot time with her going to concerts, taking walks, etc. Her husband died of cancer too, and that gave us a lot to talk and reminiscence too. And everybody says: Why not? You are both alive and have the same interests. But now the rest of the family, Ineke is talking about marriage now. Hans has a job in Delft, but it takes quite a lot of time for Liesbeth (his wife) has still a job in Groningen, and she follows a course in psychotherapy there. So they have a weekend marriage now.

My mother is very frail now, 85! I succeeded in getting her a house approximately as she has now in Schiedam, but now here. It will be ready next summer. I hope she can enjoy it. It is much better to have her here. Her brother, 87, still lives in Rotterdam and is not so good. We plan to get my mother here next Friday (23rd) for some days, but it must be very quiet!

I hope you have nice days and I greet you from whole my heart.

Your Aad

Epilogue

But the story did not end there. Even after Hanna died, Aad continued writing and even visited Ruth twice in the States where he took the opportunity to photograph the local flowers of Southern Illinois. Hans (with a doctorate in physics), his own wife and two sons whom Hanna never got to enjoy, and Ineke with her husband Frank have kept Ruth updated on their lives "as their mother would have wanted them to do."

Ruth's letters have been lost, but we owe a great amount of thanks to Ruth for having kept Hanna's correspondence over the years and sharing this touching story with others.

Hanna's family feels she is being honored by keeping the memory of their wife and mother alive to untold future readers.

As a conclusion to this book, Ruth wrote a final letter to Hanna, 19 years later, expressing her feelings.

Dear Hanna,

Although you have been gone for a few years, I want you to know that I still miss you and think of you often. So often I think of things I'd like to tell you, and share with you—things I know you'd be interested in and would like to hear.

First, I would like for you to know that your family and I have kept in touch all these years through letters, phone calls, pictures, and gifts the way we used to do. That means a lot to me, as we have all been friends for so many years. So it's always a pleasure to receive a letter or a phone call from Holland.

Hanna, you have two fine grandsons, Arjen and Karel, children of Hans and Liesbeth. I'm so sorry you never had a chance to know them while they were growing up or that they didn't have a chance to know their Grandma Hanna. I've never seen them, but I've talked to them on the phone (in English, of course), and I have many pictures showing their many activities.

In the last year or two Karel and I have become pen pals. In his first letter he wrote, "My grandma used to be your pen pal, and now I am." He writes clever letters, and if he doesn't know an English word, he draws it, and I always know what he means. I'm always amazed at how much he knows about American TV shows, sports stars, and other celebrities.

I also want you to know that in April, 1986, Aad made a visit to Illinois to see me and my family. He had just celebrated his 70th birthday the previous November. For that day Ineke compiled a scrapbook for him. She asked all his friends to write an account of their friendship and past connections with him as a birthday tribute. So I wrote a long story telling of our years of friendship and the highlights of our many years of correspondence. It was soon after that when Aad called and said he might visit us. Of course, we were thrilled. We spent the first week in Decatur with Euvera and Everett, visiting the Lincoln country, the Amish settlement, the University of Illinois, and many other well known places. Then we came to Southern Illinois. We went to many scenic places such as Giant City, Garden of the Gods, and other places of interest, including the Land between the Lakes in Kentucky. But Hanna, I thought of you everyday and wished you could have been here, too.

Also, at one time Ineke and Frank planned to visit me, but Frank became ill and they had to cancel the trip.

There have been so many changes in our lives too numerous to mention all. Zus' husband Karel died, and Zus now lives in a retirement home. She attends Aad's birthday parties and is still close to your family. Aad sold the house where you lived when Euvera and I visited you and he now lives in an apartment near Ineke and Frank. Euvera's husband died after Aad visited us, also my sister Irene and her husband from Mt. Vernon. So you see, our lives have changed so much, yet in many ways remain the same.

I truly am sorry that fate dealt so much sadness to you, especially the years in the Japanese prison camp in Java during World War II and your illness and long, drawn-out period of suffering. But your life had many happy years, and I'm glad our correspondence and friendship gave so much happiness to both of us. Even though you were ill when I visited you, I could never have been content with myself if we had never met personally. Do you remember when Hans called you the night Euvera and I arrived in Holland? When you came from the phone, you said, "Hans wants to know if I'm disappointed." We all had such a big laugh over that. Later, other people asked me the same question. No one seemed to understand that we already knew each other 'heart and soul' before we met, and from our pictures, we would have recognized each other anywhere.

When we wrote our first letters more than sixty years ago, never could we have imagined that our correspondence would last a lifetime. Nor could we ever have imagined all the memorable events that occurred during these years that cemented our friendship.

Hanna, I hope you aren't angry with me for finally permitting parts of your letters to be published. But I do feel maybe others can gain strength from your spirit and courage in years of adversity. Also, if any young people read this, maybe they will learn a bit more about the history of World War II and about the misery and suffering so many endured. Your strength and courage could be a source of inspiration for all.

So now farewell, dear Hanna, I miss you and love you and will forever treasure our years of sharing and caring.

All my love,
Ruth

Ruth Sullivan at home in
Herrin, Illinois—1996

Hanna's father and mother

Aad's Uncle Jan and
Aunt Mien Broekman

Ineke and
Aunt Clazien

Aad Muijser

Aad, Ruth, and Hanna

Hanna and Ruth together
for the first time

Ineke

Ineke

Hanna and Ineke
in Austria

Frank's mother, Frank,
Ineke, and Aad
(Frank and Ineke's wedding)

Hans

Hans and Carol Cross
in Amsterdam

Liesbeth (Hans' wife) and son

Arjen and Karel (Hans' sons)
(wearing Illinois and Herrin
Tigers shirts)

Wide canal and "driveway" for farmer's boat

Cows grazing
in unfenced
pasture in
Holland

Whimsical
modern stamp
denoting major
dairy products

Windmill and a drainage ditch which
serve as a fence to contain livestock.

About the Authors

Jean Ellen Reynolds is a former elementary teacher and administrator in the Carterville, Illinois Unit School District #5. She taught third grade for 14 years and served as principal for 12 years. She earned a B.S., M.S., and PhD from Southern Illinois University, Carbondale, Illinois. Jean retired in 1993.

Carol Cross has taught in elementary grade schools in New Haven, Connecticut, East St. Louis, Alton, and Carterville, Illinois. Her teaching career has spanned three decades. She earned a B.S. and M.S. from Southern Illinois University, Carbondale, Illinois. Carol retired in 1991.

When the authors had the opportunity to preserve this story for the enjoyment and edification of present and future generations, it was a "labor of love."

Jean Ellen Reynolds

Carol Cross

Carol, editor Molly Norwood, and Jean Ellen

About the Author